The JOY of CHRISTMAS

Books by Melody Carlson

Other Christmas Novels

The Treasure of Christmas: A 3-in-1 Collection
Christmas at Harrington's

Young Adult Novels

Just Another Girl
Anything but Normal

The JOY *of* CHRISTMAS

A 3-in-1 COLLECTION

MELODY CARLSON

Revell

a division of Baker Publishing Group
Grand Rapids, Michigan

Published by Revell
a division of Baker Publishing Group
P.O. Box 6287, Grand Rapids, MI 49516-6287
www.revellbooks.com

Combined edition published 2010

Previously published in three separate volumes:
An Irish Christmas © 2007
All I Have to Give © 2008
The Christmas Dog © 2009

Printed in the United States of America

Library of Congress Cataloging-in-Publication Data
Carlson, Melody.
  The joy of Christmas : a 3-in-1 collection / Melody Carlson. — Combined ed.
    p.   cm.
  ISBN 978-0-8007-1975-3 (cloth)
  1. Christmas stories. I. Title.
PS3553.A73257J69 2010
813'.54—dc22   2010017871

10   11   12   13   14   15   16   7   6   5   4   3   2   1

In keeping with biblical principles of creation stewardship, Baker Publishing Group advocates the responsible use of our natural resources. As a member of the Green Press Initiative, our company uses recycled paper when possible. The text paper of this book is comprised of 30% post-consumer waste.

green press INITIATIVE

An
IRISH
CHRISTMAS

1

||||||||||||||||

Colleen May Frederick

Spring of 1963

I felt certain I was losing my son. Or perhaps I'd already lost him and just hadn't noticed. So many things had slipped my attention this past year, ever since Hal's death. But lately it seemed I was losing everything. Not just those insignificant items like my car keys, which I eventually found in the deep freeze beneath a carton of Green Giant mixed vegetables, or my favorite pair of calfskin gloves, which I still hadn't located. But it seemed I was losing important things as well. Or maybe I was just losing my grip.

I studied the piles of financial papers that I had neatly arranged across the surface of Hal's old rolltop desk, the one his grandfather had had before him. I restraightened my already tidy stacks of unpaid bills, insurance papers, and miscellaneous mishmash, hoping that would help create a sense of order from what felt more like chaos. But I was still overwhelmed. So much I didn't understand. So much that Hal had handled, always somewhat mysteriously—or mysteriously to me.

Oh, I could run a household like clockwork. And I even helped out at the shoe store when needed, as long as it didn't involve keeping the books or ordering merchandise or anything terribly technical. The truth was, other than helping customers find the

9

right shoes, ringing up sales, smiling, chatting, inquiring about an aging grandmother or a child who'd had a reaction to a vaccination, I was not terribly useful. And more and more I was feeling useless. And overwhelmed.

I hadn't heard from my son Jamie in weeks, even with college graduation right around the corner, not a word. I finally resorted to calling his dorm, but even then only received vague and unhelpful answers from a guy named Gary. I wondered what Hal would do if he were still alive. Of course, I knew what he'd say. He'd tell me not to worry so much. He'd say that I should pray instead. Easier said than done.

It had been Hal's idea that Jamie attend his alma mater, an expensive private business college in the Bay Area. And Jamie had been thrilled at the prospects of living in San Francisco, several hours away from us. He longed for independence and freedom. But after a few semesters, Jamie grew disenchanted with the small college and wanted to switch schools to Berkeley, in particular to their school of music. Jamie honestly believed that he could make it as a musician. Naturally, this seemed perfectly ridiculous to both Hal and me. So Hal encouraged our dreamer son to stick it out and get his business degree first. Hal told Jamie that music was perfectly fine—for fun and recreation—but it would never pay the rent or put food on the table. I had to agree.

The plan was for Jamie to take over the family business eventually. Frederick's Fine Footwear was a successful and established business in our hometown of Pasadena. It was well respected and had been in Hal's family for more than sixty years. We felt that Jamie should be honored that he was next in line for the shoe throne. As it turned out, he didn't feel quite the same. Oh, I wasn't privy to all of those "father-son" discussions that year, but it seemed they had reached an agreement of sorts, and Jamie had given up the idea of Berkeley and returned to the business college.

Then, about a year ago, it came to a head once again. At the beginning of last summer, Jamie announced that he never planned to go into the shoe business at all—period—end of discussion.

Well, I know this broke Hal's heart, and I secretly believe that it contributed to the heart attack that killed him in July. Of course, I never told Jamie my suspicion. Although I know that he felt guilty enough. The poor boy blamed himself for most of the summer, even giving up a summer trip to work in the shoe store to make up for things, although I know he hated being there. Still, I reassured my son that Hal's faulty heart had nothing to do with Jamie and that his Grandfather Frederick had suffered the same ailment at about the same age.

At summer's end, I had encouraged Jamie to return to college for his senior year. The most important thing seemed to be that he would complete his education and get his business degree. What he did after that would be up to him. My son had a definite stubborn streak, and I knew that no one could force him into the shoe business. Especially not me!

And so on that warm day in May, less than a year since my husband's death, I reached for the sales contract that dominated the piles of paperwork on his neatly cluttered desk. I had decided the time had come to sell the shoe store, and under these circumstances, I felt Hal would agree. Still, it was terribly hard to sign the papers. My fountain pen weighed ten pounds as I scratched my name across those lines. I wished there were another way—or that I was made of stronger stuff. But I felt so terribly overwhelmed . . . as if I were losing everything. Maybe that's why I decided that since I was losing the shoe store, I might as well sell my house too. It was far too large for me, and expensive to maintain, what with the pool and the grounds and everything. Besides, if Jamie wasn't going to be part of my life, what would be the point? Especially when it seemed that Jamie had always been the reason for everything.

I picked up the family photo that Hal faithfully kept on top of his desk—the three of us, our happy little family. Jamie was about eleven at the time, still the little boy on the brink of adolescence. Still willing to hold my hand as we walked through town together—unless he spotted a schoolmate, then he'd let go. His dark brown hair curled around his high forehead and those bril-

11

liant blue eyes just gleamed with mischief and adventure. I studied my face next to his, the high cheekbones and pixie nose framed in dark hair. I was surprised at how young I looked back then, although it was less than ten years ago, but then again I was barely thirty. That seemed so very young now.

I pulled the picture in for a closer look. Although I had been smiling, there was sadness in my eyes. Had that always been there? Did anyone else ever notice it? Hal wore his usual cheerful grin. He had just started to bald back then, and his paunch was perfect for playing Santa, which he loved to do at the shoe store during the holidays.

Setting the frame back down on the desk, I looked at the image now blurred as tears welled up in my eyes. There we all stood, smiling midgets beneath our enormous Christmas tree, oblivious to the fact that life would be vastly different ten years later. Jamie had always insisted that the gilded star on the treetop must touch the ceiling, but our home had vaulted ceilings that stretched more than fifteen feet tall. Hal never once complained about how much trouble it had been to unearth a tree that size down here in Southern California, although one year he drove six hours to get just the right tree. Consequently Jamie had never been disappointed. Spoiled a bit, perhaps, but then he'd been our only child and such a good boy. He always made us happy to be his parents, always made us proud.

Until recently anyway.

And, in all fairness, just because a grown son hadn't bothered to call his mother in several weeks, well, I supposed that didn't make him a bad boy. Just neglectful. After all, he had his own life.

2

⸻

James William Frederick (Jamie)

I'd kept a secret from my parents for a couple of years now. It had started out to be a temporary thing—a quick fix. But when Dad died unexpectedly last summer, I thought that would end my little game. I'd planned to make a clean break of it with Mom—and I figured she'd forgive me, eventually anyway. But she seemed so fragile over losing Dad, and the shoe store needed attention, and life just got busy. One thing led to another, and before I knew it, another year had passed and I still hadn't made my disclosure. And I discovered there was something about secrets . . . the longer you keep them, the bigger they grow.

My life of deception began when I dropped out of college. It had been winter term of my junior year when I decided to call it quits. My main reason for giving up had been to pursue my music—well, that combined with a slightly broken heart, something that, unlike my music, I eventually got over—or mostly. To me, music was my life (as well as a form of therapy) and I believed I could make it into my livelihood. But my dad didn't agree. He felt that music was something to play at, but selling shoes was a *real* job. And, after my futile attempt to discuss my musician's dreams with him during Christmas break of 1961, I decided to take my future into my own hands and quietly dropped out of school without bothering to mention this minor fact to either of my unsuspecting parents.

After all, I'd convinced myself, it was my life. And it hadn't helped matters that I'd missed a lot of classes as a result of getting dumped by my girlfriend that winter. The choice was pretty obvious, and I'd figure out a way to break this news to my parents . . . when the time was right. My thinking was that when my music made me rich and famous, which I felt was inevitable, the truth would be much sweeter. In the meantime, thanks to my friend the dorm manager, I continued to live on campus, and I continued to collect my parents' monthly support checks as well as their tuition payments for the classes I wasn't taking. This benefit was accompanied with a fair amount of guilt, although I did my part to justify things. And I blamed my dad for trusting me. It had been his idea from the beginning that part of growing up and becoming a man would be for me to manage my own finances during college. I was managing them, all right.

When alleviating my guilt, I would remind myself that it had never been my choice to go to that college in the first place. Sure, it had been fine for Dad, back in the Dark Ages when a guy was considered fortunate to attend college at all. But I would've preferred attending Berkeley, specifically the school of music. And so I convinced myself that my parents' financial support was "my due pay." It wasn't easy to support a fledgling band back in the early sixties, so I figured it was an investment in my future. And it was my compensation for my hard work—my work that included writing music; purchasing, maintaining, and practicing my instruments; and performing with my newly created band, Jamie and the Muskrats. Thanks to twenty-twenty hindsight, I can now admit that our band's name didn't boost our career much, but on second thought it was just the beginning of the rock and roll era, and even the Beatles had a few kinks to work out.

"Selling shoes might be your bag," I had informed my dad when I came home to visit at the beginning of last summer. I'd probably been just a little full of myself since Jamie and the Muskrats had played two high school proms in the Bay Area the previous month, and I felt certain that fame was right around the corner. "But I refuse to spend my entire life handling stinky feet and trying to cram Mrs. Flemming's puffy size 8½Ds into 7Bs." By then I'd spent enough summer "vacations" working in Frederick's Fine Footwear to know what the shoe business was really like—up close and way too personal—and I had no intention of dedicating my life to shodding the fine but smelly feet of Pasadena.

"But Frederick's has been in our family for nearly sixty years," my dad had protested. "Your grandpa started it before I was even born, and it's been my dream that you'd take it over after graduation, Jamie. That's why I wanted you to get your business degree. I expect you to follow in my *footsteps*." Then he even chuckled at his weak pun, slapping me on the back as if that was all it took to pull me into the family shoe business.

"Sorry, Pops," I told him. "But I'm just not ready to fill those shoes." When it came to bad puns, the apple didn't fall far from the tree. So it was that we went round and round for about a week that June. And Dad even laid down some tempting offers for me. And when that didn't work, he actually resorted to some slightly camouflaged threats, like cutting off my spending money, although he'd never been the sort of man to carry out such a thing. But it was all of no use. Neither of us wanted to budge and it finally became a standoff. The shoe business might be fine for Dad and my grandpa before him, but I made myself perfectly clear: Frederick's Fine Footwear would have to get by without the youngest Frederick. And so I took off on a road trip with my band—my plan was to be gone all summer.

Then Dad suffered a heart attack in early July. It was only due to Steve, our band's drummer, that I discovered this since he had called home and heard the news from his mom just one day after Dad died. Thanks to my secret dropout status along with my refusal to play the "good son" by taking over the family business, I felt overwhelmingly responsible for my father's death. Talk about a guilt trip. Of course, Mom reassured me that it wasn't my fault at all, and that Dad had been having some "serious heart trouble" for a couple of years already. Still, I felt miserable about the whole thing. Plus, I really missed Dad. I suddenly realized that we don't really know what we have until it's gone.

So here I was stuck in Pasadena and suffering from many layers of guilt, which killed any desire to return to what had turned into a fairly lackluster road trip anyway. To ease my guilt, I volunteered to fill in at the shoe store for the remainder of the summer; it was the least I could do. But then September came and Mom insisted I return to my classes. And, fed up with hot swollen feet and cranky back-to-school shoppers, I was more than happy to comply with her wishes. I told myself that I'd write her a nice long letter and confess my lie to her later on—after she'd had more time to recover from losing my dad. There seemed no sense in adding to her load just then.

"The most important thing, right now," Mom told me as she handed me clean laundry and I packed my bags, "is for you to graduate. Don't worry about a thing. I'll handle the store from here on out. You just take care of your education, Jamie. Look toward your future."

I couldn't disagree with her about that either. But I also couldn't admit that, at the moment, my education and my future was all about music—I couldn't tell her that everything I wanted to learn either involved a guitar or a piano or my transistor radio and the Top Forty. Nor did I mention that the Muskrats and I had already lined up several more promising gigs for the upcoming fall. Instead, I just kissed her good-bye and said, "See ya at Christmas."

But autumn came and went and I had to excuse myself for Christmas because Jamie and the Muskrats had several good parties to play during the holidays. Naturally, this only added to my growing accumulation of guilt. The truth was, I felt ashamed to go home and face Mom, knowing that I was living such a lie. At the same time, I wasn't man enough to tell her the truth either. Instead I sent her an expensive hand-carved jewelry box, purchased with some gig money, as if I thought I could buy her off. Then I even called her on Christmas Eve and I told her how much I missed her and how I wished I was home, which was actually the truth. She sounded sad and slightly lost—sort of how I was feeling at the time. But I promised I'd spend next Christmas with her.

Jamie and the Muskrats got a few more frat parties that winter and a couple of high school dances that spring. But, despite these opportunities, the Muskrats were not making it to the big time like I'd planned. Ed Sullivan had not called, and consequently we knew we could never make ends meet on our musicians' wages. Plus it seemed that the band's earlier enthusiasm was definitely flagging. It didn't help matters when Gordon and Bill, about to graduate, both lined up "real" jobs for the upcoming summer. The Muskrats were about to become a duet with only my drummer buddy Steve Bartowski and me, and as far as I could see, a guitarist and a drummer did not equal a band. Then within that same week, Steve, shocked to hear of his girlfriend's pregnancy and in need of "some serious dough," enlisted in the Air Force! I couldn't believe it. Jamie and the Muskrats had been reduced to *just Jamie*, and I wasn't about to take my act out solo.

"I guess I'll come home for summer after all," I told Mom on the same day that Steve dumped me for his girlfriend and the Air Force. I'd called her long-distance—as always, collect.

"Wonderful," she said in a flat voice that lacked any genuine enthusiasm and actually sounded pretty depressed, and not a bit like the cheerful little mother I'd grown up with.

"And I can work at the store for you too," I added, hoping that might cheer her up.

"Uh, *the store*?" she said in this slightly higher pitch, like all was not well with Frederick's Fine Footwear. "I'd meant to tell you, Jamie. And I actually tried to call your dorm a couple of weeks ago, but you weren't there. The thing is I, uh, I sold the store."

"*Really?*" Now for some reason I felt slightly blindsided by this news. "You *sold* Dad's business and you didn't tell me?"

"Well, I knew how you felt about the shoe trade, and I have to admit I was a little overwhelmed by the whole thing myself. And you've been so busy with school and with graduation coming up . . . by the way, when is graduation, Jamie? You've been so evasive this year. I hope you didn't forget to reserve some tickets. I promised your Aunt Sally that we'd both fly up there for it. We plan to stay at the Fairmont in San Francisco, live it up a little. We need something to celebrate. Perhaps we can have you and a few of your friends for dinner while we're there. Wouldn't that be fun?"

That was when I decided my best defense might be to get defensive. "I can't believe you sold Frederick's Fine Footwear, Mom." I took on a tone that was meant to sound hurt. "I mean, just like that, you go and sell a family business that's been around for generations and you don't even consult me?"

"But I thought you didn't want—"

"How could you possibly know what I want when you didn't even talk to me about it, Mom?"

"I tried to call you . . . but I haven't heard from you for so long, Jamie."

"But I was counting on coming home this summer, I was going to work in the shoe store, Mom. I thought I might even take over running it, and now what am I supposed to—"

"Oh, Jamie!" She sounded truly alarmed. "*I had no idea!* Oh, I feel so horrible. I wish I'd known. I never would've sold it if I'd known you'd changed your mind. I'm so, so sorry."

I knew I had her where I wanted her, but I suddenly felt guilty about my tactics. Even so, I knew that before long I would have a confession to make. I knew I needed to position myself. And I guess I was feeling a little desperate. "Oh, it's okay, Mom. It's not really your fault. I guess I should've called you and said something—"

"I feel so terrible. You're absolutely right, I should've asked you, Jamie. It's just that George Hanson was so interested in buying, and I felt things were going downhill so fast, it was time to reorder merchandise for the fall season, and everything just seemed so over—"

"Really, Mom, it's okay," I said soothingly. "I just wish I'd known, that's all."

She sighed loudly.

"You really should've kept me in the loop, Mom."

"I know, Jamie. I'm *so* sorry."

"So, I'll see you in a couple of weeks then?"

"For graduation?" she asked hopefully.

"No," I answered quickly. "I decided not to do the ceremony. It's all such a production—a bunch of pomp and circumstance and stifled yawns. I just want to come home, Mom. I'd hoped to come home and take over the business and—"

"Oh, dear . . ."

"But don't worry about any of that now." I paused for dramatic effect. "I'll . . . well, I'll think of something else to do with my life."

So it was that Mom's decision to sell the business helped to counter my own dilemma and, by burdening her with layers of parental guilt, I didn't have to confess my lack of graduating with the prized business degree. But after I got home, we didn't talk too much. I wasn't sure if it was because of her or because of me. Admittedly, I wanted to avoid any conversations that might force a confession. Oh, I wanted to confess. I just wasn't sure how—or more importantly, when. As a musician, I knew that timing was everything. Still, I could tell that Mom was sad and maybe even depressed. She seemed really withdrawn and she slept a lot, but that might've been the result of some of the medication she was taking. She told me that Dr. Griswold had prescribed Valium for her nerves shortly after Dad died.

"I didn't take it at first," she told me, "but then I figured maybe it would help."

Well, I couldn't tell if it had helped or not, but it sure did knock her out. Consequently there wasn't much for me to do but hang by the pool, mow the lawn occasionally, and see if any of my old friends were in town, which didn't seem to be the case.

I'd stored most of my stuff, including my music instruments and the secondhand piano I'd purchased with my "tuition" money, in an old warehouse space that had once been used for shoe-related things but hadn't been sold along with the business. By the end of summer, I found myself spending more and more time at the rundown warehouse. I'd pulled the piano out into the open and had begun to just play for the fun of it. But unlike the tunes I'd played for the Muskrats, this sort of playing was purely for my own enjoyment and not something I felt certain I'd want people my own age to even hear. It wasn't anything like the stuff that our generation listened to nowadays. In a way it reminded me of country music, which I claim to despise, but the beat was different. I wasn't even sure how I'd explain it, or if I cared to. But I was really getting into it, and it was a good way to kill time—perhaps it was a way to postpone the inevitable and to avoid my mother. I wasn't sure how long I could hold out, and I had no plan for how I would admit that I'd squandered my tuition money as well as nearly two years of college. Mom had always been pro-education, and who knew how she would handle such news? She was already having a hard time anyway. Why add to her stress? Besides, I told myself, she was usually sleeping anyway.

As fall approached, Mom announced that she was quitting the Valium. "It makes me feel like I'm living in a cloud," she admitted. "Like I'm half dead."

"Good for you," I told her. Still, considering the fact that she was getting back on her feet, so to speak, I didn't think it was the right time to dump on her just yet.

As September ended, both Mom and I were getting pretty antsy. I even had the gall to blame her edginess on her lack of narcotics, sometimes even suggesting, "Why don't you just pop a Valium?" which made her furious.

"Why don't you just clean up after yourself?" she'd toss back at me.

I suppose I had gotten a little sloppy. But then I'd grown up having a mom to clean up after me. And when Mom started to nag me about leaving messes in the kitchen or piles of dirty clothes in the laundry room, I'd get irritated. And if I got too worked up, like I often did, Mom would start asking what I was going to do for employment now that I had graduated.

"How do you plan to use that college education?" she would ask.

"I thought I was going to run a shoe store," I'd toss back, hoping to keep her questions at bay. Then we'd really get into it. She'd point out that it had been my choice, reminding me of how

I'd made myself clear to Dad. Then I would blame her for not communicating with me. It could get pretty loud sometimes. Like that muggy evening when one of our "discussions" escalated into a heated argument, and I told Mom that I thought it was high time for me to move out.

"I need a place of my own!" I shouted at her, knowing full well that the windows were open and half the neighborhood could probably hear us.

"Fine!" she shouted back.

"And there's no time like the present!" I added, almost expecting her to back down now. Despite our disagreements, I thought she liked having me around.

"Maybe that's for the best," she said with tear-filled eyes, reaching for her pocketbook. "I'll help you get into a place, and then you can get a job and support yourself, Jamie. That would probably be good for you." She wrote me a check that would cover a month's worth of rent and buy groceries and then told me "good luck."

But by late October, I was out of money, still unemployed, about to be thrown out of my apartment, and one day, while strolling through town, I discovered that Mom had put the family home up for sale.

"What's going on here?" I demanded when I saw the real estate sign planted in the front yard. Mom was raking willow leaves and looked up at me with a weary expression. Was she tired of me or just life in general?

"This place is too big for me," she said calmly. "Too hard to keep up. Plus it's too expensive to hire someone. There's the pool and the grounds and just everything. I decided to look for something smaller, perhaps a little cottage near the ocean."

I blinked at her in surprise. *Who was this woman anyway?* What had become of my mother, that small but feisty woman who could run an impeccable household and still have time to play cards with her friends or tennis at the club? It seemed like the life had been sucked right out of this woman. It occurred to me that she probably needed my help, maybe she even wanted me to move back home. Even so, I was too proud to ask if I could come back.

21

I wanted her to ask me. Not only that, but I was too embarrassed to admit that I was still jobless. And that naturally brought up the other part of the problem. No way did I want to confess to her that I hadn't finished college or any of my other shortcomings. No, instead I just opened my big fat mouth and the escape plan I'd recently been toying with came flying out.

"Fine," I snapped at her. "Go ahead and sell the house. You make all your decisions without me anyway. But just so you know, I plan on enlisting in the Air Force. I was on my way to the recruiter's office right now. I hear they're looking for some smart guys with a college education, and I—"

"*What?*" Mom dropped her bamboo rake and her jaw in the same instant. You'd have thought I'd just told her that I was planning on chopping off my right arm or robbing a bank or something. "Are you crazy?" she demanded, the color draining from her face.

No doubt, I had her attention now. And even though my proclamation was rather half-hatched, not to mention somewhat premature, it suddenly made perfect sense to me. Joining the Air Force sounded exciting and interesting. I'd watched their exotic TV ads about seeing the world. Plus, didn't they offer three good meals a day? That was better than I'd been doing lately. Also, I'd heard they had education benefits by way of the GI bill. Maybe I could even get my degree when I finished. Plus, it would be the perfect way to delay the inevitable—confessing all to Mom.

"My buddy Steve enlisted in the Air Force last June," I told her with false confidence. "He thinks he'll be an officer. And with this business going on in Vietnam right now, I thought why shouldn't I do the same? After all, it's my patriotic duty, and President Kennedy is the one who said, '*Ask not what your country can do for you, but ask what you can do for your*—' "

"*James William Frederick!*"

"What?"

"Have you taken leave of your senses?"

"No, Mom. I'm thinking straighter than ever at the moment. And, hey, I might even become a pilot, and I could—"

"You could get yourself killed!"

"Why do you have to go and jump to that conclusion?" I asked in a surprisingly calm voice. It was fun playing the mature person for a change. "Don't you remember how Dad used to say how much he'd wanted to enlist during World War II? Every time we watched a war movie on TV, he'd get all depressed. He felt like he'd missed out on something really important, but he told me that no matter how hard he'd tried to sign up, they refused to take him."

"That's because he was *too old*!"

Well, it was no secret that my dad had been about twelve years older than Mom. But that hadn't been too old to enlist. "He told me it was because of his flat feet."

Mom blinked, then nodded. "Yes, that's right."

Flat feet or no flat feet, there was something about the way Mom had blurted out "too old" that made me wonder if their age difference had been an issue with her. Had it bothered her that he was so much older? And now he was gone and she, only forty-one and still nice looking (for a mom anyway), was all alone. I studied her more closely. Even without makeup and twigs in her hair, she was pretty. But she looked too skinny and her high cheekbones looked even higher than usual with dark shadows in the hollows of her cheeks, and dark shadows beneath her eyes. Was she okay?

"Well, what about Henry Ackley?" I demanded, pushing my sympathetic thoughts aside, at least for the time being. I had a point to make here—about the Air Force and why I should join. Henry had been Dad's most faithful employee and a proud veteran to boot. "Henry used to tell me that joining the armed forces was the best way a man could possibly serve his country."

"Henry didn't know everything!"

"What do you mean by that?" I demanded. "Henry was always telling great war stories, acting like being in the South Pacific was the greatest time of his life. And, good grief, it had to be a lot more exciting than selling pumps to old ladies, for Pete's sake. What are you talking about anyway, Mom?"

She stepped forward and looked me in the eyes. "I'm talking about a young man—a young man with a bright future and a fine education—a young man who is willing to toss everything aside just so he can run halfway around the world to shoot guns and bombs and things!"

"Whoa, Mom," I said in an almost teasing voice. "I had no idea you were anti-war. Did Dad know about this?"

Her eyes were filled with fire now and she was really fuming. She reminded me of a character in those cartoons I used to watch on Saturdays, maybe the one where Elmer Fudd got so fed up with Bugs Bunny that the steam came pouring out his nostrils and ears as he aimed a loaded shotgun at the rabbit's head. Well, my mother looked ready to blow too. But I just shrugged, picked up her fallen rake, and took over where she'd left off, scooping a big clump of leaves into her pile.

Without saying a single word, Mom turned away and stomped off toward the house. I think I actually felt the lawn vibrating with each step. And I felt pretty sure I'd missed a bullet—a mother bullet.

But when Mom came back out again, about an hour or so later and after I'd gotten all the leaves raked into one big neat pile, she informed me that I was *not* going to enlist in the Air Force, and that I was *not* going to go to Vietnam, and that I was *not* going to become a pilot. "Not until you've accompanied me to Ireland *first*," she told me in her firmest most I-mean-business–like voice.

"*Ireland?*" I said, thinking my mother had finally lost her blooming mind. "What on earth for?"

"Because I said so," she said with finality. "And I've already made the travel arrangements for us. We're going there in mid-December. *For Christmas.* You'll have just enough time to get your passport. And if you know what's good for you, you will not argue with your mother, young man!"

24

3

Colleen

"Why in the world are you going to Ireland?" my sister demanded as I refilled our coffee cups. Sally had just driven up from San Diego and we were having our second cup of coffee. I returned the chrome coffeepot to its spot by the stove, then sat back down, placing both of my palms flat on the shiny plastic surface of my kitchen table. I studied the cheerful buttercup color of the plastic laminate and pondered her question. It was a good question—one that deserved a good answer. It had been only a week since I'd announced my crazy plan to Jamie, and to be honest, I was starting to have second thoughts myself.

"Really, Colleen," she persisted as she picked up the creamer. "What makes you want to go to Ireland? And for Christmas? You don't even know anyone over there, do you?"

"No . . ." I stirred cream into my coffee.

"Not that I wouldn't love to travel too, if I were you." She let out a long sigh, looking dreamily out my kitchen window toward the bougainvillea bush. "But Ireland?"

"Jamie was talking about joining the Air Force." I said the words slowly, still trying to absorb the meaning behind his announcement.

"So?" Sally shrugged then stirred some sugar into her cup.

"So, I didn't want him to."

"Why not?" She looked evenly at me now, and I could tell I was walking on thin ice here. Especially since her husband Richard had only recently retired from a lifetime career in the Navy and their older son Larry was considering following in his dad's footsteps after high school graduation in two years. "You have something against the military, Colleen?"

"No, no, of course not." I considered my words carefully. "It's only that Jamie just graduated from college and . . ."

"First of all, what makes you so sure about that? It's not like you *saw* him graduate, did you? Has he shown you his diploma yet?"

"No, but that's not really the point."

"What *is* the point?"

"I don't want him going off to Vietnam and getting hurt."

"Why would he get hurt, Colleen? From what I hear it's mostly about peacekeeping, restoring the order. According to Richard, it should all be over before long anyway."

"But you never know . . ."

Sally frowned, then reached over and placed her hand on mine. "It's because of losing Hal, isn't it? You're worried that since you've been recently widowed, you only have Jamie left, am I right?"

I looked out the window in time to see a goldfinch lighting on a branch, then nodded. "Yes, I suppose that has something to do with it."

"But why Ireland? And if you're worried about Jamie's safety, you might want to think again. From what I've heard about that new prime minister in northern Ireland, it's not going to be the most peaceful place either before long."

"It's hard to explain . . . but I suppose I've wanted to see Ireland for a long time."

"Is it because of your name?" Sally teased. "You think that because Mom named you Colleen means you're Irish? Because I can assure you that's not the case. She just happened to like the name. If Dad had had his way, we'd all have Norwegian names like Helga or Olga or Gudrun."

I chuckled. "Can you imagine being *Gudrun*? It sounds like a bad case of indigestion. And, no, my interest in Ireland isn't related to my name. But maybe it's because of that movie . . . remember *The Quiet Man* with John Wayne and Maureen O'Hara about ten years ago? I was so taken with it. Ireland looked like such a pretty place. So romantic."

Sally seemed to consider this, then eagerly nodded. "Oh, I loved that movie too. Well, except for the part where he spanked her. *That* was uncalled for."

I laughed, then agreed.

"So, there's no talking you out of this Ireland trip then? You and Jamie won't change your minds and come down and spend Christmas with us this year?"

"No, but thanks anyway. The travel agent has it all booked and Jamie's already applied for his passport."

"And yours must still be good."

"Yes. It's been less than three years since Hal and I went to Paris."

Sally sighed. "And I'll bet you're glad you did that, aren't you? Good thing you didn't wait for your twentieth anniversary after all. Wouldn't that have been last winter?"

I nodded. "Who knew Hal would be gone by then?"

I could almost see the wheels turning in Sally's head now. Hal and I had kept quiet about our anniversary for years, and not for the first time, I could see my sister doing the mental math, calculating about how Hal and I married in February, but how Jamie was born the following July, only six months later. And, weighing in at a hefty eight pounds four ounces, he wasn't a bit premature either. Still, as usual, Sally didn't mention this slight discrepancy. I suspected she and Richard had their own secrets too. Some sleeping dogs were better left undisturbed.

"Hi, Aunt Sally," Jamie called as he slammed the kitchen door behind him.

"You're looking fit and trim." Sally nodded approvingly at his tanned and sturdy torso, still glistening with perspiration.

"He's been helping to keep the grounds up for me, cleaning the pool and cutting the lawns and whatnot." I smiled at my shirtless son as he foraged through my refrigerator. He eventually located a bottle of Pepsi and popped the lid off with the opener tucked beneath the counter. Then he nodded to us, said a polite good-bye, and headed back out.

"I noticed the real estate sign is still up," Sally said. "You still planning to sell?"

"It's been a relief having Jamie around to help, but I can't depend on him forever, and this place is really too big for me." I set down my empty cup and pressed my lips together, unsure once again about so many things.

"It's such a beautiful home, Colleen . . ." I heard the longing in her voice.

"According to Jane, my real estate lady, there's an interested party who plans on making an offer in the next week or so."

"And then what?" Sally studied me carefully as she set down her cup. "Don't tell me you plan on moving out of here before your big trip to Ireland?"

"I don't know . . . but I didn't sell the old warehouse that Hal used for the shoe business," I explained. "I suppose I could store some things there, and then sell some things. I really won't need all this furniture."

Sally frowned. "You're okay, aren't you, Colleen? The way you're talking about selling things, packing up, and all that . . . well, you remind me of an old woman who's about to call it quits. Is there anything you're not telling me? You're not sick, are you?"

I forced a tight smile and took a small sip of coffee. "No, I'm perfectly fine, Sally. I just feel overwhelmed, that's all. I want to simplify my life." I waved my hand around the big modern kitchen with its long laminated countertops, sleek white metal cabinets, and the fancy GE appliances, all those expensive things that Hal insisted I should have when we built this house back in 1950. "I really don't need all this."

Sally laughed. "I sure wish I could trade with you. My kitchen is so tiny that if all three kids and Richard are in there with me, I can barely turn around, let alone attempt to cook anything edible."

"At least it's better than what we grew up with back in Minnesota," I reminded her. "Remember Mom's old cast iron cookstove and how hot that place got in the summertime during harvest season? It was like a Swedish sauna."

"Or a steam room if we were canning." Sally nodded grimly. "I still remember how I fumed at you for leaving home after high school. I got stuck with all the cooking for the next few years."

I smirked at my younger sister. "I did my time."

"You and me both!"

We both laughed, then as usual we recalled some of the fun parts of growing up on a wheat farm in northern Minnesota, commiserating about how it felt being the only two girls in a family with six sons who all helped our dad to work the land. We exaggerated about the size of the mosquitoes and how challenging it was to have a boyfriend with all those brothers around. I even told her the story of when our oldest brother Hank found Tom Paulson kissing me in the hayloft.

"Poor Tom," I said, suppressing laughter. "After the black eye and bloody nose, that unfortunate boy never looked at me again."

"No wonder you wanted to move out to Hollywood," Sally teased. "And, you know, Colleen, I really thought you were going to make the big times too. I used to brag to all my girlfriends, telling them how you were going to be a famous movie star. I even made up some stories, pretending like you were actually getting cast in some films. I have to confess that I even told Katherine Olson that you'd gotten a small role in a movie with Clark Gable, and she believed me."

I laughed loudly now. *"She believed you?"*

"Well, we'd all seen you in the high school plays. You were the best and you were a beauty, and everyone knew it. We thought you had a real chance."

I frowned and glanced away. "Guess we were all wrong about that."

"You *could've* been a star," Sally said stubbornly. "If you hadn't given up so quickly. We were all so shocked when you wrote home and told us that you'd gotten married. Oh, sure the war was going and all, but it still took us all by surprise."

"Oh, well . . ." I sort of shrugged and tried to think of a way to change the subject.

Sally laughed now. "I suppose that's what true love does to a person."

I stood and carried my coffee cup to the sink. "Your Julie told me that she's interested in acting," I said as I rinsed my cup. "She said she plans to try out for the school play next spring. I think she'd be a good actress."

Fortunately that was all I needed to sidetrack my sister. Soon Sally was talking about Julie and how much her only daughter had matured last summer. "She gave up all her old tomboy ways, well, besides playing basketball with the boys in the driveway, I don't think that will ever end. But did I tell you that Julie's got a little boyfriend now? Not that we're letting her date yet since she's only fifteen, but it's so cute how he calls her on the phone. Richard even got her a little pink princess phone for her bedroom last week. It's so adorable."

"Julie is such a sweetheart. I'd love to see her before we go to Ireland. You know, she's the closest thing I've had to a daughter." I smiled at my sister. "I try not to feel too envious of you."

"Believe me, there are times when I'd gladly give her to you." She set her empty cup down, then just looked at me. "Tell me, sis, why didn't you and Hal have more kids? You were such good parents to Jamie, and with this great, big house, well, it just never made sense to me."

"I would've loved more," I admitted. "But Hal had an old injury . . . you know, the sort of thing that makes it impossible to conceive children."

Sally looked truly shocked at my unexpected confession, and I suddenly realized my faux pas and wondered what I could possibly say to undo my blunder. This was what came of getting too comfortable while chatting.

"Then having Jamie was a *real* miracle, wasn't it?" Sally's eyes grew wide with curiosity.

For a brief moment, I considered telling my sister the truth—the whole truth and nothing but the truth. She was, after all, my only sister as well as my closest friend. But this was a secret I had harbored and protected for so many years, and old habits are hard to break. "Uh, actually, Hal's accident happened *after* Jamie was born." I did hate to lie, but sometimes it was a necessary evil. "It happened during the holidays, years ago . . . an eight-foot shelf overloaded with boxes of shoes toppled onto him . . . nearly killed the poor man." Well, at least that was all honest. But the real truth was that the accident happened when Hal was in his early twenties, long before I ever met him.

"I never knew that," Sally said, her finely plucked brows arched high.

"Well, it's not something we ever talked about, not even privately," I admitted. "I think Hal was very embarrassed by the whole thing." Now that was totally true.

Sally nodded. "Yes, I can understand that. I'm sure Richard would be the same way. Men are just like that."

"So, I'll trust you to keep that little confidence to yourself," I said quietly. "You know, for Hal's sake . . . and Jamie's."

"Of course." Sally glanced at the kitchen clock. "Goodness, I only meant to stay for an hour or so and it's nearly noon already. I've got so much to do. Say, why don't you and Jamie come down for Thanksgiving next month? That way you can see Julie and she can ask you all sorts of acting questions. I've been telling her about her almost famous aunt."

I chuckled. "I doubt that I can tell Julie much about acting, that was so long ago and things have certainly changed since then. But I'm sure we'd both love to come for Thanksgiving. I'll check with Jamie and call you next week. Okay?"

"Perfect!"

I watched from the living room window as Sally drove away in her old blue Plymouth, the same car she'd been driving for more than a decade now. I imagined her busy family life down in San Diego, sharing a small three-bedroom bungalow with only one bath and five people—and despite wanting to be a more mature person, I flat out envied my younger sister. I think I would've traded my modern five-bedroom house, my upscale neighborhood, the inground pool, my sleek white Cadillac, my membership at the country club, and all my fancy clothes and shoes and *everything*—well, everything except my Jamie—all of it in exchange for the simple little life that my sister had been living all these years.

And feeling like that just made me sick inside. How could I be so ungrateful? How could I be so self-centered and selfish? Think of all that dear Hal had done for me, and now all I felt was regret. But not for losing him. Oh, I did feel that too, I felt it deeply. Hal had been good to me. But, no, my regret went deeper, further back. Perhaps it was a grief that I had neglected to experience at the time—a grief that would haunt me the rest of my earthly days. Or maybe Ireland would put it to rest. One could only hope.

4

||||||||||||||||

Jamie

"I hear your mother put her house up for sale," Henry Ackley said as he set a shoe box at my feet.

I'd come into Frederick's Fine Footwear for a new pair of loafers, after Mom had strongly hinted that my old ones might not be fit for international travel. I'd been trying to be a bit more congenial lately, trying to show some appreciation for the fact that Mom had invited me to move back home. I'd spent the last several days pruning shrubs, edging the lawn, washing windows, and all sorts of labor-intensive projects to make the old homestead look better—the reason being that Mom's "most serious buyer" was supposed to come by for a "third walk-through" today, and she hoped the third time would really be the charm.

"That's right," I told Henry as I slid my foot into the sleek leather shoes, lined with even more smooth leather. Now, despite my previous prejudices toward the shoe-selling business in general, I had to admit, at least to myself, that new shoes really were sort of cool. They had this certain smell and texture that just made you feel good all over. These particular loafers, with a pair of bright copper pennies tucked into the slots, would look just about perfect. And, as I extended my right foot out to admire the workmanship, a small wave of regret washed over me. Why had I so easily abandoned the opportunity to run my dad's business?

Then, as I slipped my left foot into the remaining shoe, I remembered the piece of music I'd been unable to work on this past week, and I recalled how much I missed my secret piano sessions in the warehouse, and how I planned to go over there and play for a few hours later today—and perhaps one day I'd be able to confess the whole thing to my mother, somehow make her understand. So, once again, I convinced myself that selling shoes was not what I wanted to do with my life. I sighed as I stood and looked down at this pair of swell-looking shoes.

"How do they feel?" asked Henry.

I strolled around the store now, careful to stay on the dark green carpet runners that Dad had installed himself many years ago. We always got irritated if a customer ventured off the padded surface and over to the linoleum floor, even if they did want to hear the sound of the heels clicking on the hard surface. "Nice," I told Henry. "I'll take them."

Henry grinned. "I guess that means you'll *pay* for them too. Not like the old days, eh?"

I slipped off the loafers and placed them back in the box. "Nope. Times are changing."

"How about some socks to go with them?"

I grinned at Henry, ever the salesman. "Sure," I said, going over to the sock rack and removing a couple pairs of crew socks.

"White socks with brown loafers?" He actually lifted his nose in the air.

"Like I said, times are a-changing."

He shook his head. "Brown shoes need brown socks."

I just laughed and handed him the socks.

"So, your mother really is serious about selling her house?" he asked for the second time.

"Seems to be the case." I followed him up to the cash register, wondering about his sudden interest in my mother's real estate deals. "You interested in buying it?"

He sort of laughed. "Afraid it's a little too rich for my blood."

"For hers too." I opened my billfold, feeling partially surprised to see actual money in it. My mom had been paying me for helping out these past few weeks, and for the most part, I'd been saving it. Amazing how it could begin to add up when your expenses were minimal.

Then Henry cleared his throat. "Jamie, I know it's not been much over a year since your dad passed, but do you think your mom will ever be interested in, well, you know, in seeing other fellers and whatnot?" He picked up a stubby yellow pencil and fiddled with it, obviously nervous about this out-of-character inquiry.

I blinked, then stared at him, noticing how his smooth pale cheeks were starting to flush pink. Was Henry seriously interested in my mom? "I, uh, I don't know," I said. "We don't talk usually about things like that." The truth was I couldn't imagine, for the life of me, my mother going out on a date with *any* man, let alone someone like Henry.

"Well, I can understand that, Jamie." He licked the tip of his pencil. "But your mom is a fine-looking woman and a good person to boot. I expect it won't be long before fellers start coming a-calling."

I grinned at Henry. "Would you be one of those *fellers*?"

He blushed even redder now. "Well, I might just get myself in line."

I patted him on the shoulder. "I'm sure she could do worse, Henry."

He smiled as I handed him a ten. "Thanks."

I nodded, but the image of my mother with someone like Henry Ackley made my head hurt. Oh, sure, he was a nice enough guy and all, but the two of them would be like Gomer Pyle dating Audrey Hepburn. Granted, Mom was a little older than Miss Hepburn, but she had a similar kind of class and style, and somehow I just couldn't see how Henry would fit into that picture. Of course, I'd be willing to bet there'd been those who'd said the same sort of thing about my dad. But then he'd been younger back when they'd gotten married. He'd been thinner and had a full head of hair in those days. I knew this was true because I'd seen the photos.

35

"So, what are your plans, son?" Henry was counting out my change now and sounding a little too fatherly, in my opinion. "For the future, I mean. What's next for young Jamie Frederick?"

I sort of shrugged, then quickly told him about Mom's plan to take me to Ireland next month. To be honest, that was about as far ahead as I could see anyway.

"An Irish Christmas?" he said with curious brows. "Interesting . . ."

"Yeah, something like that." Then I winked at him. "Actually, I think this little trip might be Mom's way of trying to talk me out of joining the Air Force."

Henry's pale eyes lit up now. "The *Air Force*? Are you joining the Air Force, Jamie?"

"Maybe so."

"Well, I'll be! That's the best darn news I've heard in weeks. The *Air Force*—now wouldn't that be something. I can just imagine you up there, flying high in one of those big old jets and serving your country with pride."

I stood a little taller. "Yeah, a buddy of mine joined up last spring, and it sounds like a pretty good opportunity for guys my age."

Henry slapped me on the back. "It'd make a man out of you, son."

Okay, I probably slumped some at that comment. I suppose I like to think that because I'm twenty-one, I'm *already* a man. But then again it might just be a matter of perspective. "Thanks, Henry," I said as I took the paper bag with my last name still stamped onto the side of it. "Be seeing you 'round."

"Tell your little mother hello for me."

"Will do." I waved as I walked away, and the bell jingled as I pulled the glass door toward me—a familiar sound, sometimes comforting, sometimes aggravating. Now I realized it was something I'd probably taken for granted. Like so many other things in my life. But today that little brass bell had the sound of finality to it. As if it was the end of an era. And maybe it was . . . *times they were a-changing*. Not that I wouldn't go back there to buy shoes again someday. I probably would. But this was the first time I'd ever been in Frederick's Fine Footwear when it hadn't belonged to my family. I think the whole thing just made me sad. Or maybe it was just something in the air that day.

I felt another wave of melancholy as I walked down the business loop, past other familiar shops, restaurants, my favorite bookstore . . . and although I'd walked this street hundreds of times before, I felt sort of like a stranger today. My family no longer owned the shoe store on the corner, my mother was selling the family home, and most of my old friends had moved on to jobs or had headed back to college to finish their degrees. Where did I fit in here now? Where did I fit in anywhere?

I gazed in the window at Harper's Cafe, trying to decide whether or not I was hungry since it was getting close to noon. But the window was grimy looking and uninviting, and their window display—a cluttered menagerie of crepe paper turkeys and cardboard pilgrims—wasn't particularly appetizing, although it did remind me that Thanksgiving was less than a week away. Mom had said that she wanted us to go down to Aunt Sally's in San Diego, which was fine with me since I had no other place to go anyway. Plus I hadn't seen my cousins in ages.

I continued walking until I reached Scott's Television and Appliance Shop, and that's when I observed several people clustered close to the large plate glass window out front. I wondered if Scott's had gotten in something new and amazing—maybe a color TV with stereo. But the small crowd was simply staring at an ordinary black-and-white television that was playing inside, and as usual, the sound was being piped through an outdoor speaker to the sidewalk. But I noticed the elderly woman had her hand clasped over her mouth and her eyes were wide with terror.

"Oh, no!" Mr. Garvey cried, the owner of the five-and-dime. "*No!*"

"It can't be," a woman next to him gasped.

"What?" I asked, but the small crowd was rushing into the shop.

"*The president!*" the elderly woman called over her shoulder.

"He's been shot!" Mr. Garvey said.

I followed them inside, where we all stood in silent horror, watching the nightmare unfolding before our very eyes. President John F. Kennedy had been shot while driving in a motorcade in Dallas, Texas. Everyone in the store was crying, including me. No one even tried to hide it. And I didn't care that I knew many of the people in the shop. I didn't care that I was supposed to be a grown man, a man who barely cried at his own father's funeral. I just stood there and openly sobbed with the rest of them. How could this have happened? In our own country? Our leader had been murdered, with his pretty young wife by his side. It was like a really bad movie.

I eventually left Scott's and spent the remainder of the day in a deep, dark depression. Tucked away in the gloomy warehouse, with my transistor radio blaring on an AM news station, I sat on a crate and listened to all the ongoing details of the assassination, the head wound, how long before JFK died, how Vice President Johnson was sworn in on Air Force One before leaving Dallas—I took in the whole works. And finally, when I couldn't take it any-more, I started to play my piano. I played and played. And, although I knew it was senseless and would probably matter to no one but me, I dedicated my playing to President John Fitzgerald Kennedy and his two children and beautiful wife Jackie. My heart ached for all of them. How could something like this have happened?

It was about four o'clock when I finally remembered my own mother. I suddenly wondered how she would be taking all this—and realized that it might have hit her as hard as it hit me—and so I rushed home to find her sitting in front of the television with her hands in her lap and her big brown eyes all swollen and red from crying.

"Have you heard?" she whispered, clutching a white handker-chief in her fist and looking at me with a trembling chin.

Without saying anything, I nodded and sat down beside her. I draped one arm around her frail shoulders, and together we watched the news until finally she got up, went into the kitchen, and made us some supper. But neither of us felt hungry that night.

We continued to watch the news on television, seeing that scene in the car again and again. Then we watched as they replayed the scene where Jackie stood by LBJ on Air Force One, watched as a new president was sworn in. We listened to the familiar newsmen, the ones who came on every evening at 6:00, but tonight they were discussing the terrifying events of the day and speculating over what would happen next, but it was impossible not to notice the sound of uncertainty, the uneasy caution in their voices, as if they too, like us, were afraid.

It wasn't until the next morning, Saturday, that I remembered to ask Mom about the sale of the house and whether or not the third time really had been the charm. She had already turned on the small television that Dad had insisted on putting in the kitchen, and I'm sure it was the first time I'd ever seen that television on, but the volume was turned down low.

"Yesterday?" she said as if it had been a few weeks ago. "Let's see . . . as I recall Jane had just told me that the couple liked the house and wanted to make an offer." She handed me a cup of coffee, setting the cow-shaped porcelain creamer on the table. "But that's when Sally called and told me about the shooting. She was crying and she said to turn on the television."

"And you did?"

She sighed. "Yes. Then we all just stood there in the family room and watched it. It was the strangest thing, Jamie. I'd only just met this couple and suddenly we were all sobbing and holding on to each other, like it was the end of the world and we were all we had. And then just as abruptly, they left, they wanted to go and get their children. I doubt they will want the house. Who can think of buying a house right now?"

I nodded. "It sure makes you look at life differently."

"I still can't believe it happened, Jamie."

"I know."

"He's really dead."

"I really liked Kennedy . . . I think he was the best president ever. No one can ever replace him."

"I know."

"I wanted to vote for him in the next election."

"It's all so sad." She stared down at her coffee cup.

"It was so cool having such a young president. It's like he understood young people. He wanted to make this country better."

"He was too young to die."

I swallowed hard. "Man, it just really ticks me off. And I know you don't want to hear this, Mom, but it really makes me want to join the Air Force more than ever now. I'm ready to give back to my country. I want to do it for JFK."

She nodded slightly, then looked away. I sensed she wasn't too pleased with my newfound resolve, but I could tell she didn't plan to stand against me either. At least not today.

The next few days felt like the entire country was draped in this ominous blanket of heavy darkness. Everyone seemed to be in mourning, or if they weren't, they at least had the good sense to keep their thoughts to themselves. The house was quiet and both Mom and I moved silently through the days. I was extra careful not to leave any dirty dishes on the counter, and I kept my personal items picked up, even put my dirty clothes in the laundry hamper in my room. I wasn't sure if I was growing up or if life had just suddenly gotten serious.

Finally, it was Thursday and Thanksgiving Day. Mom and I drove to San Diego, and we all did our best to "celebrate" the holiday, but even my cousins were much quieter than usual, a cloud of sadness hovered over everyone. I think we were all relieved when the day finally ended and we could put our party faces aside.

"Will we see you before the big trip?" Uncle Richard asked as we stood around my mom's white Caddie. He paused to light up a Marlborough, then took in a long drag.

"I don't know . . ." Mom jingled her keys in one hand.

"You don't still want to go over there now, do you?" Aunt Sally asked. "I thought maybe you'd changed your mind, Colleen . . . I mean with all that's happened and everything. Are you sure it's a good idea to travel now?"

"I don't know why not," Mom said. "What do you think, Richard? Any warnings about international travel?"

He shook his head, then let out a puff of smoke over his shoulder. "Not that I've heard. But make sure you check with your travel agent a day or two before you leave."

"Kennedy was Irish," I said suddenly. Of course, I instantly felt stupid for making such a childish-sounding statement, except that it had just occurred to me.

"That's right," Uncle Richard said, crushing the cigarette butt beneath the heel of his boot. "He was Irish-Catholic. First time ever in this country."

Then we all hugged and everyone said good-bye.

"They're okay," I said to Mom as she drove back up the freeway toward home.

"Yes, they are."

I decided it was some comfort to have family around at times like this. Especially since my dad was gone and he didn't really have much family still living, at least not around here. I know he had some relatives out on the East Coast, but they're like strangers to me. And the rest of my mom's family, except Aunt Sally, still live in Minnesota. I'd been out there once, back when I was about nine, before my Grandpa Johnson died, and although there were lots and lots of cousins to play with, along with tons of other relatives, I pretty much felt like an outsider. Maybe it was because most of them had Johnson for a last name, the same name as the big family farm, and I didn't really fit in too well there.

So on Thanksgiving Day, less than a week after Kennedy was shot, I was glad to have Aunt Sally and Uncle Richard and my cousins around. And I was glad to have my mom too. Maybe that was one of the good things about a tragedy . . . it made you appreciate what you had.

5

‖‖‖‖‖‖‖‖‖‖‖‖‖

Colleen

I made my best effort not to feel sorry for myself as Jamie and I walked through Los Angeles International Airport in mid-December. The terminal was busier than ever with all the holiday travelers, and everywhere I looked seemed to be wrapped in the trappings and trimmings of Christmas. From the oversized Christmas tree near the entrance, dripping in silver tinsel and blue lights, to Bing Crosby crooning "White Christmas" over the sound system, it was obvious that Christmas was just around the corner. They even had a Santa Claus wearing a flight jacket who was giving out candy canes and airline wings to young travelers.

And I think I could've dealt with all of that, if it hadn't been for all the families coming and going and saying good-bye to or greeting their loved ones. That was what got to me. Whether it was college students coming home for Christmas break or grandparents arriving with arms laden with brightly wrapped gifts—all the jubilant greetings and embraces and heading off for a joyous family reunion somewhere, well, it just got to me. And, as much as I despised self-pity or feeling like Ebenezer Scrooge, all that sweet Christmas cheer was hard to swallow.

Needless to say, I was greatly relieved when we were finally loaded onto our big jet, cozily buckled into our comfy seats, and being treated so nicely it was almost like being family. After we took off, I even allowed myself to imagine that the pretty blonde stewardess named Cindy was a relative, a cousin perhaps. And when she smiled and offered me hot tea, I actually pretended we were sitting in a parlor with a fire burning and a small pine Christmas tree in the corner.

"Do you need a blanket?" she asked Jamie with a sparkling Colgate smile. I could tell by the way she looked at him that she thought he was a nice-looking young man, and I had to agree with her on that account. And although she was probably at least ten years older than he, I could tell he was enjoying the attention.

"Sure," he said, taking the neatly folded plaid woolen throw from her. "Thank you."

"I think Cindy likes you," I whispered to Jamie as the steward-ess walked away.

He looked slightly embarrassed, then grinned. "Maybe I should ask her out."

I made a slight face—a motherly expression meant as a subtle warning—then asked him what had become of his last girlfriend. "Wasn't her name Shelly?"

"Shelly," he said stiffly. "And that was almost two years ago, Mom."

I sensed a slight irritation in his voice, as if Shelly was an unpleas-ant subject, but since I also knew we'd be stuck together for some time and conversation topics might possibly get scarce, I decided why not persist a bit. Besides, I was curious about the girlfriend. He had even talked about bringing her home to visit at one time and then that was it—not another word on the subject. Of course, Hal had passed away about the same time and life got a little stressful after that. Perhaps I'd missed something. And that made me feel sad . . . like a poor excuse for a mother. But now I really wanted to know. Not that I could force my son to talk. But I could try. Just as I was formulating my next question, Cindy returned.

"We have complimentary champagne," she said, flashing that brilliant smile again. I started to decline on her offer, but then remembered that this was going to be a long flight and perhaps a little champagne would make things more comfortable for both Jamie and me—might even loosen our tongues a bit.

"That sounds lovely," I said. "How about you, Jamie?"

He grinned and nodded eagerly. Although my son had been twenty-one for months now, it still felt strange to think that he was of legal drinking age and could casually drink a glass of champagne with me right now. Hadn't he just been learning to ride a two-wheeler last week? And when did he get his braces off? Suddenly everything about motherhood and raising my only son felt like a fast hazy blur—similar to the clouds that were passing by the window at the moment.

"Here you go," Cindy said, handing us both a glass of champagne.

We thanked her, and then I held up my glass to Jamie. "Here's to a good trip."

"To Ireland."

We clinked glasses, and despite my lapse in matters of faith these past couple of years and particularly recently, I actually said a silent little prayer just then. *God, if you're there, if you can hear me and you're not too busy, please, help this trip to turn out right. So much is at stake . . . please, please, help me. Amen.*

"So . . . ," I said to Jamie, as we were finishing our champagne, "I'm curious as to what became of Shelly."

He downed the remainder of his drink. "She went her way . . . I went mine."

"So, it was a congenial parting?"

He shrugged in a way that suggested it was not. Then Cindy reappeared with her bottle of champagne. "More?"

Jamie stuck his glass out, and thinking it couldn't hurt our conversation, I followed his lead. Then when we were about halfway through our second glass, I tried again, deciding that if he really didn't want to talk about Shelly, I would simply change the subject. But to my amazement, he began to open up.

"It was really her idea to break up," he said quietly.

I just nodded, trying to look empathetic but not overly so.

"It was right after Christmas break, back in '61. I was so glad

44

to get back to school and see her again. I'd been wishing that I'd invited her to come home with me during the holidays, to meet you and Dad . . ." He kind of sighed now. "Turned out I was a day late and a dollar short."

"Why's that?"

"During Christmas break, Shelly had gotten back together with an old high school sweetheart who'd been going to an Ivy League school back east."

"Oh . . ."

"Yeah, she told me that this guy had always been the love of her life and that he'd broken up with her to go to college, but then when they got together again, he suddenly decided she was really the one for him and they'd actually gotten engaged on Christmas Eve." He shook his head. "Can you believe that?"

"Seems like pretty fast work, not to mention a little harsh," I said defensively. "Especially since she'd been dating you."

"Yeah, you'd think she might've called me or something."

"Well, I don't mean to sound callous, Jamie, but I'm not too sure I'd like this girl. She sounds a little fickle to me. I think you deserve someone better."

"Yeah, but you never met her, Mom." His voice got that defensive edge to it again, just like when he was in high school and I questioned him on something. "She was actually very nice—smart and pretty. Everyone who knew her liked her a lot. Some of the guys in my dorm were pretty jealous of me for going with her." He paused and got a thoughtful look. "I think I might've asked her to marry me."

Well, I knew I'd stuck my foot in my mouth now. But, at the same time, I was glad that he was being so open with me. Whether it was the champagne or being away from home, it didn't matter, we were actually talking and not arguing! And yet, at the same time, my heart ached for my son. I wanted to hug him and tell him everything would be okay; I wanted to put a bandage on his owie and kiss it and make it all better. Wasn't that what mothers did when their sons were hurting? But I realized things had changed. Jamie wasn't my little boy anymore.

"She sounds like a nice girl," I finally said, "and, of course, I can't imagine you caring for a girl who wasn't nice. I'm sure that I probably would've liked her too. But I do feel badly that she hurt you like that, Jamie. I can't help feeling like a mom, you know. It's just the way God wires us."

He nodded now. "It was hard losing her, Mom."

"I'm sure it was . . ."

Then he turned and looked at me with those clear blue eyes, so striking against his dark brown hair, so reminiscent that it was painful to look at sometimes. "Did anything like that ever happen to you? Any broken hearts in your past?"

I took a quick sip of champagne, gauging my time and asking myself if this was the right moment or not. I just wasn't sure. Or maybe I just wasn't ready.

"I mean, I know that Dad was head over heels in love with you," he said quickly, relieving me of having to give an answer. "I could see it in the way he treated you, Mom. I don't know if you always saw it, but I'd see him looking at you, and it was as if he had stars in his eyes. The guy adored you, Mom. And I remember, not that long before he died, Dad was talking about how you guys met when you came to apply for a job at the shoe store, and how it was love at first sight for him, and how even though you didn't know the first thing about shoes, he hired you right on the spot. And he even confessed at how stunned he'd been when you actually agreed to marry him. I think he said he was 'over the moon for you.' " Jamie laughed. "That was pretty good for Dad, don't you think?"

I nodded, moved by my son's sentiment and blinking back hot tears that brimmed in my eyes. But, although touched, I also felt as if someone had just twisted a dull knife in my heart. I knew that Jamie would assume my tears were for Hal, because I missed him. And that was partially true. I was extremely sad that Hal was gone, and I did miss him. Every single day. There was no denying that. But in that moment, I felt like a complete hypocrite, and my heart ached with an old festering guilt—a guilt I could never seem to completely shake off. And that was because I still faulted myself with the fact that I had never been "over the moon" for Hal.

46

Oh, I had tried my hardest, I'd put on a good show, I'd been the best wife I knew how to be, and yet, in my mind, it was never enough. Never equal to what Hal poured out over me. His love for me was so natural, so easy. Sometimes it reminded me of a dance. He knew all the steps, he moved gracefully, effortlessly . . . and I sort of stumbled along. I never felt equal to him when it came to loving. And with him gone now, I felt even more like a failure—a phony. And I feared this shroud of guilt would follow me to my grave and perhaps even haunt me thereafter.

"Dad was a good guy, Mom," Jamie continued as if to comfort me, still misunderstanding my emotions. "I mean, I probably took him for granted more than anyone, and I really do regret that. But I've been thinking about him a lot lately . . . especially since President Kennedy was killed. I've been thinking about a lot of stuff. Like what it takes to become a really good man, you know, someone like Dad or JFK. And I think about what a good example Dad gave me—he was honest and hardworking and really kind. He was a great husband to you. I couldn't have asked for a better dad. Man, I still remember how he'd close up the shoe store early just so he could come see me at a ball game."

"He loved watching you play sports, Jamie. He'd never been very good at them himself. You brought a lot of joy into his life."

"And I want to make him proud, I really do."

"I know you do."

"And I think he'd be proud if I joined the Air Force. Like maybe I'd be fulfilling his dream somehow. You know?"

I swallowed hard, then nodded. This was a battlefield I wasn't ready for.

"Anyway, I realize how lucky I was to have him. We were both lucky."

"Or as your dad would say, we were blessed."

"Yeah, *blessed*."

A hot tear escaped, sliding down my cheek now. Using the cocktail napkin, I dabbed at it. "You're right, your dad was a good man. And he loved us both dearly."

"And, even though I acted like a jerk sometimes and I know

I hurt him about the shoe business and everything, I really did love him." His eyes got a little moist too. "Do you think he really knew that?"

I nodded. *"He knew."* I closed my eyes and leaned my head back, trying to contain the tears that threatened to flood. Jamie's words felt like iodine being poured into a deep wound—they burned like fire, but hopefully there was healing in them too. Still, this wasn't going to make it any easier to tell him the truth—the timing seemed all wrong just now. Maybe once we were in Ireland it would be easier. *God, give me strength!*

6

Jamie

I thought flying was fun when we started out on this trip. But by the time we landed in Dublin, I didn't think I'd be wanting to get on a plane anytime soon. "I'm glad that's over with," I told Mom as we gathered our bags. "I'm sick of planes."

"I am too," she said. "I never breathed so much cigarette smoke in my life, not even on our trip to Paris, which I'd thought was bad enough. But I think most of the passengers must've been smokers on this flight."

"Well, at least we don't have to fly again for a couple of weeks."

"Actually, that's not the plan," she said as we waited for a cab. We were trying to stay close to the building to avoid the rain that seemed to be coming down in buckets just now. "We do have another short flight on Tuesday."

"Where to?"

"Galway."

"What's in Galway?"

She shrugged and waved to an oncoming cab. "I guess we'll find out."

Then suddenly we were loading our bags in the trunk and jumping into the back of the cab. We were both dripping wet as the cabby

49

drove us into the city, and Mom was getting more and more frustrated as she tried to make herself clear to the driver, who appeared to be a bit deaf. Mom was using far too many words and actually trying to give the cabby directions, which seemed a bit crazy, plus I could tell the poor guy was ready to toss us out, fare or no fare. It didn't help matters that his thick accent was impossible for Mom to decipher, although the more they bantered, the more I seemed to be getting it. That was when I realized that Mom's ear was not too clever when it came to accents and decided to jump in.

"Why don't you let me translate for you?" I teased.

She scowled at me, but handed me the paper with the name of the hotel and other details written on it.

"The Fitzwilliam Hotel," I said as clearly as possible, even trying to sound a bit Irish myself.

He nodded. "Aye, 'at's on Sain' Stephens Green, i'tiz."

"Yes," I said eagerly. "I mean *aye*! That's it!"

Then he laughed and drove on through the dark and damp city, and soon we were pulling up to a well-lit hotel. At that point, I decided to take charge of matters. I'd already exchanged a couple of twenties at the airport, and after a quick inventory of the strange-looking Irish bills and coins, I managed to pay and tip the cabby. It was possible I overtipped him, because he seemed pretty happy, but at least we were safely at the hotel and the guy was very helpful in getting our bags into the lobby.

Mom smiled at me as she removed and shook out her trench coat. "I'll have to remember to take you on all my foreign travels."

"You planning on doing a lot of this?" I asked as I removed my soggy suede jacket and laid it over a suitcase.

"You never know." Then she glanced up to the registration desk. "Would you like to help check us in too?"

"Sure."

Then she handed me a confirmation slip. "Tell them we have a reservation for three nights, adjoining rooms."

Mom listened as I spoke to the man at the desk. This guy was a little easier to understand, and I suspect that she could've handled it just fine. But it was sort of fun taking charge, and I could tell she was getting a kick out of it too.

"I know I should be exhausted," I told Mom as we rode up the elevator, which they call a *lift*, "but I think I've gotten my second wind. I wouldn't mind taking a little stroll and checking out the nightlife."

She frowned. "In the rain?"

"Sure. Isn't that what Ireland is all about?"

She sort of laughed. "Well, count me out. All I want is a hot bath and a soft bed and maybe a little room service."

"See you in the morning then?" I said, after I got her bags and things into her room, which actually looked pretty nice. Mom was doing this thing first class.

"You be careful out there, Jamie," she warned as she hung up her trench coat. "I know you're twenty-one and think you're all grown up, but you're also a stranger in a foreign country and—"

"I know"—I held up my hand—"don't be taking any wooden nickels."

She sort of smiled. "Just be careful."

I gave her a slight salute. "Will do."

I dumped my stuff on the floor of my room, which was also pretty ritzy, then dug a dry shirt out of my big suitcase and found a slightly wrinkled sports jacket, and then I took off. I didn't know much about Dublin, but something about the look of the city as the cabby drove us here pulled me right in. I couldn't wait to do a little exploring.

I walked around for about half an hour, just enjoying the opportunity to stretch my legs and get the lead out. I passed by numerous pubs and considered going into several, but it wasn't until I heard lively music coming out of Flannery's that I decided to go in. Now, I'd never heard Irish music before, not that I could recall anyway, but something about the sound of this band felt familiar. And something about the music just drew me in. I bought myself a pint of Guinness, took a seat near the band, and just listened.

It wasn't long before I was conversing with the three guys in the band, just talking about regular stuff between songs—music talk.

They thought it was cool that I was an American and a musician, and I thought it was cool that they were Irish. Sure, that made no sense to them since they were, obviously, in Ireland. But it was as if I was getting pulled into this country—and its music. Something about the whole place just seemed right to me. After about an hour, I offered to buy the guys in the band a Guinness, and they gladly agreed. It seems musicians didn't get rich in this country either.

Sean, the outgoing redhead, played the fiddle. Galen, the short, quiet guy, played the drum. In fact he played several drums, but only one at a time. And Galen's drums were nothing like the trap set that Steve had used for Jamie and the Muskrats. These Irish drums resembled oversized tambourines, but without the jingles on the sides. And Galen played them with a collection of sticks, resulting in a variety of cool sounds. Last but not least was Mick, the leader. He played both the guitar and a flutelike instrument that he called a *penny whistle.*

We talked about music while drinking our Guinness, and to my surprise, we were all pretty interested in a new British group, The Beatles. Mick had even heard them play once in Germany.

"'Twas afore they got their new drummer," he told me with a thick Irish accent.

"Wha' is the name of the drummer?" Galen asked. "'Twas a strange un, I recall."

"Ringo?" Mick offered.

"That's right," Galen said. "Ringo! Now, where'd they come up with that?"

We were so engrossed in our conversation that the pub owner had to remind them it was time to play again. So I sat and listened some more. And they finally wrapped it up a little before midnight. By then I was actually starting to get a little sleepy, probably jet-lagged, or maybe it was that third pint of Guinness. But since the guys offered me a ride, I didn't mind waiting for them to pack it up. I couldn't help but wonder what Mom would think of my new group of friends—not that she'd still be up to see them—but I felt sure she'd think they were a little strange with their long hair and sideburns. But then Mom wasn't used to musicians either.

As we rode in their van back to my hotel, Sean and I got to talking about the recent assassination of President Kennedy. It seemed the Irish had been almost as upset by this as the Americans. Then Sean told me about his hometown.

"I grew up in ta very same place where John Fitzgerald Kennedy's ancestors come from," he said proudly.

"Really?" I was impressed. "What's it called?"

"New Ross in Wexford."

"Where's that?" I asked, wishing I'd brought my map of Ireland along.

"Near a city called Waterford," Sean said as he lit a cigarette. "Not far from Dublin. Ya take the train, an' 'tis only a day trip."

"There ya go now," Galen called from the driver's seat, which was oddly on the right side of the cab. "The Fitzwilliam 'otel."

Sean whistled. "Quite posh. You must be rich."

I laughed and confessed I was traveling with my mom. That made them laugh. But they all slapped me on the back and told me to come back to Flannery's and see them again.

"We're featured for a fortnight," Galen said as I hopped out.

"Big New Year's Eve bash," Sean called out.

"I'll be back," I promised. "Count on it!"

Then I ran through the rain up to the hotel, rode up the lift, and let myself into my room. I considered checking on Mom, but figured she'd be dead asleep by now. Hopefully she hadn't stayed up and worried about me, but just in case she was still awake and listening, I tried not to be too quiet in my room. That should set her mind at ease.

By the time I hit the sack, I was so exhausted that my eyes couldn't even stay open. It'd been an unexpectedly groovy evening, my first night in Ireland, and already I'd met some fun musicians. But what surprised me most was how much I liked Ireland, when I hadn't even wanted to come here in the first place. I don't think I could begin to explain what was going on in me, not even to myself—but something about this country felt comfortable, familiar even. It was weird but cool.

I replayed some of our conversations from tonight, thinking that if I really worked on it, I might be able to get down that Irish accent a little before we headed back home. In a way there was something almost musical about their language, and something about the sound of it—or perhaps it was the rhythm, it was hard to understand . . . but it made my fingers just itch to get to a piano. Maybe it was a combination of the music I'd heard tonight, the guys I'd talked to, and the country itself, but somehow I knew this experience was changing me as a musician, and it might even change the way I played piano. In fact, I was so jazzed that, although I was totally beat, I didn't know if I could even go to sleep.

7

〰〰〰〰〰〰〰

Colleen

It took me a few minutes to get my bearings and remember where I was, but then it hit me—*Ireland*! I was really here. I glanced at the little alarm clock to see it was past ten and felt surprised that I slept so long. Then I remembered how I woke in the middle of the night, how I worried that Jamie might not have made it back to the hotel safely. But I'd been unwilling to knock on his door and disturb him in case I was wrong, so I just sat and watched the hands slowly moving around the clock, and then I paced back and forth in the room and asking myself, why had I come here? I finally forced myself back to bed again. But I still felt anxious and uneasy, fretting that it had been a big mistake to take this expensive trip, fearing that nothing was going to help me tell Jamie the news that I felt certain he would never want to hear.

But with morning here and the Irish sun shining through the heavy lace curtains, I began to feel better. Perhaps it wasn't a mistake after all. Funny how the nighttime turns challenges into monsters. I did a few stretches and tried to calculate what time it was in Pasadena right now, but then decided, why bother? This was Ireland and I was on Irish time, might as well get used to it.

As I slipped on my quilted satin robe, I noticed a white piece of paper by my door, as if someone had slipped it under from the hallway. I went over to pick it up, seeing the word "Mom" penned across the front. Obviously it was from Jamie. I hoped nothing was wrong.

Dear Mom,
    I had a fantastic time last night. I met some musicians and they told me about the town where John F. Kennedy's family came from. I got up early so that I could look into taking the train there. I think I'll be back sometime tonight. I hope you don't mind.
    Love, Jamie

I reread the note and wondered what kind of wild-goose chase my son had taken off on today, and who on earth were these "musicians" and how had he met them so quickly? Young people these days—it almost made my head spin. But then I reminded myself that Jamie was an adult, and if he was old enough to join the Air Force, which I hoped I'd be able to dissuade him from doing, then he was certainly old enough to hop on an Irish train and see the sites. Besides, I told myself, as I leisurely bathed and dressed, a quiet day to myself wouldn't be so bad. Perhaps I would explore a bit of Dublin. Maybe even do some shopping. I'd promised Sally to look for some fisherman knit sweaters, and I'd heard there was beautiful crystal to be found in this country. Then, by evening, Jamie would return and we could have a nice dinner somewhere. I'd ask the concierge downstairs to recommend a good place.

After a light breakfast of a soft-boiled egg, served in a fragile porcelain eggcup, which was a new experience for me, along with toast and delicious jam and some nice Irish tea, I decided it was time to see a bit of Dublin. Dressed warmly and armed with my umbrella and trench coat, since it had just started to rain again, I inquired at the concierge desk. Fortunately, this man's accent was easier for me to understand. Plus, I knew it was good practice.

"I've heard Dublin has some good museums."

"Aye, we do. All sorts of museums. History and art. What sort of things are you interested in?"

"I like art," I said. "Not that I'm much of an expert. But I did enjoy seeing the Louvre in Paris." I remembered how Hal had patiently accompanied me that day. The poor man really didn't care much for art, although he appreciated the architecture.

"Do you like modern art?" he asked hopefully. "We have a wonderful place."

I wasn't terribly fond of modern styles like cubism or Picasso, but his enthusiasm caught me off guard. "Sure," I said.

Then he told me the name, which was quite a mouthful. "But you'll need a cab," he said as he pulled out a city map and pointed out some other sites as well as the better shopping areas that I might be interested in. Then he had one of the bellboys call a cab for me, and I set out for what I hoped would be a delightful adventure.

Unfortunately, within minutes I began to wish I had Jamie along to help "translate." The cabby, like the one last night, had a heavy Irish accent, and it seemed the harder I tried to understand him, the worse it got. Finally, I pulled out a fountain pen and a piece of notepaper from the hotel and wrote down exactly where I wished to go, *The Hugh Lane Municipal Gallery of Modern Art*. The note did just the trick, and before long I was dropped off by an old but impressive-looking building. And to my delight, the "modern art" in this museum featured some of my all-time favorite artists, including Monet, Degas, and Manet. I suddenly began to appreciate Ireland's history, realizing that the interpretation for "modern" was all a matter of perspective. To Ireland, an old country, these impressionist painters were considered "modern."

After that, I took another cab over to the National Museum of Ireland. The art museum had whet my appetite, and I was now intrigued by Ireland and its history. The museum was quiet, and other than a surprisingly well-behaved class of elementary school children, I had the place almost entirely to myself. So I took my time as I studied ancient weapons, beautifully carved furniture, silver and gold sculptures, ceramics and glassware, as well as lots of other things.

For some reason I felt particularly taken by the Irish harps, or perhaps it was their history. I learned that England, in an attempt to oppress Ireland, had banned the harp several hundred years earlier. The ruling Brits feared the Irish's love of harp music would lead to nationalism, and so they killed all the harpists and burned their harps. It broke my heart to think of that sweet music being stolen from the Irish like that—it felt so wrong, criminal even. However, I discovered that the Irish did salvage some of their lost music by gathering the few surviving harpists and secretly having them write down what music they could remember. I supposed it had been better than nothing, but so much of the music, not to mention those ancient harps, had been completely lost. Such a shame.

With a sense of melancholy, I decided to take advantage of the break in weather by walking back to my hotel. It was nearly one now, and I was hoping that Jamie might've gotten back earlier than expected. But there was no sign of him. I asked the concierge about the place where our former president's family had immigrated from, and he told me that it was near the town of Waterford.

"Where they make crystal?" I said.

"Aye. And there are bus tours that go up there." He pulled out a brochure and handed it to me. "If you'd like to see the factory."

"I'll think about that," I told him. Then I returned to the hotel restaurant and ordered some lunch. It felt odd eating alone for the second time today. I didn't like to think of myself as a needy sort of woman, the kind who must always have a man in tow to feel at ease, but suddenly I wasn't so sure. Hal had always taken such good care of me. He was the kind of man who opened doors, took me by the arm, carried my bags, and just generally made my life smoother. It hadn't been easy getting used to taking care of myself this past year and a half. And yet, I felt I'd made progress. I felt that I was getting more comfortable with my widowed status. Still, would I have attempted this trip on my own? Having Jamie along had seemed to make it easier, but then he certainly was nowhere to be seen today. I hoped that all was well with him. And, again, I told myself that it was for the best. We both needed our space today. Perhaps it would bolster my spirits and help me to say the things that needed saying.

Following lunch, and a continued break in the wet weather,

I walked over to a couple of sites that weren't too far from the hotel. I toured the National Museum until I felt as if I'd absorbed as much art and history as was possible. After that, I found my way to a nice little shopping district. The one thing I had learned in my world travels (although relatively few) was that shopping, particularly for women, came easy, it seemed we all spoke the same language when it came to opening up one's pocketbook and purchasing something. Shopkeepers were always friendly and willing to take time to explain things like merchandise quality, money exchange rates, or even fashion tips. And so by the end of my day, I had splurged on several fisherman knit sweaters, two mohair blankets, and other various Irish souvenirs. Most of these I had sent to Sally and her family, although it was doubtful that they would make it by Christmas. Still, it saved me from having to pack them about the country for two weeks. The rest of the items I'd had sent along to the hotel.

My biggest splurges of the day came from a shop that specialized in Donegal tweed. Ireland is known for its fine wool, and Donegal is considered the best. For Jamie, I purchased a brown tweed sports coat that I knew would look handsome on him. For myself, I was easily talked into a classy black-and-white hound's-tooth suit.

"Miss Doris Day, herself, purchased the exact same suit," she assured me.

"Really?" I said, not sure that I believed her, or that I really cared.

"'Tis lovelier on you," she said in a hushed tone, as if Doris herself was in the next dressing room. That was when I knew this saleslady was good. Still, I had to agree with her, the suit did look awfully nice on me.

"I'll take it," I told her.

"We have a lovely Irish linen blouse that is perfect with this suit."

Naturally, I was a pushover. But, all in all, it was a wonderful way to spend my first full day in Ireland. And it helped to distract me from worrying about Jamie. At least for the time being.

However, when I got back to the hotel and it was after five and dark outside and, according to the front desk, Jamie still hadn't returned, I wasn't sure what to think. So I wrote out a message and handed it to the clerk.

"Please give this to my son when he gets in." I wasn't going to take any chances of missing Jamie. I could imagine my wayward boy getting in and then popping back out without even letting me know that he'd gotten safely back to town. Jamie had always been a fairly independent boy, but he'd gotten even more so once he'd gone off to college. Not that I minded—I thought independence and confidence were good traits. But sometimes I did worry about him. For instance, the weeks preceding this trip . . . even though Jamie had been helpful at home, he'd also been known to disappear without telling me he'd even gone, and sometimes for hours at a time. And if I'd ask him where he'd been, or what he'd been doing, or who he'd been with, Jamie would often turn evasive and defensive, as if it were none of my business.

It wasn't that I thought he'd been up to no good, but I was curious. And I was aware that many of his friends didn't live in town anymore, and I couldn't help but wonder what it was he did with his spare time. Goodness, wasn't that what mothers were supposed to do? Just because our children grew older didn't mean we quit worrying, did it?

I went up to my room and began to put away today's purchases. I paused to take out the lovely mohair blanket that I'd gotten for myself. I shook it out and admired its colors, a delightful mix of mossy greens and rusty reds, then laid it across a chair. It would be nice to have this throw on these long Irish winter nights. The climate was so different than Southern California. Then I removed my new tweed suit from the box and carefully hung it up in the closet. Very classy. And then, because it was chilly in the room, I slipped on the cardigan fisherman knit sweater and checked it in the mirror. I hadn't intended on getting one for myself and hadn't even tried it on at the shop, but after finding lovely ones for my sister and her family, and a pullover for Jamie, I thought, why not? And, as I studied my reflection, I thought perhaps I'd made the right choice after all. It really did look rather good on me. I think it actually made me look younger. I struck a pose, putting one hand on my hip and jutting my chin out like a model, then laughed at myself. Sally had always thought that I looked like Audrey Hepburn, although I felt sure she was only being nice. Still there was something about this sweater with my dark hair pinned up in a French roll that almost made me think there was a faint resemblance.

Finally, it was half past seven and I still hadn't heard a word from Jamie. I'd tried knocking on his door, but no answer. I even called down to the front desk; no one had seen him. Now I hated feeling like a fretful granny, but I couldn't help but begin to imagine the worst. After all, we were in a foreign country—who knew what could go wrong? What if something terrible had happened or what if he were unconscious and no one knew who to contact for him? It wasn't as if my son was wearing a dog tag, and even his California driver's license would be useless in reaching me here in Dublin. Why hadn't I thought of this before?

What if Jamie had been robbed at knifepoint? Or kidnapped by Irish thugs? Or hit by a car? I'd heard stories of American tourists who had stepped straight into oncoming traffic, all because they were looking the wrong way, left instead of right. Oh, why hadn't I thought to warn him about that sort of thing? Soon I was pacing again, fretting and pacing, pacing and fretting. And finally I knew that the only thing I could really do was to pray. I remembered how often Hal had told me this very thing. "Don't worry, Honey," he'd say calmly if Jamie had stayed out a little late when he was still a teen. "Pray instead." But Hal's faith had been stronger than mine. His experience with God had seemed more genuine than my own. And it was in moments like this that I dearly missed that man. And so I prayed. And before long I did begin to feel calmer.

At eight o'clock, I called for room service. Although I didn't feel hungry, I thought a light meal could be a distraction. I ordered the lentil soup and a Caesar salad and hot tea. I was sitting alone in my room, barely touching my food, when I heard a knock at the door. Preparing myself for the worst, perhaps a policeman to inform me of an accident, I went to answer it.

"Hi, Mom!" Jamie said cheerfully. His cheeks were ruddy and his dark hair was curling from the moisture in the air. Suddenly I was torn between wanting to take him over my knee, or to simply hug him. Fortunately hugging won out. Although it was a damp hug.

"Where have you been?" I demanded as I pulled him into the room. "I've been worried sick." I used the linen napkin from my neglected meal to wipe my eyes, trying to conceal the fact that tears of relief were falling.

"Sorry, Mom. Didn't you get my note?"

"Yes. But you said you'd be home this evening."

"It is *this evening*."

I nodded. "Yes, I suppose so. But I guess I thought you'd be home in time for dinner."

"I actually sort of thought I would too." He glanced over to my tray. "Sorry about that."

"It's okay. I'm just glad you're safely back. Do you want to order room service?"

Soon we both had a tray of food. I ordered something more tempting than my lukewarm lentil soup, and we sat in my room, eating happily together, and Jamie told me all about his excursion. And I told him about mine.

"I think we both had lovely days," I had to admit as I went to get the items I'd purchased for him.

"Yeah, it's pretty amazing, Mom," he said with a youthful enthusiasm—a tone I hadn't heard in his voice, it seemed, in years. "I really like this place—I feel like I fit in here—in Ireland, I mean. I can't even explain it really, but it's groovy."

I suppressed a smile as I handed him the pullover. "I like Ireland too, and this is a *real* Irish fisherman knit sweater."

"For me?" He stood to examine it better.

"When in Ireland . . ."

He quickly pulled the sweater over his head, emerging with a big grin and ruffled hair. "How's it look?"

"Perfect," I said. "Very handsome."

"But do I look Irish?" he asked hopefully.

I nodded, hoping I wouldn't start crying again. "Oh, yes, very much so."

"Cool."

Then I showed him the tweed jacket, which fit him perfectly and actually gave him the appearance of a young country gentleman. "They say that Donegal wool can last for decades," I told him. "If you take care of it properly. The tag tells how."

"Thanks, Mom. I really like it." But it was the sweater that he put back on. "I was thinking about going down to that pub again tonight. It's called Flannery's and it's about a thirty-minute walk from the hotel. That Irish band is going to be there all month, and I really wanted to hear them again. Do you want to come along?"

I considered this. On the one hand, I felt flattered that he was actually inviting me. On the other hand, it was past nine now, and it had already been a very long day. That, combined with my worrying this evening, and I felt exhausted. "Maybe not tonight," I said. "I'm still a little jet-lagged plus I didn't sleep too well last night."

He nodded. "Man, was I surprised that I slept like a baby. Then I got up feeling great. I think this Irish air agrees with me."

I smiled. "Well, it's probably a lot cleaner than Southern California. But it's a lot cooler too."

"This sweater will be just the thing for that. Thanks again!"

"I'm glad you like it, Jamie. And have a good time tonight, but do be careful, okay?" Then, even though I didn't want to sound like a complete worrywart, I warned him to remember that the traffic came from the opposite direction. "Tourists have been known to get killed after looking the wrong way and then stepping out."

He just laughed. "Yeah, I know, Mom. I already figured it out."

Then, just like that, he was gone and I was alone again. And although I was hugely relieved that he'd made it back safely, and that he'd had a great day, I also felt like I might've missed an opportunity just now. I considered his high interest in Ireland, how much he seemed to love everything about the country and, well, it seemed like it had been my perfect chance to tell him the truth—to just get it over with. Then, I reminded myself, we still have lots of time, nearly two weeks. Maybe the smart thing would be to simply let Jamie have a good time, to experience the culture, the people, and to completely fall in love with the country. And then, when the timing was perfect and he was ready to hear the truth, then I would tell him.

8

|||||||||||||||

Jamie

On our second day in Ireland, Mom showed me the sites in Dublin, which was actually somewhat interesting. Then on our third day, we rode the train to Waterford to see the crystal factory. To my surprise that was fairly interesting too. Then on Tuesday, after I had a late night listening to the guys at Flannery's again, we got up early and flew in a small plane to Galway, then got onto a bus that was headed to a region called Connemara. Mom seemed to have it all worked out, and I couldn't help but be curious.

"So, what's in Connemara anyway?" I asked her as I looked out the fogged-up window to see lots of green rolling hills and soggy-looking sheep.

She shrugged in a slightly mysterious way. "To tell you the truth, I don't really know," she admitted. "I just heard about it once and wanted to see it for myself. Some people call Connemara the Emerald of the Isle, and I've heard it's supposed to be incredibly beautiful." Then she told me how an old John Wayne movie had been filmed somewhere around there. "I just loved that movie."

"A *Western*?" I stared in disbelief. Mom usually went out of her way to avoid watching any kind of Western, and it was Dad who'd been the John Wayne fan.

"Of course not. A Western in Ireland? No, John Wayne played

a prizefighter from America who came over here and fell in love with an Irish lass. It was a charming movie."

"Oh."

"I can hardly believe it's only a week before Christmas," Mom said.

"Yeah, they don't seem to make nearly as big of a deal of it as they do in America. I almost forgot it was the holidays."

"I have noticed an occasional wreath here or there, or a small Christmas tree in a shop," she pointed out.

"But not all the trappings and trimmings that get plastered all over the place back home. And none of that tinny old music."

"I think it's rather refreshing. I get so tired of all the commercialism and the pressure to do so much in so little time. By the time you decorate and send out cards and make cookies and buy far too many gifts and go to parties and cook a big dinner, it's practically over with and you're completely worn out. I don't recall it being anything like that when I was growing up. In fact, my parents always kept the holidays fairly simple, a candlelight service on Christmas Eve and a nice family dinner on Christmas. Besides a tree and a few gifts, it wasn't such a big ordeal back then."

"So, what are we doing for Christmas?"

Mom frowned slightly. "To be honest, I don't really know, Jamie. I guess I hadn't really thought that out. Of course, we'll be at the hotel in Clifden all week. But maybe we can find a church with a Christmas Eve service." She got a wistful look. "Perhaps a candlelight service like when I was a girl."

"Yeah, I guess that could be interesting."

"And then we'll find a nice restaurant for Christmas Day. I wonder what the Irish eat for Christmas . . . maybe the fatted goose and plum pudding, or is that British?"

"What if all the restaurants are closed?"

Mom's brow creased now. "Oh, dear, I hadn't even considered that."

Now I felt bad for worrying her. "We'll figure it out," I said quickly. "Worst-case scenario, we'll get provisions from a grocery store and just make do. Have an indoor picnic or something in our hotel room."

She smiled now. "That sounds like fun."

Mom returned to writing postcards and I continued to watch out the window. It really was beautiful landscape, so green that it seemed almost unreal. At first the clouds had hung so low that they gave the countryside a misty, almost haunted appearance, but after a while they began to lift and eventually the rain shower quit as well. I'd already heard that this was one of the wettest spots in the world, and I'd started to wonder if we'd ever see blue sky again, but by the time we reached our destination, the small seaport town of Clifden, the sun had actually made an appearance.

The bus dropped us right in front of our hotel, which was on the main drag, and the driver even helped us get our bags inside. On the way into town, I'd noticed there were several pubs, and one of them had a sign that said LIVE MUSIC, and I was eager to check that out.

"This looks like a cool little town," I said to Mom after we got checked in and were riding an ancient elevator up to our floor. I hoped the tiny "lift," loaded with us and our bags, wasn't going to give out before we reached the third floor.

"I think I'll be taking the stairs after that ride," I told Mom when we finally got out.

"It'd probably be quicker," she said as she handed me a large brass key. "You're in 302 and I'm in 304. And there are no phones in the rooms."

"How about TVs?" I joked. Even our big hotel in Dublin didn't have televisions in the rooms.

"I think I'll put my stuff away, then check out the town," I told Mom as I unlocked my door. "How about you?"

"I might take a little walk," she said. "Maybe mail my postcards. And I'd like to find a bookshop since I finished my paperback."

"Want to meet up for dinner?"

"Yes, that sounds good. How about 6:30 in the lobby downstairs? Maybe one of us will find a promising restaurant by then."

I tossed my bags into the room, then closed and locked the

door. "See ya," I called as I headed for the stairway. I wanted to check out that pub, the one with the live music sign. Hopefully I could talk Mom into going there tonight. But, even more than that, I wanted to find someplace with a piano. Maybe there was a music store in town. Or maybe one of the pubs would have a piano. Perhaps I could offer to play for a Guinness. I laughed to myself as I hurried down the street. Or maybe they would offer me a Guinness to quit playing.

The wet sidewalks were steaming in the afternoon sun, and the temperature felt warmer than it had in days. But it was the air that got my attention. It smelled so fresh and good, breezing in right off the sea, I thought that if a person could bottle this and sell it, they would soon become rich.

I ducked into the first pub and looked around to see if there was a piano in sight, but no luck. I checked several others, but again no luck. Even the one with the live music sign was pianoless.

"Whad'ya 'ave?" the man behind the bar asked.

"A piano?"

He laughed. "Is that some fancy American drink?"

I shook my head, then pantomimed playing a piano. "No, I was just looking for a piano that I could practice on. Is there a music store in town?"

He scratched his head. "Aye, but I don't tink O'Toole's got any pianos in his wee store."

"How about the pubs?" I persisted. "Do any have pianos?"

Now his eyes lit up. "Up at the Anchor Inn is a nice grand piano."

"Where's that?"

"Ya take the beach road an' ya go on up past the yacht club and a bit beyond there and you'll see a tall brick building with lots of windows, that be the Anchor Inn. The menu's a bit pricey, but the food's good and there's a nice view up there, if ya go afore dark, that is."

I thanked him and started walking toward the sea, figuring that must be the right direction for the beach road. It took about an hour to find the place, but sure enough there was a nice grand piano sitting in the corner of the restaurant. Other than a couple of old guys sitting at the bar on the other side of the room, the place looked pretty deserted.

"Might I be of some help to ya, laddie?" a middle-aged woman asked. Her curly hair was the exact same color as Bozo the Clown.

"I was looking for a place where I could practice piano," I told her.

She studied me closely. "Ya sound like an American."

I nodded, then smiled. "Yes, that's right. My mother and I came to Ireland for Christmas."

She smiled back at me now. "Well, I s'pose 'twouldn't hurt to let ya play a bit. Since there's no one much about." She nodded over her shoulder. "'Ceptin' for the old lads having their stout, and I doubt they'll pay you much mind. Just keep it down, though."

"Thanks."

I waited for her to leave before I slowly approached the piano. I knew that Ireland was a damp climate; hopefully this piano was in tune. I ran my fingers over the smooth wooden surface of the wood, then sat down, almost reverently, on the padded seat. Then, after stretching my fingers a little, I started to play. It felt so good to feel the ivory keys beneath my fingers again. To start with, I played the piece I'd been working on at home, back in the warehouse. Then I did some variations on it, giving it what I liked to think was an Irish flare, and it really seemed to work. I played for about an hour before the orange-haired woman returned. To my surprise, she started to clap when I finished my final song.

"That was absolutely lovely," she said. "Ya come on up here and play anytime ya like. Bring your mother too."

Now that gave me an idea. "Could I make a reservation for dinner tonight?" I asked eagerly. "For my mother and me?"

"'Twould be my pleasure," she said.

So I gave her my name and told her we'd be there around seven.

"Jamie Frederick," she said, sticking out her hand to shake mine. "'Tis a delight to make your acquaintance. And I am Kerry

McVee, and ta sole proprietress of the Anchor Inn, left to me by my late husband Bobby, God bless his soul."

"Pleased to meet you, Mrs. McVee."

"Just call me Kerry." She smiled. "So I'll be seeing you and your mother at seven then?"

"And would it be okay if I played the piano tonight? Maybe just a song or two?"

"Ya can play the whole night long if ya like, laddie. If it were my busy season, I'd even offer to pay ya for your music. Unfortunately, 'tis the slow time o' year and I'm barely able to make ends meet."

"That's okay. I don't want to be paid." Then, excited about my spur-of-the-moment plan, I decided to let her in on it. "You see, my mother doesn't even know that I can play piano. This will be her first time to hear me."

"She doesn't know?"

I shook my head. "She knows that I play guitar, but I took up piano a couple of years ago, and I never told her."

"Isn't she in for a lucky surprise."

"Yes," I agreed. "So I'd appreciate it if you didn't say anything."

"Mum's the word." She put a forefinger over her lips and winked. "And I won't mention it to your mum either."

I hoped that would be the case as I retraced my steps back to town, making it to the hotel just as it was getting dusky. I wasn't sure if Mom was back yet, but just in case she was resting or immersed in a new book, I decided not to disturb her. I wrote a note on the hotel stationery, telling her about the reservations for dinner at the Anchor Inn, then slipped it beneath her door.

My plan was to play for her, maybe between dinner and dessert, giving us both time to relax and enjoy the evening. And then, after playing, I would lay my cards on the table and tell her the truth about dropping out of college. I knew this would be a tough conversation. And in some ways, I'd just as soon avoid it altogether. But I also knew that music was a huge part of my life, and I didn't want to hide it any longer. Besides, I had several things working in my favor. First, I would be breaking this news in a public place so that Mom wouldn't be able to get too angry since she never did like to make a scene; and second, Mom and I had been getting along better than ever these past couple of days and her sympathy levels should be good; and finally, Mom actually liked good music and hopefully she'd be proud of what I'd done and this new direction I'd taken. At least that's what I hoped. It seemed to make perfect sense.

Even so, I was incredibly nervous as I waited for Mom to join me in the hotel lobby. I hadn't been this uptight since Jamie and the Muskrats had made our debut at a high school fall formal back in '61. I nervously stood near the stairs, pretending to study the small rack of tourism information while I waited. I even stuck one of the fishing excursion pamphlets into my pocket. I'd already asked the desk clerk to call a cab for us since I knew that it would be too far for Mom to walk, plus it was dark out now anyway. He told me there weren't any cabs in Clifden, but that he could get us a Hackney car. I wasn't sure what that meant, but if he thought it would do the trick, it was fine by me.

I'd even dressed carefully, putting on the new tweed jacket that Mom had gotten for me, along with a clean white shirt and a striped tie. I wasn't too sure about the stripes with the tweed, but I'd only brought along a couple of ties and this one seemed to work the best.

"Jamie," Mom said as she emerged from the geriatric elevator. "Don't you look handsome."

I grinned at her. "You look nice too." Mom had on her blue suit, complete with matching hat and gloves. I think that suit was made by some famous designer with a name like Coco Puffs or something I could never quite remember. But Dad had always liked how it brought out the color of her eyes.

I held the door for my mom. "I think our Hackney car is out here."

"What?" she asked curiously.

So I explained about the cab situation and where we were going. "This place has an amazing view of the ocean in the daytime,

71

and the lady who runs it is really nice," I told her as I helped her into the car.

"How did you find out about it?"

"Just asked around," I said casually.

The wind was picking up a little as we went up the walk toward the restaurant. "I hope our good weather isn't about to blow away," Mom said as she kept her round, little blue hat from going airborne. "It was so nice out this afternoon."

The Anchor Inn was well lit inside, complete with a crackling fire in the big rock fireplace. I noticed now that there were even sprigs of holly about, hanging over pictures and across the mantel. A nice bit of Christmas cheer, understated but charming. Mom should like that. Also, there were candles lit, one in each windowsill. A nice touch and great atmosphere. And there, just as it had been earlier today, sat the grand piano, the dark wood gleaming as if it had just been polished, almost as if it were waiting for me.

"Welcome," Kerry said as I introduced my mother. "I hope you're enjoying your visit in Ireland."

"We're both falling in love with your beautiful country," Mom said as Kerry led us to a table not far from the piano. There were a couple of other parties here tonight, but most of the tables were vacant, and I could understand the concerns about lack of business. It was a wonder the place even stayed open.

Kerry smiled brightly. "That's what we like to hear from our neighbors across the sea. One day we hope to have a bustling tourist trade here in Ireland."

Dinner turned out to be very good, and despite the high prices Mom seemed completely pleased with my choice of restaurants. Our quiet but attentive waiter, Dolan, introduced himself as Kerry's younger brother. But other than that bit of info and bringing us our food and drinks, he kept to himself.

"Dessert?" he asked as he cleared our dinner plates.

"Sure," I said quickly, worried that Mom might try to get the check before I had a chance to do my mini concert. "What do you have?"

Dolan went over a short list, and Mom chose the custard and

I went with chocolate cake. Then I excused myself to "the men's room." And I actually did go to the men's room, but it was only to take some deep breaths and to calm myself. Then I went out, walked straight to the piano, and sat down. I was within plain sight of my mother, but she wasn't looking that way, which was just fine. It gave me another moment to compose myself and to focus. And then I began to play, glancing at Mom but focusing on the music.

To begin with, she didn't even look my way. She appeared completely absorbed by her cup of tea. And then quickly, almost as if she'd heard a gunshot, she turned around and just stared at me with wide eyes. I couldn't quite read her expression. It seemed a mixture of astonishment and horror, which really made no sense. Good grief, it wasn't like I was dancing on a table; I was simply playing the piano. Feeling even less at ease, I diverted my eyes but continued to play. When I finished my first piece, the small group of diners actually clapped. Even my mother clapped, although I could tell by the mechanical way that she moved her hands back and forth like a stiff marionette that she was still in some kind of shock. So I decided to play another piece. Then another. I suppose it was a delay technique, buying myself enough time in the hope that the next phase of my little dinner show might proceed a bit more smoothly. Finally, I stood up after the fourth piece. Once again I was pleased to hear the applause, even more enthusiastic than before. Even Kerry and Dolan and workers from the kitchen were clapping.

"Well . . . ," my mom said when I rejoined her.

"Well?" I studied her face. It seemed unreasonably pale, and I couldn't figure why she was reacting like this. My intention had been to please her with my musical skill. It was no secret that my mother enjoyed music, particularly piano, although her leanings were more to classical and light jazz. But I had hoped to gain her approval with my performance and then to gently break the news about what I'd been up to these past couple of years. It had seemed the perfect ploy.

But she just slowly shook her head, and her brow creased as if she were deeply troubled about something. She kept twisting the linen napkin between her fingers, something she often told me not to do, and her untouched dessert was pushed away to the side. "Wherever did you learn to play *like that?*"

Now it's possible that she didn't mean those words to come out the way that they sounded to me, but it was hard not to feel just a little offended. "Like *what?*" I said crisply, suddenly on the defensive.

She waved her hands, as if searching for words. "Well, it's a different sort of style," she said carefully, as if weighing each word. "Not the sort of thing one hears every day."

"So, you didn't like it?" I demanded.

"No . . . that's not it, Jamie." Her eyes looked slightly misty now. "I just wondered where you'd learned to play like that. That's all. One might think you'd taken music classes somewhere."

The time had come. I knew I might as well get this over with as quickly and painlessly as possible. If she took it badly, there wasn't much I could do. I cleared my throat. "There's something I need to tell you, Mom."

9

Colleen

I stared at Jamie as if staring at a complete stranger. How had this happened? What was the meaning? The whole thing was unsettling, disturbing, eerily haunting even—almost like seeing a ghost. Yes, that was exactly what it was like! It was as if I'd seen the ghost of Liam O'Neil just now, sitting there at the piano and playing like *that*. Of course, Jamie had no idea why my reaction to his music was so irrational, so unlike me. And, while I felt badly for catching him off guard and putting him on the defensive, I also felt that I was maintaining rather well not to have fallen out of my chair.

"There's something I need to tell you," he was saying and I was attempting to focus, but at the same time thinking, *No, Jamie, there's something I need to tell you*. Still he continued, the words poured out quickly, in the form of a confession of sorts.

"I didn't graduate from business college," he said. "I used the money that Dad sent to take some music classes at Berkeley. Then I quit school completely, supporting myself and my band with the tuition money while I seriously pursued music. I had meant to tell you guys. But then Dad died and I didn't want to upset you. And time passed and the lie just kept going."

"You didn't graduate?" I said, trying to absorb this new fact.

Perhaps even using it as a distraction from the emotions that were raging through me—memories of Liam and how he once played like that.

He nodded. "I'm sorry, Mom. I know I should've told you. But there just didn't seem to be the right opportunity." Then he smiled, that same little half smile that he'd used on me since he was a toddler. "But I *love* music. It's all I want to do and—"

"How long had you been lying about school, Jamie?" I knew my words sounded harsh, and much colder than I meant them to be, but it was as if all my emotions had risen to the surface, hammering to get out, and I didn't even know where to begin. Focusing on Jamie seemed the easiest route.

"It was winter term in '61 that I quit."

"And you kept this a secret the whole time?" I frowned as I considered how this would have hurt Hal. "You never told your father?"

"I tried to once, Mom. But he was so insistent that I'd take over the shoe store. All he wanted was for me to get my business degree and start selling shoes. I didn't want—"

"But you continued taking his money?" I stared at my son, seeing how much he looked like his birth father, and feeling shocked by this. But I made myself believe that my shock was because he had deceived us and that we had never even suspected. "That whole time you kept taking his money and pretending that you were going to school? What else were you keeping from us?" I could hear the venom in my voice, and yet I felt helpless.

He pressed his lips tightly together, as if he were biting his tongue, holding back the words he probably wanted to say. And his hands were curling into fists, as if he wanted to pound them on the table, to make his point. Instead, he just stood. "I know you're angry, Mom. And I don't blame you for that, but somehow I thought—" He looked longingly at the piano now. "I thought that maybe if you understood how much I love—" Then his voice broke.

"I'm sorry," he said then turned and walked away. Heading straight for the big carved door, he slowly opened it and, without looking back, walked out.

Suddenly my anger seemed foolish . . . and, in some ways, even selfish. And now I felt desperate. My son had laid his heart on the table, confessed to his deception, and I had treated him like a criminal. I knew I had hurt Jamie deeply, and I didn't know what to do next. I glanced around the quiet dining room, curious as to whether or not we'd made a spectacle, and yet not really caring either. But the other diners seemed fine, as if they hadn't noticed a thing. Or perhaps they were simply being polite.

"Everything all right?" asked the owner, the woman with bright orangey-red hair that had to have come out of a bottle. I couldn't remember her name.

"I, uh, I'm not sure," I admitted. "I think I'd like the bill, please."

Then she left, I assumed to tell Dolan to bring the bill, but a few minutes later, she was the one who returned. With the bill in her hand, she sat down across from me, the same spot where Jamie should've been sitting right now.

"Jamie's a fine musician," she said. "'Tis a boy 'twould make any mother proud."

I blinked in surprise. Who was this woman and how did she know my son? I simply nodded. "Yes. He's always been a good boy."

"But you're unhappy with him now."

"I'm frustrated," I admitted, still wondering who she was and why she felt the need to intrude into my personal affairs. "We had a little misunderstanding."

"About his piano playing?"

I glanced over to the door, curious as to whether he'd come back or not. Maybe he was just taking a little stroll, to cool off. Maybe the right thing to do was to wait for him to come back.

"Jamie told me that ya did not know—'twas meant to be a surprise."

I stared at this strange woman. Just how much did she know anyway? "I'm sorry," I said, "but I totally forgot your name."

She smiled. "Kerry. Kerry McVee."

I swallowed hard. "Kerry, you seem like a nice person. And I'm not sure how much Jamie told you. But . . ." I paused then shook my head. "Let's just say this is a little bit complicated."

"Yes, the best things in life usually are." She waved at her brother who had just given another table their bill. "Dolan," she called. "Bring us a fresh pot of tea, will ya?" Then she turned back to me and smiled with warm eyes. "Why don't ya tell me all about it?"

I felt my eyes getting moist now. I wasn't sure if it was due to her unexpected kindness or the tumultuous emotions I'd just experienced with Jamie and the piano, but I felt as if a thick wall inside of me was crumbling. The dam that had held back my secret for so long was about to break. I knew it was time to open up, and Kerry seemed a safe person to confide in. "It's a long story . . ."

She nodded. "I have time." Then she glanced at the door too. "Let's just talk until he comes back."

"*If* he comes back . . ."

"He's a grown lad, dear. And a smart one too. He'll be all right."

So I took in a deep breath and I began. "I was so shocked when Jamie started to play the piano. I had no idea that he knew how to play, that he had any interest in it. I mean, he'd gotten a guitar in high school, like so many boys who wanted to be the next Buddy Holly. And he and some of his friends would play out in the garage. Mostly that loud crazy music that I can't stand. I just figured it was a phase."

"But perhaps 'tis something more?"

"Yes. You see, Jamie's father was a musician too. Oh, Jamie doesn't know this. In fact, he doesn't even know who his *real* father is—" I took in a sharp breath, shocked that I'd just made this confession.

"Go on, Colleen. This is not a new story, you must know that."

"No, I suppose it's not." I gathered my thoughts, turning back the clock, back to twenty-two years earlier, back to the fall of 1941. "I had moved to Hollywood, from a farm in the Midwest," I began. "I thought I was going to become a movie star." I laughed and told her a bit about my high school acting days. "Of course, that did not prepare me for Hollywood in the least. Although I did manage to get a few small jobs, a couple of photo shoots for soap advertisements along with some runway modeling. But after two years, it wasn't really working out like I'd planned. It was a week before Thanksgiving, and I had actually considered giving the whole acting thing up and going home for good. You know it was wartime and several of my brothers had been shipped off to Europe and I knew my family missed me. But my roommate Wanda, who was also trying to get her big Hollywood break, talked me into going to a party with her. She thought we might make some good connections, meet somebody important, a director or producer, someone who could change our lives." I remembered everything about that night. How Wanda and I had both dressed carefully, how we split the cab fare, knowing we'd be broke tomorrow, both hoping this could be it—our big night.

"And did you meet someone important?"

"Oh, I'll admit there were some impressive people at that party. And, yes, I did meet someone who changed my life . . ." I remember the crowded room now, seeing the handsome man at the piano, the way his head bent ever so slightly as he played, just the way my son's had done tonight. He was a friend of the host's, just playing for the fun of it. "But not in the way I had planned." I sighed, remembering the way I felt when he picked me out of the crowd, the way he spoke to me as if he really knew me, knew everything about me, and later the way he touched my face, our first kiss. A delightful shiver ran down my spine just to remember the feel of his touch, how my heart raced when we danced, when he held me close. It was like nothing I'd ever experienced before . . . or since.

Kerry smiled. "And you fell in love?"

"Is it that obvious?"

"Your cheeks are flushed."

I touched my face. "Oh . . ."

"It's lovely."

I took in another deep breath, trying to decide how much more to say to her. And yet it felt good to finally tell this to someone—

79

like a confession, wasn't it supposed to be good for the soul? Especially if I could tell someone who I would, in all likelihood, never have to see again. "I'd never been with a man," I admitted. "I was saving myself for marriage. But something happened when I was with him—something wild and uncontrollable. We spent the next three days together, and I felt as if I would follow that man anywhere . . . I'd do anything to be with him forever. Do you know what I mean?"

She had a wistful expression now. "It's been many years ago, but I do remember that feeling. So, what happened?"

"He was an officer in the Navy, a communications specialist, and was being shipped to Honolulu. Pearl Harbor."

Her pale brows arched. "Oh . . ."

"Yes. It was 1941 and he shipped off a few days before Thanksgiving. He was due to arrive the third of December. But before he left, he asked me to marry him. He told me he loved me and he wanted us to go down to city hall and do it right then and there, but I wanted to wait . . ." I bit my lip and for the millionth time asked myself why—why didn't I agree to marry him that day?

"So, you didn't marry?"

"No. I wanted to plan a small wedding. I wanted some of my family to come out and meet him. He was so wonderful, I knew they'd all love him. And Liam didn't think he'd be in Honolulu more than a couple of weeks. He felt certain he'd be back for Christmas."

"Liam?" she said with interest. "Was he Irish by chance?"

I nodded eagerly. "Yes! Rather, his parents had been—they had immigrated before he was born. But it had always been his dream to come to Ireland someday. That was why I wanted to come here now, and why I brought my son. I thought it would be a good place to tell him . . . the truth."

"So am I correct to assume that Liam died in the bombing of Pearl Harbor?"

I swallowed hard, then nodded. "Because we weren't married . . . I was never notified of his death . . . but all my letters were returned. I searched the Red Cross lists, but I'd heard that many names hadn't been included yet. But then I never heard a word from him either."

Kerry reached over and put her hand on mine. "And you were with child."

"Yes . . . and I knew that Liam had been going over there to work on the Arizona," I said. "So many were killed . . . I knew in my heart that he was gone."

"What did you do?"

"I considered going home and lying to my parents, telling them that I'd been briefly married, then widowed, and I could almost convince myself that it was true. And I wanted to stay in California, in case he came back. But while I was waiting, hoping to hear from Liam, Wanda got married, and I couldn't afford the apartment. So I took a job at a shoe store in a nearby town and rented a room there. I knew my Hollywood dreams were finished by then."

"Not much call for actresses with a bulging belly, I'll venture."

I shook my head. "The man I worked for, the owner of the shoe store, was so kind and generous to me. He was the one who helped me find a room to rent. Although it didn't take him long to figure things out. I tried to cover it up, but I began to show in the spring. Plus I had morning sickness for nearly half of the pregnancy. One day, when I'd been late for work again, he called me into his office and I just knew that he was going to fire me. But, instead, he proposed."

"And you accepted."

"I didn't know what else to do. I told Hal the truth, the complete truth. He said it didn't matter and that we would raise the child as our own. The only thing he asked of me was to never speak of it again. So I didn't."

"Until now."

"Yes. He died a year and a half ago."

"I'm sorry."

"So am I. But I feel that Jamie needs to know the truth. Perhaps more than ever after hearing him tonight. He is his father's son."

"'Tis amazing . . . a son would play music like the father, and yet they never met." She just shook her head.

The dining room was quiet now. All the other diners had left, and I suddenly realized it was getting quite late. "I should be going," I said, standing and opening my purse. "I'm worried about Jamie. I should check on him." I reached for the bill.

But Kerry got it before I could and she crumpled it up in her hand. "Dinner is on the house tonight."

"No," I insisted. "You must let me pay."

She gave me a stern look. "You need to respect Irish hospitality, Colleen. If I say you're my guest for dinner, ya should not argue with me."

"May I leave a tip?"

She smiled. "Certainly."

I slipped what I hoped would be a generous tip beneath my teacup and thanked her.

"Do come again," she said. "And bring Jamie along. I would love to hear the lad play some more of that lovely music. He has a gift, you know, a real gift."

I forced a smile, unsure if I'd ever be able to talk my son into playing anything again. At least not for me. "I'll tell him you said that."

"Or if you'd like to come on up here for a spot of tea," she said hopefully. "Please, drop by. We have a lovely view in the daytime and I make some scones that are renown in the region."

"Yes," I said suddenly. "I'd like that. Thank you!"

10

||||||||||||||||||||||

Jamie

I didn't know how things had gone so crooked for me tonight. Everything had seemed just about perfect, and then—bam—it all went sideways. I was walking back toward town, trying to find my way in the dark, and wondering why there weren't more streetlamps out here. Although, to be fair, I was still a ways from town. I could hear the sound of the ocean to my right, the waves smashing onto the rocks in a lonely way, a way that made me long for something . . . something I couldn't even put my finger on.

Finally—feeling like, what was the use, why try to figure it out?—I found a boulder planted next to the gravel road and just sat down on it. I could see some sort of light off in the distance, and to my surprise it turned out to be the moon, rising up over the sea. I watched with fascination as it came over the surface of the ocean, reflecting a long, cool slice of blue light over the water. It wasn't a full moon, but it was getting close. Maybe three-quarters or seven-eighths. I'd never been great at geometry.

Like an LP record with a deep scratch, I kept replaying Mom's reaction to my confession tonight, trying to understand where it had gone wrong, and why. Why hadn't I been able to use the music and some of the charm I've been accused of misusing to bring this whole thing around and make her understand that my choices had really been for the best in the end? Why had she gotten so upset? I knew that no parents want to be deceived, but sometimes it just happened. To be fair, it had happened all my life. Mom was well aware that her son was no angel. But she'd always forgiven me before. I usually got off pretty easily too—even my friends thought I was a little spoiled. And yet, my mother just didn't seem like herself tonight. As if she'd been caught off guard, she'd seemed so shocked, so taken aback, and so unlike her usual cool, calm, and well-mannered self. Looking back, it was just plain weird.

I picked up a stone and chucked it out as far as I could, trying to make it to the sea, but hearing no splash. I thought about my dad, wondering how he would've reacted to all this, and I honestly felt like he might've taken it better. Sure, he would've been shocked at first, but then he would've listened, he would've tried to see my side. Despite the fact that he'd always wanted me to go into the shoe business, that he'd never thought music could ever provide a means to live, but something a guy ought to do just for the fun of it, I still think he would've understood me eventually. Oh, he would've been disappointed in me for lying to him. No doubt about that. Especially since Dad lived by a strict code of ethics, a code that was ruled by his faith in God. But he would've gotten over it. And because of his faith, he would've forgiven me too. I knew that for a fact. Plus he probably would've forgiven me a whole lot quicker than Mom, that was assuming that she ever would. Man, I wished I had told the truth sooner, back when Dad was still alive. I thought about that old saying about weaving tangled webs by telling lies. It seemed to be true.

I didn't know how long I'd been sitting there, but I finally decided that I was cold and I should probably get back to the hotel. I knew that Mom would be worried about me, but I thought maybe that was a good thing. Maybe she'd have time to think and maybe even feel bad about her reaction. It seemed the least she could've done was to compliment me on learning to play piano. Even if she didn't like the style or whatever it was that seemed to displease her. Who could figure out mothers these days? That reminded me of her main purpose in bringing me to Ireland. How could I have forgotten? Oh, she hadn't really spoken of it lately and I was sure if I confronted her now, she'd deny it. But I had no doubt that her plan was to talk me out of joining the Air Force while we were here. I knew that she wanted to keep me home, and I suspected she thought if she kept me on a tight leash, playing the handyman around her house, that I would be safe and sound.

Well, my mother still had a few lessons to learn. As far as joining the Air Force went, I was more committed to it now than ever before. The first thing I'd do once we got back home would be to go sign up. And I knew they'd take me too. I'd done sports throughout high school and for fun afterward, so I was in pretty good shape. Plus nearly two full years of business college wouldn't hurt either. Hopefully it'd get me a better status once I enlisted, maybe even an officer. I'd have to look into that.

So, as I stood up and started walking toward town, it was with a new authority. I was going to join the Air Force. I might even become a pilot. And eventually, like it or not, my mother would learn to respect me for it.

Once I got to town, I decided I wasn't ready to face Mom quite yet. It wasn't even ten, and I suspected that she'd still be up. Probably waiting for me. So I went into the pub where the live music was playing, and although this band wasn't as good as the one in Dublin, probably because they were older and maybe a little more traditional, they were still good. Very good. And I enjoyed listening to them. I decided to stick around until the place closed up. That way I could probably avoid seeing my mother altogether tonight. And even if it made her worry a little, I didn't see how that could hurt. As I drank my second pint of stout, I wondered if my mother had any idea of how deeply she had hurt my feelings tonight. Or if she even cared.

11

‖‖‖‖‖‖‖‖‖‖‖‖‖‖‖‖‖‖

Colleen

I tossed and turned until after midnight, worried sick about Jamie, but hoping he was all right and that I hadn't hurt him too badly. Although I knew I had. Oh, I'm sure he expected me to be upset, but normally, we would discuss such things in a civilized way if we were in public. I knew I'd have to explain myself. Jamie had no idea that I was reacting more to his music and my memories of Liam than I was to the news that he dropped out of college. In fact, I think I suspected he hadn't graduated. My own sister had suggested as much. Somehow I needed to make him understand. I needed to tell him the truth . . . perhaps even tomorrow.

Finally when it was nearly one, I heard footsteps down the hallway and then a key turning in the door next to mine, and I knew he'd made it back safely.

Still, it was hard to shut down my mind. So many old and new feelings tumbled inside my head; like my old Whirlpool washer when it got stuck on the spin cycle, things just kept spinning round and round. Would I ever be able to sort it all out? And how was I going to explain it all to Jamie? Telling my story to Kerry tonight had been a relief of sorts, but at the same time it had stirred up the pot, a pot that I'd managed to keep quiet for a long time. Now I was plagued with old questions, haunted by forgotten longings, and even obsessing over that old *what might have been*. . . . What if things had gone differently? What if I'd said *yes* to Liam, instead of *wait*?

But I'd been through all that before . . . so long ago that it seemed like another person, another lifetime. At the time I'd picked up the only survival skill that seemed to work—I learned to move on. I learned to focus my emotions and energies on the task at hand, whether it was having a baby, being a new mom, helping to sell shoes, or volunteering in the community. I simply moved on.

But I felt blindsided by this misunderstanding with Jamie—without even making my disclosure, our relationship had already hit the rocks. What if things got worse? What if I lost him completely? I wasn't sure I could survive that. Maybe I needed to rethink my plan. Maybe I was being too hasty.

Suddenly I wondered why I'd ever felt the need to tell him about his birth father in the first place. What difference did it really make? What was done was done. Nothing I could say or do would change the past. Why not let sleeping dogs lie? Then I remembered how he'd announced his intention to join the Air Force, and the chill of fear that had rushed through me when I imagined him going to war. It seemed just my luck that Jamie wanted to follow in his birth father's footsteps—whether he knew about him or not. Hadn't his style of music been a clear sign of that tonight? I was stunned to hear him playing—so like Liam that it was eerie. And, for one brief, crazy moment, I thought I'd gone back into time. I thought that Liam was still alive, still young and handsome, still playing the piano. It was as if Pearl Harbor had never happened. And then I actually pinched myself, realizing it wasn't Liam, it was *my* son. And Liam's son. So strange.

And who could tell with fate? Perhaps the son was designed to be a shadow of the father, something predisposed even before his birth. What if my attempts to intervene made no difference? What would be, would simply be. *Que será, será.* Why try to fight what seemed written in stone, or perhaps in the stars? What if God's cosmic sense of humor was cynical? Maybe he got a kick out of watching history repeating itself. My dear Liam had played the piano, gone off to war, and died. In all likelihood Jamie would do the same. I callously wondered if Jamie might even get a girl pregnant before he trucked off to war and an early grave.

Finally I told my mind to *be quiet*—to just *shut up*! Quit dwelling on all that was negative and pessimistic and frightening . . . I reminded myself of what Hal had often said, whenever I was fretting over Jamie or life in general. He'd quietly put his hand on my shoulder and say, "Why work yourself into a fit over things you can't control, Colleen? Why not simply pray?"

Maybe he had been right. Perhaps prayer was my only ally now. And so I did pray. But first I had to apologize for imagining God as some heartless practical joker. I had a feeling that wasn't quite right. Then I prayed for help and mercy and wisdom. And then I fell into a fretful sleep and dreamed some crazy, mixed-up dreams involving Liam, Hal, and Jamie.

The next morning, I got up early, but I was not refreshed. I didn't feel the least bit rested or peaceful, and I wasn't even happy about being here in Ireland. Doubtful thoughts clouded my head as I pulled on my quilted bathrobe and opened the curtains. It was still dark out, but the sky looked as if it might be clear again today, and I could see a sliver of golden light off to the southeastern horizon, out over the ocean. It seemed likely that we could have another nice day, not that I cared since I felt certain another storm brewed, one between Jamie and me. Yet, I knew what had to be done. I knew I must place one foot in front of the other, and I must speak to my son, and somehow I must make amends. I would take the high road and apologize for how things went last night. I would forgive him for his wasted college money and his deceptions, and I would tell him that we needed a fresh start.

But would I tell him the truth about his father? I still felt unsure. Was it best to just get these things out in the open, to lay my cards on the table and see what happened next? Or was it wrong to burden him with my mistakes? It was too early to figure that out. Instead, I slowly bathed, then dressed, shivering in the cool air of the bathroom and wondering why the Irish hadn't discovered the lovely convenience of bathroom wall heaters.

Then I busied myself in my room until 7:30, and although I knew it was still pretty early for Jamie, I went out and tapped on his door. When there was no answer, I tapped a bit louder. Surely he hadn't gotten up and left already. I hadn't heard a peep from his room since last night. And he'd come in so late. I knocked even louder now, calling out his name, and eventually I heard some thumping around, and he opened the door, blinked sleepily at me, and asked me what time it was.

"It's after 7:30," I told him. "I was going down for breakfast and wondered if you'd like to join me. I think we should talk."

"Give me a few minutes," he said groggily as he closed the door. "Gotta wake up and stuff."

This seemed reasonable, so I got my new book, an Irish novel set in the eighteenth century, and went down to the lobby to read for a while. Then, when it was a quarter past eight, I went on into the dining room. I figured forty-five minutes was plenty of time for Jamie to clean up. I knew that, if in a hurry, like back in high school and he had slept in too late, that boy could be out the door in five minutes flat.

I ordered a pot of tea. But after another fifteen minutes, with no Jamie, I went ahead and ordered my breakfast.

"My son seems to be running late," I told the waitress as she brought me my bacon and eggs. Then, although I ate slowly, glancing every now and then to the door, I was finally finished with my meal, and the only thing left to do was to sign for the bill and go back upstairs to see what was keeping Jamie. I hoped he hadn't sneaked out on me. It was nine o'clock when I knocked on the door again and after a couple of minutes, Jamie answered, looking exactly as he had the first time.

"I waited for you," I told him in a slightly irritated tone. "For an hour and a half."

He yawned. "I must've fallen back asleep."

I studied his red-rimmed and slightly puffy eyes, then remembered he'd had a late night, which made me suspicious. "Were you out drinking last night?" I demanded.

"I had a couple of pints, no big deal." He frowned.

"Look, I didn't bring you all the way over to Ireland just so you could go on a drunken binge every night." I instantly regretted my words, aware that my voice sounded just like an old fishwife. But it was too late; like a gun that had been shot, my bullet words were out and they had hit their mark.

"I haven't been on any *drunken binges*, Mom." He was closing the door now.

"I heard you coming in after one in the morning." I wedged my foot in the door, keeping it open. Part of my brain warned me to be the grown-up here, to talk reasonably and make peace, but the other part was putting up its fists, ready to go the next round.

"I was listening to a band."

"After midnight?"

"What is this?" he shot back at me, eyes narrowed. "The Irish inquisition?"

"Well, *I'm your mother*, Jamie. And I brought you here to—"

"Yes, you are my mother," he said loudly. "Although I doubt that anyone would've known that last night when you raked me over the coals and didn't even acknowledge my music. What kind of mother does that anyway?"

I pushed open the door now, worried that our voices might be disturbing other hotel guests, not that there were many this time of year. Still, this was uncomfortable—and embarrassing.

"We need to talk, Jamie," I said firmly as I went into his room and closed the door. I stood before him with my hands on my hips, just the way I had done so many times while he was growing up, times when he had to be nagged to clean his room, or to finish his homework, or to undo some childish prank. More than Hal, I had been the disciplinarian with my son, and it seemed I wasn't ready to give up my role yet.

"Sit down," I commanded him, pointing to his unmade bed. To my surprise he did this without arguing, and I sat on the chair across from him.

He perched on the edge of his bed just staring at me, but I could see the hurt in his deep blue eyes, and I knew I was the one responsible for it. And I knew why. But I wasn't sure I wanted to face that just yet.

Suddenly it occurred to me that I was coming at this thing completely backward. After all, he'd been the one to make that shocking confession last night. I still couldn't believe how casually he had lied to both Hal and me, pretending to go to college when he'd been wasting our money and just playing around. For two years he'd kept up this deception. What made him think it was acceptable to take our money, abuse our trust, and then lie about graduating? We hadn't brought him up to be like that, and I had every right to be indignant and angry. And yet . . . was I using these emotions for a smoke screen?

"Just say it, Mom," he said, breaking into my internal battle-field. "Tell me that you're ashamed of me, that I'm a good-for-nothing son, that I'm useless and hopeless, and that I stole the tuition money from you. Just say it. I know that's what you're thinking."

I blinked, then took in a sharp breath. "Yes, I *am* disappointed in you, Jamie." I reminded myself I had meant to be in control here. I had planned to be mature, whether or not I felt like it. I wondered how Hal would handle this. Probably much better than I was doing. "I really did want you to go to college, and I wanted you to graduate too. I thought a college degree would be your ticket, your way to get a solid heads-up in life, a key to success. And I wanted it even more after you decided not to go into the family business. I can't deny that it hurt me to hear that you'd deceived us, Jamie. I think it would've hurt your father too."

"Yeah, I know, Mom." He held up his hands in a helpless gesture. "But at least Dad would've forgiven me."

Now that stung. "I'll forgive you too, Jamie."

He scowled. "Yeah, maybe you'll forgive me, but not until you get good and ready. Not until you've punished me first."

"I don't *want* to punish you," I said. "I just want you to understand how I feel. You used your father's money . . . pretending to go to school . . . you took advantage of him, Jamie. And he's not even here to defend him—"

"Are you trying to lay some big guilt trip on me? Maybe you really do think it's my fault that Dad had a heart attack. And he's not here to set us straight."

"No . . . no, that's not it." I felt lost now. I was saying things that really didn't matter, going down rabbit trails that had nothing to do with why I brought Jamie to Ireland in the first place, or what I felt I needed to tell him. I leaned over and placed my head in my hands, trying to figure it out. What was I supposed to do here?

"Then what do you want, Mom? You want me to get a job and pay you back that money? Would that make it better? I can do that if that's what it'll take to—"

"No, Jamie," I said, sitting up and looking at him, preparing myself for what I knew I had to do. "It's really *not* about the money."

"It's just that I'm a loser, isn't it? That I dropped out of college, and now you'll have to tell all your friends that I'm just a—"

"Jamie, that's not it!"

"*Well, what is it, Mom?* What is making you act like such a weirdo? Why are you making such a humongous deal out of something that's over and done with—something I can't change even if I wanted to? I told you that I'm sorry. And I can work to pay you back, if that's what it takes."

"That's not—"

"And I don't know why you're so opposed to my music. It's not even rock and roll. Man, I actually thought you would like it." His eyes glistened as he stared at me, looking like a lost and confused boy now. "I cannot believe that I actually thought that you would like it!" He picked up his pillow and slammed a fist into it. "What a complete dope I've been. About everything."

"I *did* like it, Jamie," I spoke quietly now, measuring my words, trying to gauge if this was really the right time or not. I had imagined it happening so differently. I'd planned to tell him when we were doing something fun, perhaps on a ferryboat ride, or driving through the countryside, or enjoying a nice meal. Not like this. Not with him still wearing his rumpled pajamas, sitting here in his messy hotel room, punching his pillow like an eight-year-old. I hadn't imagined myself feeling this close to the edge, sitting here with clenched fists and on the verge of tears. This was all wrong. But maybe that didn't matter.

"So why did you act like that?" he demanded. "Like you thought it was so weird when I played the piano, as if my music made you miserable and that you'd just as soon never hear me play again? *Why, Mom?*"

"Because . . ." I took a deep breath. "It was the *way* you played the piano last night, Jamie." The words were coming out so slowly, one at a time in a mechanical way, as if someone else was doing the talking for me, like one of those new "chatty" dolls—you pulled the string and out came the words. "It was the style that you played, Jamie . . . it sounded exactly the same as . . . well, it was the same *way* that your father used to play . . . and when I heard it I was shocked and it felt as if someone had punched me in the stomach or pulled the rug out from under me . . . I felt confused and upset and I just didn't know how to deal with it and consequently I reacted poorly."

Jamie just sat there with the most confused expression. I knew he was trying to put this together, to make sense of my completely senseless confession.

"Huh?" His head actually cocked to one side, like a bewildered puppy. "I didn't know Dad played the piano."

"Yes, that's right. Your dad, I mean Hal, *didn't* play the piano . . ."

"But you just said—"

"Your *father* played the piano, Jamie." I took in a deep breath, bracing myself. "Your *father*, a man you never met, a man named Liam O'Neil, played the piano—in almost the exact same way that you played it last night, Jamie. And it was just too much for me to deal with at the time."

Jamie's eyes were huge now. "What are you saying?"

"I'm trying to tell you something," I continued. "It's not easy, and it's a big part of the reason that I brought you to Ireland in the first place. Hal Frederick was not your *real* father. Certainly, he was your *dad*, Jamie. And he was a fine dad. But your real father, your *birth* father, was Liam O'Neil."

Jamie shook his head as if he was trying to get water out of his ears. *"What?"*

"I know you must be shocked by this," I said calmly. "Probably similar to the way I felt last night, only far more so."

"Shocked?" He stood up now. "Shocked doesn't even begin to describe it. What exactly are you saying here, Mom?"

So for the second time in twenty-four hours, I told my story. Only this time I edited a few things, telling the story in the way that a mother would want her only son to hear it. "I was young and foolish and in love," I finally admitted. "Liam did ask me to marry him, but I had no idea I was, uh, with child. And being young and foolish, I wanted to have a real wedding, so I told your father that I'd wait for him to come back. He was only supposed to be in Hawaii for a few weeks, working out some communications problems on a battleship. But he arrived just a few days before Pearl Harbor . . . and he never made it back."

"My *real* father died in Pearl Harbor?" Jamie was pacing across the room now, running his hand through his already messy hair. "My *real* father was a stranger named Liam—what was his last name again?"

"O'Neil."

"Was he Irish?"

"His parents were Irish; they had immigrated before he was born. Liam grew up in the Boston area. He'd gone to Annapolis and was an officer in the Navy when we met."

"A military man?"

"Yes, one who was killed in a battle where they never even got to fight back."

Jamie was still pacing, shaking his head as he tried to absorb all of this, trying to make heads or tales of my crazy mess. I felt sorry for him. It was a heavy load for a young man to carry.

"So my whole life has been a complete sham?" He turned and glared at me now, as if I had planned this whole thing just to hurt him. "A total lie?"

"No, Jamie. It has not been a sham or a lie. You are who you are no matter who your parents were or what they did."

94

He narrowed his eyes and studied me. "So, are you *really* my mom?"

"Of course!"

"How do I know for sure? For all I know, you and Dad might've kidnapped me at birth. Maybe I have real parents living somewhere else right now. Maybe it's Barney and Martha Smith of Little Rock, Arkansas."

"It is *not* Barney and Martha Smith of Little Rock, Arkansas!"

"How do I know?"

"Why would I lie to you?"

He shook his head. "I don't know, Mom, you tell me. Why *did* you lie to me?"

"How in the world was I supposed to tell a little boy that his birth father had died? What difference did it make?"

"It makes a difference, Mom!"

"How? How could this change anything?"

"Remember all the crud I went through with Dad and not wanting to go into the shoe business?"

"Of course." I felt a small stab of guilt now. Perhaps I should have told him sooner.

"Well, maybe if I'd known that my real dad was actually someone else, well, maybe things would've made more sense."

"I don't see how."

"You said my *real* dad played piano too?"

I nodded without speaking.

"And something in me was just bursting to play piano, Mom. Don't you get that? And if I'd known, I could've told you and Dad the truth about quitting college and getting into music. It would've made sense."

I considered this. "And it would've hurt your dad, Jamie. He felt you were his son. He treated you like a son. He loved you, believed in you. We were his family. And when he married me, knowing full well that I was expecting, he only asked one thing."

"What?"

"For me to never mention a word about Liam again."

"You broke your promise, Mom."

"Not to Hal, I didn't. I never did say a word to him, or anyone, not while he was alive." I swallowed hard. "But I thought you had a right to know, Jamie. Would you rather I hadn't told you?"

He sat down and punched the pillow several times. "I don't know, Mom. I don't know much of anything at the moment. Except that you lied to me. My whole life has been nothing but a great big fabrication. James William Frederick is nothing but a fraud."

"That's not true, Jamie. You are blowing this way out of proportion."

"It's *my* life, Mom!" He stood and opened the door now, obviously a not-so-subtle hint that this conversation was over. "If I want to blow it out of proportion, or just blow altogether, well, I guess I can."

I stood and walked to the door. "Well, just know this, Jamie. Liam O'Neil was a fine man. A good man. And you are very much like him. And that's nothing to be ashamed of."

Jamie studied me. "Maybe I'm not ashamed of *him*, Mom."

I stared at my son. I knew what he was saying. He was ashamed of *me*. And why not? For all these years, I'd been ashamed of myself. It only made sense that he would feel the same.

12

||||||||||||||||||||

Jamie

It felt like my world turned upside down this morning, or maybe inside out. But as soon as my mom left my hotel room, I packed a small bag and I took off. I wasn't sure where I was going or when I'd come back. All I knew was that I had to get away from her. It felt as if my mother had turned into someone else, like one of those weird B movies—a sci-fi or horror film—where aliens possess people, making them speak and act like complete strangers. That was what Mom seemed like to me. A complete stranger.

My parents raised me with a certain set of morals. Not that I'd always practiced them myself, obviously, but it was a standard I'd grown to accept and even respect—especially in my parents. It was comforting to know that they were rock solid and predictable. And I assumed that eventually I'd adhere to their standards myself.

But suddenly that whole thing seemed like a hoax, a great big charade where nothing was as it seemed. Everything about my life felt phony to me now. My dad had not been my *real* dad. The family business that he tried to force me into wasn't even my own family's business. My mother, the woman who always insisted on truth and integrity, had lived out a great big lie, a lie that was created to cover up her own indiscretions. It was like, while my back was turned, someone had dropped an H-bomb onto my life. In a split second, everything was changed.

I walked through town and just kept on going, following the road before me as I mulled over what had just happened, replaying all the words that had been said. After about an hour, I figured it was possible that I had overreacted to this. And yet, I felt like I'd been tricked or robbed or hoodwinked. And by my very own parents—rather, the people I had assumed were my parents. Now I knew that Dad, or Hal, really wasn't. Well, I supposed that explained some things about me. We were so completely different, he and I. And yet I really did like him. Oh, sure, I'd taken the poor guy for granted and I'd taken advantage of him. But after he died, I had realized how much I really did love him. I had decided that I even wanted to be like him—in time.

For some reason this whole thing reminded me of President Kennedy. His death had knocked me sideways too. I remembered how lost I'd felt after he was assassinated, so confused and hopeless and alone. And yet that was exactly how I felt again today—only more so. I grappled with the thought that I'd not only lost the man I'd called "Dad" for most of my life but now my biological father as well. A man I'd never even known—or known about. Well, it was just too much. It wasn't fair that all the father figures had been stripped from my life—*bam*—just like that.

I mulled over these things as I walked and walked, just following the curving country road to wherever it led and not thinking about whether or not I would follow it back again. After a couple of hours, I realized that I'd walked clear out of town and was now entering another town. Another sea town, but not as picturesque as Clifden, this one also had a large dock, and I noticed what appeared to be a ferryboat docked there. People who looked like they knew where they were going were starting to board, and I suddenly decided to see if I could join them.

I quickly located the small ticket office, and without having the slightest idea where Inishbofin might be, or even caring much, although it was the ferry's destination, I bought a roundtrip ticket and boarded the boat. Since the sun was still shining, although clouds were gathering on the western horizon, I sat out on the upper deck, waiting for the boat to sail, which it did rather quickly. Then, once it was moving away from the dock and cutting through the ocean, I felt a small wave of concern, or perhaps it was regret or remorse . . . I wasn't even sure. But I simply blocked these feelings away by focusing my eyes at the bright blue sea and the sky, wondering where I would ever fit into this mixed-up world. Maybe I should join the Navy instead of the Air Force.

After about twenty minutes, I actually started to get a little worried. The ferry appeared to be going straight out to sea, and suddenly I wondered just what I'd gotten myself into. Just where was Inishbofin anyway? I had assumed it was another small seaport on up the shore, but the mainland was quite a ways behind us now, and besides the big, blue sea and a bank of gray clouds, who knew what lie ahead? I wanted to ask another passenger for information, but realized how stupid that would make me sound. Why had this crazy American guy gotten onto a boat without even knowing where it was headed? Then, I reassured myself, these other passengers seemed perfectly normal and well adjusted. They appeared completely unconcerned over the fact that we seemed to be going due west, heading straight toward America. Obviously, they knew something I didn't, so why should I be worried?

Finally, I saw a mound of land up ahead, as well as something that looked like a fortress. Inishbofin had to be an island. Well, that was fine with me. I didn't mind exploring an Irish island to take my mind off of things.

"I've never been to Inishbofin," I said to a pretty girl who had just come out onto the deck. The wind was picking up now, and she was attempting to tie a pink scarf over her curly auburn hair. She looked to be about my age and had a nice sprinkling of freckles over an upturned nose. "Do you know much about the place?"

She laughed. "Probably a bit too much since I was born and raised there. Are you an American?"

"Yes." I smiled at her. "Just visiting."

"Seems an odd time to be visiting," she said. "What with holidays and all."

"Yes. Well, it was my mother's idea to spend Christmas in Ireland. We've been staying in Clifden."

She nodded. "I see. And ya decided to do some explorations on your own today?"

"That's right."

"Some say that Inishbofin is one of the loveliest islands in Ireland. And I suppose it does have some keen spots of interest, although I've taken them for granted myself, and I've known more than one tourist that got disappointed." She sighed, shading her eyes as she peered up ahead. "Still, I'm glad to be coming home for Christmas. I can't wait to see my family."

"Where have you been?" I asked.

"In Galway. I finished my nurses' training last year and I'm working for a pediatrician in the city now."

"So do you come home to visit a lot?"

"When I can. I suppose I do miss it a bit."

"Hello, Katie Flynn!" called an old man in a plaid jacket who had just made his way to the top deck. He was lighting up a pipe.

"Hello, Mr. Kelly." She waved, then turned back to me. "Inishbofin is a rather small place. Everyone knows everyone there."

"Then maybe I should introduce myself," I said. "My name is Jamie Frederick."

"And, as ya heard, my island friends call me Katie Flynn, although I go by Katherine in the city. It sounds a bit more sophisticated than Katie, don't ya think?"

"So, tell me, Katie, what do I do when I get to Inishbofin?"

She peered up at the sky. "Depending on the weather, which is about to change, there are a few things you could do."

"For instance."

"Well, on a good day there's plenty of fishing. And we do get scuba divers in the summertime. Of course, there's bird-watching, although it's not the best season for that right now, and we do have some gorgeous beaches . . ." She studied me for a moment. "Do ya know how to ride a bike, Jamie Frederick?"

I laughed. "Of course."

"Lots of tourists rent bikes. They tour the island that way. But you don't have to rent a bike. You come on by my house and I'll loan you one of my brothers' bikes."

I grinned at her. "But how will I find my way around the is-land?"

"It's a bit hard to get lost, ya know, we're not terribly big." Then she seemed to catch my clue. "I suppose I could show you about for a bit though. After I've spent some time with my family, that is—I can't be taking off as soon as I darken the door."

We continued to talk as the ferry pulled into the dock. Then Katie went below to get her bags, and we met again once we were on land. I carried my small bag as well as her larger suitcase, and we walked into town together. Then once we got to what appeared to be a main street, she paused and wrote some quick directions for getting to her house on a small slip of paper.

"Thanks," I told her, wondering what I'd do until she was freed up to take that little bike ride with me. It was already after two o'clock, and I didn't want to waste time.

"Looks to be gettin' thundery," she said, glancing up at the sky as she took her large suitcase from me.

"Thundery?"

"A storm's a-coming." She nodded to the big, rounded dark clouds that hovered directly overhead.

"Oh." I nodded. "Not so good for riding bikes then?"

She laughed. "Not unless you want to light up like a Christmas tree. You best keep inside. If I were you, I'd get myself checked into Murphy's straight away."

"Murphy's?"

"You do have a reservation, do you not?"

"For what?"

"For a room." She frowned at me.

"A room?"

She shook her head as if questioning my mental capacity. "For overnight, Jamie Frederick." Then she pointed back to the dock, which was empty now. The ferry was already making its way back to the mainland. "You do know that's the last ferry for the day, do you not?"

I felt my eyes getting wide. "The *last* ferry?"

"Aye." She glanced at my bag. "You did mean to stay the night, didn't ya?"

I took in a quick breath. "Oh, I hadn't really thought about it. But at least I came prepared." I forced a confident smile. "So, which way to Murphy's?"

She pointed to a large gray stone building with a sign that said MURPHY'S INN in bright blue letters. "That's it. I hope they have a room."

I wanted to ask if there was a room at her house, but thought better of it. I'd already shown her that I wasn't the smartest tourist around.

"Come by the house tomorrow," she called over her shoulder. "If the weather's willing, we can take a ride."

"Right." I waved good-bye and hurried over to Murphy's Inn. I just hoped it wouldn't turn out to be like Murphy's Law and have no vacancy. I couldn't imagine sleeping out in the rain tonight.

After a brief explanation as to why I had no reservation, and an admission to my general American naïveté, I was eventually given a room.

"You're lucky we weren't full up," the woman said, "what with the holidays and all, we sometimes don't have a room to spare this time o' year."

"Is there a phone I can use?"

She looked at me as if I had two heads, then laughed. "A *telephone*?"

"Yes. I need to make a call."

"We do not trouble ourselves with such things."

"Are you telling me there are no phones in Inishbofin?"

She nodded, suppressing more laughter. "'Tis wha' I be telling you, laddie."

"Oh." I tried to regain a bit of composure as I picked up my key and my bag and made my way to my room, but I could hear her chuckling as she repeated my story to a man named Sean, who I supposed was her husband. Well, I told myself as I unlocked the door to a small and sparsely furnished room, maybe it was for the best not to call my mother just yet. Maybe she and I both still needed some time to stew, then cool down. Still, I felt a little guilty. And I knew she'd be worried.

My guilt was soon distracted by the "thundery" weather that quickly set in. The wind picked up and the thunder boomed. I left my bag in the room and decided to check out what I was guessing was the only pub in town, just a couple doors down from the inn. I'd just finished my first Guinness when the lights went out.

"Does this happen a lot?" I asked as the pub owner lit a kerosene lantern and a couple of candles as if this were no big deal.

"Now and again," he said as he blew out a match.

The wind was howling now. That, combined with the booms of thunder and flashes of lightning, and I wasn't too sure that I wanted to venture out on the streets just yet. What kind of a mess had I gotten myself into anyway?

"Do you serve food here?" I asked the pub owner. I was his only customer, and I had a feeling he wouldn't mind if I made myself scarce just now. But I also knew that although the Murphy Inn served breakfast, they didn't have an actual restaurant for the other meals. Plus I hadn't eaten anything since I'd put away a stale bag of pretzels and a lukewarm lemonade on the ferry today. My stomach was growling like a wild beast.

"I reckon the wife can fix somet'ing," he said, disappearing through a door that I figured must lead to some kind of living quarters. I was alone in the pub now, just me and the lantern and flickering candles. I longed for some music, but there was no jukebox or radio or anything to break the silence. Just the sound of the occasional clap of thunder, which usually made me jump.

After what seemed an unreasonable amount of time, and I was tempted to just leave, the pub owner came back with what appeared to be some sort of meat sandwich and a bowl of brown-looking soup. I ordered another pint to go with this and quickly ate. I couldn't say it was the best meal I'd ever had, but it certainly wasn't the worst either. I paid the man, setting on the counter what seemed like a generous tip for his wife.

103

"Thank ya," he said, as if he really did appreciate my business after all. "Mind the storm now, an' keep the wind to yer back."

I thanked him and pushed open the door just in time to get hit with a blast of wet wind. Fortunately, the inn was downwind, and propelled by the blustery air, I ran all the way. Even so, I was soaked by the time I got there. I paused in the tiny lobby to shake off some of the rain. It looked like the inn was without electricity too. Other than a smoky kerosene lantern on the registration desk, it was shadowy dark in here too.

"There ya are now." The woman who'd given me the room reached under the counter for something. "Ya haven't blown away with the storm then, have ya?" She handed me several white taper candles and a small box of matches. "Candleholders'll be in your room. This should get you through the night."

I thanked her, then headed up the stone stairs to my room. Fortunately someone had set out a couple of burning candles to light the way, but the shadows these cast on the old stone walls was a little eerie, and I felt I was starting to understand why the Irish had such a reputation for ghosts. The inn hadn't been exactly warm and cozy when I got here this afternoon, and I had a feeling it was going to feel pretty cold before the night was over. I lit a candle to see to unlock the door to my room, cautiously going inside. Before long I located several metal candleholders in the drawer of a small dresser over by the window. I lit two of the candles and set them out, then peeled off my soggy fisherman knit sweater and hung it over a wooden chair, hoping that it would dry, or at least be slightly less damp, by morning.

It wasn't even seven o'clock now, but I knew there was nothing to do in this place. I wasn't the least bit sleepy, and after several minutes of shivering in the cold and dimly lit room, I got into bed just hoping to get warmed up a bit. I kicked my feet back and forth in an attempt to defrost the sheets, but it seemed useless. Why had I come here anyway? What had I been thinking? Obviously, I wasn't thinking at all. Otherwise I'd be back at the relatively nice hotel with heat and electricity—maybe off listening to music in one of the local pubs and eating something that actually tasted good.

What a fool I'd been to go stomping off like that. Oh, sure, it had been hard and shocking to hear what Mom told me—it still was. But why had I reacted so strongly? What good had it done? And what was I thinking to hop on a boat without knowing where it was headed? Look where it had gotten me—locked up in this dark dungeonlike room on a tiny island where the next ferry to the mainland wouldn't be until tomorrow. What a complete imbecile I'd been! You'd think a "grown" man of twenty-one would have more sense.

Then I began to wonder about the man who had been my biological father. I wondered how old he might have been when he and my mom had met. Perhaps he'd been about my age. Maybe he'd faced the same kinds of questions I struggled with now. I wondered what he looked like and how he felt about going to war or what it felt like to be in Pearl Harbor when it was attacked that day. *Liam O'Neil.* Who had that guy really been? A musician who'd graduated from Annapolis? And hadn't Mom said he'd been an officer in the Navy? But how long had he been in the Navy? And what about his family, who would also be my family? Did I have aunts, uncles, cousins? And what about the fact that his parents had come from Ireland? Were any of their relatives still here now?

Maybe that's why I felt such an affinity for this country—the Emerald Isle. Well, until today, that is. I wasn't too sure how I felt about Ireland, particularly Inishbofin, at the moment. Mostly it felt inhospitable. It was cold and damp and dark, and I wanted to get out of this place, the sooner the better. But Ireland, in general, meaning the people, the music, the land . . . it had all seemed to speak to me at first, to welcome me, as if I actually belonged. And then when I'd finally sat down at a piano—was that only just yesterday?—it had all seemed to fall right into place for me. I had begun to feel as if I was finding myself, knowing who I was and what I wanted out of life. But then came my mother's stunning confession, and now, stuck in this strange and isolated island called Inishbofin, I'd never felt so lost in my life. Lost and alone and hopeless.

Still shivering, I wondered if it was only because of my birth father that Mom had brought me to Ireland. There really seemed no other logical explanation. And, really, it made some sense. I could imagine her planning this whole thing, assuming it would be the perfect way to break the news to me—Mom had always cared a lot about settings and doing things in certain ways. And I had to give her credit, coming probably had been a good idea, but then I'd gone and messed it all up. I felt pretty certain that I'd derailed my mother when I confessed about college and squandering my tuition money. I'm sure I threw a great big wrench in her works.

Maybe it had something to do with freezing to death and being stuck somewhere I'd rather not be—a prison of sorts—but I felt that the time had come to get honest with myself. And I had to admit I'd probably overreacted to Mom's revelation in order to create a smoke screen of sorts. It was my sorry little attempt to cover my own mistakes. I'd blown her revelation out of proportion just to get the limelight off of me and back onto her.

Sometimes the truth was ugly.

Still, and to be fair, I was pretty stunned to think that Mom— *my mom*—had been involved *like that* with another man. And they weren't even married. It was equally shocking to think that she'd then married my dad, rather Hal, while pregnant with another man's child. Man, she would've had a fit if I'd pulled a stunt like that. My mom, the same woman who'd given me all those speeches about what kind of girls were nice and what kind were not, back when I first started dating. But didn't this change things? How could my mom have been so opinionated about what she called "fast" girls. Was it possible that she had been a "fast" girl herself? I even recalled how sometimes, like right before a date, she pressured my dad into giving me *the speech*, although it made him extremely uncomfortable, even more so than for her. Now I had an idea of why she'd been so worried that I might get a girl "in trouble." She'd been a girl "in trouble" once. It was really mind-blowing.

I'd heard the phrase "dark night of the soul" before, I think it was in my English lit class, but I guess that would pretty much

106

describe how I felt that night in Inishbofin. Combine thunder, lightning, darkness, and lack of heat with an overall lost feeling, and I couldn't recall a darker or longer night. And before the torturous night was to end, and before I would finally find relief in sleep, I wrestled with many demons. I had moments when I questioned the state of my mind—I wondered if maybe this was all my own doing. Then finally I remembered how Dad, the dad who raised me, had always told me that God *was there in times of trouble.*

"God wants you to call out to him, Jamie." Dad told me this right before I set off on that crazy summer road trip—the last time I'd seen him alive. "God knows you're going to have some hard times and challenges ahead, son, and that's okay. He just wants you to know that he's there, always ready to help. He's a lifeline. Just grab onto him and don't let go."

At the time I'd taken those words completely in stride. To be polite, I had even pretended to listen, but I knew I'd dismiss his advice, right along with most of the other parental warnings that were so generously dished out whenever I got ready to attempt something new. And that's exactly what I did. I felt that I had control of things, that I was the master of my own fate, and that I could do whatever I pleased and everything would turn out just fine.

But suddenly I wasn't so sure about that. In fact, I wasn't so sure about much of anything. Maybe the time had really come to call out to God. Maybe I wasn't doing such a fantastic job of handling everything on my own. And so, after struggling with my demons and my selfishness and the cold and the dark of the night, I finally did cry out to God. I did admit my weaknesses, my failings, my insecurities, and my fears. And then I cried like a baby, crying to God. And I pleaded with him to help me. And at last I went to sleep.

13

⦚⦚⦚⦚⦚⦚⦚⦚⦚⦚⦚⦚⦚⦚⦚⦚⦚

Colleen

I felt like a cat on a hot tin roof as I got ready for bed. Not that it was particularly warm in Ireland, especially since a storm had stirred up that evening. But I felt edgy and anxious and unable to settle down. As far as I knew, Jamie had not returned to the hotel at any time today. At least no one had seen him. For a while I'd held out the faint hope that perhaps he'd sneaked in when the clerk was away from the desk, but I'd tried knocking on Jamie's door just a few minutes ago and there was no answer. Still, I reminded myself, it wouldn't be the first night my son had stayed out late. And I had no doubts that he needed some time to himself just now. For that matter, so did I.

Now, I hadn't expected this to be easy. But I'd hoped it would go more smoothly than it had. I had known my news would be a shock to Jamie, but I had no idea it would drive such a wedge between us. Perhaps it had been unrealistic to think that Jamie would be interested in hearing about his biological father. Yet somehow I had convinced myself that once he recovered from the shock, he would've been understanding, perhaps even compassionate. And I'd thought he'd have questions. But, as I'd walked the streets of Clifden earlier today, I'd come to grips with the possibility that I'd been wrong. Perhaps about everything.

The next morning, after I'd had breakfast and waited what seemed a reasonable amount of time for a young man to sleep in after a late night, I tried knocking on Jamie's door again. Still no answer. It was nearly ten o'clock and I'd kept a close eye on the front door while eating, so I felt certain he hadn't slipped past me and gone out again. I knocked even louder now, calling out his name. But the door remained firmly shut. Silent. That's when I suspected that he hadn't returned to the hotel at all last night. But, if that was the case, where could he be? He didn't have too much money on him. Oh, enough for a night or two in another hotel and some meals. But he didn't have enough to get far away, and if he did, he wouldn't last long.

The storm that had started up yesterday evening grew even more violent as the following day wore on. By midmorning, the wooden shutters on the ocean side of the hotel had been closed up tight, blocking the light and giving the interior of my room a dark and somber appearance. Despite the dismal-looking weather, I took a morning walk, which was really an excuse to search for my son again, but I noticed shopkeepers taking signs and things inside, and they too were closing shutters, bolting things down tight.

"The cat's tail is in the hot ashes," an old woman said as she scurried away from the grocery store with a bag of provisions. I had no idea what she meant by this strange comment, but her eyes looked foreboding. Also, the wind whipped at my skirt, slapping it back and forth against my legs as I walked back to the hotel. It seemed that everyone in town was holing up and hiding out, and as I rushed into the lobby, followed by a gust, I was informed by the hotel manager that we might be in for "a class ten gale."

"What does that mean?" I asked.

"It means ya best stay inside unless ya want to be blown clear to Dublin." Then he hurried off, I felt sure, to batten down more hatches.

As far as I could tell, Jamie still wasn't back yet. He didn't answer his door, and when I pressed my ear to it, all I heard was silence—that and the howling of the wind outside. Now I was beginning to feel seriously alarmed. What if he was out in the

109

elements during this storm? Maybe he wasn't aware that we were in for a class ten gale, whatever that might be. Or what if he'd been hurt or was in some kind of danger? Once again, anything and everything seemed possible.

Suddenly I felt completely enraged by my wayward son. That he dared to do this to me—*his mother*—that he dared to treat me like this! After all I'd done for him, all I'd given up to secure his future, making sure that he had everything he needed, everything he wanted, setting my own needs and feelings aside! After all that—that he would put me through something like this—it seemed unpardonable. All I'd ever done in my life, every decision I'd ever made, every sacrifice . . . it had all been for Jamie. Well, for Jamie and Hal. But everything about my whole life had been to make them happy. It had always been my primary focus and concern. And this was the thanks I got?

I probably spent a couple of hours going through this rage, working my way through these feelings, trying to make sense of what seemed totally senseless.

I finally wore myself down. No more rage, no more fury. These emotions were replaced with worry. And so, as I sat alone in my darkened room with shuttered windows just waiting for this storm to pass, my imagination was assaulted with all the horrible possibilities. Instead of being angry at Jamie, I became obsessed over his safety. Where could he be during this horrible storm? What if he was injured? Or dead? Finally I knew that my only recourse was to pray. It was all I had left. But, as I prayed, I couldn't help but imagine how my life might be without my son. And that picture was bleak and dismal.

I'd never wanted to be one of those controlling mothers, the kind of women who doted on an only child, expecting that son or daughter to bring fulfillment and happiness to her, a comfort in her old age, make a life where none existed. I didn't really want that and I knew that wasn't fair. It was selfish and wrong. And yet I just didn't think I could survive losing Jamie. I'd lost Liam twenty-two years ago, and not long after that I'd lost my father, and then most recently Hal. How much more loss could I handle?

"I can't take any more!" I yelled out to God. The wind was blowing so loudly now that I wasn't even concerned that other guests would hear me. "I don't think I can stand it!" I cried. Then, pouring out all my tumultuous feelings and heartaches and worries, it was as if I just dumped the whole sorry load at God's feet. Finally, I had nothing more to say, nothing more to do, nothing more to think. I felt completely emptied. And yet somehow I believed that God could deal with it.

For the first time in my life, I knew I must completely trust God to handle this. Or maybe I was simply at the end of my rope with no place left to turn. Perhaps for the first time ever, I realized that there was really nothing I could do to control anything. Not a single thing. Just one look at my life, and it should've been obvious to me long ago. For, no matter how hard I tried to hold it together, whether it had been with Liam or Hal or Jamie . . . it had never worked. Or if it appeared to work, it was only a temporary illusion. A false moment. Because then, just as if a class ten gale had swept through, it could all be blown away. Just like that—now you see it, now you don't. It was gone. I might as well give it up.

Somehow I fell into an exhausted sleep in the midst of the storm, and when I woke up, everything was quiet. The weather outside and my internal storm had both quit howling. I left my room and knocked on Jamie's door, but still no answer. And yet I didn't feel terribly upset by this. It was as if something in me had simply let go, and I knew it was up to God to work this thing out. I returned to my room, got on my coat, and went downstairs to inquire about my son. Just in case.

"I haven't seen him," the desk clerk said. "But if da lad was smart, he'd a stayed put during that storm. 'Twas a bad one."

"Is it over now?"

He nodded. "Aye. It seems to be. Go outside and have a look for yourself."

So I went outside and was surprised to see that not only had the sky cleared up, but the sun, now dipping low into the western horizon, was shining its spotlight onto a wet and sparkling world, and there was a glorious rainbow out over the ocean. And the crisp sea air was so fresh I wanted to drink it! But the day was coming to a swift end, and although it was barely four o'clock, it would soon be dark again. And yet I still didn't feel that sense of panic that I'd felt earlier. Something in me, probably my strong will, had completely surrendered itself to God during today's storm. For the first time in my life, I felt that I was really in his hands. Even with Jamie missing in a foreign country, I felt at peace. And I *would* get through this. God would help me.

I ate a quiet and early dinner at the hotel, and although I still found myself thinking of Jamie, it wasn't that old obsessive sort of fearful thinking. I wrapped my thoughts of my son in layers of prayers. And I eventually was able to go up to my room and to bed—and finally to sleep.

The following morning, I wasn't quite sure what to do. This was the third day that I had not seen my son, and despite my resolve to trust God, it was becoming more of a challenge. After all, I did have a missing son. I considered calling the authorities, but I had no idea what I'd say—and would I need to tell them that we'd had a squabble? And, if so, would they even take me seriously? I thought about asking the manager for advice, but wasn't really sure that it would do much good. Finally I thought about Kerry and the Anchor Inn. She seemed such a wise and caring soul and the only actual friend I had in Connemara. And so, since the weather had continued to be clear today, I decided to walk on up there in time for afternoon tea. I was surprised to see some trees had fallen and some roofs had lost shingles and tiles and a small boat had blown onto shore. But other than that, it was a splendid day with sunshine and temperatures much warmer than the previous week. And as I walked up the hill toward the Anchor Inn, I was stunned by the gorgeous view of sea and sky. Really breathtaking!

As I walked up to the restaurant, I hoped that I hadn't made a mistake in coming up here. I didn't see any cars or signs of customers. Perhaps they weren't even open.

"Welcome, welcome," Kerry called out as she opened the door for me, waving me inside. "Isn't it a lovely day!"

I smiled at her. "Yes. A perfect afternoon for tea."

Soon we were seated at a small table near the fireplace, and I was pouring out my story, or most of it. And, once again, she proved a sympathetic listener.

"So you haven't seen the lad in three days?" she said as Dolan set a rose-covered porcelain teapot on our table, along with a silver plate of cookies and miniature tea sandwiches, all prettily arranged on a paper doily.

I shook my head. "And I'm not sure what to do about it."

"But ya did tell him about his father, the way you'd planned to?"

I nodded now. "Unfortunately, that seemed to be the final straw." Out of respect for Jamie, I hadn't told her about his surprising confession that came first.

She frowned. "Jamie seemed a sensible lad, to me. Perhaps he only needed a bit of time—to clear his head so to speak."

"I thought about that too. But now that he's been gone two nights . . ." I sighed. "Well, I'm just not sure. What if something happened to him?"

She waved her hand as if to dismiss my concerns. "Oh, now, what could've happened? Jamie is a strapping young man and I'm sure he's quite able to look out for himself. Don't ya think?"

"Yes, I hope so . . ."

"But you're a bit worried all the same."

"I'm really trying to trust God right now." I paused, wondering how much I wanted to share about this—in some ways it seemed rather personal, and yet . . . "You see, I've been such a worrier, and I spent so much time and energy trying to control everything about my life . . . and only recently I came to understand that, well, it seems I really can't control much of anything."

"Isn't that the truth?"

"So I might as well trust God."

"Sometimes 'tis all we can do." She refilled both of our dainty teacups. "'Tis a long road that has no turning, Colleen."

"What does that mean?"

She seemed to consider this. "It means it may take him awhile to get there, my friend, but your Jamie will eventually find his way home—meaning home to you."

"I hope you're right."

"What are you two doing for Christmas Day?" she asked, and I suspected she had changed the subject for my benefit.

"Goodness," I said, trying to remember what day it was today. "I'd almost forgotten all about Christmas."

"'Tis only a few days off now."

"I hadn't really thought that far ahead," I admitted. "To be honest, what with how things have gone lately, if Jamie were to come back today, I'd just as soon change my flight and go back home immediately and we'd have Christmas at home."

She frowned. "So you've gone sour on our country already?"

I thought about this. "No, I really *do* love Ireland. But what with the storm yesterday . . . and Jamie being gone . . . well, I suppose I feel that it might be safer to be at home for the holidays." Then I laughed. "Oh, there I go, thinking I can control things again."

"If you and Jamie find yourselves still here in Ireland by next week, I hope you'll come on up to the old Anchor for Christmas dinner. We stay open for some of the older folks in town, ones who have no family about, and I'd be pleased to have you join us. We'll have turkey and goose and all of the trimmings. Dinner is at two."

"Thank you, Kerry. That sounds wonderful, and I'll keep that in mind."

"And tell your wayward laddie, *when* he comes home, that I'd be delighted to hear him play again. In fact, we have quite a crowd coming tonight. Dolan said we are almost full up. But then it's the Saturday before Christmas, and folks like to go out, so it's not so unusual."

I frowned. "Well, I don't even know that Jamie will be back today."

She patted my hand. "Aye, I understand. Whether he comes back tonight or next week, just know that you're both welcome . . . anytime."

The clear weather had continued to hold out, and so I walked back to town, praying as I went. Then, just as I turned the corner to the hotel, I noticed a familiar figure walking down the street directly toward me.

"Jamie!" I cried, as I ran toward him, throwing my arms out to embrace him. "I'm so happy to see you!"

"I'm really sorry, Mom," he said immediately. "I know you must've been worried and I couldn't—"

"Never mind about that," I said, which I knew must sound crazy after I made such a big deal of this only days ago. "I'm just relieved that you're safe and sound."

"I really would've called you, Mom." He kept one arm wrapped protectively around my shoulders as we walked side by side toward the hotel. "But I went to this island and then the storm hit and there were no phones and—"

"What?" I blinked at him as he held open the door to the hotel. "No phones?" Hopefully my son hadn't taken up the gift of blarney while he'd been gone. Come to think of it, maybe he'd been born with it.

"Yeah, Mom," he continued as we went into the lobby. "This place is called Inishbofin and they really don't have phones there and—"

"Ah, so that's where ya been, laddie," said the desk clerk, the one I'd haunted with my regular inquiries regarding the possible whereabouts of my long-lost son. "'Tis no wonder you were not able to make it back, nor to call your ma."

"Why's that?" I asked him.

"The ferryboat captain will not go out to the island during a class ten gale." He looked at me as if questioning my state of mind for not already knowing this. "And, certainly, Inishbofin has no telephones. Everyone knows that."

I turned and stared at my son in disbelief. "You were really there? Out on this island with no phones?"

He laughed. "Yeah, trust me, Mom, this isn't the kind of thing a guy makes up."

14

Jamie

Mom and I got a cup of coffee in the hotel restaurant, and I told her all about my strange visit in Inishbofin, which I learned was Irish for *Island of the White Cow*, and I actually thought might make a good name for a band if I ever started one again. Probably better than Jamie and the Muskrats. Apparently that name was the result of someone a few centuries back seeing a white cow there during a dense fog. I asked my new friend Katie how anyone could see a white cow through dense fog, and she just laughed.

"I got stuck on the island for two long nights," I explained, "all because of that storm and the ferryboat not coming. And it was pretty creepy for a while. But by yesterday afternoon, the storm cleared up and Katie gave me a bicycling tour of the island, which was actually kind of interesting. Then this morning, before the ferry came, she took me to see these amazing tide pools."

"Really?" Mom looked impressed.

"Yeah, at first all I wanted to do was to get out of that place. I mean, it felt like a prison and, man, was it ever cold and wet. And, oh yeah, did I mention that they lost their electricity?"

"Sounds like quite an experience."

"You got that right. But now I'm glad I went and I'd like to go back again, maybe just for a day. Only I'd make sure to tell you.

I really did feel bad about being AWOL and not able to call—especially after I got stuck there for the second day. I knew you'd be frantic."

Then Mom told me about how it was actually good for her having me gone, and how she really learned to pray and to trust God. "I need to lean on God more," she admitted. "Instead of trying to hold everything together myself."

"Yeah," I told her. "I kind of learned the same thing too."

"I know it's just the beginning for me," she said, "and I have a feeling there are still a lot of things I need to work out . . ."

"Like what?" I was starting to see Mom with a new set of eyes. She wasn't just Mom anymore. She had been in love with a man I'd never known, kept this hidden for years. It really was pretty mysterious.

She studied me, as if trying to decide how much to say. Then she sighed. "Things about your dad . . ."

"You mean Hal, that dad?"

She smiled faintly. "Yes, that dad. Sometimes I feel that I cheated him, Jamie. I feel guilty that I didn't love him enough."

"Oh, Mom." I reached over and put my hand over hers. "Like I told you before, Dad was 'over the moon' for you. I don't know how you could've possibly made him any happier."

She shook her head. "But I feel guilty."

"Look," I began, "you told Dad what was up before you guys got married, right?"

"Of course."

"He knew exactly what he was getting into."

She nodded.

"And he was thrilled about it. You were a really good wife to him. You made him happy. And I know he was proud of you. He loved everything about you, the way you took care of us, your cooking, your housekeeping, your looks—the works. Honestly, Mom, what more could you have done?"

She sighed. "I don't know . . ."

"You gotta let that go."

Now she smiled at me. "You're probably right."

"I know I'm right."

Mom laughed. "Oh, the confidence of youth."

"You should've seen me the night of the storm," I admitted. "I didn't look too confident then."

"I almost forgot," Mom said. "I went to see Kerry at the Anchor Inn today, and she invited us to join them at the restaurant for Christmas Day."

I slapped my forehead. "Man, I almost forgot Christmas. When is it anyway?"

"Wednesday."

I nodded, reminding myself to pick up a present for her. It seemed the least I could do, considering how I must've worried her. And I was impressed with how she was taking everything so well. It seemed like we'd really moved on now.

"And Kerry invited you to come up and play the piano again."

"Really? That'd be cool." But suddenly I wasn't so sure. What if it was hard on Mom hearing me play? What if it reminded her too much of my father? "But, you know, I don't have to . . ."

"But don't you want to?"

"Of course, I *want* to. But not if you don't want me to. I remember how it was that night, the first time you heard me play . . ."

"Oh, I loved hearing you play, Jamie. It was just, well, you know . . . everything I told you. About Liam and all. That was hard. But I do love hearing you play."

"Maybe we could go up there tonight," I said, glancing at the clock. "It's getting close to dinnertime anyway."

Mom frowned slightly now.

"That's okay . . ." I had a feeling that she didn't really want to go, and although I wanted to understand this, it made me feel bad too.

"I know what you're thinking," she said quickly. "But you're wrong. I really do love hearing you play. In fact, I've decided to get a piano when we get back home."

"You mean if the house hasn't been sold," I teased.

"Even if it does sell. I'd still get a piano for the next house."

I considered telling her about my old secondhand piano, but figured that could wait. "But you don't want to go to the Anchor Inn tonight?"

"I think I'm a little worn out. I already walked up there and back once today. And I just had a lovely tea with Kerry." She paused. "Why don't you go on up there and play tonight, if you like. Then, if you aren't tired of the place, we could go up there again tomorrow. You could ask Kerry to reserve a table for us on Sunday night."

"Really, you don't mind?"

"Not at all." She smiled brightly. "I'm just so glad that you're back. And that we're okay. I think it'd be wonderful if you went up there. And I know Kerry will be so happy to see you."

"Cool!" I studied Mom closely. "I'm really interested in hearing more about Liam. And I'm curious about where his parents were from. Do you think I might have any living relatives in Ireland?"

She nodded. "I think it's a possibility. And all I can remember was that Liam wanted to come to Connemara someday. It was the first time I'd heard of the place, but it stuck in my mind."

"Wow, so he could have relatives around here?"

"Maybe so. Although I know a lot of people emigrated about the same time as his parents did. I'd meant to ask around, about the name O'Neil, but I haven't really gotten around to it yet. I guess I was a little distracted . . ."

"Sorry. Maybe we can both check around some. Did you ask Kerry if she knew any O'Neils?"

She shook her head. "I told her about Liam and all that, but I don't think I even mentioned his last name . . . we were talking about so many things."

"We'll have to see what we can find out," I said.

We talked awhile longer, but I think Mom could tell I was getting antsy, and she finally suggested I head on up there.

"Are you sure?" I asked, feeling a little guilty for leaving her.

She winked at me. "Yes, I'm absolutely positive. I'm actually looking forward to a quiet evening with my book."

I knew she meant an evening when she didn't have to be worried about her mixed-up son, but I didn't say this. "Well, I better go change." I nodded down to my fisherman knit sweater. "I finally got this thing dried out, but I'm sure it doesn't smell too fresh after all the weather and everything I've been through."

She laughed. "Maybe we can find a dry cleaners."

So I freshened up, and although it was dark, I went ahead and walked on up to the restaurant. Kerry was so warm when she welcomed me that I felt right at home. The place wasn't full, but lots busier than last time, and Dolan insisted on bringing me some complimentary fish and chips even before I sat down to play.

"Don't ya even think of paying," he whispered as he set the plate down, "or my sister will be fit to be tied."

I hurried to finish my dinner, went to wash my hands, then sat down to play. It felt so good to have my hands on the keys again. It was as if they belonged there. And, even though I hadn't played for several days, it seemed that my playing had actually improved. Or else it just felt like it. The diners clapped their approval after each piece, and when I took a little break to have a sip of the lemon soda that Donal had brought me, Kerry approached the piano with an attractive blonde woman with her. I was guessing that the woman was about my mom's age.

"This is my dear friend," Kerry said. "She was so impressed with your playing that she wanted to meet you. Margaret, I'd like to introduce you to my young American friend, Jamie Frederick."

The woman stared at me with a curious expression. "You play quite well, Jamie Frederick." Her accent was Irish, but something about her appearance seemed American. Maybe it was her pink knit dress. It reminded me of something my mother might wear.

"Thank you."

"It's a most unusual style," she said, glancing over her shoulder as if she were nervous about something. "*Very* unusual, I'd say."

I shrugged. "Well, I'm sort of self-taught. I kind of do my own thing."

"Interesting . . . you taught yourself to play piano?"

"That's right." I studied her, curious as to why she didn't go back to her table so I could continue to play.

"And you're an American?"

I nodded. Kerry had returned to the kitchen by now, and I wasn't quite sure what more I could say to this lady, but I figured I should be friendly, even if her questioning did make me uneasy. Who was she anyway? "Yeah, I used to play guitar and I had my own band"—I rambled just to fill the space—"but then I got interested in piano and just took it up on my own. I took a few music classes, but haven't had any real piano lessons or anything."

Her pale eyebrows lifted slightly. "That's quite impressive."

"Thanks." I smiled at her, wondering if perhaps she was some kind of music professor or a recording person. Who knew? At least she seemed to like my music. Still, I wished she'd leave. Something about those pale blue eyes just staring at me as if I were a monkey in the zoo made my skin sort of crawl.

"The way you play . . . your style . . . it reminds me of someone." Again, she glanced over her shoulder, then back at me with an odd expression. I was starting to feel like a character in *The Twilight Zone. The* Irish *Twilight Zone.*

"Yeah?" What was this lady after anyway? Was she a groupie? Did she think I was famous and wanted an autograph?

"Yes. You play in a style very similar to my good friend . . . and what's even odder is that you look quite a bit like him—or rather the way he looked when he was about your age. You could almost be brothers."

I suddenly remembered what my mom had said about my biological father and how I played piano and looked so much like him. Could she possibly know a relative of mine? Or maybe she'd known him, long ago. I felt my heart starting to pound now, like something really weird was going on here, but I couldn't think of a thing to say.

"Would you mind if I introduced him to you?"

"Who?" I managed to blurt out.

She waved to a table in the corner of the room. "My friend William," she said.

"Oh . . ." I took in a quick breath, trying to steady myself although I was still seated. "Sure."

She waved to a middle-aged man now, motioning him over here. He slowly stood and, using a cane, walked toward the piano with a slight limp. He was a nice-looking guy, fairly tall, with dark hair.

"William," Margaret said, "this is Jamie Frederick. I was just complimenting him on his fine musical abilities."

I stood and the man shook my hand. Now I could see his hair was tinged with gray at the temples, and he peered at me with a pair of intensely blue eyes—eyes that seemed familiar somehow.

"I'm so pleased to meet you, Jamie. I was taken aback by your distinctive style of music. Perhaps Margaret mentioned it, but I play in a similar style and I have to say it's not something you hear every day." His accent was mostly Irish, but I sensed a hint of an American mixed in there as well.

"Jamie just told me that he's self-taught," Margaret said.

William seemed to consider this. "That's how I learned too."

My heart had started to pound again. It thumped against my chest, reminding me of when I'd played the bass drum in marching band. Something really strange seemed to be going on here. I couldn't explain it, but I felt as if I already knew this man. "Excuse me," I said without allowing myself time to reconsider. "But do you know anyone by the name of O'Neil?"

Margaret blinked. "William's last name is O'Neil."

I sank down to the padded piano bench now, unsure as to whether I really heard her correctly or if I was imagining this. "Your name is William O'Neil?" I said slowly, letting it sink it. William, not Liam.

He nodded. "Yes, that's right."

"By any chance, did you have a brother by the name of *Liam*?"

Margaret laughed. "Liam is a nickname for William." She nodded to William. "He used to go by Liam when he was younger. Didn't you, William?"

He nodded, but his eyes were fixed tightly on me.

I reached for my glass and took a big gulp of soda. The bubbles burned as it went down, making my eyes water.

122

"Are you feeling all right, Jamie?" Margaret asked. "You don't look well."

By now Kerry had returned. "How are you doing, Jamie? Dolan said some of the folks are asking if you're going to play again. They so enjoy your music."

"He seems unwell," Margaret said.

I looked up at Kerry and swallowed hard. "Margaret just told me that Liam is a nickname for William."

Kerry looked puzzled by my curious statement, but she just chuckled and picked up my soda glass and sniffed at it. "Is that all you've been drinking tonight, laddie?"

I nodded uneasily, but continued anyway. I needed to know the truth, the sooner the better. "You see, my father's name was *Liam O'Neil*."

Now they all looked slightly shocked, and I felt pretty stunned myself. I couldn't believe I'd just said this out loud. Good grief, there must've been hundreds of William O'Neils in Ireland. And, yet, I knew. Something in me just knew.

"What is your mother's name?" William asked in a quiet voice.

"Colleen."

William took in a deep breath, clasping his hand to his chest as if in pain. *"Colleen Johnson?"*

"Johnson was my mother's maiden name."

"May I sit down?" he asked slowly, steadying himself with one hand on the piano, the other clinging to his polished wooden cane.

I scooted over and made room for him on the bench beside me.

"Are you okay, William?" Margaret asked, her voice filled with concern.

He was taking slow deep breaths, and for a moment I thought perhaps he was having a heart attack. Just like my other father. Maybe I was a jinx—older men should keep their distance from me. Then William turned and looked at me with kind eyes. "How old are you, Jamie?"

123

"I'm twenty-one, sir. I was born July 27, 1942."

William took in another slow breath and just stared at me as if I were an apparition, then he slowly nodded again, as if this was all beginning to make perfect sense. His voice was calm now, but his hands trembled as he wrapped them around his cane. "I tried and tried to locate your dear mother . . ." He closed his eyes for a moment, as if trying to remember something long ago. "Johnson was such a common name . . . I called every Johnson in the Los Angeles area, asking for a Colleen May Johnson. I tried to find her old roommate. But it was as if they had both disappeared. I wondered if I'd imagined Colleen Johnson. But I knew she was real. I did an exhausting search for her, but with no luck. After a year or so, I even wondered if she had died."

"She thought you'd been killed in Pearl Harbor," I told him.

He sighed. "Nearly . . ." He put his hand on my shoulder and I could see tears in his eyes. "Your mother was the only thing that kept me alive. I wanted to get back to her."

"Come, come," Kerry said, taking me by the arm. "You both go on over to that quiet table over there and sit down. You need to talk about these things in private."

Soon we were seated by ourselves, and we both just sat and stared at each other for several long moments. It was so much to take in, and I think we were both in shock. Dolan had set a whiskey in front of William and a glass of water in front of me.

"I can't believe it," he finally said.

I shook my head. "Me neither."

He asked me questions and I told him what I knew. How my mother thought he had died, how she had married my dad. "Well, I guess he wasn't really my dad," I explained. "But I thought he was. Just until recently . . . my mom only told me the truth a few days ago."

"This is so amazing . . . so incredible . . ." He shook his head again. "I can just hardly believe it." He reached across the table and grasped my forearm, giving it a squeeze. "You're really here? You're really my son? It's like a dream."

I nodded. "Yeah, I feel the same. So what happened? Mom said you were an officer in the Navy, that you'd gone to Honolulu, but that you weren't supposed to be there long."

"I had gone to work on some communications things . . . on the SS *Arizona*. I'd only been there a couple of days when we were attacked. So many people died that day. I should've been one of them." He nodded toward his lap. "I lost my left leg in the explosion, lost so much blood that it was a wonder I survived at all. I don't actually remember much of it because I had a severe blow to the head and a concussion. The story I heard was that someone picked me out of the water, put a tourniquet on, and got me to a hospital. I was out of it for weeks, and when I came to, I kept thinking of Colleen. I would imagine her face, and that kept me alive."

"Wow."

"You can say that again. It really was a miracle."

"And Mom didn't know you were alive?"

"I sent letters to her address, but they were returned."

"The same happened to her."

"That may be because I wasn't considered officially stationed in Honolulu at the time. I'd only gone over to do some work, after that I was supposed to return to San Diego for further orders. And it's possible that I was listed as missing in action for a while. The world was a mess back then."

"And then Mom got married," I said sadly. "And her name changed. No wonder you couldn't find her."

I asked him more questions and discovered that he'd been living in Ireland since the late forties. "After the war and all . . . I just couldn't find anywhere I felt at home in America again," he said. "I drifted from town to town, job to job, and finally I came over here to visit and liked it so well that I never went back to America."

"I like it here too."

Then he asked me lots and lots of questions. I told him my whole life story, and he sat there and listened to me as if I were the most exciting guy in the world. Ironic, considering all that he'd been through.

125

"I hate to ruin the party," Kerry said, "but we've been closed for nearly an hour."

I glanced at my watch. "Man, it's nearly eleven."

So William and Margaret and the couple with them gave me a ride back to town. "Is it all right if I call you tomorrow?" he asked as they dropped me in front of the hotel.

"Sure," I told him, getting out. "My mom is going to have a fit."

"A fit?" Margaret said.

"American slang," William said, winking at me.

Then I got out and waved, but as I went into the hotel, I had to wonder . . . what would Mom think of this? I'd have to be careful how I broke it to her—she might have a heart attack for real!

15

Colleen

It wasn't even seven in the morning when I heard knocking at my door. I sleepily pulled on my robe, then opened it to find Jamie standing in the hallway. He had an odd expression—I couldn't quite read it.

"Is something wrong?" I asked instinctively, then noticing that he was fully dressed, added, "Have you been out *all* night?"

"No and no," he said quickly. "I just got up really early and I couldn't wait for you to sleep any longer."

I smiled as I fastened the belt of my robe. "Now, isn't that a switch."

"Can you get dressed and come to breakfast?"

"Can I have twenty minutes?"

He frowned with impatience. "Yeah, I guess."

"Be right down." I closed the door and hurried to clean up and quickly dress, barely putting on makeup or doing my hair. I could tell by his nervous demeanor that despite his claim that nothing was wrong, something most definitely was up. I hoped it wasn't anything serious. Had he gotten into some sort of trouble when he'd been on that island, Inabobbin or whatever it was called? As I pushed my feet into my shoes, I reminded myself that worrying would not help. I remembered my resolve to trust God. And so as I hurried downstairs, I prayed. *Please, let me take whatever this is calmly. Let me trust you implicitly, God, and help me to remember that you are able to fix anything. Amen.*

"You're here," Jamie said brightly, pulling out a chair for me. We were the only ones in the restaurant and I wasn't even sure they were open yet, although I thought I smelled coffee drifting from the kitchen area.

"What is going on?" I asked in a controlled voice, forcing a smile. "You have me quite curious."

He slowly inhaled, then placed both of his hands palms down on the table and exhaled. "You are *not* going to believe this, Mom."

I thought I could feel my blood pressure rise, but I kept my face expressionless and just waited. "Try me."

"My father is alive."

I blinked and steadied myself. Had my son taken leave of his senses? "No, Jamie," I said calmly. "Your father is *not* alive. I saw him . . . uh, in his coffin . . . before the internment, and Hal was most assuredly—"

"No, not *that* father, Mom. William, I mean *Liam* O'Neil—he is alive."

"Jamie . . ." I glanced toward the kitchen now, longing for someone to come out and help me make sense of this or at least bring some coffee to clear my head. "I think you must be confused—"

"No, Mom. I know it probably sounds crazy, and I had a feeling it would be hard for you to believe this. It wasn't easy for me either. But, really, I met him last night. Liam O'Neil is very much alive."

I considered this. "Do you mean you met someone by that name, because if that's the case, I'm sure there must be dozens of Liam O—"

"No, Mom, *really*, this is the guy—the real deal. We talked for a couple of hours. He told me everything—about Pearl Harbor, about you, and how he lost his leg."

I blinked and leaned back in my chair, trying to catch my breath and to take this in. Was Jamie crazy? "What on earth are you saying?"

"Liam O'Neil is alive. He's been living in Ireland for about fifteen years and he's a really great guy."

I felt like I couldn't breathe just now, like someone had wrapped a thick corset around my rib cage and pulled it tight. I wondered if I should lean over and put my head between my knees, allow some oxygen to my brain, but instead I just sat there, staring at my son. Was it possible that he'd been smoking some of that marijuana that I'd just read about? Or perhaps that other new drug LDS or SLD or whatever that mind-altering chemical was called?

"Jamie?" I tried again, my shaky voice coming out in a hoarse whisper. "Are you certain you weren't hallucinating?"

He actually smiled now. "Listen to me, I *really* met him. It was my piano music that brought this whole thing up. This lady named Margaret came up and told me that I played just like him, and she talked to me for a while, then introduced me to the guy, and it really was him." He was so excited that I couldn't help but almost believe him. "Isn't it great?"

I just shook my head, still trying to absorb all of this. Liam was alive . . . a woman named Margaret . . . they had spoken to my son. "And who is Margaret?" I finally asked. My voice sounded like that of a small child, and it felt as if the earth were moving beneath my feet, like I was losing my balance, tipping sideways.

"I don't really know exactly," he admitted. "I mean, she was with Liam and everything. But when she introduced herself, I think she said she was his friend." He brightened. "She's also a friend of Kerry's. Kerry introduced me to Margaret. And Liam and Margaret were with this other couple, I can't even remember their names, but they live near Clifden. Liam and Margaret live in Galway. I think they came to visit for the weekend."

I took in a shaky breath. "And what did Kerry think of all this? Was she convinced that this Liam person was really your father as well?"

"Of course. Because *he is*."

"But, Jamie . . . it just sounds so—so impossible."

So then he went into detail about how Liam had been on the SS *Arizona* when the bombs fell that day, and how he'd been seriously injured, unconscious for a long time, and how he lost a leg . . . and slowly it all began to sink in. It began to make a tiny speck of sense. Those were strange times back then. So much going on. I supposed people, papers, records . . . maybe it could've gotten mixed up.

"But what about the Red Cross?" I tried.

"Liam said he wasn't actually stationed in Honolulu," Jamie continued. "He was only supposed to be there for a couple of weeks. That's why they didn't have a record of him and probably why your letters were returned."

I nodded. Everything seemed fuzzy and blurry just now, as if the restaurant had filled with smoke, but no one was smoking. Although I wasn't a smoker, I almost felt as if I could use a cigarette. "Yes," I said meekly, "that sounds possible . . ."

"So, do you believe me now?"

"To be honest, I don't know what I think just now, Jamie." I glanced to the kitchen. "Could you see if someone could get me a cup of coffee . . . or a glass of water or something?" My throat felt tight and it was still difficult to breathe. I wasn't sure if I was about to cry or laugh or have a stroke. But Jamie left and came back after a couple of minutes with a cup of coffee.

I took a cautious sip, then a slow breath. "Thanks."

"Are you okay?"

"I don't know . . ."

"It was a shock. I understand. I wanted to tell you as carefully as possible."

"You did just fine, son." I took in another slow breath.

"It'll get better," he reassured me. "After it sinks in some. I was pretty stunned at first too."

I just nodded and took another sip of coffee. It was black and hot and I usually drank mine with cream, but right now I didn't care. Jamie waited patiently as I sat there slowly sipping my coffee in amazed silence. I felt like I wasn't really there just then, like I was just floating around and watching this woman and her son. Finally, I remembered the prayer I'd prayed in the stairs. I silently prayed it again. *God, help me with this.* That was all. I thought I could breathe again.

"Do you feel better now?" Jamie asked after I finished my coffee.

"Yes. I think so. But I suppose I'm still in shock. It's a lot to take in."

He reached over and put his hand on mine. "I know."

Then I smiled at my son. Despite my tumultuous feelings, I had to appreciate how mature he was being just now. How supportive and understanding. When had he grown up so fast? "Thanks."

We talked about it some more. Jamie told me how Margaret had mentioned how much he looked like Liam when he was younger. "She must've known him for a long time."

I nodded, almost afraid to admit it. "You do look like him, Jamie. Strikingly so."

"He seems really nice."

"Did he play piano for you?"

"No." Jamie frowned now. "But I'd sure like to hear him."

"That would be nice." Even as I said these words, I wondered at myself. How was I calmly sitting here? How was I able to hear all this without falling completely apart?

"You're going to see him too, aren't you?"

I considered this. "Do you think he wants to see me?"

"Of course!"

Finally the waitress appeared, refilled my coffee cup, and took our order. I didn't feel the least bit hungry, but I ordered a bowl of oatmeal anyway.

"I told him he could call today."

"Here?" I asked stupidly. "At the hotel?"

"Sure. Is that okay?"

My hand flew up to my hair. I knew I must look disheveled and how, feeling so rushed, I hadn't dressed very carefully, hadn't even put on lipstick. "When?"

"I don't know. Probably not this early."

"Yes, of course."

As I picked at my oatmeal, I wondered about Liam. What would he think of me now? I was so much older. And who was Margaret?

"Did Liam tell you if he married?" I asked suddenly. "Does he have children?"

"He didn't mention it."

"Oh . . ."

"How do you feel about him now, Mom?"

I stared at my son, looking so much like his father. "I don't know, Jamie. It's been so long that it doesn't even seem real to me. If I didn't have you, I might even doubt that I'd ever known someone named Liam O'Neil. It's like an old movie that I watched a long time ago."

"But it's real, Mom. He's real. You know that, right? You do believe me?"

"Yes, of course, I believe you." I looked down at the table. "Do you mind if I excuse myself, Jamie? I still need some time to process all this."

"Sure, Mom." He even stood as I got up. Such a gentleman. When had he grown up so nicely?

"I'll be in my room," I said as I set the linen napkin on the chair.

"I'll finish up my breakfast and then be in my room too."

Then, feeling slightly robotic, I mindlessly walked out of the dining room, mechanically up the stairs and into my room where I locked the door, then sat down on my still unmade bed and just cried. I wasn't sure exactly why I was crying—were they tears of regret? Fear? Anger? Relief? Or perhaps just a cleansing of sorts.

But, after the tears subsided, I knew I had only one resort. I knew that I needed to give all of this to God. It was far too much for me to carry alone. And so I did. Then I took a long, soothing bath, adding some salts that I'd picked up in town. After that, I carefully did my hair and my makeup. Then I put on the lovely black-and-white Donegal suit that I'd purchased in Dublin. I studied myself in the mirror, and although I was much older than the last time Liam had seen me, I thought perhaps I didn't look too bad.

I wasn't sure what to do then. I certainly didn't trust myself alone with my thoughts. If not for my prayers, I felt I was hanging by an emotional thread. So I went and knocked on Jamie's room and told him that I was going to take a walk.

"You won't be gone long, will you?" He looked worried.

"No, I just want to stretch my legs while the weather holds. I heard it's going to rain again this afternoon."

He grinned. "What a surprise."

"I may stop at McGinney's for a cup of coffee," I said. "And to read the paper."

He nodded as if making a mental note of this. "Okay."

Then I went for a little walk, but most of the shops were closed and the streets fairly deserted. Then I realized it was Sunday and people were probably at mass or church. Fortunately, McGinney's, as usual, was open. So I got my coffee and then sat and distracted myself by reading the paper. I'd been curious as to what was going on in the United States lately. Life had seemed tenuous since the Kennedy assassination, and I had meant to keep up on the news. I felt as if the future was shaky. Not just for me personally but for our whole country, perhaps the whole world.

"Colleen?"

I looked up from my paper and instantly knew who this tall handsome man was, but I was unable to answer.

"May I join you?"

I nodded and set the newspaper aside. "Liam?" The word emerged as a whisper.

He smiled as he sat. "Colleen, you look just as beautiful as ever."

I felt myself blushing. "You look fine too." I liked the distinctive gray hair that had gathered at his temples and the fine creases by his eyes, as if he smiled a lot. This made me feel happy.

"I'm still in complete shock." He slowly shook his head. "This is all so unbelievable."

"I know . . ."

"I have so many questions."

"So do I."

"Ladies first?"

133

I wasn't so sure I wanted to go first. I wasn't even sure where to begin. "I wrote to you in Honolulu," I finally said. "Over and over. My letters were all returned."

"That's what Jamie said."

"I was frantic when I discovered I was pregnant." I shook my head as I recalled the horror at that discovery.

"I wish we'd gotten married."

"I was so stupid."

"You were trying to be sensible."

"No," I admitted. "I was being selfish and vain. I wanted to have a real *wedding*. I wanted my family to come out and meet you. I wanted to show you off." I looked down at the table, swallowed hard against the lump in my throat.

"I *tried* to find you, Colleen. I really did."

"Jamie told me that."

"When I got back to the mainland, you and Wanda weren't at the apartment. No one knew where either of you had gone, there was no forwarding address. I made so many phone calls to Johnson families in Southern California, all with no results . . . finally I just gave up. It seemed like you had vanished into thin air."

"We lost the apartment. Wanda got married, her name changed. And my family is just one of thousands of Johnsons in Minnesota, not California." I sighed at the hopelessness of two people separated by war and life and death and desperate circumstances. "I got a job selling shoes . . . I moved to Pasadena in December, then got married after a couple of months . . . my last name changed to Frederick."

"Jamie told me that your husband died a year and a half ago."

"Hal was a good man, he took good care of us."

He nodded sadly. "Did you love him?"

"I was desperate . . . I didn't think I could raise a child by myself. Hal loved me and in time I learned to love him . . . in a way . . . and he was a good dad to Jamie."

"Jamie is a fine young man. You did an excellent job raising him."

This made me laugh. "Jamie is what Jamie was going to be. I think you've had as much to do with it as I have—he is so like you."

He seemed to consider this. "I just couldn't believe it when I heard him playing the piano last night." Liam's eyes lit up. "It was so amazing to find out who he was. I'm sure my friends thought I was about to have a heart attack. I never dreamed I had a son, Colleen—that we had a son. It was so incredible, surreal. But hearing him on the piano, well, I just *knew*."

"I sort of know what you mean about the piano." Then I told him about my own experience less than a week ago, how Jamie had taken me so by surprise and how I had only told him the truth about Liam after that. "That's why I brought him to Ireland," I explained. "I thought it was the perfect place to tell him."

"More perfect than you knew."

Liam's eyes seemed to look right into me—past my calm veneer and straight to my soul. I wasn't sure what to say now. "I'm curious about your friends," I finally ventured. "Jamie mentioned them to me."

"Devin and I have been friends for years. He and Myrna have a lovely home a bit outside of Clifden. We came out here for the weekend—a little getaway. And Margaret is an old friend of mine."

I nodded as if that was all very nice, but I really wanted to ask him more about Margaret. What kind of "old friend" was she?

"Did Jamie tell you about my leg?" He held up his cane as if it were a prop. "Lost it in Pearl Harbor."

"Yes. I was so sorry to hear that. That must've been hard."

"Not nearly as hard as losing you . . ." Was there a trace of bitterness in his voice? Was it about me or the leg?

"I'm so sorry, Liam."

"I eventually resolved myself to my unlucky lot in life. It could've been worse . . . so many didn't survive that day. I finally convinced myself it might've been for the best—not finding you, I mean. I wasn't sure how you'd react to a one-legged husband, and I wasn't sure how I'd react to being rejected."

135

"And I might've been married by the time you found me," I said, which was sad but true.

He looked down at the table, tracing a long, graceful forefinger over the grain of the wood.

"So, did you marry, Liam? Have children?"

"No to both."

"I'm sorry."

His eyes twinkled now. "Wait. I take that back. I *did* have a child."

"Oh, yes!" My hand flew up to my mouth to think of this. "Jamie."

He leaned forward eagerly. "I want to get to know him better."

"I don't know why you shouldn't."

"He said you were going back to the States after the holidays."

"Our tickets are for the twenty-sixth," I admitted. "Jamie had insisted we keep the trip to two weeks. He wanted to be home for New Year's Eve."

"Big plans, eh?"

I shrugged. I still wanted to ask him more about this Margaret person. But how did one do this gracefully? At least they weren't married. That was some consolation. But what if they were involved? Besides, it was quite possible that Liam had no feelings left for me. After all, I was the one who gave up so quickly. I was the one who got married.

We continued to talk, filling in some of the blank spaces, telling each other bits and pieces of so much that had happened in the past twenty-two years. I told him a lot about Jamie. And he told me about how returning to Ireland was a life-changing experience for him, explaining how he found himself as well as God here on the Emerald Isle. It was quite a moving story. I even told him about how I'd been learning to let go of my hold on Jamie and trusting God instead. Perhaps it had to do with Ireland.

And to my surprise, after an hour or so, I felt fairly relaxed—almost as if we hadn't been apart all those years. It was amazing, really. And I loved hearing about Liam's life. How he'd returned to college on his GI bill and gotten his music degree, how he'd taught at several universities and occasionally did concerts here in Ireland. "Music is an enormous part of my life."

"How exciting," I said, marveling again at the color of his eyes—still as intensely blue as ever. "Does Jamie know about any of this?"

"We didn't get terribly far last night. To be honest, I was so stunned that I hardly recall what we did speak about."

"He'll be thrilled to get to know you. He loves music dearly, more so than I even knew, and I'm afraid I haven't been terribly encouraging."

"This is all so incredible," he said suddenly. "I feel as if I should pinch myself. To think I have a real son—a talented son who appreciates music as much as I do." His eyes got misty now. "It's such a fantastic gift! What a grand Christmas this will be!"

Of course, I was thrilled that he was so excited about Jamie. But I wanted to ask him where I fit into this picture. I knew it was unrealistic to assume we could pick up right where we left off. But how did he really feel about me? Was it too late for us? And what about Margaret? What was she to him? But it was as if these questions were bottled up tight, the cork jammed down. I couldn't get a single one out.

"I'm sure you guessed that Jamie was the one who told me where to find you this morning." Liam looked at his watch. "And I told him that I'd love to spend some time with him before we have to head back to Galway. Margaret has a function there at two this afternoon, so our time today is limited."

"Oh . . ."

He reached for my hand and gave it a warm squeeze. "It's been so great seeing you, Colleen. Really amazing."

I nodded, forcing a bright smile as I held back tears. "You too, Liam."

"Are you going back to the hotel now? Shall we walk together?"

I glanced at the paper still at my elbow. "I think I'll stay here a little longer," I said in a restrained voice. "I, uh, I think I'll get another cup of coffee and finish the newspaper first."

He nodded and stood. "Take care now."

"You too." Then as soon as he was out the door, I picked up the newspaper, and using it like a privacy screen, I started to cry.

16

Jamie

I knew this Christmas was going to be the best ever! For one
thing, we were in Ireland and that was pretty amazing in itself.
But besides that, I was going to spend the holidays with Liam,
my biological father. Before leaving Clifden on Sunday, Liam had
invited me to come to Galway for the holidays. Of course, he extended the invitation to my mom as well. But since he had to get
back to Galway and Mom wasn't around, he asked me to ask her
for him. Even so, I could tell he wanted her to come.

"You just missed Liam," I told Mom as she came into the hotel
lobby.

"Actually I saw him being picked up in front just now."

"Did you talk to him?"

"Well, no . . . but I saw him getting into a nice Mercedes Benz
with a pretty blonde woman at the wheel."

I smiled. "Yeah, that was Margaret. Did you know that she's
a musician too?"

"No, I didn't."

"Yeah," I told her. "Liam said that she plays several instruments—they both do. And they're having this huge Christmas Eve
party with all their musical friends. And everyone will be playing

music and Liam invited me to join them. He said I can play the piano or borrow his guitar or whatever. Isn't that cool?"

"I'm sure you'll have a good time, Jamie."

"But you're coming too," I said quickly. "Liam said I could invite you."

"That was nice of him." Mom sighed as if she was bored, or perhaps it was something more.

"You do want to come, don't you?"

"Oh, I don't know . . ."

"Come on, Mom. It's going to be great. You have to come to Galway. After all, it's going to be Christmas." I knew how Mom felt about the holidays. Family was supposed to be together. I'd broken that cardinal rule last year, and I didn't intend to repeat that same mistake.

Her brow creased and I was afraid she was about to say no.

"Is it because of Liam?" I asked suddenly. "Are you uncomfortable with him?"

"It's hard to explain . . . I'm not even sure how I feel. Or how he feels . . ."

"Even more reason to come," I urged. "Liam seemed like he really wanted you there in Galway. You've got to come."

She smiled. "Okay, Jamie, I'll come to Galway with you." She glanced over to the front desk. "That is if I can get it all arranged. It's awfully late notice and it's the holidays. We might not be able to find accommodations."

"I already asked the concierge to do some calling for us."

She looked surprised at my assertiveness. Then she smiled and I knew it would be okay. As it turned out, the concierge knew just the place, and by the end of the day, it was all set.

So it was that on Christmas Eve day, following a leisurely lunch with Kerry and Dolan at the Anchor Inn, we checked out of our Clifden hotel and a hired car took us to Galway, where we checked into a very posh hotel right in the center of town.

"Merry Christmas, son," she said as she handed me a key to my room. "I hope this is really what you wanted."

I hugged her. "It's perfect. Thanks so much. Liam said to come over anytime after six. It's not a sit-down dinner, but they'll have plenty of food."

"Oh, I don't know that I'll go to the party," she said in a tired tone. "I'm feeling a little worn out and—"

"You have to come. It won't feel like Christmas without you."

"I don't know . . ."

"Come on," I persisted. "It's only one night. And we'll be going back home in just two days. You need to make the most of it."

"I suppose you're right. But I can't be ready by six. You can head on over there ahead of me if you like—"

"Not a chance," I told her. "I'll wait and go with you."

She looked slightly relieved. "Okay. Then I plan to take a nice, long bath first. And I won't be ready to leave until seven."

I grinned. "That's fine. I'll meet you in the lobby, okay?"

She frowned slightly, then nodded. I wasn't completely sure why Mom was having such a hard time with this. Was it because of her old relationship with Liam? Was she feeling nervous about where things stood with them now? Of course, that made some sense, but it had been such a long time ago that they'd been involved. Still, it seemed possible she could still have feelings for him. Although she hadn't said anything to make me think this. If anything, she'd been pretty tight-lipped about the whole thing. Well, other than asking about Margaret. She had tried to sound disinterested and casual, but I could tell she was concerned that Margaret and Liam were involved. To be honest, I wasn't sure. They did seem to be pretty good friends.

As I went into my room, I wondered what it would be like to be Mom's age and suddenly have an old flame popping back into my life. I suppose if it was Shelly, telling me she'd made a mistake and that she wanted me back, well, I'd probably stand up and take notice. Still, it'd be awkward. I had to admit that much. But if nothing else, I hoped that Liam and Mom could be friends. What kid wouldn't want that much from his parents?

Mom was a few minutes late, but when she came into the lobby, I felt proud to think that this lady was my mother. She had on a dark red velvet dress that looked fantastic. She even had the mink stole that my dad had gotten her for Christmas a few years ago. And as we waited for our taxi, a gentleman going into the hotel really checked her out and even tipped his hat.

"You look like a million bucks," I told her.

She thanked me and we got into the back of the taxi.

"Since this side trip to Galway is your Christmas present to me," I began as I pulled a small bundle from my pocket, "I thought I should give my present to you too."

She smiled and looked curious. "You really got me something?"

I nodded and unwrapped the tissue paper to expose a small silver ring that I'd bought in Clifden. It was shaped like two hands holding a heart. "It's a traditional Irish ring," I explained.

"A Claddagh?" she said with excitement.

"Yes," I said, suddenly remembering the name.

"Oh, I had wanted to get one."

"It's only silver," I said. "And the lady at the shop said that you're supposed to wear it on your right hand with the heart pointing away from your fingers."

"Really?" She slipped the ring on. "It fits! How did you know?"

I grinned. "Just lucky, I guess."

Then Mom hugged me. "Thank you, Jamie. I will treasure this always."

We were out of the city and driving through a neighborhood now, probably getting close to the place. And I could tell by the way Mom started twisting the handle on her little black evening purse that she was getting nervous. I hoped I wouldn't be sorry that I'd talked her into coming tonight. I was starting to feel worried about the status of Liam's relationship with Margaret. Even though Margaret was older, probably in her late thirties, I had to admit she was really good-looking. I glanced at Mom and mentally compared the two women. While Margaret was pretty in that flashy blonde sort of way, I thought my mom had a very classic sort of beauty.

"Liam said they play a lot of traditional Irish folk music," I said for no apparent reason, except that I was hoping to fill in the dead silence of the taxi. "It's supposed to be like an old-fashioned Irish Christmas." I said a few more random things, but I suspect that Mom knew I was trying too hard. And I was probably just making both of us even more nervous.

Liam's house was on the outskirts of town. Situated in an impressive-looking neighborhood, it was a large stone house with lots of tall windows. Each window had a candle burning in it—I'd heard that was an Irish Christmas tradition—but it gave the house an inviting appearance. There was a huge holly wreath on the shiny red door, and we'd barely rung the bell when it was opened wide and we were welcomed by the happy sound of music.

"Come in," said a man in a dark suit as he held the door and took our coats, pointing us in the direction of the music.

I spotted Liam immediately. He was playing the fiddle along with several other musicians on other traditional Irish instruments, including Margaret, who was playing a lively piece on the mandolin. Margaret stood right next to Liam, looking up into his face with an expression that seemed to convey more than just a casual musician friendship, although I hoped I was wrong. I glanced at Mom in time to see her nervously fingering the strand of white pearls that circled her neck. It was possible that this evening was going to turn into a great big mistake. As badly as I wanted to participate in the music and all, I hated to think that I was ruining Mom's Christmas.

"Want to sit down?" I asked, pointing to a comfortable-looking chair near the fireplace. "I can get you something to drink or some food or something."

"Something to drink would be nice." She spoke to me, but her eyes were on the mandolin player. And it was hard not to stare at Margaret since she had on this silver sequined dress that was cut low in the front, and showing a fair amount of leg as well. Mom sat down and I went off in search of something to drink just as the song ended.

"I didn't see you come in," Liam said when he joined me at the large cut crystal punch bowl. "Is your mother here too?"

I nodded. "I was just getting her something to drink."

"This is a traditional Irish Christmas punch," he told me. "It's Margaret's special recipe, but I should warn you it has a bit of rum in it."

I considered this. Mom wasn't much of a drinker. But perhaps this wasn't a bad idea tonight. Maybe it would help her to relax. "That was a great song you guys just played," I said as I filled a cup.

"Do you want to join us on the next number? Are you good at improvisation?"

"I'd like to give it a try."

He grinned at me, then nodded toward a large table with an assortment of musical instruments arranged upon it. "Pick your instrument and come on up."

I took Mom her punch, then excused myself to join Liam and his friends.

"Don't worry about me," she assured me. "I'm perfectly fine, Jamie. You go and have fun. It'll be a delight just to listen."

I still felt a little guilty, but appreciated her attitude. This was such a great opportunity—a once-in-a-lifetime Christmas. I chose the guitar and joined the others, and before long I was picking and strumming to a lively Irish folk tune. It felt so natural to play like this, like it really was something in my blood. It seemed to be the same sort of feeling that I'd been putting into my piano playing this past year. But I could never quite figure it out or even put a name to it. Now I wondered if it was simply "Irish." I didn't know how many songs I'd played with the others before I remembered my mom. I hoped she didn't feel abandoned.

"How are you doing?" I asked as I joined her again.

She smiled happily. "I'm absolutely fine, Jamie. And the music is lovely. Please, don't feel that you need to entertain your poor old mother."

I laughed. "There's nothing poor or old about you."

She smiled at a gray-haired woman sitting to her right. "And I've made a new friend tonight." Then she introduced me to Mrs. Flanders. "She's Liam's neighbor and an artist. We've been having a great time getting acquainted."

"And you are a talented lad," Mrs. Flanders said. "I nearly fell over when Liam informed me that he had a son joining us tonight." She shook her head. "Remarkable!"

Mom smiled at Mrs. Flanders, but her eyes seemed a little sad. "So, really, Jamie, please, don't worry about me. Just enjoy this evening. I love watching you play. I had no idea you were this good."

"I take after my father." I winked at her.

"You sure do." Her smile looked genuine now. "And I'm so proud of you!"

So, feeling relieved that Mom at least had someone to chat with, I returned to the musicians, and this time, seeing that no one was at the piano, I slipped in and began to play along. Liam grinned at me as he picked up the discarded guitar and surprised me with some very tricky fretwork. This guy could teach me a lot!

As the evening wore on, we began to play more Christmas music and some of the less musical spectators even started to sing along with us. Margaret was a pro at getting the crowd enthused. She'd shout out the words and they'd join in. It was such a happy evening and such a great mix of people. Not to mention that the music was amazing. And, for the first time that I can ever recall, I felt as if I completely fit in. It was better than when I'd led Jamie and the Muskrats and better than when I'd met the Irish musicians in Dublin and wished I could join their band.

This was unlike anything I'd ever experienced before. It felt as if I'd finally come home. I was so comfortable here, playing with my biological father and his musician friends, that it was indescribably cool. Extremely groovy. The only disappointing part of the evening, and something that seemed completely out of my control, was the aura of sadness that seemed to drape itself around my mother. Oh, she was smiling and clapping and even singing along when she knew the words. But her eyes . . . they were full of sadness. And I feared this was probably the longest evening of her life—and she was doing it for me. And, despite my guilt, it was so hard to quit playing. But when I checked on her, she reassured me that she was having a good time. And so I was back on the guitar again, and as we played and played, I honestly thought I could carry on like this for hours. Maybe even days.

Finally it was nearing midnight and the crowd was still going strong, but I noticed that Liam had taken a break. And so I decided this was a good time for me to call it a night. I didn't want to leave, but I knew Mom had made her sacrifice in coming here tonight. I could make mine by leaving early.

But when I went to look for her, she wasn't in the chair. Neither was Mrs. Flanders. Maybe they'd gone off together, although that seemed unlikely. So I got a bite to eat, then looked around for Mom, but didn't see her anywhere. Had she called a taxi and gone back to the hotel by herself? And, if so, why didn't she let me know? I decided to see if I could find Liam, perhaps I could use his phone to call the hotel. But I didn't see him anywhere either. Finally I spotted Margaret, adding some more rum to the punch.

"Have you seen Liam?" I asked.

She glanced around. "No, but he might be in the library. He sometimes takes a break in there." She pointed to a hallway near the stairs. "Second door to the left."

I thanked her and headed in that direction, pausing by what I thought was the door to the library. Other than a slit, it was mostly closed, but I could hear voices talking quietly—male and female. I strained my ears to hear better, unsure as to whether I wanted to interrupt or not, when I realized it was Liam talking to my mother. I couldn't quite make out the words, but there was a sound of urgency in Liam's tone. And it almost sounded as if my mother was crying, which worried me.

I actually leaned over now and, feeling like a snoop or maybe just a kid trying to sneak a peek at Santa, I peered through the crack just in time to see Liam taking my mother into his arms—and she was not resisting—and kissing her with such force and passion that I had to look away. There was only so much that a son wants to know about his mother's love life. Besides I knew this was a private moment.

But I retreated back to the kitchen feeling just slightly victorious. Of course, this didn't really make sense. But somehow I felt just a little responsible for reuniting my two parents like this. If it hadn't been for me, Mom never would've come to Ireland. If we hadn't come to Ireland, we never would've met Liam.

"Did you find Liam?" Margaret asked as I returned to the punch bowl.

"Yeah." I studied her for a moment, wondering how she was going to take this new development.

"Were they together?" she asked as she ladled out some punch. "I mean your mother and Liam?"

I blinked. "You know?"

She shrugged. "I've known for years, Jamie."

"Seriously?"

She took a sip of punch, then nodded.

"How did you know?"

"For starters, I'd have to swear you to secrecy."

I held up my fingers in the old pledge. "Scout's honor."

"Can I really trust you?"

"Yes," I urged. "Now tell me what it is that you've known for years."

She let out a big sigh. "That if Colleen ever walked back into Liam's life . . . well, let me just say that I've always known that he never quit loving her."

"And you're okay with that?"

She nodded with misty eyes. "Liam is a very good friend. How could I not be happy for him? Colleen was the love of his life and he thought he'd lost her forever." Then she threw her arms around me. "And you, young man, are one of the most amazing young musicians that I've had the pleasure to meet. Has your father talked to you about attending university here in Galway yet?"

"Not yet."

"Well, he should!"

17

Colleen

On the day after Christmas, also Saint Stephen's Day and an Irish holiday, I stood in the relatively quiet Dublin airport by myself. I felt surprisingly torn about leaving Ireland. But I felt even more torn that I was leaving my son behind. Of course, I was glad that he wanted to finish college, even if it was in Galway, halfway around the globe from our home in Pasadena. And I'd been especially touched when he told me that he also planned to get a job. "I want to pay you back for what I wasted on my phony education," he told me over breakfast yesterday. Now my first instinct had been to say no and that the debt was forgiven and not to worry about it, but on second thought, I wondered if this was something he needed to do—another step in becoming a man and a responsible adult. So I bit my tongue and hid my motherly pride.

But I missed Jamie more than ever just now as I waited to board my plane. The idea of going home—alone like this—was overwhelming and nothing I had ever imagined when I started this trip, oh, a lifetime ago. Still, I reminded myself, it was time for me to accept my independence. I didn't need anyone to hold my hand. I was a grown woman and perfectly capable of carrying my own bags, sitting on a plane by myself, catching a taxi back to the house, making plans for my future . . . even if that meant

I would be the only one in the picture. And, after all, I did have God to lean on. I wasn't really alone.

"But what about Liam?" Jamie had demanded in my room just last night, right after I'd informed him of my plans to go home on the regularly scheduled flight. For some reason he'd gotten the idea that, like him, I planned to extend my visit.

"What about Liam?" I had calmly asked as I carefully packed my bags.

"He loves you," he said. "Don't you love him?"

I smiled patiently at my son. I knew he meant well. "This really isn't your problem, Jamie."

"But I saw you kissing on Christmas Eve," he confessed.

I blinked back surprise. "You were spying on us?"

He nodded sheepishly. "Sort of. I mean I hadn't meant to, but I did see you two together. And it looked pretty obvious that you were both in love."

"I'd had too much of that Irish punch," I told him. "I was impaired."

"That wasn't the case, Mom."

"Jamie, I know it's every child's hope that his parents would be in love and stay in love and that everyone would live happily ever after, but it can't always be like that."

"But Liam *does* love you."

I studied Jamie closely. "How do you know that? Has he told you that?"

"No, he hasn't said that, not in so many words. But I know it's true. I have my reasons to believe it's true. You have to trust me on this, Mom."

I turned my attention to the folding of my red velvet dress, the same dress I'd been wearing that night. And I had to admit that I had felt that way too. I had honestly believed that Liam did still love me—especially on Christmas Eve, when we had kissed. But he had never *said* so. Consequently, I hadn't told him how I felt either. Although it seemed obvious that night—to me anyway. But then Jamie and I had left. And then there was the next day. And there was Margaret.

On Christmas Day, when we got together with Liam and some of his friends again, he privately admitted to me that Margaret had been in his life for years—and even that she had recently been pushing him toward marriage. He seemed very confused and uncomfortable with all this. He didn't say it, but I felt that I was an interruption, a distraction, and an inconvenience. And, after all, Liam had known Margaret much longer than he'd known me—they'd spent years and years together. Simply because Liam and I had made a son together didn't mean that we were meant to be together. And then I'd seen how compatible he and Margaret appeared to be—so much in common with their music, their lives, and Ireland. And she was so beautiful. How was I supposed to compete with that?

"You can't leave, Mom."

"I'm sorry." I turned and faced him with a firm chin. "But I have to go home. For one thing, I have the house on the market, and the last time I spoke to the realtor, right before Christmas, she thought she had a buyer for it."

"Great," he said. "Sell the house. But why do you have to go home to do that?"

"It's the mature and responsible thing to do," I explained as I rolled a pair of stockings.

And so, as I stood there so carefully dressed in my Donegal suit with matching shoes and handbag, waiting for my flight to begin loading, I thought I was being remarkably responsible and mature. Or at least I looked that way. Despite how I felt inside, I wasn't crying or fretting or fuming or any other childish thing. I was simply waiting to get on my plane and go home. And, once I got home, I would begin to sort out my life again. Perhaps the house would be sold by then. Maybe I would find that little cottage near the beach after all. And who knew, I might even get a job. The possibilities were endless.

"Colleen?"

I didn't turn at the sound of his voice. Not immediately, anyway. But my stomach grew fluttery and there was a catch in my throat as I slowly pivoted and faced him.

"Liam." I studied his eyes, trying to read what was behind them. "What are you doing here? Is something wrong? Is it Jamie?"

He took a tentative step toward me. "Jamie is fine."

"Oh . . ."

"It's Jamie's father who is having trouble."

"Jamie's father?"

"Yes, Colleen. I am perfectly miserable."

"Oh . . ."

"I can't let you go like this."

"Like what?"

"I can't let you go without telling you the truth first."

I nodded now, bracing myself for the worst. Perhaps he and Margaret had gotten engaged last night, after Jamie and I had left. Perhaps Liam felt that the mature thing for him to do was to come here and tell me this news in person. Maybe Jamie had said something to make Liam think that I would need to know. "Yes?" I heard my voice shaking.

"I love you, Colleen."

I blinked, then stared, unable to speak. Had I heard him correctly?

"I never quit loving you."

"But why didn't you say something . . ."

He held out his cane. "I don't like to talk about it, Colleen. It's hard to admit . . . but being a man with one leg, well, it's not been easy. To be honest, it's probably one of the main reasons I never asked Margaret to marry."

I sucked in a quick breath. "So, you would've asked her?"

He nodded then sighed. "Yes. I probably would've."

"Why don't you ask her now?"

"Because I don't *love* her. Not like this."

"Oh . . ."

"I love *you*, Colleen." He peered at me with those intense blue eyes. "And are you going to just hang me out to dry now? Do you have nothing to say?"

I took a step toward him, our eyes still locked. "I love you too, Liam. I always have. I always will. I never quit loving you."

Then he took me into his arms and held me tight. "Please, don't go."

"But I need to take care of things back home," I began meekly. But suddenly he was kissing me, his lips pressed into mine with passion and intensity—the kind I had longed for since that November of 1941. And in that moment I felt both lost and found, and without holding back, I returned his kiss.

"Please, don't go," he said again. "Stay here and marry me, Colleen."

I almost said no, not now. I almost told him that I needed to go back to Pasadena and that I needed to take care of business—that I needed to be a grown-up and to sell my house, that I needed to store my furniture, that I needed to tell my sister the good news, and I almost told him that we should wait—but I stopped myself.

"Yes!" I said with excitement. "I *will* stay here and I *will* marry you!"

His brows shot up with surprise. "You will? You really will?"

"Of course! You don't think I'm going to make the same mistake twice, do you? I'm not taking any chances this time. *Yes, I will marry you!*"

Then he took my right hand in his and carefully removed the silver ring that Jamie had given me for Christmas.

"What?" I frowned and felt slightly worried.

"Now you must wear the Claddagh like this." He took my left hand and slipped the ring onto my ring finger with the point of the heart aiming toward me. "Worn like this means your heart is taken."

I nodded. "You took it long ago, Liam."

"Let's go get married!" he said as he pulled me close for another long kiss.

"You just name the day and the time, and I will gladly marry you, Liam O'Neil."

"Let's go round up a preacher." He grinned down at me. "And I know a certain young man—a man who's waiting outside in my car right this minute—who will be extremely happy to hear about this."

I grabbed Liam's hand. "Let's go tell him!"

ALL
I HAVE
to
GIVE

1

||||||||||||||

"Do you think Michael's experiencing a midlife crisis?" Anna mused as she dipped a serving bowl into the sudsy water. She and her younger sister Meredith were cleaning up after a Thanksgiving dinner that Anna had hosted for her extended family. It was the first time she'd entertained this many people at one time, but the meal had gone relatively well, especially considering twelve people had crowded into their rather small dining room. The food had been reasonably palatable, and the table, which was actually a piece of plywood secured to a pair of sawhorses and hidden beneath a tablecloth Anna had sewn, had been elegantly set. Although Anna was now rethinking her choice to use Great-Grandma Olivia's Meissen china. She hadn't considered that, thanks to the elegant gold-leaf trim, all twelve place settings and the numerous serving dishes would need to be hand washed.

"I think your hubby is too young for a midlife crisis," Meredith said with her typical skepticism. "I mean, what is he . . . like, thirty-seven?"

"Thirty-eight in January."

"Even so, that seems pretty young for a midlife crisis."

"Maybe he's mature for his age."

Meredith laughed as she carefully dried a platter. "Okay, what's really going on here, Anna? Trouble in paradise?"

Anna sighed as she scrubbed some stubborn gravy from a dinner plate. "No, we're okay. It's just that Michael has seemed sort of distant lately . . . but then he's been putting a lot of overtime into this new business, and, oh, I don't know—I guess I'm probably just obsessing."

"Meri?" Todd called from where the guys were huddled in the nearby family room, cozily gathered around the TV in their usual holiday ritual. "I hear the baby crying."

Meredith rolled her eyes at Anna as she hurried to dry her hands. "Todd hears Jackson crying, but he can't get off his duff and go pick up his own son?"

"And I'm guessing the womenfolk can't hear him."

"Not over the roar of that ball game." Meredith tossed the towel aside. "Sorry to bail on you, sis, but it is Jackson's feeding time."

"No problem." Anna ran some hot water into the sink, preparing for the next go-round. "I'll be fine."

"Want me to send Celeste in to take my place?" Meredith's tone was teasing now.

"That's okay," Anna said quickly. "I can handle it."

Meredith chuckled. "You just don't want to hear our sister-in-law going on again about how 'our big new house will be oh so perfect for a great big ol' Thanksgiving dinner.'" Meri even had the southern accent down just right.

Anna smiled at her sister, then nodded. She didn't add that she was also getting tired of hearing her sister-in-law complain about how none of her size-two clothes fit her anymore. "I can't believe I'm only three months pregnant and I'm going to have to go out and get maternity clothes," she had whined when she'd seen the pumpkin and apple pies Anna had made for dessert. What Anna wouldn't give for that kind of wardrobe challenge! It seemed such a small price to pay in exchange for a baby. But Anna didn't want to go there today. She also didn't want any more help in the kitchen. It was barely large enough for two people anyway.

She held the clean plate up to the window now, allowing the afternoon light to come through the china's translucent surface. "You can tell it's fine china when you can see daylight through it," Great-Grandma Olivia had told her more than thirty years ago, back when Anna was a little girl and had admired the lovely set. With pink rosebuds and gold-leaf trim, Anna couldn't imagine anything more beautiful. Of course, her tastes had changed somewhat as an adult, but she still felt honored that her great-grandmother had chosen Anna, as the oldest granddaughter, to bestow this treasure upon. "Glad it's you and not me," Meredith had admitted ten years ago when Anna had gotten engaged to Michael and received the china as a pre-wedding gift. "I'm sure not into pink rosebuds." Anna had appreciated the china even more when Great-Gran passed on shortly before her wedding. The sweet old woman had been ninety-six and still living in her own little house when she'd died in her sleep. Although saddened that Great-Gran had missed her wedding, Anna had thought it was a lovely way to go.

"I'll bet you could use a hand," Donna said as she came into the kitchen. Donna was Anna's stepmother, but she'd been in their lives for so long that Anna and her siblings had pretty much accepted her in the role of mom, although Anna still called her by her first name. "I didn't realize that Meredith wasn't in here still."

"She's feeding the baby. But you can dry if you want." Anna rinsed the last plate and set it in the drainer. "I'm going to start getting things ready for dessert now."

"It was a lovely dinner," Donna said as she picked up a fresh dish towel.

"Albeit a little crowded in my tiny house?"

Donna smiled. "You'll have to excuse Celeste. She's so excited about their new house and everything."

"Well, she can host Thanksgiving at her big ol' house next year."

Donna laughed. "Yes, I can just imagine Celeste dressed in silk and pearls as she stirs the gravy and balances her six-month-old baby on her hip."

"Meaning that David won't be much help?"

Donna frowned slightly. "I do wish he was a little more excited about becoming a daddy."

"I know . . ." Anna shook her head as she remembered her

brother's negative reaction when Michael had toasted him and his wife on their impending parenthood. "I couldn't believe what he said during dinner."

"Oh, I don't think he really meant it." Donna reached for another plate. "It's just that David wanted to be married for at least five years before starting a family."

"I think he should just be thankful," Anna said a bit too sharply. "After all, it is Thanksgiving," she added to take the sting out of her words. Then she changed the subject, telling Donna about the Thanksgiving party that one of her room mothers had put together for her second grade class. "It was totally over the top," Anna admitted, as she went into detail to describe the fancy decorations and foods that had probably been very expensive. "But the kids actually seemed to like it."

"Where does this china go?" Donna asked as she set the last plate with the others on the countertop.

"Back into its crates."

Michael poked his head in the doorway from the dining room. "Need any help in here?"

"Sure." Anna turned the flame up under the teakettle. "You can help me get the crates and pack up these dishes and get them out of here."

"Nice dinner, Anna," Michael said as they walked back to the spare bedroom.

"Thanks."

Michael picked up a plastic crate, then paused to glance around the guest room. "You know, I've been thinking about converting this room into a home office."

"But where would we put company?"

"Well, I thought maybe the, uh, the *other* room . . ."

Anna bit her lip but didn't say anything.

"It has really nice light in there," he added.

Anna felt her throat tighten. "That's true, it does."

"And I thought if I had a home office, maybe I could work at home more. You know it's been hard starting up the new business, but if I could get set up at home, I could spend more time here. And I thought maybe I could repaint this room, like a dark blue or green or burgundy, sort of like a den or library, with some bookshelves. Maybe you'd want to use it too, for lesson plans or grading or whatever."

Anna brightened a bit. "That does sound nice, and dark paint would look good with the woodwork and crown molding."

"So maybe we should store your china set in the, uh, other room for now," Michael said as they carried the empty crates back to the kitchen. "It'll be one less thing to move out when I start to paint in there."

"I guess so . . ." Even as she said this, Anna knew she lacked enthusiasm. Still, she tried to process Michael's suggestions as she walked back to the kitchen.

"Want me to make coffee now?" Donna held up the empty carafe.

"Sure." Anna unzipped one of the many quilted containers, slipped in a china plate, and topped it with a circular pad to protect it from the next plate—just the way Great-Gran had shown her.

"Goodness." Donna paused from measuring coffee and watched Anna and Michael carefully putting the delicate pieces away. "I didn't realize that china was so much trouble."

"It's just that I don't have a proper place to keep it."

"You need a china cabinet, Anna."

"That would be nice."

"I don't know why you didn't just use your regular set of dishes," Donna continued. "They're pretty enough."

"Because this china is special," Anna said. "And I thought the family, especially Grandma Lily, would enjoy seeing it out again."

Donna examined a teacup. "I suppose so . . . but it's certainly a lot of work."

"I don't mind." Anna picked up a full crate and carried it back toward the spare bedroom.

"Let's put it in the other room," Michael said from behind her. "Remember?"

"Oh, yeah . . ." She paused, actually holding her breath as he balanced the crate on one side and reached for the doorknob. She hadn't seen this room for a while. Probably not since last summer when she'd retrieved a diaper bag that she knew Meredith could use, since her other one had split at the seams. And she knew Meredith had put Jackson down for a nap in here today, but Anna had been busy in the kitchen at the time . . . and now they were probably out in the living room with the grandmas.

Anna cautiously walked into the room, feeling almost surprised to see that it was just as cheerful as ever. The walls were still a warm buttery yellow, and the creamy white nursery furnishings—the changing table, crib, dresser, and rocking chair—were still in their places, although Meri had left a red and blue baby quilt behind. Anna had long since stowed the pretty pastel bedding and stuffed plush animals. It had been too difficult to see those cheerful baby items placed around the room . . . so expectant and waiting.

Michael set his crate down against the wall, then slowly removed the one that Anna was still holding. "I know this isn't easy, honey, but I've been thinking we should clear this room out," he said quietly.

She nodded, a hard lump forming in her throat. "I'm sure you're right."

"Maybe we could give the furniture to David and Celeste. I mean, despite how she goes on about how great they're doing, your brother admitted to me that he wasn't financially ready for this baby yet, what with recently getting that new house and all."

"Yes, that's a nice idea, Michael." She tried to feign enthusiasm as she ran her hand over the smooth surface of the crib's head-board, then picked up Jackson's bright quilt and folded it neatly, placing it under her arm. She remembered how she had carefully researched this line of infant furniture online, looking for the safest manufacturers available. Making sure that it was nontoxic paint, and that the railing posts weren't too far apart, and that there were no fancy knobs or things for a baby's clothing to get caught on. No, she would have no concerns over the safety of her brother's baby with this well-made line of furniture. Still, it was so hard to let it go—such a final good-bye to old dreams. And

160

what about the possibility of adoption? Yet that seemed unlikely since their savings account was gone, plus they'd incurred a small mountain of debt when they'd "invested" in every imaginable fertility treatment available.

Anna was blinking back tears now, staring down at the ugly tan plastic crates that were now cluttering what she had once considered something of a sanctuary. "Do we really need to store the china in here?"

Michael reached over and put his arm around her shoulders. "I know it's hard . . . but we need to move on, Anna."

"I know, but I just don't like seeing the crates in here."

"Well, like I said, I want to paint that other room . . . and, as you know, we're a little short on storage in our little house, and I—"

"Fine!" She turned and glared at him. She knew she was being unreasonable, but suddenly she felt angry. Really angry. "Your old MG—a car that doesn't even run—takes up our entire garage, Michael. And whether it's raining or snowing or sleeting, I have to park my car on the street. But do I complain about that? Do I?"

"But, Anna, that's because it's—"

"It's just *fine*, Michael. You come and you go. You do as you please. You'll get your home office and you'll ruin this little room— this nursery that I—I love. Well, fine, it's just perfectly fine. Don't worry about me. Just as long as you're happy. *I'll be just fine!*"

Michael blinked and stepped back. "But, Anna, that's not what I want—"

"Excuse me, Michael, I need to go serve dessert now!"

As she turned and stomped back to the kitchen, she knew that she was acting totally crazy, not to mention completely out of character. She knew that she was being irrational, and if any members of her family had overheard her little tantrum, they would wonder what on earth had come over her. This was so unlike her. But for a change, Anna didn't really care what anyone thought. Let them wonder. Let them speculate. Maybe it was time she acted up.

2

||||||||||||||||

As she got ready for bed, Anna still felt bad about her temper tantrum. Really, what had come over her? Maybe she was simply stressed. Certainly, it had been a long day. And she'd spent the previous afternoon, and late into the night, preparing things for Thanksgiving. Still, there was no denying that she hadn't felt like herself for several weeks now. She leaned against the bathroom vanity and peered at her image in the brightly lit mirror. Naturally, she looked tired. But who wouldn't be exhausted after a full house of relatives and a long day like today? And judging by the dark circles beneath her eyes, she was probably slightly iron deficient again. No big surprise there. Out of habit, she had taken prenatal vitamins plus iron for years . . . well, up until a few months ago when she just couldn't stand to see that *prenatal* label one more time. She'd promised herself to pick up a regular brand of vitamins but then had forgotten.

She leaned even closer to the mirror now, examining the gray hairs that seemed to be multiplying daily. Like her mother, she had been blessed with a full head of thick, dark, curly hair. And like her mother, she had been going prematurely gray since her late twenties. At first she'd tried to cover it, but then she'd heard that rumor about cancer being linked to hair dyes, plus Michael had insisted he liked her hair just the way it was. And so she'd decided to go with the flow, letting nature take its course, which was apparently the fast track. But didn't the Bible say that silver hair was a crown of glory? At this rate, she'd be glorious by the time she reached forty.

Anna reached for her bottle of Tums, noticing that it was nearly empty. Hadn't she just gotten it last week? But her stomach felt worse than usual tonight. Probably from too much rich food . . . although she'd tried to go light on dinner and hadn't even touched dessert. She popped a couple of the chalky tablets and even considered mentioning her stomach problems to Michael, just to hear his thoughts. He had a knack for distributing good medical advice. But he was probably asleep by now anyway. As usual, they'd already kissed and made amends—maintaining their promise to never go to sleep mad. But the truth was Anna still felt a little out of sorts over his comment about her needing to move on. That was easy for him to say.

Yet, as she brushed her teeth, she told herself that Michael was right. She knew it made perfectly good sense to turn their spare room into a home office. In fact, it was a great idea, and she'd probably enjoy the room too. As she flossed, she knew she would love to have him at home more. It seemed he'd been gone so much these past couple of weeks. Furthermore, she was well aware that the baby nursery had a great southern exposure and would make a delightful guest room. It all made total sense.

Except for the fact that she just didn't want to let it go yet. Despite that it had been nearly three years since she'd miscarried the only pregnancy that, with the help of modern medical technology, she'd actually managed to carry for almost six months, and despite that they had exhausted their financial resources as well as their limited supply of frozen eggs and sperm, Anna still didn't feel she was ready to give up. Good grief, she was only thirty-seven. Besides, she believed miracles could still happen. Well, at least she believed that on a good day. Today had not been a particularly good day. But tomorrow might be better. Especially if her stomach felt better . . . and if she could just get her energy back. As Anna applied moisturizer to the fine lines that had recently fanned out around the edges of her eyes, she promised herself that she would eat sensibly tomorrow, whole grains and fruits and vegetables, and she would go for a nice long walk with Huntley, their elderly beagle, and she would not forget to take her vitamins—prenatal or not. Although she wondered if the iron might aggravate her stomach even more.

For good measure, she popped another Tums tablet and hoped that it would do the trick. At first she'd assumed that these digestion problems were just a lingering case of a pesky strain of flu that had swept like wildfire through the elementary school last month. But now she wasn't so sure. And about a week ago, an old nagging fear had begun to gnaw at her again—tugging at the corners of her mind and trying to get her full attention. But she had put it off, telling herself that she'd think about it later . . . sometime when she wasn't so busy—perhaps during winter break, which was only a couple of weeks away now.

Anna rubbed lotion on her elbows and reminded herself that she was overdue for a gynecologist appointment, but after that last one—a year and a half ago—when Dr. Daruka had given her the hopeless prognosis on ever getting pregnant, Anna hadn't bothered to reschedule her annual checkup. She'd had enough doctor appointments to last a lifetime, and if she ever put her feet in those horrid stainless steel stirrups again, it would be way too soon.

She clicked off the bathroom light and went to the kitchen to make sure that Huntley had fresh water in his dish. He'd been slightly neglected today. She gave him a Milk-Bone, a pat on the head, and a promise for a walk in the morning, then turned off the kitchen light. But on her way back to the bedroom, she paused in the hallway, stopping to gaze at an old family portrait. Anna had been about thirteen when it was taken and nearly as tall as her mom, plus her feet had gotten big enough to wear Mom's shoes. Feeling rather grown up, Anna had been trying out a new eighties-style hairdo that made her head look enormous, but at the time Anna had thought she was styling. Meredith had been eleven at the time, smiling broadly to show off her shiny new braces that she would later come to hate. And David, at nine, was gangly with an impish look in his eyes. Mom and Dad were seated in front, holding hands and looking generally pleased about life, as if they had no idea what was just around the corner.

Once again Anna got hit with that eerie sense of déjà vu—that haunting feeling that history was about to repeat itself. Of course, this time it would be different. There wouldn't be three children left behind to grieve—only a husband and an aging beagle. She stared into her mother's dark brown eyes, so much like her own, and attempted to discern whether or not Mom had known the truth when the photo was taken. She'd been so urgent about getting everyone to the portrait studio that Anna had later been suspicious—as if there wasn't much time left and Mom had to get this shot while everyone was still able to smile . . . and while Mom still had a full head of hair. Anna's mother had been only thirty-six when the family portrait was taken . . . and thirty-seven when she'd succumbed to ovarian cancer just a bit more than a year later—only months older than Anna was now. A chill ran through Anna, making the hairs on the back of her neck stand up. She shivered and wrapped her arms tightly around herself, then realized that she was standing in the drafty hallway with bare feet and only a summer-weight cotton nightgown to keep her warm. Who wouldn't be cold?

She hurried to the bedroom, slipped quietly into bed, and wished she could warm her chilly feet on Michael. But she knew that would wake him . . . and then she might suddenly begin to talk—about everything. She might toss aside all inhibition and simply unload these things on him, dumping all her anxiety and concern, as well as Dr. Daruka's numerous warnings that Anna needed to watch out for that "genetic connection."

Everyone in her family had always acknowledged that Anna looked "just like Mom." But Anna's secret fear had always been that she and her mother had more than their outward appearances in common.

Everything in her wanted to wake Michael now. To sob out her fears and to feel his arms wrap around her as he assured her that everything was going to be okay. But tomorrow was a workday for him. And, she reminded herself, he had enough stress on the job these days. Building a new business wasn't easy—especially during the holidays. He didn't need her worries added to his ever-growing pile. Plus she knew that this kind of angst was always the worst at night. By the light of day, she would probably laugh at her silly paranoia.

3

||||||||||||||

Anna hadn't really meant to sleep in the next morning, but by the time she woke up, it was nearly nine o'clock and Michael had already gone to work. But right next to the coffeemaker, which was half full and still hot, he'd left a note saying that he'd be working late again tonight and that he expected to be home after eight. Then he'd added, "Have a nice day. Love, Michael."

"I intend to have a nice day," she said aloud as she poured herself a cup of coffee and picked up the newspaper. Huntley's tail began to thump, and she wondered if he remembered last night's promise to take him for a walk this morning. Well, she would keep that promise . . . as well as the others she'd made. With a three-day weekend to look forward to, Anna planned to start taking better care of herself. Sure, last night's panic attack did seem rather ridiculous in the light of day, but just the same it was a good warning to pay attention to her health. Then, after just a few of sips of coffee, she got that same uneasy twisting in her stomach again, followed by the feeling that all was not well.

Anna shoved the newspaper aside, went to find her laptop, and set it on the dining room table that Michael must've moved back in here before going to work earlier. The table was an old beater that she'd gotten at a garage sale shortly after they were married. She'd painted it pale green and found some mismatched chairs that she'd sewn chair pads for, promising herself that someday she'd

166

get a real dining room set—something worthy of Great-Gran's china. But, like so many other things, "someday" hadn't come.

Anna opened the laptop and turned on the power, then went back to the kitchen to heat up the teakettle. What she needed right now was a nice hot cup of green tea. It would be part of her new "get healthy" plan. But as she waited for her sluggish computer to get online and for the teakettle to whistle, she started to feel slightly panicky again. What if something really was wrong? To distract herself, she popped two slices of wheat bread into the toaster and went to the pantry in search of some orange marmalade.

She returned to her computer with her tea and toast and, seeing that it was now online, went directly to Google.com. Her topic was *ovarian cancer,* and as soon as she hit *search* more than seven million results popped up. She narrowed the search to include "symptoms," and the list shrunk to less than two million. Then she scanned for a website that sounded reliable and waited for it to open up. She knew this information should be familiar to her. After all, Dr. Daruka had given her numerous pamphlets in the past. Then again, had she ever actually read them? Or had she stuck them away to read "later" as she hid beneath a protective blanket of denial?

Anna felt herself growing more and more tense as she studied the list of symptoms. Her palms were sweating, and she knew that her pulse rate was increasing as she began to mentally check off all the symptoms that she'd been experiencing. Everything from abdominal discomfort and bloating to gastrointestinal symptoms like gas, indigestion, and nausea, to fatigue and even urinary problems. There was hardly one symptom on the list that she hadn't experienced. To make matters worse, she discovered that ovarian cancer was sneaky . . . because symptoms often didn't appear until the case was quite advanced. Not only that, but women who hadn't given birth were at a much higher risk. And the risk climbed even higher when family history was involved—particularly on the maternal side.

Anna slammed her laptop shut, then raced to the bathroom, where she barely made it to the toilet in time to lose her green tea and toast. With tears streaming down her cheeks, she stood over the sink, rinsing out her mouth and splashing cold water onto her face. She knew what was happening . . . history was repeating itself.

Unless she was overlooking something. Oh, it seemed impossible and too much to hope for. Especially considering all the times she'd been disappointed before. But what if this time was different? What if she really was pregnant?

Anna opened the small storage cabinet in the bathroom, digging past toilet paper packages and tissue boxes until she found what she was looking for—a pregnancy test kit. She'd almost tossed it out several times before, but doing that would have felt like giving up for good. Besides, there was still one test remaining, and one was all it took. Really, what could it hurt to just try?

After several minutes, Anna stared down at the used strip. Of course it was negative. Why should that surprise her? She wondered why she'd even bothered as she tossed the kit into the wastebasket. Then she took it out again. She didn't want Michael to see it and wonder about it. Instead she wrapped the kit in newspaper and took it to the trash can outside. On her way back through the kitchen, she paused at her computer again, then sat down to read some more. Although there were informative sites that boasted of new procedures and improved treatments, Anna felt a growing sense of doom and foreboding. It seemed obvious . . . She *was* her mother's daughter.

She picked up the phone and called Dr. Daruka's office but immediately got a recording. "Dr. Daruka will be out of town during the Thanksgiving holiday weekend. You may reach her on Monday during regular office hours. If this is an emergency, please call 911. Thank you."

"Right." Anna hung up. "911 . . . you bet."

Anna took a long, hot shower, got dressed, leashed up Huntley, and headed for the neighborhood park. As she walked, Anna attempted to pray. She wasn't a stranger to prayer, but, she suddenly realized as she struggled to come up with the right words to pray, she hadn't prayed much during the past couple of years—not since losing the baby. Oh, it wasn't as if she blamed God. She didn't. Not really. But she had wondered why he hadn't helped out just a little . . . Giving them a baby had seemed such a small thing at the time—especially in light of all the harder-to-resolve problems of the universe. It wasn't as if she'd been asking to win the lottery or to be handed a leading role on *Grey's Anatomy*. She had simply wanted a baby.

But then again, God had probably known that Anna was going to get sick like her mother . . . and perhaps he hadn't wanted for her to leave a motherless child behind. If her pregnancy had gone full-term, her baby would've been nearly three by now. A girl, Dr. Daruka had somberly informed her at the hospital. Anna hadn't wanted to know the baby's sex before the birth—she had wanted to be surprised. If it was a boy they were going to name him Edmond, and a girl would be named Olivia after Great-Gran and Mom. Maybe it was just as well that little Olivia was safely in heaven with her namesakes now. Maybe God knew that Anna would be with her baby girl before long.

Anna walked and walked around the little park. She circled it so many times that even Huntley began to slow his pace, glancing up at her as if to question this odd behavior. The poor old dog was going on twelve, and his stubby legs weren't as strong as they used to be.

"I'm sorry, Huntley," she said. "Am I wearing you out?" She paused at a park bench, and Huntley, obviously relieved for this break, stretched out on the footpath in front of her.

Anna sat there on the bench, looking up at the bare trees. Okay, if her worst fears were really coming to pass, what was her next step? Well, besides making a doctor appointment, and that wasn't even possible right now. She knew she needed to talk to someone, but she wondered how she could possibly break this news to Michael. He'd already been through so much with her—all those years of useless fertility treatments combined with all those desperate nights when she'd cried herself to sleep in his arms. She replayed all that he'd sacrificed for her since their marriage. How he had reluctantly gone into what he called "that nasty room" to "donate" sperm for her, or how he'd continued at a job he'd hated just to keep up their health insurance policy (mostly for her, since the private school where she taught had no coverage). Not to mention how he'd willingly emptied their savings and gone into debt—all in an effort to make her happy. Or at least that had been the goal. And now, after she'd given up on more fertility treatments as well as a baby, and he'd finally been able to quit the detested marketing job to start up his own design firm with his buddy Grant, she was going to tell him this? It was just too cruel.

That's when it hit her—they had no health insurance! Not a speck! They had known it was risky, but it was only temporary. Michael had quit his job in August, and they'd decided to save a few precious bucks—money that was needed for the new business—planning to purchase a health insurance plan after the New Year. But by then it would be too late . . . unless there was no diagnosis. Okay, perhaps keeping her illness a secret might be considered devious or dishonest. She wasn't even sure. But, to be fair, she didn't know for certain she had ovarian cancer. In a way, she'd been jumping to conclusions since no professional had examined her yet. And surely they wouldn't be able to call this a preexisting condition without an official diagnosis.

Anna did some quick calculating, counting the weeks off on her fingers. January was less than six weeks away. Whatever was going on with her would simply have to wait. Most of those weeks would be vacation time anyway. And, really, what difference would it make in the end? Anna felt fairly certain that her fate was already sealed, and she cried as she walked home. And, although she may have been imagining it, she felt that Huntley understood what was going on with her. At the end of each block, he would look up at her with those big, sad eyes, and it seemed they were full of compassion—as if he was saying he was sorry.

By the time she got home, Anna knew what had to be done. She had to "buck up." And that's exactly what Dad used to tell her and her siblings in the months following their mom's death. Dad hadn't been very tolerant of emotional outbursts. He took the stance that what was done was done, and no one should carry on about it. And so that's what Anna would do about this. She would follow her father's example and pretend like everything was just fine. Not only that, she had to make sure—mostly for Michael's sake—that this was the best Christmas ever!

4

"You're putting up lights this year?" Bernice, the elderly neighbor from across the street, observed.

Anna forced a smile as she continued her attempt to untangle the strands of small white bulbs, stretching them out across the lawn. "Yes, I decided it was time to get back into the Christmas groove."

"Not me," Bernice said. "Ever since Harry died, I just don't have it in me to decorate much anymore."

Anna peered at the white-haired woman. "I'm sorry," she said with compassion. "Holidays must be hard."

Bernice nodded. "Particularly Christmas. Harry just loved Christmas. He didn't mind climbing on the roof to put up Santa and the reindeer and the works. Every year I was certain he was going to fall and break his neck, but he never did. And, oh my, the grandkids thought he was the greatest. I can still remember their eyes lighting up when they saw the house glowing from one end to the other. And the tree—good grief, Harry always had to get one that reached clear to the ceiling." She tossed her thumb back toward the contemporary-style house. "And we have twelve-foot ceilings." She sighed. "It was really something."

"Do the grandkids still come for Christmas?"

"Mercy, no." She shook her head. "They all have their own lives now . . . other relatives to spend time with."

"So, what do you do for Christmas?"

Bernice just shrugged. "Oh, I usually pop in a microwave dinner . . . watch a Christmas special on TV . . . go to bed early."

Anna frowned, suddenly feeling guilty for not having this conversation with her neighbor years ago. "Well, how about if you come to our house for Christmas this year, Bernice?"

Bernice's eyes grew bright. "Really?"

"Sure. We usually go to my dad's house for Christmas Eve and someone else's for Christmas Day. But this year I'd like to do Christmas dinner at home, and I'd love to have you join us."

"Well now, I'd like that. Thank you." She smiled. "Thank you very much. And you let me know if there's something I can bring. I used to make a very nice Waldorf salad."

"That sounds great."

"I'm going to run home and see if I can dig up the recipe this afternoon."

Anna laid down the last strand of lights. "And I think I'm about ready to get out the ladder and get these lights hung."

"You're going to do it all by yourself?" Bernice looked slightly alarmed.

"Well, Michael's very busy with a new business . . . so I thought I'd surprise him."

"Do be careful."

"Thanks, I will."

Anna plugged in the lights to test them. She was relieved to see that, other than a few burnt-out ones here and there, they worked. Heights had never bothered her, and once she got out the ladder and started hanging the lights around the eaves of their bungalow, she decided to climb to the peak of the roof and have a look around. She was surprised at how different things looked from that vantage point. She could see over fences and into neighbors' backyards. Some backyards, like theirs, were neat and orderly—everything in its place. Well, except for the strip of worn grass in Huntley's doggy run, but even that was fairly tidy. Others were messy and chaotic looking. Like the one a couple houses down with bright-colored plastic toys strewn all about—what she wouldn't give for a yard like that.

Finally her work was done. She couldn't wait until dark to see them really lighting up the place. It had been several years since they'd done Christmas lights, and Michael would probably be pleasantly surprised. Hopefully he'd remember this in years to come . . . when he, like Bernice, had to rethink the holidays and come up with new traditions. She wondered if Michael would remarry after she was gone. Part of her hoped so, and yet a part of her didn't want to share him with anyone.

In the house, she made a list of all the things she wanted to do for Christmas this year—all the things it would take to make this the best Christmas ever. Of course, her resources were pretty limited. Most of her salary, which wasn't a lot since she taught at a private school with a limited budget, was going to pay off their bills these days—trying to wipe out the debt that had accumulated during those despicable fertility treatments. And now, more than ever, she knew she needed to stick to that financial plan. If all went well, she might have the debt completely wiped out by the end of the school year. That is, if she could remain healthy enough to teach until June. She sure hoped so.

She tried to remember how her mom had been during that final year. Of course, she hadn't worked outside of the home, but even so, taking care of a husband and three kids couldn't have been easy. Always their house had been neat as a pin with homemade dinners every night, bag lunches ready to take to school, and even the laundry neatly folded and sitting on their beds when they came home from school. Anna marveled at this now. These were chores that Anna still struggled to get done herself, but she rationalized that a full-time job took its toll on the housework. Plus she hadn't really been herself this fall. And perhaps, if her energy continued to falter, she'd need to enlist Michael's help with a few of the household tasks—like laundry, which she abhorred. But not until after the New Year. And not until their insurance dilemma was settled and her diagnosis was certain. Until then, she would manage somehow.

So, although her Christmas to-do list was fairly long, she tried to keep it economical. Fortunately she still had a couple boxes of unused Christmas cards . . . only because she hadn't sent them out the past two years. And she'd already tucked away a few things she'd bought for relatives during the year. It was something her mom had always done, sticking away gifts for future holidays. Even after Mom had died, Anna's dad had discovered numerous presents all wrapped and ready for them. Sure, there'd been bittersweet tears when these packages were opened, but Anna always knew that her mother had meant well. She just wanted to do her best by her family. And that's what Anna wanted to do. She wanted to leave Michael with only happy memories of this Christmas.

She was pacing in the kitchen now, trying to think of what she could give him for Christmas—what was it that he really wanted? Well, besides a long, happy marriage and a child—two things that were out of her reach now. What could she possibly give him that he would thoroughly enjoy? What could she leave behind for him to remember her by?

Then it hit her. His little midnight-blue MG convertible. The same car she had complained about just yesterday, whining about how it took up all the room in their tiny detached garage. As if she'd ever use that garage anyway, with its funky old wooden door that wasn't exactly easy to open, let alone allow her to drive a car into the garage without hitting something. But right now the 1966 MG was sitting in there with a gray dustcover draped over it, like a ghost car. Michael had purchased the little roadster shortly after graduating from college, back before they'd even started dating. His plan had been to restore it to its former glory, but dating, work, life, and marriage had gotten in the way. Still, they had enjoyed the car for a while, during their courtship period and the first couple years of marriage. And then the engine had overheated and now needed to be completely rebuilt or replaced.

If only she could come up with a way to get Michael a new engine for that car. She could just imagine him driving it around—after she was gone—and remembering her. It was perfect. Well, except for the cost. She didn't know much about engines, except that Michael had said it was very expensive . . . and that they could not afford it. And so the car had just sat for the past eight years. Of course, Anna didn't know the first thing about cars or engines. But she knew someone who did.

"David?" she said when her brother answered his cell phone on the first ring. "This is Anna, and I have a car question. Do you have a minute?"

"Go for it. I'm stuck in traffic at the moment."

"You answer your phone while you're driving?"

"I wear a headset."

"Oh." She presented her idea for getting Michael an engine for Christmas.

"Wow, that's not going to be cheap, Anna."

"I know, but do you have any idea how much? Or where I'd go? Or any of that stuff?"

"Well, I'm guessing you could probably get a rebuilt engine for, oh, I don't know, maybe five hundred. But a new engine would be more. Then you have to pay to have it installed."

"Oh . . ."

"Want me to do some research for you on it?"

"Would you?"

"As long as you guys let me borrow the car sometime."

"I'm sure that could be arranged." Suddenly Anna got a lump in her throat as she imagined David and Michael taking the roadster for a spin without her . . . after she was gone.

"I'll let you know what I find out."

"Oh, yeah," Anna said suddenly. "I almost forgot. I still have that, uh, nursery furniture . . . and, well, since we're not going to have a baby . . . I thought . . ."

"Oh, Anna . . ." His voice sounded sad now.

"I mean, it's really good quality, and I know it's very safe. Do you think Celeste would be interested?"

"To buy?"

"No, of course not. I couldn't sell it. It would be a gift."

"Wow, that's really generous, Anna. I'll tell Celeste, okay?"

"Okay."

"And I'll let you know what I find out."

"Thanks, David. And, oh yeah, please don't tell anyone about the engine for Michael. Not Dad or Meri or even Celeste. I want this to be a complete surprise, okay?"

"My lips are sealed."

Then they said good-bye and hung up, and Anna just sat there by the phone. She hadn't really thought about how all this might affect her family. They'd already gone through this once. She hated to take them through it again. Perhaps it would be best to keep quiet about it even after January. Maybe she could hold out until the end of the illness before she broke the news to them—sort of like her mother had done. She had no idea how Meredith would react. Ever since losing their mom, they had been extremely close. Even when they were teenagers, friends would comment on the fact that the two girls rarely fought. Of course, she and Meri would say it was because they were so different. Where Meredith was outspoken and extroverted, Anna tended to be quiet and shy. Somehow their opposite natures helped to glue them together. Well, that and losing Mom.

Anna looked down at her to-do list and quickly tallied up what it would cost to create what she hoped would be a wonderful Christmas. Not that Anna thought money could buy happiness. She knew better than that. But she did want to do all she could, whether it was food or decorations or gifts, to make this year truly special—and memorable. Of course, she knew her biggest challenge would be that expensive car engine. How could she make some extra money quickly? She considered tutoring, but it really wasn't the best time of year for that. She knew that some retailers were looking for part-time workers, but she'd have difficulty explaining something like that to Michael. Besides, spending time with him seemed more important right now. And with him working so much overtime lately, their time together had been diminishing steadily as it was.

Perhaps she should've told her brother that she would sell that nursery furniture after all. But, no, that just seemed wrong. Besides, she knew that David and Celeste's finances were tight just now. Plus it had been Michael's idea to share the baby furniture in the first place. It would be nice to see that pretty set put to good use, as well as kept in the family. She might've given the pieces to Meredith for baby Jack, but Meredith had already been set on a very contemporary nursery with sleek designs and bold colors. Meri thought that babies preferred bright primary colors, claiming that it increased their IQs. Well, no offense to her nephew, but Anna wasn't too sure about her sister's theory, and besides, she preferred calming pastels for baby nurseries herself. Still, what did it matter now?

Anna looked out the kitchen window to see that it was just getting dusky outside. It was that purplish-gray time of evening, with just a bit of haze in the air. Probably leftover smoke from a smoldering leaf pile. Anna knew it was the perfect time to turn on the Christmas lights. She went out to the porch and unceremoniously stuck the plug into the outlet, catching her breath as her house burst into cheery light.

She went down the steps and into the front yard to step back and admire her handiwork. Very, very nice. Happy and bright and inviting. She smiled as she wrapped her arms around herself to stay warm. There was a definite nip in the air, and she wouldn't be surprised if it froze tonight. Perhaps if this cold spell kept up they might even have a white Christmas this year. She sighed to think of how beautiful their little bungalow would look all lit up like this, with a fresh white blanket of snow all about. She imagined how sweet that front window would look with a tall Noble Fir standing in front of it, glowing with colored lights and her collection of old-fashioned ornaments—things that had remained in the attic the past two Christmases. Well, that would not be the case this year. Anna knew that she would do whatever it took to make this a truly remarkable Christmas.

5

||||||||||||||||

"You want to get a tree *today*?" Michael frowned over his coffee at Anna. "It's still November."

"Barely." She set down her mug of green tea. "Monday is December 1." She reached for the calendar behind her just to be sure.

"Yes . . . but it's four weeks until Christmas."

"More like three and a half." She flipped the page and pointed out the day. "Besides, a lot of people get their trees right after Thanksgiving. Loraine Bechtle, a third grade teacher, told me they usually put theirs up even before Thanksgiving just so the grandkids can enjoy it that much longer."

"That seems crazy."

"Not to Loraine."

"But won't the tree be all dried out by Christmas? And what about fire hazards? Don't forget this is an old house, Anna."

"I know, Michael. You just have to take care of the tree correctly. Loraine was telling us about it last week. Did you know you're supposed to cut the trunk again before you put it into the stand? And then you simply make sure the water never runs out. She also suggested you mix the water with 7UP."

"7UP?" He tossed her a skeptical frown.

"Or Sprite . . . it probably doesn't matter which brand. But Loraine said that the sugar helps to keep the tree fresh."

He sighed as he set down the newspaper. "Look, Anna, I think it's great that you're excited about Christmas this year. And I'm glad that you put up the lights yesterday. I'd been thinking about doing it myself except that things are so hectic at work these days."

"I know you're busy." She smiled. "That's why I did it."

"And it's great seeing your enthusiasm about getting a tree. I have to admit that I've missed that. But the fact is, I really need to get some work done today. I plan to work at home, but it'll take most of the day to rework a design that has to be done by midweek. How about if we get a tree next weekend? We could even go to a tree farm and cut one ourselves."

She looked at the calendar. "That would be fun . . . except that Saturday night is the school Christmas concert and the dress rehearsal is at two."

"How about Sunday?" He looked hopeful. "After church?"

She pointed to the date. "The Christmas bazaar is that afternoon—remember it's a fundraiser for Darfur this year?" She shook her head as she realized that she'd completely blanked out that commitment over the past couple of weeks. "And that means I need to get some more sewing done sometime before then."

In October, Anna had agreed to do a craft project with her sister and their mutual friend Nicole Fox. Meredith had gotten a great deal on a bunch of willow baskets, which she thought would be perfect for mini picnic baskets. Anna had agreed to sew colorful napkins and small tablecloths, which were mostly done. And Nicole was providing sets of colorful plastic plates and utensils that she'd bought with a deep discount from her mom's craft store. They'd only put one basket together so far, but it had turned out really cute, and Meri was certain they could pull at least thirty dollars apiece for them.

"See," Michael said, as if this settled it. "We both have a lot to do during the next two weeks, so why not just wait and get the tree . . ." He paused to study the calendar, then pointed to Saturday the thirteenth. "Then!"

Anna felt her lower lip jutting out, just like one of her second grade boys after being informed that recess would be inside due to rain. "But that's not even two weeks before Christmas."

"Yeah." He nodded. "Perfect."

Anna knew that it was somewhat crazy, not to mention obsessive, to get all bent out of shape over when they got their Christmas tree. After all, they hadn't even gotten a tree for the last two years. But perhaps that was just the point. She wanted to make up for it this year. And less than two weeks was not going to cut it. "What if the trees are all picked over by then?"

"That probably won't happen."

"But why take a chance?"

He just shook his head, clearly exasperated.

"I just want this Christmas to be special, Michael," she said. "We haven't done much these past few years. I just hoped this could be, well, the best Christmas ever."

His brows lifted slightly. "The best Christmas ever?"

She shrugged. "Sounds corny, huh?"

"Or maybe just a case of bad timing."

Anna looked down at the table. She had already imagined the two of them decorating the tree this weekend. She had even considered making popcorn and stringing it with cranberries, the way Great-Gran used to. And Michael could make them a crackling fire in the fireplace, and she'd make mint cocoa and . . . well, Anna just knew that she couldn't wait two long weeks before getting a tree. She needed it now. And somehow she would get it.

She stood, took her empty mug to the sink, and slowly rinsed it. "You go ahead and work today if you need to, Michael. I've got some errands to run anyway."

"You see," he said, picking up his newspaper again. "It makes sense to wait on the tree, doesn't it?"

She forced a smile and nodded. "Yes . . . very sensible." Of course, she didn't admit that just because it made sense didn't mean she agreed. Christmas wasn't something you celebrated with your head . . . but with your heart. And before the sun went down today, Anna intended to have a tree in the living room. Already she could imagine that sweet piney smell.

Anna tried not to indulge in self-pity as she drove by herself to a tree farm about twenty miles out of town. She had considered bringing Huntley but wasn't sure how tree farmers felt about pets. But she was determined to enjoy this—cutting down a tree would be fun. And wouldn't Michael be surprised. Besides that, it was a perfectly gorgeous day. Yesterday's overcast skies had completely cleared up, and although it was crisp and cold, the sun was shining brightly. She had brought along an old pair of boots and hoped that the tree farm would provide things like saws and ropes to tie the tree to the top of her old red Toyota. As she drove, she even started singing Christmas carols, really trying to get into the spirit of things. Still, she felt slightly sneaky, and she missed having Michael along with her. But it would be worth it later . . . when they were decorating the tree together, sipping cocoa, and enjoying the fire. She would make sure to have the camera out and ready to go. She wanted Michael to have plenty of photos for later . . . happy memories for when she was gone.

The tree farm was busier than she'd expected. After hearing Michael going on about how it was too soon to get a tree, she'd almost started to doubt herself. But seeing the muddy lot nearly full of cars, trucks, and SUVs, she knew that it was probably a good idea after all. She walked over to an area where people seemed to be waiting. She'd never been to a tree farm before and wasn't quite sure what to do.

"The next wagon will be here in about ten minutes," announced an old man wearing overalls, a red plaid hunting jacket, and a Santa hat. "There's complimentary hot drinks over there by the wreath booth. Come get your ticket for a tree, then go ahead and help yourselves to refreshments, if you like."

Anna waited in line to buy her tree ticket and was slightly stunned to discover that an eight-foot Noble Fir would be $72.

"And, boy, are the Nobles pretty this year," the woman assured her. "Plus we're having a great deal on the wreaths when you purchase a tree that's more than fifty bucks. You can get a gorgeous evergreen wreath with holly sprigs for just an extra twenty dollars. Normally they go for thirty, so you save yourself ten bucks."

"Okay," Anna said slowly. Then she quickly did the math and realized that this little expedition, by the time she calculated in her gas mileage, would probably be close to a hundred dollars total. Still, this Christmas needed to be special. And by getting the tree today, she would have three and a half weeks to enjoy it. What was a hundred dollars compared to that?

She picked out a nice, big wreath and put it in the backseat of her car, then got a cup of cocoa, which wasn't very hot and tasted slightly watery. But she sipped it and pretended to enjoy it as she waited among parents and squealing children for the wagon to come and pick them up. She tried not to feel sorry for herself as she realized that she was the only person who appeared to be alone. Besides, she reminded herself, it had been her choice to come without Michael today. She smiled as she watched a pair of preschool-aged brothers playing tug-of-war with a length of rope until the younger one finally gave up and let go, causing the older boy to plunge backwards right into a muddy spot. Anna chuckled, but the boy's mother did not look amused.

By the time they got onto a wagon, which was loaded with hay and pulled by a pair of draft horses, Anna was feeling like maybe this had been a mistake. She sat on a corner of the wagon bed, observing the couples happily interacting with their children, talking about what kind of tree they wanted and who would get to use the saw and where would they go for lunch later . . . and she suddenly felt very sad. She fumbled for the sunglasses in her purse, quickly slipping them on so that no one would see her eyes filling with tears as she realized that this—happy families with children—was something she would never experience. She swallowed hard, reminding herself that at least she had Michael. If only he had wanted to come here with her today!

"This is the Noble Fir section," the young man who was driving the wagon announced. Anna and another family climbed down off the wagon, and, taking the handsaw that had been loaned to her, Anna made her way to a small sign that said "8 Ft." She tried not to watch the other family—a dad and mom about the same age as Michael and her, a boy who looked about the same age as her second graders, and a girl who was probably still in preschool. They had on matching red sweaters, and the parents took turns getting photos of them with the trees. But the best they could do was one parent with the kids.

"Want me to take one of all of you?" Anna said.

"Oh, would you?" the mom said.

"Sure." Anna went over and waited as the dad explained how the digital camera worked, although it wasn't much different from the one she and Michael had at home.

The mom arranged the kids in front of a tall tree. "If it's a good shot, we might use it on our Christmas card."

"Okay," Anna said. "I'll count to three and everyone smile big." So she did. And they did. And she thought it looked pretty good. "Just to be safe, I can take another," she called out.

"That would be wonderful," the mom said as she adjusted the little girl's stocking cap. "We really appreciate it."

Anna's eyes got blurry as she snapped the second picture. Still, it was probably just fine. "Here you go," she said, quickly handing the camera back to the dad as she replaced her sunglasses.

"Thank you so much!" the mother said.

"No problem." Anna turned, blinking back tears. "Happy tree hunting!"

Anna walked into the thicket of trees, going down one row and then the next, but without really looking at the trees. She mostly just wanted to get away from that happy family, wanted to block their smiling faces out of her mind. Finally, realizing that she might get lost in this maze of trees, she paused and took in a deep breath, then looked up at the clear blue sky. She stood there for a long moment, just staring up past the branches and toward the heavens. "Why me?" she whispered to God. "Why?"

She stood there for several minutes, as if waiting for an answer, but other than the sound of some crows cawing back and forth not far off, all was quiet. Then she took in another long, deep breath and, getting her bearings, made her way back to the edge of the Noble Fir section, where she examined some of the eight-footers more closely until she finally decided on one that seemed to look just about perfect.

Of course, sawing it down turned out to be a challenge of its own. She hadn't counted on the thickness of the trunk or her lack of skill when it came to using a handsaw. She tried to recall if she'd ever cut down a tree before, then remembered back when she'd been a girl and had gone out with her parents and siblings to cut a tree from the woods a few times. And, since she was the oldest, her dad had finally let her use the saw. But that tree's trunk had been much narrower, and she'd had Dad there to help her. It had seemed easy. Still, she continued sawing, pushing the blade back and forth and trying to keep it from sticking. When she was only halfway through, she decided to try cutting it from the other side. Perhaps that would be easier. So she sawed and sawed some more, and then, just as she paused to catch her breath, down came the tree, flattening her smack down in the damp dirt.

She fought to push the tree away from her, and although she wished she could make light of her lack of lumberjack skills, she felt close to tears. She stood and brushed the dirt and debris from the back of her jeans, then picked pine needles from her wool jacket and even a few from her hair. She gathered up her purse and the handsaw and reached down to pick up the trunk of the Noble Fir. But it was much heavier than she'd expected. She gave it a hard tug, but it barely even moved. How was she supposed to get the tree back to the road where the wagon would be returning? And how in the world would she get the heavy tree on top of her car? Oh, why hadn't she saved this holiday errand to do with Michael? Why had she been so stubborn? Not only was it excruciatingly lonely getting a tree on your own, but it was downright difficult too.

She gave it a couple more tugs, then finally gave up and went to stand by the road. At least she could flag down the wagon, and maybe someone would take pity on her and offer to help.

"Where's your tree?" the mom from the photo session asked. She and her husband and kids were lugging an even taller tree to the side of the road.

184

"It was too heavy," Anna said.

"We can help," the woman said.

"Sure," the guy said. "Come on, kids, let's help the lady with her tree."

They all went back to where Anna's tree was lying like a fallen soldier, and together they carried it back to the side of the road. Along the way, they exchanged names, and Anna, feeling somewhat self-conscious for being alone on what it seemed should be a family outing, explained that her husband was busy today but this had seemed the best weekend to get a tree.

"Oh, I definitely agree," the woman said. "We always get ours on the Saturday after Thanksgiving." She smiled at her husband. "It's a tradition."

"And we make a gingerbread house too," the boy said, using his hands to show how big it was. "It's more like a castle, really," he explained.

"With a gingerbread princess," the little girl said, her brown eyes wide with excited anticipation.

"Wow," Anna said, "that must be fun."

"Do you want to help us make it?" the girl offered.

"Oh, no," Anna said quickly. "But thank you—I'll bet it'll be really cool."

"Where are *your* kids?" the boy asked with a furrowed brow.

"Marcus," the mom said with a warning tone.

"That's okay," Anna said, forcing a smile. "I don't have children . . . at home, that is. But I am a teacher." She patted Marcus's curly dark hair. "And I have twenty-three kids in my second grade classroom."

"I'm in first grade," he admitted.

"Well, you look old enough to be in second grade."

He grinned. "Yeah, I'm kinda big for my age."

"Oh, here comes the wagon now," the mom said. She seemed relieved by this, and Anna hoped she hadn't made the family too uncomfortable. She wondered why it was that many people seemed to feel ill at ease when they encountered someone who didn't have what they had. Maybe it was simply human nature—a protective intuition that someone might want to take what you had. Or maybe it was just Anna's overactive imagination.

She tried not to think about these things as they rode back to the parking lot. And when the young man driving the wagon offered to help her unload her bulky tree and then get it tied securely on top of her car, she didn't protest. Mostly she just wanted to get out of this happy Christmas place. She was tired of watching families, of feeling like a poor kid with her nose pressed against the toy store window and knowing that all she saw—all those desirable things—were not meant for her.

6

Michael's car wasn't in the driveway when Anna got home. So much for his "I'll be working at home all day today" excuse. Although it was possible that he'd gone to the office, where the big printer and other pieces of expensive electronic equipment were kept. Anna got out of the car and studied the tree still tied securely on top. Perhaps it wouldn't be too difficult to get down, what with gravity working with her. So she untied it and slid it down, laying it next to the car, then stepped back to admire her prize.

"Nice tree," Bernice called as she checked her mailbox.

"Thanks," Anna called back. "I cut it down myself."

"It looks very Christmassy against your red car."

Anna laughed. "Maybe I should leave it out here, although I was hoping to get it into the house at some point."

"Need some help?"

Anna considered her elderly neighbor's offer, then shook her head as she imagined Bernice stumbling under the bulky weight of the tree and breaking a hip. Anna wanted the tree inside the house, but not that badly. "Thanks anyway, Bernice. I'll wait until Michael gets back."

She went inside to see if he'd left a note. But all she found was his empty coffee cup and the newspaper still spread out over the dining table. She straightened things up, then went to the living room to make room for her tree. Her plan was to get everything in order and ready so that when Michael got home they could easily put the tree into place and begin decorating.

She moved some furniture around, freeing up the space in front of the window, then went up to the attic in search of Christmas decorations. Anna had begun collecting hand-blown glass ornaments even before she got married. She'd gotten off to a good start by adopting some of her mother's fragile pieces after Dad married Donna and she brought in her own style of Christmas, featuring a white-flocked tree and silk flowers in shades of pink and purple. Not Anna's favorite look. Anna preferred the old-fashioned ornaments that, lucky for her, neither Meri nor David had the slightest interest in at the time. Although if David knew their collectible value, he might see it differently now.

Anna removed the dusty cover from an old cardboard box, then carefully picked up a beloved Santa ornament from where it was snuggled down into layers of tissue paper. This was the very piece that her mom had said was the beginning of her own collection back in the sixties. She'd purchased it in Switzerland during a college trip, and somehow she'd managed to carry it all over Europe without breaking it.

What would become of these precious ornaments after Anna was gone? She picked up a snowman ornament and held it up to the faint light coming through the small attic window. Would Michael want to use them? Or perhaps Meri or David should have them, saving them for the next generation. Anna decided that she should put together some kind of will, saying who should get what after she was gone. Not that she had much to leave anyone. But some of the family things should probably be shared with her siblings and their children. Of course, she knew that neither David nor Meri would want Great-Gran's china. Meredith had never liked it much, and Celeste already had a very contemporary set of china that they'd gotten for their wedding.

Oh, well, Anna didn't have to resolve everything in a single day. Right now she just wanted to focus on Christmas. She picked up the tree stand and, upon closer examination, knew that it would be too small for that big trunk. One more thing to add to her growing list

. . . which once again reminded her of their limited finances. Already she'd stretched their budget with what Michael might consider an extravagant price for the tree. Nearly a hundred dollars! But that was with that lovely wreath that she'd totally forgotten about in the backseat. Well, at least she could have that up before Michael got home. She couldn't wait to see it hanging on their front door.

Anna carried the boxes of ornaments down the steep attic stairs, pausing in the kitchen to dust them off before adding "bigger tree stand" to her list. Then she fetched the big wreath from the car and was even more pleased with it. At the tree farm it had seemed nice enough, sitting there among the others, but now that it was home, she could see that it was perfectly beautiful with its varied selection of lush evergreens and shining holly with bright red berries. Even the big red-velvet bow was perfect. Anna stood back to admire it. Really, it was the best wreath she'd ever hung on their front door.

Suddenly she remembered their first Christmas in this house, seven years ago. She'd just started doing the infertility treatments, and that, combined with the purchase of the house, had made finances tighter than ever. To be thrifty, she'd created a homemade wreath using a wire hanger and tying on greens she'd clipped from shrubbery around the yard. The sad wreath had been slightly lop-sided and limp, but better than nothing . . . until a strong wind, just a few days before Christmas, managed to dismantle it com-pletely. All that was left were a couple of sad sprigs of pine and the crooked hanger. Well, this year would be different.

Anna grabbed her list and her purse and made a Wal-Mart run, where she found a big tree stand as well as some other Christmas decorations that were on sale. And then, with Michael still not home, she put many of the decorations up. As it started to get dark outside, she turned on the exterior Christmas lights, made a fire in the fireplace, lit candles, and even had Christmas music playing. The only thing missing now was Michael. After several unsuccessful attempts to reach him on his cell phone or the office phone, Anna was getting worried. But then she heard the front door opening.

"Ho ho ho!" Michael shouted from the entryway.

She dashed out in time to see him dragging in a Christmas tree. Not her tree, but another one. It was about the same height as hers, but not nearly as pretty. And it wasn't a Noble Fir.

"You got a tree?" she said in a slightly accusatory tone.

He looked disappointed. "Hey, I thought you'd be happy."

She held out her arms and sighed. "Yes, of course I'm happy. Except that I got a tree too. Didn't you see it out front?"

His brow creased. "You got a tree too?"

So she told him the story of the tree farm. And he told her how he'd noticed a Christmas tree lot on his way home and thought he'd surprise her. "But you don't like it?"

"It's a nice tree," she admitted. "But the one I got is nicer." She tugged him by the arm. "Come on outside and see it."

Of course, once they dragged the tree up to the porch where it was illuminated by the Christmas lights, he had to agree that her tree was much nicer.

"So, what'll we do with this one?"

"I don't have a tree in my classroom yet . . ."

"You do now."

She hugged him. "Thanks!"

"You're really getting into the spirit of Christmas this year," he said as they went back into the house and examined her holiday decorating.

"That's right. And I thought maybe you'd help me get that tree in here tonight." She showed him the oversized tree stand. "You just need to recut the trunk and—"

"Can't it wait until tomorrow?"

She shrugged. "I guess . . . but I thought it would be fun to decorate it tonight."

"I'm worn out." He kicked off his shoes and flopped into his favorite chair.

"I guess I can do it myself," she said. "Is there a saw in the garage?"

He sat up in the chair now, reaching for his shoes. "Okay, Anna, if you're that determined . . . I guess I can do it."

She could tell by the tone of his voice that he wasn't nearly as enthused about this as she was, and she was surprised he was doing this without an argument, but she just smiled. "And since you're being such a good sport, I'll go start dinner."

He turned and looked curiously at her. "You mean we're not going out?"

Saturday night was usually their date night, but Anna had already decided that she'd fix dinner at home tonight. An effort to economize after her big day of spending. "I've already got something ready to fix," she told him. "And then we can decorate the tree—that'll be more fun than dinner and a movie anyway."

"If you say so . . ."

By the time dinner was ready, Michael had managed to get the tree in its stand, and the two of them then wrestled it into the living room. "That is one heavy tree," he said as they stood back to see if it was straight.

"And one beautiful tree . . . don't you think?"

He nodded, then pulled a twig from her hair. "I hate to think how much it must've cost, Anna."

"Probably about as much as dinner and a movie," she said. "Let me get some water for the tree and then we can eat."

She quizzed him about work while they ate, asking him how long this crunch time of working late and on weekends was going to last. But his answer was vague, and she suspected that he didn't see an end in sight.

"Are you still glad you got your own business?" she asked. "No regrets?"

"We knew it would be hard to get it going at the start," he said as he took another serving of spaghetti. "But it'll be worth it . . . eventually."

She wondered. Now more than ever, time seemed very precious to her. And the idea of Michael putting in long hours was unsettling. "How long do you think it'll be before . . . 'eventually'?"

"I know the business seems demanding right now, Anna, but trust me, just one year from now things will be a lot different."

Anna swallowed hard and looked down at her plate. Chances

were things would be a lot different. But not different in the way that Michael was hoping for. Anna looked back up at him, tempted to say something.

"I'm glad you decided to do all this Christmas stuff early," he said. "I know I probably seemed like a wet blanket earlier . . . but now I think it's just what we needed. I've missed Christmas in this house."

She smiled at him. "Me too."

After dinner, he willingly helped her to decorate the tree. And he listened as she told him the various histories of each of the ornaments. She made them big cups of cocoa and popped some popcorn, and although he helped to string some, she was pretty sure he was mostly eating it. Still, it didn't matter. This was more about making memories than anything else. And she knew, for her, tonight would always be special.

Anna felt her throat tighten as she sat there looking at the tree and Christmas decorations . . . at Michael and Huntley sitting next to the fireplace. It was picture perfect. "Are you crying?" Michael asked her.

She blinked, then smiled. "Just because I'm so happy," she said.

He sort of frowned, as if he wasn't convinced.

Now she forced herself to laugh. "And I'm sure my hormones are messing with me too."

He nodded as if he could buy into that. And Anna decided that it wasn't exactly a lie either. In fact, it seemed quite likely that her hormones would be playing havoc with her emotions from here on out. She remembered how her mother had been during that last year, often crying over what seemed like nothing. Dad had told the kids not to be too concerned, saying that Mom's ups and downs were simply a part of the illness. But then, he had played down a lot of things.

Sometimes Anna wondered if Dad had been in some sort of denial. Or maybe he had simply shut down his own emotions. Because even when Mom died, Anna never saw her father cry. And if she or her siblings cried occasionally in the months following their mother's death, Dad would scowl his disapproval, telling them to "buck up" and "get over it." He'd even said that their mother wouldn't have wanted them to carry on like babies. But Anna wasn't so sure. She thought that Mom probably would've wanted them to express their grief—she probably understood that tears were part of the healing process. And when Anna died, she hoped that her loved ones would cry for her. At least a little. After that they could move on.

7

||||||||||||||

"David said that he and Celeste planned to swing by our house on their way home from church," Michael said as he pulled into the driveway. "David wants her to see the baby furniture."

"Oh . . ." Anna nodded, trying to take this in. She knew she'd offered them the furniture, but suddenly she wasn't so sure she could part with it.

"I know it's hard." Michael took her hand and squeezed it. "But David sounded relieved that it might save them a few bucks."

"I know." She took a deep breath. "And, really, I'm fine with it. I like the idea of a little niece or nephew using those things."

Michael looked relieved. "And I like the idea of having a home office."

She squeezed his hand now. "So do I."

"That looks like them now," Michael said as a silver SUV pulled up.

"Wow, you've already decorated for Christmas," Celeste said as the four of them went into the house. "Kind of early, isn't it?"

Anna shrugged. "Maybe . . . but I thought we could enjoy it longer this way."

"What a good-looking tree," David said as they paused in the living room.

Anna told him about how she'd cut it down herself and then been tackled by it. "It's a lot heavier than it looks."

"You went to the tree farm by yourself?" Celeste said with a frown.

"I know." Anna laughed. "I guess it was a little desperate. But we haven't had a tree for a couple of years, and I think I was feeling Christmas deprived."

"If I'd known she was that determined, I would've gone too," Michael explained. "But I was working."

"It's okay," Anna said. "It all worked out in the end."

"And it looks great," David said.

"Want to see the baby furniture?" Anna asked.

"Sure," David said, but Celeste just nodded with seeming reluctance.

"I'll put on some coffee," Michael said as Anna led the way to the nursery.

"Anna said it's really well made," David said as she opened the door.

"Oh . . ." Celeste said with a slight frown. "It's painted."

"Yes," Anna said as she ran a hand over the rail. "It's nontoxic paint, of course, with a very hard finish. And it's all solid wood underneath."

"But it's very old-fashioned," Celeste said. "I suppose it would be okay for a girl . . . but it seems kind of feminine for a boy."

"It's just a nursery," David said. "Who cares what it looks like? As long as it's safe and sturdy and—"

"I care," Celeste protested. "And I don't want hand-me-down furniture for my baby."

"But it's never even been used," David said.

"And you can put any kind of baby linens with it," Anna said. "If you guys are having a boy, just get boyish-looking things and—"

"I already had my heart set on another set of furniture," Celeste said. She turned and glared at David. "Are you saying I can't even pick out my own baby's furniture?"

"I'm saying that this will save us a few bucks," David said.

"But the set I want is designed to grow with the child. The crib can be converted to a bed, and the dresser doesn't look so—so babyish."

David leaned his head back and let out a groan. "And I'll bet it costs a fortune too." Then he turned and walked out of the room.

"I don't see why he's being so stubborn about this," Celeste said in a wounded tone.

"I think he just hoped to save some money."

"But we're talking about our baby. Don't you think our baby deserves the best?"

Anna sighed. "Well, of course . . ."

"I mean, you got to pick out what you wanted, Anna. And even though I don't like it, I'm sure this furniture wasn't cheap. And then you didn't even have a baby. I'll bet Michael doesn't get on your case over the wasted money."

Anna blinked and swallowed over the lump in her throat. "No, of course not."

"I don't see why David can't be more like Michael. It's like he doesn't even want this baby." And suddenly Celeste was crying.

Anna knew that she should hug her sister-in-law, but everything in her wanted to just run from the room and escape her.

"David acts like I got pregnant just to aggravate him." She sniffed loudly. "Like he thinks I'm enjoying all this pregnancy crud." She pulled up her shirt to reveal the top of her pants, which were unbuttoned and partially unzipped. "It's not exactly fun watching your waistline disappear. Before long I'll be as big as a house."

Anna didn't say anything.

"You probably think I'm being really stupid, don't you?"

"No."

"I just want David to be happy for us," Celeste continued. "Is it too much to want him to want this baby?" She started crying even harder, and now Anna opened her arms and gathered up her sobbing sister-in-law.

"I'm sure David will be happy . . . eventually," Anna assured her. "It's just that your pregnancy has taken him by surprise. But trust me, I know that David is going to make a really good dad. And he'll totally love having a baby. He just needs some time to adjust to this whole thing. It's a big change."

"Well, he's got until May to get used to the idea," Celeste said. Then she stiffened slightly, and Anna dropped her arms limply to her sides and stepped back, feeling uncomfortable.

"Maybe that's why God designed a pregnancy to last nine months," Anna said.

"All I can say is that David better get with the program."

"So . . ." Anna glanced around her forlorn baby nursery. "It doesn't sound like you're going to change your mind about the baby furniture then?"

Celeste's brow creased as she studied the furniture more closely. "I don't know. I suppose if we were having a girl . . . and if David refuses to give in . . . well, maybe it would be okay. I guess I could think about it."

"Right." Anna wanted to tell Celeste to forget the whole thing and that she'd changed her mind about giving it to them, but instead she just pressed her lips tightly together as she reached for the doorknob. "Let's go see what the guys are up to."

The guys were in front of the TV, already tuned in to a football game, and Anna knew it was going to be a long day. Eventually she excused herself to the kitchen to put together some lunch for the four of them. It was as much to escape Celeste as anything. And when Celeste halfheartedly asked if she needed help, Anna quickly declined the offer. Her plan was to make grilled cheese sandwiches and tomato soup. She knew it wasn't a very exciting lunch, but she didn't care.

"Need any help, sis?" David asked as he slipped into the kitchen.

"Nah," she told him. "As you can see, this isn't going to be a very fancy meal."

"Hey, you know I love this kind of thing." He plucked a dill pickle from the jar on the counter and took a big bite.

"Hopefully Celeste does too."

He sighed loudly. "Celeste doesn't seem to like much of anything these days."

"She said she'd think about the baby furniture."

David brightened. "Really?"

197

"She said if you guys are having a girl, she might be able to work with it."

"That'd be great."

Anna lowered her voice. "But she thinks you don't want this baby, David."

"I'm not crazy about the timing."

"I know . . ."

"But it's not that I don't want it."

"Well, that's how she feels. Maybe you could try a little harder to see her point of view."

"Maybe . . . but she could try a little harder too. Celeste is so self-centered sometimes. Like it's all about her."

"Maybe having a child will change that," Anna said. "She'll have someone else to take care of."

"She's already talking about a nanny."

"A nanny?" Anna tried not to look too stunned.

"Yeah. Sometimes I think that Celeste thinks we're made of money."

"Well, at least she's considering my hand-me-down nursery furniture."

"Thanks for that, sis. I really do appreciate it. You know what old Ben said, a penny saved is a penny earned." He glanced over his shoulder as if worried that someone might be listening. "Hey, speaking of money, last night I did a quick online search for that particular item you asked me about."

She looked up from flipping a sandwich. "Any luck?"

"There are some options out there . . . but they're a little spendy, Anna. You didn't mention what you can afford yet."

"How spendy are they?"

"You can get a new engine for about seven hundred, but it'll cost that much again—maybe more—for the mechanic to install it. I'm assuming you want it installed, right?"

"Of course." She flipped another sandwich.

"Okay. I just thought you should know. Do you want me to order one?"

"Not yet. I need to figure out some things first."

"Well, just let me know."

Anna carefully put the lid back on the butter dish. It was from her china set, something that had been missed when they were cleaning up on Thanksgiving. "Hey, David," she said as she picked up the lid again. "You don't think Celeste would like this set of china, do you?"

David frowned. "Why? I thought you liked it."

"I do." She studied the delicate floral pattern. "But it's not very practical. It has to be hand washed, and I don't even have a place to store it."

"You want to get rid of it?"

"I don't know . . . I mean, I realize it's been in the family and—"

"It's yours, Anna. You should do whatever you want with it. And in answer to your question, Celeste would definitely not want it. Don't kid yourself."

"And I know Meri doesn't like it either." Anna sighed and replaced the lid.

"But I thought you liked it," David persisted.

"I do like it. But like I said, I never use it." Anna was thinking about what would happen to the heavy crates of china after she was gone. "And I just got to thinking that maybe it's worth as much as an engine . . ."

David nodded. "Yeah, it might be. I mean, it's a pretty big set, isn't it?"

"Twelve full place settings plus every serving piece imaginable."

"And it's in perfect shape?"

"Absolutely."

David put a hand on her shoulder. "Anna, you're breaking my heart here."

"Huh?" She peered curiously at him.

He shook his head. "I guess I'm just trying to imagine Celeste doing something like that for me." He laughed. "Yeah, right. Maybe in my dreams."

"Or maybe when you guys have been married longer," she said, although she wasn't so sure. "You need to remember that Michael and I have been together for more than ten years . . . and we've been through a lot. That makes a difference."

David still didn't look convinced. "But I remember you guys from the get-go, Anna. You've always been like that."

"Like what?" Michael asked as he joined them.

Anna slipped an arm around his middle, then smiled up at him. "Like in love," she murmured.

He pulled her closer to him and leaned down to kiss her on the forehead. "Yeah, so what else is new?"

"Is this a private party?" Celeste asked as she joined them in the small kitchen space. "What's going on in here anyway?"

"Just lunch," Anna said as she turned down the gas under the burner. "And it looks like it's just about ready too."

Fortunately lunch, with a somewhat caustic conversation between Celeste and David, ended relatively quickly. Then the guys declared the football game "hopeless," and Celeste announced that she and baby needed to go home for a nap.

"I need a nap too," Michael said as he closed the door behind them. "What did you put in that soup anyway? Tryptophan?"

"Yes," Anna teased. "I thought it would be a sure way to safely get rid of our guests."

"That Celeste," Michael said, shaking his head. "She's a real piece of work."

"Poor David." Anna headed back to the kitchen to finish cleaning up.

"I thought she was going to rip his head off when they started talking about the nursery furniture again. Made me wish I'd never suggested you give it to them." Michael rinsed a dish and handed it to her.

"I was tempted to rescind my offer several times today." Anna slid a plate into the dishwasher. "I mean, it's not that I want to be selfish . . . but I'd just hoped the nursery furniture could be enjoyed by someone who actually appreciated it."

"I know how you feel. But give Celeste some time. Maybe she'll come around."

"I guess . . ."

But the truth was Anna felt like she'd rather just sell the furniture to a perfect stranger now. And that way she could put the money toward the cost of Michael's engine. But then she thought about her brother again. For David's sake, she would wait on Celeste. And maybe they'd have a little girl. Anna could imagine the pretty white furniture in a pale pink room. Although Celeste didn't care much for pastels. Well, even a hot pink room would make the white furnishings stand out nicely. And David would certainly be happy with the compromise.

8

▌▌▌▌▌▌▌▌▌▌▌▌▌

"I hate Christmas," Monica Meyers announced as the teachers gathered around the big table in the teachers' room to quickly devour their lunches. This was the only real break in their schedules and a time when they liked to let their hair down. Particularly Monica. She was a first grade teacher and sometimes a little on the impatient side, which made Anna wonder why she'd decided to become a teacher in the first place.

"Why?" Loraine asked. "I adore this time of year."

"For one thing, we have to do all these extra things at school," Monica pointed out. "The Christmas concert, the parties, the special Christmas crafts, and then we're expected to make gifts for parents . . . you know, that whole hoopla."

"Which is one reason I love teaching at a private school," Loraine said. "Christmas traditions are fading fast in public schools."

"But it's exhausting," Monica complained.

"I find it exhilarating," Loraine argued.

"And I agree with her," Anna added. "I already decorated and put my tree up, and I think Christmas is wonderful."

"See," Loraine said, "that's the spirit."

"Yes, but your children are grown," Monica said. "And Anna doesn't have any. But I do. And I do all this stuff at school, and then I have to go home and do it all over again for my own kids. On top of that, there are Christmas cards to send, which means another yearly Christmas letter, and the decorating, and buying

202

gifts . . . Have you guys heard what the average family spends on Christmas each year?"

"How much?" Anna asked with slight interest.

"About a thousand dollars." Monica just shook her head. "And they say that it's probably even more, but people don't want to admit it. Furthermore, most average American families use credit to cover holiday spending. So they're just going further into debt."

"You're starting to depress me," Nina, a fifth grade teacher, said.

"I'm just telling you the facts." Monica crumpled up her brown paper lunch sack and tossed it into the garbage can.

"Well, I don't care," Loraine said. "I still love Christmas."

"I can see Monica's point," Nina said. "I mean, I have kids at home too. And it is tiring. It's like we have to do Christmas twice. Once at school and once at home."

"See," Monica said, "Nina gets it."

"If you guys really dislike Christmas so much, maybe you should consider teaching in public schools," Anna suggested.

Loraine laughed. "Yes, that would teach them, wouldn't it?"

"And people don't have to spend so much at Christmas," Anna said. "I mean, isn't it up to the individual to decide what's best? There are lots of homemade things you can do."

"Who has time?" Monica asked.

"Not everyone gets Christmas vacation," Loraine said. "I find that I have more time than most people during the holidays."

"And I don't think we've ever spent a thousand dollars," Anna said. Although, knowing the cost of what she wanted to get for Michael, she knew this year would be different.

"You know how I've made extra money for Christmas?" said Victor, the sixth grade teacher who usually couldn't get a word in edgewise when the women were going at it.

"How?" Monica asked.

"EBay."

"You sell things?"

"Sure. Already I've made close to five hundred dollars."

"What kinds of things do you sell?" Nina asked.

"Just stuff we don't need. Not only do I make money, I clear things out too."

"You don't worry about fraud?" Monica said. "I heard that sometimes people buy things and then scam you out of actually paying for them."

"There are ways to ensure that doesn't happen."

"I have a set of china," Anna ventured. "Do you think I could sell it on eBay?"

"I don't know why not," Victor said.

"What kind of china is it?" Loraine asked.

"Meissen." Anna described the delicate floral pattern and gold trim. "It's twelve full place settings and I don't know how many serving dishes. All in perfect condition."

Loraine nodded. "Do you know what you'd ask for it?"

"Are you interested?"

"I am."

"That would probably be better than selling it on eBay," Victor said. "Because you do have to pay for shipping and pack it so that nothing gets broken."

"Do you have a price in mind?" Loraine persisted.

"Well, I need to do some research," Anna said. "But I'd like to get at least, well, maybe fifteen hundred for it . . . if I could. There's something I really want to get for Michael this year."

"That sounds reasonable," Loraine said.

"Really?" Anna blinked in surprise. "You're still interested then?"

"Quite possibly. But I'd like to do some checking on the prices first. And then, of course, I'd like to see it."

"Naturally," Anna said, trying not to sound too eager.

"It may be worth more than you think," Loraine said. "And I wouldn't want to take unfair advantage."

"I actually have no idea what its value might be," Anna said. "But I can do some checking myself."

"Speaking of checking . . ." Monica pointed to the clock. "Two minutes until recess ends."

They scurried about, finishing their lunches and clearing things up, but as Anna hurried to meet her kids in the classroom, all she could think about was the possibility of Loraine buying her china set. And, although Anna didn't really want to let the pretty china go, she knew that Loraine was the kind of person who would love it and take care of it. After Anna was gone, what more could she hope for anyway? Now if she could just think of a way to find out what the set was really worth. Maybe David would know how to figure this out.

After school ended and her classroom was empty, she called David at his office. "I hate to bother you," she said quickly. "But do you know how to find out what my china set is worth? I might have a buyer for it."

"Easy breezy," he said. "But I don't have time to explain it to you right now. How about I email you some information later on tonight?"

"That'd be great." She thanked him and hung up. Maybe she was going to make enough money to get Michael his engine after all.

"Ho ho ho," Michael called as he suddenly appeared in her doorway, bearing, once again, his Christmas tree. "Anyone in need of some Christmas cheer?"

"Thank you," she exclaimed as she helped him set it up in the corner she'd already cleared out. "The kids will be thrilled."

"Well, I needed to head downtown for a meeting, and I decided to stop by the house and pick this up for you."

"A meeting?" Anna looked up at the clock. She'd been just about ready to go home. "Does this mean you'll be working late again?"

"Sorry." He leaned down and pecked her on the cheek. "We're still in crunch mode."

She sighed. "I guess I can get some sewing done tonight."

"Good idea," he said. "And don't worry, this overtime thing should come to an end in a couple of weeks. That's a small price to pay for what we're accomplishing."

A couple of weeks might seem like a small price to Michael, but Anna was looking at things differently now. Still, she knew that it was pointless to talk him out of it. Really, he needed to get this business solidly launched now. Besides, that might afford him more time to be with her later on down the line—perhaps when she would need him even more.

"Thanks again for the tree," she said as he was leaving.

"My pleasure. See you later tonight."

"Don't forget to eat something for dinner, Michael."

"Same back at you."

Well, Anna told herself as she drove home, perhaps she would use her evening alone to figure out the value of her china set. And maybe, if Loraine was really interested, she could get that engine ordered this week. She hadn't even asked David how long it would take to get the motor here or any of the details on how they would get it into the car in time for Christmas. Hopefully she could get it all worked out tonight without worrying about Michael overhearing her. Really, an evening alone wasn't such a bad thing.

Even so, it was hard coming home to a dark house by herself. It was different when she knew Michael would be home soon, but as she walked up to the door, she knew that wasn't the case tonight. Maybe she should get a timer for the Christmas lights. Wouldn't it be nice to come home to a cheerfully lit house? Well, at least it would be like that when Michael came home.

Anna's stomach had been a little better today. But she still had to pass on coffee at school. Even with creamer, it was just too acidic for her sensitive digestion. And now she didn't feel like having anything much besides soup and toast. If Michael had been coming home, she might've considered making homemade soup. But as it was, she was grateful to pour a can of chicken and vegetables into a bowl and put it in the microwave. As it heated, she popped a piece of whole wheat bread into the toaster, then turned on her laptop.

As she ate her meager meal, she checked her email and was pleased to see that David had delivered as promised. He'd listed several sites that would be helpful for figuring out the value of her china set, and by the time she finished eating, she realized that her set (if in excellent condition, which she felt certain was the case) might be worth close to two thousand dollars. But to be fair, one of the sites said that the value of antique china was determined by the market. If you had an eager buyer, it was worth more. If not, it was worth less. She wondered how eager Loraine would be, and how she would show Loraine the china without tipping off Michael as to her plan. Finally, she decided to simply call.

"Oh, I'm so happy to hear from you," Loraine said. "I just looked up your Meissen design online, and it's just what I'm looking for. It's absolutely perfect."

"Really, it's what you wanted?"

"Yes. It's so similar to a set my grandmother had that I was stunned. I literally had to pinch myself."

"What happened to your grandmother's set?"

"Oh, my aunt has it. And she doesn't even use it."

"Will you use it?"

"Only for special occasions . . . but, yes, I would plan to use it."

"I was surprised to see what it's worth," Anna said.

"Yes . . . I was a little surprised myself," Loraine admitted.

"One site suggested I could get close to two thousand for it."

"Yes. It sounds as if we visited the same site."

"And my brother found a set on eBay for $1,400. But it sounded as if that set had some chips, and some of the plates had scrapes and markings on them. I can assure you that my set is just about perfect."

"I'd love to see it, Anna. I mean, if you're really serious about selling it."

"I am serious. But here's the problem: I don't want Michael to know that I'm selling it. I want his gift to be a surprise, and if he knows I've sold my china, well, he would probably get suspicious."

"Oh, I understand completely."

"And he's not here this evening . . . but I'm not sure when he's coming home. I mean, I'd hate to get it all set out and have him walk in."

"Yes. That wouldn't be good."

"I could bring it over to your house," Anna suggested.

"You wouldn't mind?"

"No. In fact, the timing might be good for sneaking it out of here without him knowing."

"Oh, that would be wonderful, Anna." Loraine gave her directions.

"Okay, I'd better hurry," Anna said. "It'll take me awhile to get it all loaded into the car. I assume you'll want to see all the pieces?"

"You might as well bring them, Anna. My guess is that I'll be writing you a check tonight anyway."

Anna was so excited that she had to remind herself to be careful as she carried the crates through the house and down the stairs. One misstep and she could ruin this whole plan. But finally they were all loaded into her car and she was driving across town to what turned out to be a very nice neighborhood. One of those old and established areas where the trees were big and the houses were beautiful. Loraine's house turned out to be a Queen Anne Victorian on a corner. What a great match for this set of china!

Anna carried one of the boxes up to the door with her, and then both Loraine and her husband Rich helped to carry the crates into the house. Soon they had unpacked enough place settings to set the large cherry dining table in Loraine's high-ceilinged dining room.

"Oh, they are exquisite," Loraine gushed. She turned and looked at her husband. "Don't you think so too?"

"I think that if you like them, I like them." He smiled. "Merry Christmas."

"What a wonderful Christmas present," Anna said.

"Well, Loraine's been pining after her grandmother's dishes ever since we got married more than thirty years ago. I even tried to buy them from her aunt several times, but nothing doing."

"And they really do look perfect in your home," Anna said. She sort of laughed. "Much better than they looked in my small bungalow. I didn't even have a place to keep them—besides in the crates."

"And they really do deserve a place of honor," Loraine said. She showed Anna the cherry china cabinet that matched the table.

"What will you do with those dishes?"

"Those will be my younger daughter's wedding present in June."

"Katy is going to be over the moon," Rich said.

"Now, Erika—that's my older daughter—she'll probably want me to leave this set to her," Loraine said as she held up a fragile plate, allowing the light from the chandelier to glow through it.

Anna swallowed hard against the lump that was suddenly growing in her throat. How she had longed to pass these dishes down to her own daughter someday. Of course, that was a dream that wasn't meant to come true. A dream she needed to forget about.

"You really don't mind letting them go?" Loraine asked as she set the plate back down. "You don't think you'll regret this decision later on?"

"No," Anna said firmly. "I want to do this for Michael." Then she explained about his little MG and how it had been sitting in the garage for so long.

"Wow," Rich said. "I wouldn't mind getting my hands on a car like that. Say, if your husband decides he wants to sell—"

"No way," Anna said. "He adores that car. In fact, I do too. And once it's running, I doubt that he'll ever want to get rid of it."

Rich nodded. "Understandable." Then he pulled out his checkbook and wrote out a check for $2,000.

"Oh, I was only going to ask for $1,800," Anna said when he handed it to her.

"These dishes are in mint condition," Loraine said. "Two thousand dollars is a good deal."

"You're sure?" Anna tried not to stare at the check.

"Absolutely. And I can't wait to serve Christmas dinner on them."

"Well, thank you." Anna slipped the check into her purse.

"Thank *you*!" Loraine said.

Anna knew she should be happy as she drove home. And for the most part she was, although she knew she would miss her dishes. Still, she could hardly believe that not only had she made enough to buy an engine, but she also had enough to pay to get it installed. She couldn't wait to give David the green light on this thing. Hopefully it would work out that the MG would be ready to roll in time for Christmas!

9

As it turned out, David got so busy that he didn't order the engine until Thursday. "And it could take up to three weeks for delivery," he informed her.

"Three weeks?" she cried. "That could be *after* Christmas."

"I know."

"Isn't there a way to rush it?"

"I asked and they said it could get here before Christmas, but that this is a hard time of year to make promises on deliveries. I emailed you a photo of the engine, though. I thought if nothing else, you could print that out and put it in a card for him."

Anna knew it was unreasonable to feel so disappointed, but she did. She had wanted this to go perfectly. "I suppose I could do that . . . but I'd really hoped to have the engine in the car by then."

"Well, that's not very realistic, Anna." He'd already explained that getting a mechanic to install an engine just days before Christmas was pretty unlikely.

"Yes, I'm starting to see that now."

"But I did get another idea for you," he said. "You could get Michael a gift certificate from British Motors and make an appointment to get the installation right after Christmas. I talked to my friend Ron this morning—remember I told you about him, he owns British Motors—anyway, he said that he might be able to get the engine put in for you by New Year's if you get it scheduled now."

"New Year's?" She considered Michael taking her out in the sporty little car on New Year's Eve and smiled. "That might be okay . . . although I'd really counted on having the car all ready to go for Christmas."

"The main thing is that you're doing this, Anna." David sighed. "Seriously, Michael is one lucky dude."

Anna knew that her brother was thinking about his own wife. She could hear the defeated tone of his voice. "How's Celeste doing?" she asked. "Has she said anything about my nursery furniture yet?"

"I think she's still pouting."

"Oh . . ."

"Sounds like we'll find out whether the baby's a girl or a boy the week after Christmas."

"That'll be nice. Do you have a preference?"

He laughed. "Just whatever will make my wife happiest."

"What does she want?"

"Depends on her mood. If she's mad at me, she wants a boy. I think she hopes she can raise a son to replace me. If she's not mad at me, she seems to want a girl, and she acts like she's agreeable to using your baby furniture. But you should see what color she wants the nursery painted."

"What is it?"

"Psychedelic green."

"What?"

"Or maybe it's chartreuse, I'm not sure, but she painted a sample on the wall, and I think it's atrocious. Not that my opinion is worth much around here. But even Celeste's mom thought it was odd. She called it acid green."

"*Acid* green?"

"Of course, Celeste calls it *apple* green, but I call it sickening—it makes my teeth hurt."

Anna laughed. "It sounds, uh, very interesting."

"Honestly, Anna, our baby's vision could be at serious risk if Celeste gets her way on this one."

"Well, maybe she'll change her mind."

211

"That's possible. But at this rate, she might go for something like fire-hydrant yellow or traffic-cone orange."

"Maybe she should wait to see whether it's a girl or boy to make up her mind."

"That's exactly what I told her."

⌒✺⌒

Later that day, as Anna and Meredith met at their friend Nicole's house to put together their picnic baskets, Anna relayed the story of the "acid green" baby nursery.

"You gotta be kidding," Nicole said as she bent down to wipe the nose of one of her fifteen-month-old twins. Anna wasn't sure if it was Evan or Derrick, but she wondered if they'd get much done with three toddler boys clambering about in the family room. So far it seemed that Nicole and Meri were spending more time refereeing their boys than assembling the baskets. As a result, Anna was trying to work twice as fast.

"I think Celeste should try getting up in the middle of the night and, while she's still half asleep, turn on the light in the nursery. Then see what she thinks about that color," Meredith suggested. "The world looks a lot different at three in the morning."

"Poor David said it actually made his teeth hurt," Anna said.

Meri laughed. "I can just imagine it."

"Here's another thought," Nicole said. "When Celeste gets up at three a.m., David should pop in a soundtrack of a screaming baby—then ask her how she likes that color."

Meri nodded. "And I have just the baby to make a recording."

"You guys should tell David about our little plan," Nicole said.

"I think I will," Meri said. "I mean, just one sleep-deprived night and a simulated screaming baby, and I'll bet Celeste decides that she hates that bright color."

"But I thought you preferred bright colors for babies, Meri."

212

Anna rolled up a yellow-checked tablecloth and inserted it into a basket, nestling it next to the matching yellow plates.

"If you've noticed, I don't have bright colors on my nursery walls," she pointed out. "For my peace and for sanity's sake, I picked out a nice sky blue shade. But, for the sake of Jackson's brain development, everything else in there is pretty bright and colorful."

"But you said he's crying a lot at night?" Anna asked.

"I think he's teething." Meredith sighed. "Just when I thought he was beginning to sleep through the night too. It's like they say . . . a mother's job is never done."

"Tell me about it," Nicole said. "When Kent heard we were having twins, he acted so supportive, like he was so into this. He told me over and over how he was going to help out with everything— how he couldn't wait to be a daddy."

"But he's not doing that now?" Anna glanced at Nicole in time to see her roll her eyes.

"Yeah, right." She tore open the plastic on a package of plates. "I keep telling him that as soon as the boys are potty trained and a little older, he's going to be taking them with him everywhere he goes on the weekends. I don't care whether it's fishing or a ball game or going to Home Depot or whatever—boys need their daddy time, and trust me, they're going to get it." She sighed. "And me . . . well, I'll just be relaxing in a bubble bath or reading a good book or getting a pedicure or eating chocolates . . . or all of the above."

"Sounds like a good plan to me," Meredith said. "Mind if I send Todd and Jackson along with them? I could use a little downtime myself."

"Yeah, we'll send them on boy trips," Nicole continued. "Like camping for the whole weekend."

"Better make sure they can swim first." Meredith set a finished basket off to one side. "The way Todd keeps an eye on Jackson is frightening."

"I know what you mean," Nicole said.

"I asked Todd to watch Jackson while I fixed dinner last night—

you know, a home-cooked meal for a change—and after a while I noticed it was really quiet in there. So I look out, and Todd's sitting on the couch, reading the paper, and Jackson is sitting on the floor with a piece of newspaper shoved into his mouth, like he's eating it. At first I think it's kind of funny, but then I realize that Jackson has shoved so much newspaper into his mouth that he's literally gagging. So I run over and stick in my finger and pull out this huge, gray gob of wet newspaper that's nearly suffocating my baby, and Todd doesn't even look up from his paper."

"You're kidding," Anna said. "Was Jackson okay?"

"Well, as soon as I got the gunk out of his mouth he started crying really loud, and I think he was scared. But other than ink stains all over his face, hands, and tongue, he was okay. Although it may set back his reading skills."

"What'd Todd say?" Nicole asked. "Was he sorry?"

"He acted like it was no big deal, like Jackson was fine—end of story."

"So typical."

"Surely Todd felt bad," Anna said. But the glances the moms both gave her looked skeptical. So Anna got quiet. And she just packed baskets and listened as her sister and friend went on with more horror stories of daddy neglect and how men were basically useless when it came to babies. These were occasionally interrupted by settling squabbles between the three toddlers.

Anna didn't comment on their stories, but she felt certain that Michael would've been different as a dad. If only they'd had the chance. She'd always imagined Michael taking an active role with their baby. Of course, she had nothing to base this assumption on. And, to be fair, she was feeling a bit neglected herself these days— what with him putting in so many hours on the new business. How much worse would she feel if she were stuck home with a baby and no help? But, no, she knew that would be different. For starters, she would be so thankful for a baby that she felt certain she would rarely complain, if ever. And, although she would never mention it, she secretly resented the way Meri and Nicole took their gifts of motherhood so lightly. What if the tables were turned?

214

"Oh man, do you remember how it felt to sleep in on weekends?" Nicole said. "You'd see the sun coming in the window and just roll over and snooze."

"Now I can hardly remember what it felt like to sleep uninterrupted through a whole night."

"Or how about how it felt to take a nice long shower or use the bathroom without little fists pounding on the door, saying 'let me in!'?"

"Are you kidding?" Meredith said. "I don't even bother to close the bathroom door anymore—the second I do, Jackson starts howling like I've abandoned him."

Nicole laughed. "Speaking of closed doors . . . what about when you want a private moment with your man—it's like the twins have this special radar, like they have some sixth sense that I've slipped into a sexy nightie and dabbed on some perfume—and suddenly they're dying of thirst and they both desperately need a 'dink a wata.'"

"Well, that's not a problem in our house," Meredith said in an uptight voice. "I told Todd that he's not getting any until I start getting a full night of sleep."

"Seriously?" Nicole looked concerned. "That can't be good for your marriage."

Meri just shrugged. "It is what it is."

Nicole pointed at Anna. "You're the lucky one, you know. You and Michael totally have it made."

Anna didn't know how to respond to this. So she didn't. She just kept focused on filling the basket in front of her.

"Not having kids can be very rewarding," Nicole continued blithely. "Do you know how good you have it, Anna?"

"Oh, I wouldn't say that," Meredith said quickly, her eyes flashing a warning at their friend. Anna knew that Meri was fully aware that this was still a sore spot with her. For that matter, so was Nicole.

"There are lots of times when I'd gladly trade places with you, Anna." Nicole sighed loudly as she adjusted the bow on the basket. "Seriously, you are so lucky to be able to call your life your own."

"Yes," Anna said slowly, trying to prevent the bitterness from overcoming her, although she knew that it was useless. There was no way she could ignore Nicole's insensitivity any longer. "I am so lucky . . . like when I went by myself to get a Christmas tree last weekend, I so enjoyed watching other parents with their children while I so conveniently had none. And I'm so lucky to have an empty nursery with expensive baby furniture that my sister-in-law, who doesn't even want to be pregnant, feels isn't good enough for her baby. And I'm so lucky that Michael and I are still in debt over all the painful, and did I mention humiliating, treatments that we endured all for noth—"

"Oh, Anna," Nicole said quickly. "I'm sorry. I didn't mean to say that. Really, I didn't. I was just getting carried away with my stupid little mommy pity party. Please, forgive me!"

But Anna was crying now, and Nicole's apology only made her feel worse. Why hadn't Anna just kept her mouth shut—allowed this to pass like she usually did? Tears only made it worse.

"Please, don't be upset," Meredith said with worried eyes. "We're obviously just a couple of morons, Anna. Please forgive us."

"That's right," Nicole agreed. "We're just a couple of selfish mommy morons."

"We weren't thinking clearly," Meri continued. "I mean, here I am totally sleep deprived, and Nicole's bickering twins could drive anyone nuts—surely you can understand that we're not at our best just now."

"It's okay," Anna said, standing and wishing for a tissue to blot her tears. "I think I'm just, you know, hormonal or something." She wished she could stop crying, but it only seemed to be getting worse. And she was embarrassed to be reacting like this. She usually took this kind of thing in stride, at least on the outside.

"I'm sorry, you guys . . ." Anna grabbed her coat and her purse. "I hate to bail on you, but do you mind if I leave a little early?" She looked at the line of finished baskets. "It looks like we're almost done anyway."

"Please, don't go because of what I said," Nicole persisted.

"I'm just—" But her words were cut short by a fight between her twins, and it looked like one of them was in serious peril of being clobbered with a red plastic baseball bat.

"Go ahead and take off, Anna." Meri waved dismissively. "We can easily finish the rest of these." She shook her head. "But really, I am sorry."

"It's okay," Anna said again. "I'm probably just overreacting."

"Drive carefully, sis," Meri called as Anna made her way toward the door.

Nicole paused from where she was still attempting to disengage her boys and made a feeble wave. "See you on Sunday, Anna."

"The baskets really look good," Anna called as she blinked back more hot tears. "We should make a lot of money at the bazaar." Then she was outside, the cool air chilling her still-wet cheeks. She quietly closed Nicole's front door, shutting out the noise of the three toddlers and their disenchanted mothers, and hurried to her car. But once inside, she just sat there, continuing to cry. She knew that this was about more than simply being childless. More than ever, she was feeling like such an outsider. It was as if her illness was building a wall around her, isolating her from people she loved—people who loved her. And yet, she saw no other way to handle it. At least not until after the New Year.

Besides, she thought as she started the car, it was wrong for her sister and friend to joke like that in front of her. It was selfish to complain and commiserate over something that Anna could never hope to fully understand, something she would never be able to relate to. Sure, maybe they were tired of being mommies, but even so.

To be fair, Anna suspected that if she and Michael had been able to have children, she might've acted similar to her sister and friend. Maybe she would've grumbled about those very same problems—sleepless nights, fussy teething babies, or a husband who was less than helpful. Anna was no saint, and she would've likely participated in her share of whining. If nothing else, she would've indulged in their complaint department simply to fit in.

But underneath it all, Anna felt certain that she'd still be very, very thankful for motherhood. And, she told herself as she pulled into her driveway, Nicole and Meredith were probably thankful too—at least on a good day. She felt certain that, despite their frivolous words, they wouldn't exchange being moms for anything—not a lifetime supply of chocolate, massages, bubble baths, pedicures, or anything.

10

"Beth," Anna said with surprise as she returned to her classroom, "you're still here?"

The little girl nodded from where she was sitting quietly at her desk with her jacket on and her hands folded in front of her. But it was nearly four o'clock and the classroom had long since been vacated. "My grandma was supposed to pick me up," she said. "But I think she forgot." Beth had only been in Anna's class for a few weeks now. There had been some undisclosed problem with her parents, and now, as Anna understood it, her paternal grandmother was taking care of her.

"Do you want me to call her for you?"

"The office lady tried already."

"She's not home?"

Beth shook her head, looking up with sad blue eyes. "Is it okay for me to stay here, Mrs. Jacobs?"

"Of course," Anna said. "Maybe you'd like to help me."

Beth brightened. "Sure. I love helping. What do you want me to do?"

Now Anna had to think quickly. "Well, it's Friday," she said. "That means the goldfish must be fed for the weekend. And you could check the water of the Christmas tree . . . we want to be sure that it doesn't dry up before Monday."

"Okay," Beth said.

Anna thought of a few more tasks, and Beth turned out to be a good helper, but the clock was still ticking and Anna wasn't sure what she should do about this seemingly forgotten child. "Does your grandmother have a cell phone?" Anna asked.

"Yes. But I can't remember the number."

"Oh." Anna frowned. "How about other relatives? Aunts or uncles?"

"No . . ."

"How about your parents?" Now Anna suspected this wasn't an option, but she was curious about Beth's circumstances.

Beth just looked down at her feet and shrugged.

"Hmm . . ." Anna was ready to go home, but she couldn't just abandon her student. "And Mrs. Scott tried all the numbers in your records."

"It's just my grandma's phone number."

"You don't have an emergency number?"

"I don't know."

"Maybe we should check." So Anna gathered up her things and Beth got her backpack, and they went to the office to discover that no one was there. In fact, it seemed that everyone except the janitor was gone now. Not that it was so unusual for this time of day, or for a Friday.

Anna knelt down to look at Beth. "Well, what do you think we should do?"

Beth shrugged and played with the zipper on her puffy pink jacket. "I dunno."

"I could take you with me, and we could try to reach your grandmother."

"Okay." Beth looked up and smiled.

Still, Anna was unsure. In her eight years of teaching, she'd never taken a student home with her before, and she certainly didn't want to be accused of kidnapping. "Let's try your grand-mother's phone one more time first," she said after they got into the car. Beth recited the number, and Anna used her cell phone to call. When she got an answering machine, she left a very clear and concise message, informing the woman of what she was doing and giving her phone numbers as well as her address.

"Okay," Anna said. "That should do it."

"Do you have kids?" Beth asked as Anna started her car.

"No. But I do have a dog."

"What's your dog's name?"

"Huntley. And he happens to like kids."

"I like dogs too."

"Do you have a dog?"

"I used to have a dog . . . back before . . ."

"And your grandma doesn't have a dog?"

"No. She's allergic."

"Oh . . ."

"Do you know about my parents?" Beth asked suddenly.

"No . . . not really." Anna wasn't sure whether she should encourage Beth to talk about it or not. For some reason Anna suspected it wasn't a happy story.

"I can tell you," Beth said.

"If you want . . ."

"My grandma doesn't like to talk about it," Beth said. "But I go to see a counselor. Her name is Julie, and she says it's good for me to talk about it."

"Julie sounds like a smart woman."

"She is. I see her on Wednesdays, after school."

"That's good."

"My mommy killed my dad."

Anna felt a cold jolt going through her, but she didn't want Beth to notice. "Really?" she said evenly.

"I wasn't there when she did it . . . I was at school."

"Oh . . ." Anna sneaked a peek at the calm little girl sitting next to her.

"My dad was mean to Mommy. I think that's why she did it."

"Uh-huh." Anna swallowed hard.

"But Mommy is in prison now."

"That must be hard."

"Yeah. I miss her."

"Do you write letters to her?"

221

"Yeah. Julie helps me with that. Grandma doesn't want to talk to my mommy."

"Your grandma is probably very sad about what happened."

"She is."

"I'm sure you must be very sad too."

"Yeah. At first I cried a lot."

Anna nodded. "I think it's good to cry sometimes." Then Anna told Beth a little about her own mom. "I was really sad when she died, but sometimes my dad didn't want me to cry."

"Like my grandma?"

"Maybe so. But now I think that it's good to cry when you're sad. I think God made us this way for a reason."

"Maybe it's because he knew we needed to get cleaned out," Beth said.

"Yes," Anna agreed as she parked in her driveway. "I think you're right."

"Is this your house?"

"It is." Anna was glad she'd gotten that timer for the lights now.

"I like it," Beth said. "And I like your Christmas lights."

"Wait until you see the tree," Anna said.

Beth had barely had time to see the tree and meet Huntley before her grandmother called. "I am so sorry," she told Anna. "I completely forgot that I was going to pick up Beth. I left work early to go to a dentist appointment and then got distracted and totally forgot to pick her up. I thought she'd ride the school bus like usual. Then I get home and find all these messages. I just feel so terrible."

"It's okay," Anna assured her. She patted Beth's head as she spoke. "Beth is a delight to have around, and I've enjoyed her company."

"Well, I'm on my way to your house right now," Mrs. Albert said. "I so appreciate you looking out for her like this. You know, this being a parent again is taking some getting used to."

"I'll bet."

"And I'm a single woman," she continued. "It's just little Beth and me now."

"Well, she's a great kid," Anna said. "You're blessed to have her."

"Yes . . . that's true."

They said good-bye and Anna hung up. "Your grandmother is on her way," she told Beth. "And she feels terrible for forgetting about you."

"It's okay," said Beth as she petted Huntley. "It was fun coming to your house, and I like your dog."

Anna was just about to offer Beth a snack when she heard the doorbell ring. "I'll bet that's your grandmother now."

And it was, but Anna was surprised that this "grandma" didn't look too much older than herself. Also, she had on a short skirt and knee-high boots. Not your typical grandma type.

"I am so sorry," Mrs. Albert repeated. She knelt down and hugged Beth. "You must think that your grandmother is a complete nincompoop."

Beth laughed. "No. You just forgot, Grandma. It's okay. Mrs. Jacobs took really good care of me."

"I enjoyed her company," Anna said.

"Mrs. Jacobs doesn't have kids," Beth informed her grandma. "But she has a really cool dog."

Anna smiled.

"Well, thanks again," Mrs. Albert said. "Have a good weekend."

"Don't forget about the school Christmas concert tomorrow," Anna reminded her.

"Oh, yes." Mrs. Albert actually slapped her forehead. "I have the flyer on the refrigerator, but after today, well, who knows?"

"Well, I'll bet you won't forget, will you, Beth?" Anna asked.

"No way!" Beth grinned. "See ya tomorrow, Mrs. Jacobs." Then she and her grandma trotted off toward what looked like a fairly new Mustang convertible. It seemed that Beth's grandma was setting a new youthful standard for grandparents.

Anna closed the front door and went back to the kitchen, where Huntley looked up at her expectantly, like he wanted to know what had become of his young playmate.

"I suppose you miss Beth now," she said. His tail thumped back and forth as if to confirm this. "Well, sorry, old boy, but we can't keep her."

Yet even as Anna said this, a lump formed in her throat. Of course she hadn't expected to keep her student. But why was it that now her house felt much emptier than usual? And why was it that some people were "blessed" with children that they didn't really want or couldn't take care of? The idea of Beth's mother killing her father and now doing time in prison actually made Anna's head hurt. She didn't want to judge them, but what about poor Beth—why should she suddenly be parentless and be raised by a grandma who forgot to pick her up from school? What else might she forget? And what about people like Anna and Michael who wanted desperately to be parents but were forced to be childless? What was fair about that?

These were not new questions. But they were some of the things she intended to ask God about someday. Maybe someday in the not too distant future too. But Anna didn't really want to think about that right now—she wanted to pretend like she didn't know what was going on or that her stomach hadn't bothered her a lot today. Denial seemed to be her only protection for the time being, and she planned to wear it like a warm winter coat until January. She turned on the teakettle, but even green tea didn't sound very appetizing. Maybe some saltines would be better. She wondered how advanced this thing really was—how long it had been since she'd experienced the first symptoms. Or what kind of prognosis she was risking by delaying treatment. Not that it had made any difference with her mother. Why would it with her?

Again, she told herself not to think about such things. Focus on Christmas instead—make memories and happy times. Celebrate each day fully. But even as she tried to do this, she could feel those all-too-familiar tears filling her eyes once again. Anna reached for a tissue, and as she blew her nose, she reminded herself of what Beth had said—how crying cleaned them out. Anna thought she should be pretty clean by now.

Somehow Anna made it through the weekend's blur of activities and commitments without having any more emotional breakdowns. Perhaps being busy was the best defense against the blues. Oh, sure, she'd been somewhat overcome while watching her class of second graders performing their rendition of "Little Drummer Boy" for the Christmas concert—for which Beth was on time and was wearing an adorable red velvet dress. But then, Anna always got a little weepy at that particular event. And she'd been so happy that all their baskets sold at the bazaar—bringing in more than $500 for the Darfur fund—that she'd been a little teary-eyed for that too. But then so had Nicole and Meredith. Or maybe they were still feeling bad about the other night.

But by Monday, after all the busyness of the weekend, Anna realized that she really hadn't had much quality time with Michael. And this was driven home further when he announced that, once again, he would be working late tonight.

"I miss you," she complained as he filled his travel mug with coffee.

"I miss you too," he said. "But trust me, this overtime thing is not going to last forever."

"Maybe 'forever' is in the eyes of the beholder," she told him.

He laughed, then leaned down to peck her on the cheek. Still, she hadn't meant to be funny. More and more she was realizing that time—each precious, one-of-a-kind day—was not a renewable resource.

11

"Anna, this is Meri. It's Wednesday, around two o'clock, and I really, really need to talk to you. As soon as possible. Please, call me when you get this message. Really, it's urgent." Anna replayed the message just to make sure she'd heard it right, then hit the speed dial for Meri's cell phone.

"What's wrong?" she asked her sister as soon as she answered.

"Thanks for calling," Meri said in a voice that sounded much calmer than the message she'd left. "Where are you right now?"

"In the school parking lot." Anna unlocked her car. "Just getting into my car. But tell me, Meri, is something really wrong? Is it Dad? Or David? Or—"

"No. Dad and David are fine. Well, as far as I know. But this isn't about them."

"What then?"

"It's about me. Can you meet me at Starbucks on Fifth Street?"

"Sure."

"Okay, I'm on my way."

Anna's heart was still pounding hard as she started her car. What was wrong with Meri? Was it possible that she, like Anna, was experiencing the symptoms for ovarian cancer? What if they both were sick? How devastating would that be for the rest of the family?

"Please, God," Anna pleaded as she turned onto Fifth Street.

"Please, don't let Meri be sick too. That would be too much. Please, let her be fine. Please!"

Anna parked in front, then jumped out of her car just as Meri pulled up. Anna ran over and hugged her. "Are you okay?" she demanded, stepping back to look right into her sister's eyes.

"That depends . . ." Meri glanced away. "Come on, let's go inside. I'll explain."

Anna's stomach had been worse than usual again today, so she simply got a bottle of water, then went over to a quiet table and waited for Meri to join her with her latte.

"Please, tell me what's wrong," Anna said after Meri sat down. "I can't take the suspense. Is it your health?"

"No. Well, not my physical health anyway. Some people, Todd in particular, might question the state of my mental health, though."

Anna stared at her sister with impatience. "Explain."

"I think I want a divorce."

Anna blinked. "A divorce?"

Meredith nodded, then looked down at her latte.

"Are you serious?" Anna wanted to grab Meri by her shoulders and violently shake her. She wanted to say things like, "Are you crazy?" or "Have you lost your mind?" or "Have you forgotten that you and Todd have a child?"

Meredith looked back up at her. "I am serious."

Anna sucked in a quick breath. "Why?"

"It's a long story . . ."

"I have lots of time." Okay, maybe that was an overstatement.

"And Jackson still has an hour left at the babysitter's."

That was another thing that Anna silently disapproved of. Meredith had gone back to work after only six weeks of maternity leave. Todd had encouraged her to stay home for the first year, pointing out that they would spend nearly half her salary on child care, but Meredith had insisted. And Anna still didn't get it.

"Okay, Meri," Anna said, trying to sound a lot more understanding than she felt just now. "Tell me what's going on with you and Todd."

227

"Remember how I felt we were drifting apart before I got pregnant?"

Anna nodded. "Yes. But then it seemed like things changed."

"Things did change. But not between Todd and me. I was so obsessed with having the baby, I thought it was going to magically fix everything. But I was wrong."

"It seems unfair to expect a baby to fix everything, Meri."

"Yes, I know." She sighed. "But I thought maybe it would make Todd and me closer. I thought it would ignite that old spark."

"From what I've heard, it's usually just the opposite, isn't it? I mean, the way you and Nicole were going on about it . . . well, it didn't sound too good."

"Yeah, well, at least Nicole and Kent still love each other."

"Meaning?"

"Meaning I don't love Todd. And, despite the fact that he doesn't want a divorce, I don't think he loves me either." Her eyes glistened with tears.

Anna reached across the table and took her sister's hand. "Oh, Meri . . ."

"I wish it was different, Anna. Really, I do. But how can I be expected to stay in a marriage without love?"

"Maybe it's just a stage."

"That's what I used to tell myself too."

"Maybe when Jackson is a little older . . . a little more independent . . . maybe things will get better."

Meri just shook her head. "I don't think so."

"How can you be so sure?"

"I just know."

"I don't see how you can know that, Meri. I mean, Michael and I have had some rough times too. And that didn't involve children . . . well, not exactly anyway. But we weathered those times. And we love each other more than ever now."

Meri looked at Anna with hopeful eyes. "Yes. And that's what I want too."

"But you have to work at it, Meri. That's what I'm saying. You can't just throw in the towel."

"Sometimes you have to."

"But why? And what about your vows? You guys are Christians too. You're supposed to take this kind of thing seriously."

"I do take it seriously."

"Then how can you give up?"

Meredith looked down at her latte again, and something in her expression—perhaps that quick sideways glance—reminded Anna of when they were teenagers. It was the same look that Meri had gotten when she'd done something wrong—something that Anna had to try to cover up for her. Anna let go of her sister's hand and sat up straighter.

"What's really going on?" Anna asked.

"What do you mean?"

"You know what I mean, Meri. What's really going on here?"

Meredith pressed her lips together, then looked around, as if to see if anyone was near enough to hear her. "I'm in love with someone else."

Anna felt dizzy. She took in a deep breath to steady herself, wondering if this was another symptom of her illness or just an emotional reaction to Meri's confession.

"I know, I know . . ." Meri shook her head. "It's wrong. And I'm not proud of it. But it's the truth. And I just really needed to talk to someone—besides Todd, that is."

"Todd knows?"

"Not really, but he might suspect something." Meri looked down again.

"Have you—have you been having an affair?"

Meredith looked up with an offended expression. "No, of course not."

Anna held up her hands. "Hey, I don't know. You have to admit, this is pretty shocking news, Meri."

"Like I said, I'm not proud of myself."

"Who is the guy?"

"He's a social worker too. His name is Cooper, and he's—well, he's everything that Todd is not."

"Is he married?"

"Divorced."

"Oh . . ." Anna really didn't know how to react to any of this. She couldn't have been more surprised if Meredith had announced she'd just booked a trip to Mars on the next space shuttle. How had this happened? Why hadn't Anna known?

"I know you're shocked, Anna. But really, who else could I talk to?"

"It's a lot to take in . . . I mean, I never would've guessed this in a thousand years, Meri. So, how long have you been, you know, in love with this Cooper dude?" Even saying that name felt foreign to Anna—like something acidic on her tongue. She had never met the guy, and she felt like she hated him already. And Anna didn't hate anyone.

"I've always admired him. He's so great with people, and he loves kids."

"Does he *have* kids?"

"A five-year-old daughter."

"But he's divorced."

"Yes."

"How long?"

"Not quite a year."

"Does he have custody?"

"They share it."

"Oh . . ." Anna wanted to point out how complicated Meredith's life would become. She'd seen these situations at school. Stepparents, stepchildren, stepsiblings . . . everyone trying to figure out where they fit in, trying to remember whose turn it was to have the kids. Kind of like Beth's situation, only with more people involved.

"And Cooper really loves Jackson," Meri said.

"He's met him?"

"Well, yeah . . ."

Anna wanted to ask how but didn't. "How does Cooper feel about you?"

"The same."

"But you really haven't slept with him?"

"No." Meredith firmly shook her head. "I wouldn't do that, Anna. I'm not like that."

Anna wanted to scream, "You're not like this either!" But it seemed pointless. Instead she said, "So, what am I supposed to say?"

"I don't know . . ."

"You must know that I'm not supportive of this. You must know that all I can do is recommend that you work things out with Todd. Have you considered seeing a marriage counselor?"

"I asked Todd to go with me more than a year ago, but he refused. He thought it was a waste of time and money."

"What about now?" Anna asked.

"Now it's too late."

"Really?" Anna peered curiously at her sister, trying to determine who this person was—and had she always been this way? Or had something changed? Was it partially Anna's fault for not paying closer attention? In some ways, Anna had taken a parental role in her younger sister's life, although they were only two and a half years apart. She'd helped her in school, with relationships, with planning her wedding; she'd even been Meri's birthing coach when Jackson was born. What more could she have done? Paid closer attention, perhaps.

"I knew you would take this hard," Meredith said. "But I also knew that I needed to talk to someone—I felt like I was about to explode."

"And you can," Anna said. "Talk to me, I mean. It's just that I can't see how getting a divorce will be the best thing for you. A marriage is a lifetime commitment, something you have to work at, invest yourself into, and when it's hard, you simply try harder . . . and eventually it smoothes out, your efforts pay off."

"Maybe for you."

Anna bit her lip.

"I'm sorry to disappoint you."

"What about Todd?"

"I feel bad about Todd. But I do not see how staying with him will help anything. We're both miserable, Anna. Staying together won't improve that."

"What about Jackson?"

"Same thing. Staying in a lousy marriage isn't good for children."

"Will you marry Cooper?"

"I don't know . . . maybe . . ."

"But he's been divorced, Meri. Don't you see a pattern here?"

"His wife had an affair."

"Oh . . ."

"You'd like him, Anna. I know you would."

Anna felt certain that Meri was wrong.

"He's very sweet and genuine. And if you met him, you'd be shocked that I love him. I mean, he's not even handsome."

Anna blinked. This was surprising. Meredith had always been attracted to the tall, dark, and handsome types. Like Todd. "You're saying that he's not attractive?"

"He's attractive to me, Anna. But he's not what you'd call handsome. He's actually sort of geeky looking."

"Geeky?"

"Yeah. He's starting to bald and he's pretty skinny and he's about the same height as me, so I can't wear heels when I'm with him."

Anna shook her head. This was just too weird. Her sister sitting here in Starbucks talking about what kind of footwear she could sport with her new boyfriend. "So . . . what happens next?" Anna asked.

"For starters, you can't tell a soul."

"Why?"

"I don't want to ruin Christmas."

"Right." Anna shook her head.

"I know, it sounds dumb. But it's Jackson's first Christmas, and I just wanted to get through it, you know? Dad and Donna are having us all over for Christmas Eve . . . and David and Celeste are expecting. And I just want everyone to be happy, you know. I don't want to rock the boat."

"So, what then? The day after Christmas . . . you sink the boat?"

"I'll wait a week or so."

"Right . . ."

"You think I should tell everyone now?"

Anna considered this. She also considered the secret she was keeping from her family until after Christmas—or New Year's. Perhaps between her and Meredith, they would simply cancel out the shock for one another.

"You know I love you, Meredith," Anna said finally. "And no matter what you do, I'll always love you. But I really want what's best for you."

Meredith smiled. "Then you should be happy for me."

Anna closed her eyes and took a deep breath. She felt sick again and dizzy still. She slowly opened her eyes and took a sip of water.

"Are you okay?"

"Just a stomach thing," she admitted. "Leftover flu bug."

Meredith studied her closely. "I thought that stomach flu was months ago."

"Maybe this is a new one." She forced a smile. "One of the fringe benefits of working with kids, you know."

"At least you only have two more days before Christmas break. That's got to feel good."

"Yes. I can't wait. Hey, you haven't been over to see my Christmas tree yet."

"How about if I bring Jackson by on Saturday?"

"Great."

"I want Christmas to be perfect for him. I know some people don't believe that babies can remember things at this age, but I feel certain they can. And I want Jackson's first Christmas to be happy and unspoiled."

Anna wanted to ask about the following Christmases. What about sharing custody? Who got Thanksgiving? Who got Easter? Surely Meredith had to realize that those holidays might not all be "happy and unspoiled." But mostly Anna felt tired. All she wanted to do was go home and go to bed. Meredith was right about one thing today: Anna was counting the hours until Christmas break. She was ready for a rest.

233

12

||||||||||||||||||||

"You're working late again?" Anna said.

"I'm sorry, sweetie," Michael told her. "Can't be avoided."

"But it's Friday night and Christmas break has officially begun. I wanted to celebrate!"

"Can we celebrate tomorrow?"

"I don't know." She felt like pouting. "For all I know, you'll decide to work again."

"I won't. I promise. Tomorrow night I'll be home and we'll do something special. Okay?"

"Okay."

"And if it makes you feel any better, you know that I'd much rather be home with you than working, don't you?"

"Yeah, I guess so . . ."

"Come on, Anna. You know that's the truth."

"Yes, I know. And I do appreciate how hard you're working to make your business a success, Michael. Sorry to sound so grumpy. It's just that I miss you."

"I miss you too."

"And I was going to make lasagna for dinner tonight."

"Oh, now you're really making me feel bad."

"Good."

He laughed. "Well, just enjoy your leisure, little lady. Three and a half weeks to do whatever you please. I'm starting to feel jealous."

"Why don't you take some time off too?" she said suddenly. "Maybe we could go do something—take a trip or something?"

"It sounds great, honey. But you know how finances are just now."

"Oh, yeah . . ."

"Maybe next year, when we're all caught up."

"Yeah, sure . . . next year."

Anna tried not to feel sorry for herself when she hung up the phone. Then, as she was putting away the lasagna ingredients, she thought about poor Michael, slaving away at the office, probably sending for takeout again. Well, that settled it. She'd just go ahead and make the lasagna tonight after all. If she jumped right on it, she could have it delivered to Michael and his partner Grant in time for dinner.

⌘

She could hear the hot lasagna still bubbling beneath the foil as she slipped it into the cardboard box that she'd lined with kitchen towels. She'd already put a green salad, a loaf of French bread, and some plates and silverware in the car. She couldn't wait to see the expressions on Michael's and Grant's faces when they saw their feast.

She'd meant to call them but had gotten so busy that she'd forgotten. But they didn't usually order out until around 6:30 anyway, so she thought she was safe. But when she got to the office, it looked like the lights were off inside. Still, she carried the box containing the lasagna up the stairs and knocked on the door. No answer. Had they gone out for dinner? Was she too late?

"Hey," a male voice called from the bottom of the stairs. "Is that you, Anna?"

"Grant?"

She could hear him clomping up the stairs now. "What are you doing here?"

She held out the box. "Dinner."

"Wow, that smells amazing. But why did you bring it here?"

"Aren't you guys working late tonight?"

"I'm not. Suzy and I have a Christmas party to go to."

"Oh . . ." She frowned.

"But maybe Michael planned to work tonight." Yet, even as Grant said this, she detected a question mark in his voice. As if he wasn't too sure but thought maybe he was covering for his partner, which she found irksome.

"Well, maybe I got my wires crossed," she said. "I thought he was working tonight."

"Maybe he's at home by now," Grant said. "Wondering what happened to dinner."

"Maybe so," Anna said. And maybe Grant was right. Perhaps her lonely plea had gotten to Michael and, realizing that Grant was going to a Christmas party, Michael had changed his mind and gone home. For all she knew they might've passed each other in traffic just now—like the old proverbial ships in the night. "I better go," she said quickly. "Before the lasagna gets cold."

"Lasagna?" He smacked his lips loudly. "Now I actually wish Michael and I *were* working late tonight. I haven't had a good lasagna in ages."

"Maybe next time," she called out as she headed back down the stairs.

But when she got home, Michael wasn't there. And, as far as she could tell, he hadn't been there either. She set the lasagna box on the counter and frowned down at Huntley. "Guess it's just you and me tonight, old boy."

She took her time serving up a plate for herself. She knew it was because she was hoping that Michael was going to pop in and surprise her. Perhaps with flowers or a bottle of wine. He did that sometimes—just for the fun of it. But it had been awhile since he had surprised her like that. And when she finally sat down to eat, it was by herself. And, although she loved lasagna just as much as Michael, it didn't taste quite right to her tonight. She'd only eaten a few bites when her stomach began to feel upset again.

So she focused on the bread and salad instead, but she soon realized it was useless. She had no appetite, just an uneasy feeling deep inside her. She didn't want to think about it, but she couldn't help imagining the insidious mass of cancer cells quietly growing deep within her. She cleared the little dining table, then set up her laptop and before long was surfing the Internet, looking for more information on ovarian cancer. She wanted to find something new and hopeful . . . something encouraging. But mostly it was just the same old story. The same list of symptoms, all the very things she was experiencing. And always, the same old advice to see your doctor as soon as possible. She even searched out some "alternative" sites, but their suggestions sounded a little scary to her. Plus she read from other more reliable sites that alternative medicine for the treatment of ovarian cancer was questionable and highly discouraged. Finally, feeling dejected and even more sick to her stomach, she turned off her computer and went to finish cleaning the kitchen.

But where was Michael? More disturbing than the question of her health was the question of her husband's whereabouts tonight. And perhaps that was contributing to her stomachache as well. She wanted to call him and ask what was up, but she knew that would sound suspicious. Besides, it was possible he'd run out to grab a bite to eat, then returned to the office. It was possible he was sitting in front of his computer right now, immersed in some important project—and a phone call might interrupt his chain of thought and force him to work even later. No, the bottom line was that she trusted Michael. She knew that in her core. She just wished she knew for certain where he was right now—and if he was okay.

As she turned on the dishwasher, she even considered driving back over there to see if the office lights were on or if his car was parked in its space. Just to make sure he was all right—kind of like a guardian angel. But she was bone tired. Cooking that dinner had sapped what little energy she had . . . and now all she wanted to do was to sleep. She freshened the water in Huntley's bowl and turned off the kitchen lights, then took a comforting shower, using some lovely lavender shower gel that a student's mother had given her for Christmas. And then, though it wasn't even nine yet, she went to bed.

"You must've been tired last night," Michael told her the next morning as he held out a steaming cup before her. "Care for some coffee in bed?"

She made a face. "No, no thanks. My stomach is a little upset."

"Oh . . ." He blinked and stepped back. "Sorry. I just remembered how you used to like coffee in bed on Saturday mornings."

"Not this morning." She quickly got up and hurried past him toward the bathroom. Was he trying to make up for something with her? Coffee in bed? It had been years since they'd done that. She splashed water on her face. What was he up to anyway? Was he acting guilty? And why was she feeling so suspicious? Was her illness inducing paranoia too? Maybe she should check for those symptoms on the Internet. Or maybe her worries over Michael were related to her sister's confession this week. As she brushed her teeth, she thought about Meredith's marriage situation and this Cooper guy. It still just made her really mad. What was Meri thinking? Perhaps she wasn't thinking. And perhaps Anna was doing some kind of transference thing with poor Michael, suspecting him simply because of Meredith's irresponsible attitude toward marriage.

She continued to hash over these things until she finally decided that she was being unfair to her husband. But by the time she was dressed and ready to face the world, Michael was gone. Fortunately Huntley was gone too, so she figured they were out on a walk together. Good thing too, since poor old Huntley hadn't been walked in days. Anna turned on the flame under the teakettle, reassuring herself that all was well. She was just pouring a bowl of cornflakes, one of the few food items that didn't seem to bother her digestive system, when the phone rang.

"Hey, sis," Meredith said lightly. "When can Jackson and I come by and check out your Christmas tree?"

"Whenever you like." Anna turned off the flame under the teakettle right before it started to whistle.

238

"Well, I was thinking this morning would be good. That way I can get in some Christmas shopping later while Jackson is still in good spirits. And then he'll need an afternoon nap and I'll need to stop by the dry cleaner and—"

"This morning is fine," Anna said quickly. She could tell by the way Meri was chattering away that she was still uncomfortable about her situation. Overcommunication had always been one of Meredith's favorite smoke screens—her way to obscure what was really going on. Well, whatever. Anna was just as glad to pretend that nothing was going on too.

"Okay," Meredith said. "We're on our way."

Michael and Huntley had just gotten home from their walk when Meredith and Jackson arrived. And suddenly the house felt overly full and somewhat like a circus. Naturally, all that Jackson wanted to do was to attack their Christmas tree and eat the popcorn strings and pull on Huntley's ears, although the poor dog finally retreated to the sanctuary of the laundry room. Anna had forgotten what a handful her young nephew could be. But at the same time, it was hard to resist those rosy cheeks, curly hair, and sparkling brown eyes. To Jackson, every new thing was a great adventure that he felt compelled to explore.

"I see you have your hands full," Michael said as Anna set some of the more precious glass ornaments on a high shelf. "I'm going to run to the office to check on some things."

She tossed him a questioning look.

"Don't worry, Anna, I haven't forgotten about tonight. I'll be back in time."

After Michael was gone, Meredith gave Anna a dark scowl. "You told him, didn't you?"

"Told him what?" Anna pried Jackson's chubby fingers from their grasp around the pole lamp, then lifted him up so that he could see the top part of the tree.

"You know what."

239

"About you?" Anna shook her head. "No way. A promise is a promise."

"But he acted strange. Like he wanted to get away ,from me, Anna. Like he knew something. You told him, didn't you?"

"No, I did not." Anna was trying to distract Jackson with the stuffed bear that she'd set in a child-sized rocker underneath the tree, although he seemed more interested in turning the rocker into an acrobatic prop than cuddling the bear.

"Then why was he acting like that?"

"Honestly, Meri, he doesn't know a thing. If he looked like he was trying to escape anything, it was probably me." But as soon as she said this, she regretted it.

"Escape you? Yeah, right."

Anna swooped up Jackson just before he tipped over the rocker. "You are a handful, little man," she cooed at him. "No wonder your mom is plum worn out sometimes."

"You're telling me," Meri said as she collapsed into the club chair.

"I can't believe you're taking him Christmas shopping with you today," Anna said. "Talk about being a glutton for punishment."

"I couldn't find a sitter." Meredith looked hopefully at her now. "That is, unless Auntie Anna wants to have a little visitor."

Everything in Anna said to say no. Everything except that part of her that loved babies. Still, she rationalized, she wasn't at her best. It might not be in Jackson's best interests to be watched by her. What about her stomach problems, her lack of energy? And what if she needed to use the bathroom suddenly? Plus her house was in no way baby-proof. "I don't know if that's a good idea, Meri . . ."

"Oh, I didn't figure you would want him. Good grief, his own daddy doesn't even want him. Maybe this is a baby that only a mother can love."

"No, that's not it. I do love him. And I'd love to watch him. But my house isn't really baby-proof, you know? I'd feel terrible if he got hurt."

"How about the nursery? It's safe, isn't it?"

Anna nodded slowly. "Yeah, actually, it is."

"And Celeste hasn't taken the crib yet. Couldn't Jackson have a nap in there?"

"Sure," Anna said suddenly. "Why not?"

Meredith stood up now and hugged her. "You are the best, Anna. I really don't know what I'd do without you."

Anna forced a smile. Unfortunately that was a problem that Meredith would have to figure out on her own . . . someday.

Meredith handed over the diaper bag along with a few directions, then, just like that, she was gone. For the next couple of hours, Anna chased her nephew around the house, trying to prevent him from harm as much as to prevent him from harming something. She tried to put him down for a nap a couple of times, but whenever she placed him in the crib, he began to howl like he was being tortured. She changed his diaper a couple of times, tried to get him to eat some of his baby food, then gave him his bottle. And when it was nearly three and Anna was exhausted and ready to call her sister and let her know that it was time to pick up her little darling, Jackson finally started to look sleepy.

Anna set the empty bottle aside and quietly carried him to the nursery, where she'd already pulled the blinds down and gotten the bed ready. She gently rocked him in her arms, making sure his pacifier was secure, then softly sang a couple of lullabies. It really was amazing how this child, who'd been bouncing off the walls just minutes ago, could suddenly grow limp and relaxed in her arms, like a hyperactive marionette whose strings had been clipped.

She leaned over and kissed his warm, moist forehead and then, for the third time, gently eased him into the crib. She tucked the comforter—the one she'd picked out for their own baby—snugly around him, then slowly stood back up and just watched him. She was literally holding her breath as she waited for his eyes to pop open and for him to start screaming again. But miraculously he did not.

She tiptoed out of the room, leaving the door ajar so she could hear him if he woke. Then, still tiptoeing, she went into the living

241

room and flopped down onto the sofa. Right now all she wanted was a nap as well. But just as she closed her eyes, she heard a noise at the front door.

"Hello?" Meredith called quietly. "I thought Jackson might still be asleep, so I didn't ring the bell. Hope you don't mind I let myself in."

Anna glanced up from the couch. "Not at all. Excuse me for not getting up, but I don't think I'm able."

"Did he wear you out?"

"He's got a lot of energy. And he just went down for his nap."

"You mean just now?"

"Yes. Like about three minutes ago. I tried to put him down a couple of times earlier, but he was not interested."

"Wow, you look wiped out, Anna."

Anna leaned her head back into the couch and sighed. "I am. Toddlers are exhausting."

Meredith laughed as she sat down in the club chair. "You're telling me."

"What took you so long anyway?"

"I'm sorry. But seriously, it was a total zoo out there."

"So, did you find what you were looking for?"

"I guess." Meredith gave her a puzzled look now. "Hey, are you feeling okay, Anna?"

"What do you mean?"

Meredith's frown lines deepened. "I mean, you don't look so good—and, come to think of it, you haven't seemed like your old normal self lately. How are you doing?"

Anna sat up now, hoping to look more like her old self—whatever that was. "I'm perfectly fine."

Meredith looked really skeptical now. "No, you're not."

"What do you mean, no I'm not?"

"I mean, I know you, Anna. Something's wrong. I can tell."

Anna felt her eyes getting hot with tears again. She really did want to talk to someone about all that was going on in her life right now. Someone besides God, although she knew that he had been

242

listening, and she knew that she would be lost without that. But this was Meredith . . . what should Anna tell her? Where would she begin? And where would she end? To be fair, her health problem, at this point, was only a suspicion on her part. Okay, it was a very strong suspicion and the symptoms were real, but it could be nothing. And this thing with Michael, well, that was probably nothing too. In fact, it might simply be her imagination.

"I'm fine . . . really." She forced a tired smile for her sister.

"You mentioned your stomach earlier this week, Anna. Is it still bothering you?"

Anna nodded. Perhaps there was no point in keeping this from Meredith. If anyone knew Anna, besides Michael, it was her sister. "Yeah."

"How long has it been bothering you?"

"I'm not sure . . ." Anna glanced at the clock on the mantel, like that was going to help her. "Maybe a month or two."

"And what's going on exactly? Describe how you feel."

So Anna told her about feeling bloated and unable to eat and the other things. "It's probably nothing."

Meredith came over to sit by Anna on the couch and, with a very serious expression, asked, "Have you been to the doctor yet?"

That did it. The tears were coming now, hot and heavy this time, like the floodgates had been knocked open. Meredith put her arms around Anna and pulled her close. "What's going on, Anna? Please, tell me. What's wrong?"

Finally, when Anna recovered enough to speak, and after she'd blown her nose long and hard, she took a long, deep breath. "I think I might have ovarian cancer."

This time it was Meredith who broke down. She was sobbing now, and Anna was the one comforting her. "It's going to be okay, Meri," she said again and again, although she had no idea how it was going to be okay.

"Oh, Anna," Meredith said finally. "Why didn't you tell me?"

"I don't want anyone to know yet."

"Why not?" Meredith picked up a pillow and punched it hard.

"Because . . . it's Christmas, Meri. I don't want to spoil it. Sort of like you and your marriage troubles. My news can wait."

"But you are getting treatments, right?"

Anna explained the insurance dilemma and how she didn't want to get a diagnosis before they had a policy in place. "They would consider it a previous condition."

"Who cares about insurance! We're talking about your health."

"Don't you understand? Without insurance, we could go bankrupt, Michael could lose his business."

"I don't care. You need to get in to see a doctor, Anna. ASAP."

"A couple of weeks won't hurt and I—"

"Baloney, Anna." Meredith stood up now. "I've read up on this thing. Once I hit my midthirties, I started going in for a checkup every six months. You know that we're both subject to it . . . because of Mom. And you, Anna . . ." Meri shook her fist. "Oh, I should've thought of this sooner. I mean, not only do you look like Mom, you even act like her. You probably have identical DNA."

"I'll take that as a compliment."

"And it is . . . except that it places you at higher risk."

"I'm also the same age as she was."

Meredith blinked in surprise. "Really? That doesn't seem possible."

Anna nodded. "I know . . . but it is."

"And being childless, Anna, you know that places you at higher risk too."

"I know . . . I just read up on it recently myself."

"You mean, you weren't aware of this before—you didn't know what the symptoms were, or what the risk is?"

"Not really."

"But you do know now?" Then Meredith began quizzing Anna, naming all the symptoms as if going over a checklist. And each time, Anna nodded.

"I think it's pretty much a textbook case," Anna admitted.

"And you haven't gone to the doctor?"

"I thought it was the flu, Meri. You know we had a bout with it at school in early October—everyone got hit."

"That was months ago!"

"I know. And I finally put two and two together. I know it's not the flu now. Right after Thanksgiving—just two weeks ago—I sat down and figured it out."

"But you didn't see a doctor."

"I will."

"When?"

"I'll make a doctor appointment next week." She didn't add that she'd make it for January and that she'd pretend like she was simply scheduling a routine gynecological checkup.

"Oh, Anna," Meredith said. "I feel so terrible that I burdened you with my marriage problems and here you are dealing with something like this."

"It's okay." Anna forced a smile. "And maybe I'm okay. Maybe I'm just run-down and need to take better care of myself."

"And here I go leaving Jackson for you to care for."

"It was fun. I love him."

"Does Michael know?"

"No one knows, Meri. Except you."

"And you'll call the doctor on Monday?"

"Absolutely." Anna would call her too. The appointment would be scheduled.

"And maybe you're right," Meredith said. "Maybe you are just run-down. But you need to find out. Knowledge is power, Anna. Especially when it comes to something like this."

"I really do think I'm just worn out from school and everything. It's not unusual for this time of year. And I'm so glad to have Christmas break just now. I'm sure I'll be back to my old self in a week or so."

Meredith nodded. "Yes, you're probably right."

"And I can trust you not to tell anyone."

"Of course." She looked up at the clock. "And now I'm going to slip my little sleeping angel out of here so that you can get some much-needed rest."

"Oh, don't wake him."

"It's okay. He'll go to sleep again . . . as soon as we get home. And that way I can get a few things done too." Meredith hugged Anna. "And everything's going to be okay, isn't it?"

"Definitely. I know that God's in control of this," Anna said, partly to reassure Meri and partly to convince herself. "I really do have a sense of peace about it."

"Good. Just don't forget to call the doctor, okay? First thing on Monday."

Anna nodded. "It's as good as done."

"Because I need you, sis."

"I need you too."

13

|||||||||||||||||||

Michael made good on his promise to be home on Saturday night and even offered to take her out, but Anna told him she was too tired. She said that watching Jackson had worn her out, which was partially true. So they stayed home, eating leftover lasagna and watching an old movie. Anna had thought perhaps it would turn into a "romantic" evening, but Michael fell asleep in front of the TV, and Anna was so tired that she headed off to bed herself. But as she brushed her teeth, she realized that she'd never asked him about where he had been the previous evening when she'd attempted to deliver dinner. She had repressed her worries and had told herself that there was some logical explanation and that Michael would tell her all about it and they would laugh and that would be the end of it. But it hadn't happened.

As she turned back the comforter, noticing how Michael's side of the bed was empty, her mind began to churn. Where *had* he been? And what if something was wrong? Seriously wrong? What if he had fallen out of love with her? What if he was involved with someone else? What if he was cheating on her? The mere idea sliced through her like a jagged knife. She could endure a horrible terminal illness, even undergo painful and debilitating treatments for it, but she knew that losing Michael would hurt more than anything else could. In fact, she felt it would kill her. She fluffed the pillow and sighed. She was letting her mind run away with her. Surely Michael was not having an affair. She knew he loved her. She knew their love was the kind of love that only grew stronger over the years. And yet . . . how many other women had thought the same thing, only to be devastated when they learned the truth?

Finally, as she climbed into bed, she told herself she was being completely ridiculous. As Grandma Lily liked to say, she was making a mountain out of a molehill. She decided to simply push it from her mind. *Don't worry*, she reminded herself, *just pray*. And so, before she slipped off to sleep, she did pray.

Sunday passed uneventfully, and by the time they went to bed, Anna told herself that everything was just fine between them. Her suspicions about Michael—not that she called them that— were totally ungrounded. As always they were in love. And Anna couldn't wait to see his reaction when she presented his fabulous Christmas present this year. She was hoping and praying that the engine would arrive early and that David would help her to get the car to the mechanics and then parked in the driveway on Christmas morning. With a big red bow. It would be perfect.

The next day Anna called the doctor, scheduling a routine exam. "How about January 16?" the receptionist suggested.

"You don't have anything sooner?"

"Not unless it's urgent."

"The sixteenth is fine." Anna wrote it down, thanked her, and hung up. Hopefully Meredith would be so consumed with her own life and problems that she would forget to ask Anna about her appointment. Anna's plan now was to wait until the week after Christmas before she told Michael that they would need to get some health insurance in place. That was less than two weeks away. And she figured it would look better if they had the insurance for a few weeks before her doctor delivered the diagnosis. So perhaps the sixteenth was for the best anyway.

In the meantime, Anna planned to make the most of Christmas. She had shopping and baking to do and cards to send and packages to wrap, and she wanted to enjoy every bit of it—to lose herself in her efforts to make this the best Christmas ever. Anna remembered how her mother had loved Christmas and how she'd always strived to make things perfect. That's what Anna wanted this year. Still, she knew she needed to pace herself. And, like she'd promised herself earlier, she would keep her health at the forefront. She would try to eat healthier and get in a little exercise and plenty of rest.

⚬⚭⚬

On Wednesday, Anna studied her image in the mirror. She really did look like Mom. Not just her petite frame and prematurely gray hair, but the color of her eyes and the dark shadows beneath them, the structure of her cheekbones and the beginning signs of hollowness in her cheeks. This was how Mom had looked during the last year of her life. Still, Anna felt determined to fight. She might be dying, but she could do it gracefully. Couldn't she? For one thing, she hadn't had a proper haircut in ages. Lately she'd taken to pulling her shoulder-length hair back in a barrette. Unfortunately this only made her look older.

Anna found the envelope in which she was keeping the leftover money from the sale of her dishes. She pulled it out from her underwear drawer and counted the bills inside. She'd already paid for the engine, giving David the cash so he could use a charge card, which he seemed to appreciate since he was low on cash. And then she'd given him the amount to purchase a gift certificate from British Motors, which was also safe in her underwear drawer, along with the picture of the new engine. She still had a fair amount of money left, and some was already budgeted for gifts for her family. But she decided it would not only be acceptable to use some of it to improve her appearance, it would also be wise. Meredith had already guessed Anna's secret just by looking at her. How many others would begin to be suspicious? Besides that, Michael would probably appreciate her improved appearance.

Anna made an appointment for a "holiday mini-makeover" for Friday morning. She felt a flutter of excitement as she hung up the phone. That would be just six days before Christmas and just in time for the Christmas party that Grant and Suzy were hosting on Saturday night. And perhaps she'd even get something new to wear. Oh, wouldn't Michael be pleased when he saw her? In the meantime, she would finish the other holiday chores on her list— and make sure she got plenty of rest.

Meredith had called a couple of times during the week, but Anna had managed to "miss" those calls, and she'd managed to "forget" to return them. But on Friday morning, just as she was getting ready to leave for her mini-makeover, she saw her sister's white minivan pulling up in front of the house.

"Meredith," Anna called. "So good to see you. I'm on my way to an appointment right now, but maybe we could meet up later— are you off today?"

"Yes," Meri said as she came closer and peered into Anna's eyes. "Why haven't you returned my calls?"

"Oh . . . I've been so busy." Then Anna started rattling off a list of all the things she'd been doing.

"But you did see the doctor?"

"I made an appointment."

Meredith brightened. "Is that where you're going now?"

"Well, I am going to an appointment." Anna glanced away.

"To the doctor?"

"Not today." Anna smiled. "Today I'm having a holiday mini-makeover at La Bella. Hey, why don't you come along? Maybe they can squeeze you in."

"What about the doctor?"

"I made the appointment," Anna said. "But really, I have to run or I'll be late." She unlocked her car. "Sorry."

"Why don't we meet up for lunch?" Meredith suggested. "When will you be done?"

"Around one, I'm guessing."

"Okay, meet me at 1:30 at Renaldo's. It's just a block down from La Bella."

"Sounds great." Anna got in her car and wondered how she'd be able to get her sister off her case about the doctor appointment. Perhaps her best defense would be to fake it. Act as if she was feeling better. And, really, wasn't she? She'd managed to eat and hold down a whole bowl of oatmeal this morning. That was something.

"So what would you like to do?" Veronica asked as she turned Anna around in the chair to look at her reflection.

"I look pretty bad, don't I?"

"You look a little tired."

"Yes, that's the problem. I want to look healthy and happy and ready for some holiday fun."

Veronica laughed. "Don't we all? Well, do you trust me, Anna?"

Anna frowned slightly. "Well . . . yes. Although I have to draw the line at any hair color. I know the gray makes me look older, but my husband actually likes it."

Veronica fingered her hair. "I think it's kind of pretty. But how about if we gave it more sparkle—without using dye?"

"Sounds great."

"Okay." Veronica wrapped the black cape around Anna's shoulders. "Just relax and we'll see what miracles can happen."

Anna did relax. In fact, she closed her eyes and nearly went to sleep as Veronica and a young woman named Fawn took turns working on her. Veronica was in charge of hair, and Fawn gave Anna a facial and then applied makeup.

"Voilà," Fawn said as she spun Anna's chair around again. "Take a look at you."

Anna opened her eyes and peered at her reflection. "Wow, that really is like a miracle." Her hair was cut short and curling prettily around her face. And although the gray was still there, it did have a sparkle to it. She patted it to discover that it even felt good. "And the makeup," she said. "It looks so soft and natural. And yet it looks fantastic." She turned to Fawn. "But how will I accomplish this again?"

Fawn grinned and handed her a DVD. "That's part of our makeover package. We record what we did so you can do it again at home."

"Of course, you'll need the products," Veronica pointed out. She handed Anna a list. "Everything we used on you is available right here in the salon."

"Thank you," Anna said, looking back at her reflection again. "Really, I think I look ten years younger. Well, except for the gray."

"You look beautiful," Veronica said.

"Absolutely," Fawn agreed. "And that dusky violet on your eyes is stunning. If nothing else, I recommend you get that one."

"That and the hair product," Veronica said as she pointed to an item on the list. "See how your gray hair looks silvery and shimmers? Very pretty."

"And the lip color," Fawn added. "You have to get that too."

Anna laughed. "I might just have to get it all."

She thanked them and went over to see the products and review her list. Although it would've been fun to get all the products, her usual frugality kicked in when she saw the staggering total. So she limited herself to a hundred dollars' worth of beauty products. And to be fair, that was far more than she'd ever spent before. When it was all said and done, Anna knew it had been an extravagant morning, but she thought it was worth it. And she couldn't wait to see what her sister's reaction would be.

"Wow, Anna," Meredith said when they met in the foyer of Renaldo's. "You look fantastic."

Anna patted her hair as the hostess led them to a table. "I feel great too. Really, I wish you'd come with me. It was such fun."

"Maybe I'll make myself an appointment too." Meredith frowned now. "Well, not until after Christmas. Sometime before New Year's though."

"Meaning you have a date planned for New Year's?" As much as Anna didn't want to encourage Meri about this, and as much as she didn't want to hear any more about Cooper, Anna thought the question might distract her sister from pestering her about seeing the doctor.

252

"I might."

"So, you're still certain about this thing?"

"The way you say 'this thing,' Anna—it's like you're talking about polio . . . or cancer."

"I'm sorry," Anna said as the hostess filled their water glasses. "I'm trying to be understanding . . . really, I am." She waited for the hostess to leave. "But I still don't see how divorcing Todd is going to make you happy."

Meredith let out a long sigh and picked up her water glass. "That's because you are not me, Anna. If you had to live my life for just one day—twenty-four hours—you might get it."

"I suppose . . ."

"It's not easy living in a loveless marriage. It's even harder when you have a child together."

"But didn't you used to love Todd?" Anna peered at her sister.

"I don't even know. Sometimes I think I just married him because it seemed the thing to do. Everyone else was married. I was done with college." She shrugged. "Planning a wedding sounded like fun." She pointed a finger at Anna. "And you acted like it was so great."

"So great?"

"You know, getting married, having a wedding, possibly starting a family."

"You were talking about your biological clock then," Anna pointed out.

"I was only thirty." Meredith shook her head. "I think I was being influenced by you and your biological clock. I should've waited."

"But you were thirty-four when you had Jackson. Just how long would you have waited?"

"I don't know . . . long enough to have met Cooper, I guess."

Anna felt bad now, like maybe this was partially her fault. "How long have you known Cooper?"

"Three years."

"Oh . . ." Anna realized that was only a year less than Meredith had been married.

"I'm not trying to blame you," Meredith said.

Just then the waiter came to take their order, and Anna, thankful for the interruption, quickly perused the menu before settling on soup and salad. Somehow she ought to be able to get that down.

"I'd like the house dressing," she told him. "On the side."

"Certainly." Then he turned to take Meredith's order.

"How's Jackson doing?" Anna asked after the waiter left.

"He's fine. At the sitter's."

Anna wanted to question this but picked up a piece of bread instead. Then, taking her time, she pretended to butter it and slowly broke off a small piece and took a cautious bite. Bread wasn't usually a problem, but just sitting in the restaurant and smelling the various foods was making her feel a little queasy.

"How are you feeling?" Meri asked.

Anna looked up and smiled. "Great."

"Really?"

"Absolutely. I think all I needed was some rest. And my energy is coming back." She started listing off all the things she'd been doing this week, not mentioning the naps or occasional stomachaches.

"That's great," Meredith said. "I was starting to get worried when you didn't call."

"Sorry. I meant to, but it's funny how you can waste more time when you have it. I can hardly believe a whole week of Christmas break has gone by already."

"Or that there are only five more shopping days until Christmas."

"You're still shopping?"

"Not really, but I just heard that on the radio." Meredith buttered a piece of bread. "Hey, Todd mentioned seeing Michael on campus Wednesday night."

"Huh?" Anna frowned. "On campus?"

"Yeah. Todd had popped into the Night Owl to meet his brother, and—"

"The Night Owl?" Anna shook her head.

254

"Yeah, I thought that sounded kind of weird too. Why would Michael be on campus and hanging out at the Night Owl?"

"Michael was working Wednesday night," Anna pointed out. "Maybe Todd mistook someone else for him."

"No, he was certain it was Michael."

"Well, maybe he was meeting someone for something work related."

"At the Night Owl?"

"We used to go there for coffee sometimes," Anna said defensively. "It's not just a bar, you know. Lots of students hang out there."

"Yeah, but Michael's not a student."

"Well, maybe it wasn't Michael." Anna stopped talking as the waiter brought their food, but all she could think about was what her husband was doing at a college hangout on a Wednesday night when he was supposed to be working.

"Hey, I didn't mean to upset you," Meredith said as she forked into her Cobb salad.

"I'm not upset."

"I just thought it was weird."

Anna nodded and took a cautious taste of the pumpkin soup. Not bad.

"You guys aren't having problems, are you, Anna?"

"No, of course not."

Meredith pointed her fork accusingly at her. Anna wanted to remind her that it was bad manners to point eating utensils at others, but she didn't. "Anna, I remember you saying something about Michael having a midlife crisis once."

"Oh, I was probably just joking."

"You didn't seem like you were joking."

"Well . . ."

"And then, the other day, when I thought Michael was acting weird with me, you said if he was acting weird, it was probably toward you. What was up with that?"

"Nothing, Meredith." And then, in a last-ditch effort to distract her sister, Anna asked Meredith to tell her more about Cooper.

"I've been curious," she said. "What's he really like—and what makes you so attracted to him?"

Naturally this got Meredith going, and soon their lunches were eaten, or mostly, and suddenly Meri was urging Anna to check out a sale at a new boutique a couple of doors down. "I saw the sale sign, and the things I spotted in the window were totally amazing." She smiled at Anna. "And you look so hot with your new makeover, we really should get you something fun to wear for Christmas."

Anna admitted that she had been thinking the same thing, and before long she and Meri were in the boutique trying on all kinds of things.

"You have to get that," Meredith said as Anna modeled a garnet-colored dress. "It is so awesome on you—you look totally hot. Michael is going to have a meltdown when he sees you."

"But it's too expensive," Anna protested.

"It's 30 percent off," the saleswoman said.

"It's still too much," Anna said. Even with the reduction, this dress was still more than $150. And she'd already spent more than she planned with the makeover this morning.

"Fine! Just take it off then. Let's get out of here. I need to pick up Jackson now anyway."

Anna blinked, then returned to the dressing room where she carefully removed the pretty dress. It really was stunning—and surprisingly sexy too. But still it was too much. And yet she hated for Meri to be mad at her. Perhaps she could smooth it over.

"I'll find something at Ross," she whispered to her sister as she hung the dress back on the rack.

"The heck you will," Meri said as she snatched up the dress. "I'm getting this for you, Anna."

"No," Anna said as she chased Meredith to the cashier. "You can't. It's too much."

"No, it's not," Meredith said. Then she turned and actually smiled. "Merry early Christmas, Anna. Now don't look a gift horse in the mouth, okay?"

Anna didn't know what to say, but she also knew it would be

pointless to argue with her stubborn younger sister on this. Besides, it was incredibly sweet.

"Well, thank you very much," Anna said as Meredith handed her the sleek silver bag.

"You are very welcome. Now, promise me you'll wear it to the party tomorrow and knock everyone's socks off."

Anna laughed. "I promise you, I most certainly will."

Meri glanced at her watch. "Now I really do need to go pick up Jackson."

They hugged and parted ways, but Anna blinked back tears as she hurried to her car. She wasn't even sure what the source of the tears was this time. Was it Meredith's unexpected generosity? Anna's suppressed fear of cancer? Or was it the startling news that Michael had been seen hanging out with college kids on a night when he was supposedly working late? Anna could not think of one good reason why her husband would be at the Night Owl. But unfortunately she could think of some bad ones.

14

||||||||||||||||||||

"Okay," Meredith said on the phone. It had been just a couple hours since they'd parted ways downtown, but now Meri had a bee in her bonnet. "You managed to distract me from asking you the exact day and time of this mysterious doctor appointment, Anna. Now I demand to know." Anna muttered the date, and Meredith immediately went ballistic. "No way! You cannot wait that long. That's like a whole stinking month away. Do you know how fast cancer cells can grow in a month? Do you have any idea how much more can be done with early detection these days?"

"But we don't have insurance."

"I don't give a rip about that! Your life is worth more than that, Anna. You cannot wait that long. Do you understand?"

"I can't go in until we have insurance." Anna tried to sound patient, but she wanted to tell her sister to mind her own business.

"Then get insurance. Get it today."

"I don't think that's possible."

"Sure it is, you just pick up the phone and call. Lots of people do it. You just fill out the forms, let them take your blood pressure and some basic stuff like that. No big deal. Just do it, Anna."

"I can't."

"Why not?"

"I don't want Michael to know what's going on."

"Then don't tell him. Just get a policy for yourself."

"He doesn't live under a stone. He'll figure it out."

258

"Then just tell him. You'll have to sooner or later anyway."

"I don't want to spoil Christmas."

Now Meredith actually cussed. Anna hadn't heard her younger sister use bad language since they were teens. "Meri," she said in a shocked tone.

"I'm sorry. But you are making me mad. If you don't tell Michael, maybe I will."

"You will not!"

"Yes, I will." Meredith swore again. "And for all we know, Michael has some things he's not telling you, Anna. I mean, what if you're doing this heroic thing, trying to protect Michael, trying to give him some stupid perfect Christmas, and trying to save him a few bucks on insurance—and the whole while he's out there messing around."

"What do you mean?"

"I mean, the writing is on the wall, Anna. You said yourself you were concerned that he might be having a midlife crisis. He works overtime all the time . . . and then he's seen hanging out with college kids at the Night Owl. Use your head, sis."

"Why are you doing this to me, Meri?" Anna felt tears coming again.

"Because I love you. And I refuse to lose you like we lost Mom. You have to see the doctor."

"I will."

"But January 16 is too far out."

"What if I change the date?"

"What if you get insurance today?" Meri said. "And what if you make an appointment for Monday?"

Anna swallowed hard. She knew she couldn't do that. She wouldn't do that.

"Or what if I tell Michael?"

Anna was angry now. "I trusted you!"

"And I'm glad you did. Someone needs to watch out for you."

"Listen, Meredith." Anna's voice was steely calm. "If you tell Michael, I swear to you, I will tell Todd."

"You wouldn't."

"Do you want to try me?" Anna cleared her throat. "Imagine what a lovely Christmas we can all have with everyone hurt and mad and—"

"Fine! You win."

"So you won't tell Michael?"

"No. Christmas is less than a week away. But I swear to you, Anna, if you haven't told him by December 26, I will."

"Fine! And I'll do the same with Todd for you."

"You won't need to," Meredith said. "I'll tell him myself." And then she hung up.

Anna felt sick to her stomach again, but she knew it was probably as related to emotions as anything. And, to be fair, would she act any different toward Meredith if the tables were turned? What if Meri was sick and refusing to see a doctor? But Anna didn't want to think about that. All she wanted was some lukewarm, watered-down ginger ale and a nice long nap.

She had just fallen asleep when the phone rang again. This time it was Michael. "Hi, sweetie," he said.

"Hi."

"Did I wake you?"

"Yeah."

"Sorry about that. And you're probably going to guess what I'm about to tell you," he said.

"Working late again?"

"Yeah. But this will be the last night for a while."

She thought about the Night Owl but didn't say anything.

"Really," he said. "No more overtime until after Christmas."

"Right . . ."

"I'm sorry, really."

"That's okay. I'm pretty tired anyway . . . it's been a long day."

"We'll make up for it tomorrow night, okay? And don't forget it's Grant and Suzy's annual Christmas party."

"Yes . . . I remember." Anna looked at the pretty red dress hanging on the door of her closet and sighed.

The next day, Michael acted perfectly normal. Not only did he rave about her new haircut, but he fixed blueberry pancakes for breakfast as well. But as Anna picked at hers, she wondered if this was some sort of guilt offering. Then he cleaned up the breakfast things and took Huntley for a walk, which only seemed to prove her theory. Why else would he be so nice? Then, shortly after Michael left, her dad called.

"Is everything okay with you?" she asked. They'd already covered the perfunctory hellos, but she was worried now. Her dad didn't usually just call like this—straight out of the blue—without a reason.

"Yeah, sure, I'm fine," he told her. "I just had to run to town this morning—doing a little Christmas shopping for Donna, you know how that goes—and I thought maybe my oldest child would like to meet me for coffee."

"Meet you for coffee?" She tried not to sound too shocked, but this was so out of character for Dad. She hoped he was okay.

"Yeah. I thought we could meet at Hole in One, you know, get a donut and coffee . . . maybe you have some ideas for Donna's Christmas present. You know how I usually don't get it right."

"Well, sure, Dad. That sounds great. When were you thinking?"

"How about ten thirty?"

"Sounds great." She said good-bye and hung up, but as she got ready to go, she couldn't help but think this was very strange. And the most obvious reason for this unexpected coffee date had to be Dad's health. She wondered if he'd gotten some bad news . . . something he didn't want to tell Donna about. As she drove downtown, she braced herself. And, as she parked her car and walked over to the little donut shop, she realized that her dreams for "the best Christmas ever" were not only unrealistic, they were becoming downright impossible.

"Hey there, Anna," Dad said as she came into the donut shop. "Pretty cold out there, isn't it?"

She nodded and unbuttoned her coat. "Do you think it'll snow?"

"Maybe so." He tipped his head toward the glass case filled with pastries. "What will you have?"

Anna picked a plain cake donut and a cup of herbal tea, then they went to sit in a booth. "So, Dad, how's it going?"

He frowned slightly. "Well, I guess that's what I want to ask you."

"Me?"

"Yes, that's why I wanted to meet you today."

"But why? I mean, what do you want to ask me about?"

He shrugged as he wrapped his hands around the coffee mug. "How are you doing, Anna?"

She thought for a moment. "Okay."

"Well, that's not what I hear."

"Huh?" She peered curiously at her dad. His hair, cut in his regular crew-cut style, was completely white now, but his blue eyes still had a youthful twinkle. Except that right now they looked worried.

"I hear that you might have something you need to talk about . . . you know, to your old man."

"Who told you that?"

He pressed his lips together, lifting his brows slightly, as if to suggest he wasn't about to reveal his source.

"Has Meredith been talking to you?"

Again the same look.

"What has she told you, Dad?"

"She just said that I should talk to you."

"About?"

"She wasn't specific, Anna. But she acted like it was serious. She told me that a good parent would step in and do something. I think those were her exact words." But now he looked puzzled. "Problem is, I don't know exactly what I'm supposed to step in and do. You got any ideas?"

"Oh, Dad . . ." Anna sighed. "I think it's really sweet that you wanted to help, but trust me, there's nothing you can do for me. Okay?"

"If you say so." He took a slow sip of coffee, then looked curious again. "If you're sure you don't want to talk about it."

but he didn't question her words. He just sat there silently. And Anna wondered if he knew . . . if he suspected. Still, she was determined to keep her secret as long as possible. And she felt furious at Meredith for this lame attempt to spill the beans for her.

"Well, I think you've got Michael all wrong too," Dad said. "If anything ever happened to you, that man would be brokenhearted and beside himself with grief."

"You guys really stick together, don't you?"

"I'm just saying what I know is true."

Anna sighed. So many things that her father didn't understand . . . would probably never understand. She wanted to ask him if he would cry when she died, but she knew that would only complicate things more. Instead she asked him what he planned to get for Donna this year.

"Well, I was thinking about one of those diamond necklaces they keep advertising on TV. You know, the ones with three stones. Every time that ad comes on, I hear her sigh."

"It's an emotional advertisement, Dad. It's supposed to make you sigh."

"I know. But, just the same, I think she'd like one of those necklaces."

"You're probably right. I'm sure she'd love one."

"That settles it then." He grinned and picked up his ball cap. "Thanks for helping me to figure it out."

"Thanks for inviting me here for coffee." She grinned back at him. "Maybe we can do it again sometime."

"Maybe so."

Well, at least Dad's not dying, Anna thought as she returned to her car. Still, he could be a little dense about some things. But maybe that was good—probably some sort of protective device. Just the same, it was aggravating how easily he stood up for Michael. Like they were in some secret boys' club together—a wink and a handshake and everything's just fine. Her dad was a nice guy, but he really could qualify as the king of denial. Of course, Anna could probably win the crown for queen.

And since everyone seemed so deep into denial these days, maybe she'd just continue to play along. So she acted like everything was just fine all day. She and Michael went through their ordinary Saturday routines, and then, when it was time to get ready for the Christmas party, she took her time to apply the makeup just like the DVD showed her. She fixed her hair and then slipped into the garnet dress.

"Wow," Michael said when he saw her. "You look fantastic, Anna." He slipped his arms around her and pulled her close. "Maybe we should scrap that party and just spend the evening alone?"

She smiled. "Well, that'd be nice. Grant's own partner blowing off the Christmas party."

"Yeah, I guess that's a little rude." He bent down and kissed her, lingering in a way that suggested her suspicions about him were ludicrous. "But we could always come home early."

She laughed as they headed out the door. "Sure . . . why not?"

⚮

Grant and Suzy's parties were always the best. The tradition had started back when Grant and Michael were still at the marketing firm. It was probably due to Suzy's gift for entertaining combined with their lovely hillside home that looked out over the city—they were always the first pick for parties. Not that Anna minded, since their bungalow was pretty small. Plus she knew she didn't have the flare that Suzy did. And Grant and Suzy had a full bar, which always seemed to make a lot of people happy. Sometimes a little too happy, in Anna's opinion.

"You look stunning," Grant said as he handed Anna a glass of something red.

"What's this?" Anna watched as Michael was swept away by an older gentleman, probably a client.

"It's a sweet little cabernet that I thought would go nicely with your beautiful dress." He chuckled. "I know you're a lightweight when it comes to alcohol, but you can just carry it around and look pretty."

She laughed. Grant had not only a sharp artist's eye but a quirky sense of humor too. "Well, thank you. I'll try to wear it well."

"I'm still thinking about that lasagna you brought by the other night." He smacked his lips again. "I told Suzy that we'll have to weasel a dinner invite from you guys."

"Of course," she said. "Consider yourself invited. How about after Christmas though."

"Perfect."

"And you guys won't be so busy then."

"Busy?"

"Well, you've really been putting in a lot of hours these past few weeks."

"Oh." He looked uneasy. "Yes . . ."

"You have to admit, you guys have pulled a lot of late nights."

"It's not easy starting up a new business." Now he glanced across the room. "Speaking of which, here comes Thomas Sanders, one of our newest clients. I better go greet him and make him feel at home."

Anna watched as Grant cut through the crowded room. She could tell by his answer that something was wrong. And she decided to get to the bottom of it. She went to the kitchen to find Suzy speaking to one of the caterers about the crab cakes. "That last bunch wasn't even lukewarm," she told the woman. "They really need to be hot when you put them on the tray."

"Yes. We'll take care of it," the woman promised.

"Oh, Anna," Suzy said. "I haven't even had a chance to say hi to you tonight. You look so great. What have you done with your hair?"

Anna told her about La Bella and the holiday special.

"I think I'll give them a call."

"They're miracle workers."

"Well, you look gorgeous."

"I thought I needed to spruce up for Michael's sake," Anna said in a quiet voice, then chuckled. "You know, the guys have been putting in so many late nights, I thought I might need to compete with this new business."

Suzy's eyebrows lifted, but she just nodded. "Yes, it's been pretty demanding, but it sounds like things are really coming along well."

"Yes, Michael has assured me that he won't be putting in any more late nights after Christmas."

Suzy looked truly concerned now. She leaned forward and spoke quietly. "So, has Michael been working late a lot?"

Anna nodded. "Yes, about three nights a week. And sometimes on weekends too."

"Really?" Suzy's brow creased.

"Do you mean that Grant hasn't been?"

"Oh, he works late occasionally. But not three nights a week. I don't think I could stand for that."

"Especially with the demands of your job. I heard that you might be made partner at the law firm before next year."

Suzy smiled. "Well, I don't believe in counting my chickens too soon, but it is looking good."

Anna patted her on the back. "Congratulations. I'm sure you deserve it." Then Anna excused herself to the powder room, which she really did need to use. But once there, it took all of her self-control not to break into tears. Instead, she pulled out her cell phone and called her sister.

"Hey, what's up?" Meredith asked. "I thought maybe you weren't speaking to me."

"You mean after you set Dad on me today?"

"How'd that go?"

"I'll tell you later—" Anna's voice broke.

"What's wrong?"

"Just—just everything," she sobbed. Then she poured out all that she'd just learned and begged Meredith to come rescue her from the party.

"Sure," Meri said. "Jackson's already in bed and Todd is parked in front of the TV. I'll be right over."

"I'll meet you on the street," Anna said. "I think I can sneak out the back door."

"Okay. Give me ten minutes."

"Thanks."

15

||||||||||||||||||||

After making a smooth getaway, Anna reassured her sister that she would be fine at home by herself. And after she changed into her pajamas and calmed herself with a glass of warm milk, she wondered if she hadn't simply overreacted to everything. The truth was, she had no proof that Michael was cheating on her. Naturally Meredith assumed that was the only possible explanation. And Anna had to admit it didn't look good. But then Anna remembered Michael's tenderness toward her earlier that evening. The sweet way he'd walked her into the party.

Anna turned and looked at the clock. The party! It was after ten now, and Michael was probably looking for her. She grabbed the phone and called his cell. It wasn't turned on, but she left a message anyway.

"I'm sorry," she said. "But I got sick to my stomach at the party. I could see you were having a good time, so I called and asked Meri to pick me up. I'm at home now and feeling better. Please, don't worry about me and stay as long as you like. Bye." *There,* she thought, *that should smooth this over. At least for the time being.* She had no idea what she'd say to him tomorrow.

But tomorrow came, and Michael, other than being concerned for her health, seemed perfectly normal. But as they were driving home from church, his cell phone rang, and she listened as he talked. It sounded like he was talking to Grant, but she couldn't

268

be sure. And it sounded as if he was going to leave for a business trip, maybe even by tomorrow.

"Are you sure it can't wait until after Christmas?" he asked, then waited. "No, I understand. And no more than two days? You're positive?" He sighed. "Okay. No, it's fine. I don't mind." Now he chuckled. "Well, that would be great. Let's hope so." Then he closed his phone and slipped it back into his blazer pocket.

"Was that Grant?"

"Yes. We have a big account that we've been working on, and they're about to make up their mind. But Grant says if one of us doesn't go up to Seattle, we won't have a chance."

"Why doesn't he go?"

"It's Martha's Christmas ballet tomorrow night."

"Wow, they scheduled that pretty close to Christmas."

"You know how crazy schedules get. Anyway, he can't miss it."

"So you're going to Seattle?"

"Yes."

"Hey, maybe I could go too?"

He turned and glanced at her. "You could . . . but I'll mostly be in meetings. And airfare at this late notice, and during the holidays, well, it won't be cheap. Plus it'll be a madhouse at the airports. You really want to subject yourself to that?"

"I guess not."

"And you said you weren't feeling well last night. What if you're coming down with something? It'd be a drag to be sick for Christmas."

She sighed. "I suppose so . . ." Then she tried not to imagine some pretty college ingenue flying up to Seattle with him, snuggled together in the plane, holding hands, sharing a blanket. She tried not to think of some swanky city hotel and the cool restaurant where the two of them would sit, head to head, laughing about how they had pulled off this little holiday rendezvous. She knew she was being ridiculous.

As it turned out, Michael left that evening. That way he would be there first thing in the morning, ready to make his presentation and schmooze as needed. "I'll just leave the car at the airport," he had told her as he packed his bags. "It's only for two nights."

Two nights . . . what could happen in two nights? What had already happened? But she hadn't voiced these fears, she had simply nodded and said that it sounded like a good plan. But when he kissed her good-bye, she held back. He assumed it was because she felt left out, and he promised to make good when he came home on Tuesday night. "And don't forget," he reminded her. "You said this was going to be the best Christmas ever, Anna."

How could she forget? Those words would probably come back to haunt her for—for how long? Realistically, it probably would be only a matter of months . . . certainly not years. If anything, her longing for a perfect Christmas could haunt Michael for years. Who knew what his next Christmas would be like? But then again, perhaps it would be a relief for him. It would make everything so much simpler. He would be the sad widower. And Dad was right, Michael probably would cry. It would seem unnatural if he didn't. And he'd probably wait an appropriate amount of time before he remarried his new young love. She tried to imagine next Christmas. Meredith would probably be married to this mysterious Cooper by then. And Michael would probably bring his new girlfriend. How different things would be in just one year.

For two long days, Anna tormented herself with these thoughts. She also did all the things that she figured a wife who suspected her husband of cheating might do. She went through drawers and pockets, and checked bills and receipts and phone records. But really she didn't find anything very questionable. There seemed to be only two distinct possibilities: (1) Michael was an expert at hiding his trail, or (2) Michael was innocent. By Tuesday afternoon, she decided—after much prayer—to do her best to accept option two. She even planned a nice dinner for him—a welcome home. And while they ate dinner, she would confess to him all that she had heard and her concerns. And he, naturally, would explain everything. And then, somehow, they would make the most of Christmas.

Of course, by now her expectation level for the holiday had

diminished greatly. Despite the fact that snow was beginning to fly, she knew that this Christmas wouldn't be the perfect one she'd dreamed of. For one thing, the car engine had not arrived, and at this rate, she knew it was totally impossible to have it installed by Christmas even if it did get here. Still, she had her placeholder gift all ready for Michael. She'd found a very cool card with a picture on the front of an MG that looked a lot like his, and she'd put the gift certificate and the picture of the engine inside. And the mechanic was scheduled for the following week, and according to David, it was highly likely that the car would be running by New Year's Eve. That seemed the best she could do now. And, to be honest, there was a part of her that had ceased to care. And . . . she missed her dishes.

As Anna organized things for the dinner she planned to serve on Christmas for some of her family, including her neighbor Bernice, she longed for a fine set of china to serve it on. She tried not to imagine her elegant Meissen set on Loraine's table, and, although she knew it would look beautiful, she also knew she would feel jealous to see other people using it. And she knew it was immature and selfish, but she wished that china was still hers.

So what if it had been stored in crates. And so what if it didn't go with the style of their house . . . she had loved it anyway. And now she missed it desperately. Even so, she knew that it was worth the exchange. She knew she'd done the right thing. What good would those dishes be after she was gone anyway? No one but a person like Loraine would appreciate them like Anna had. And at least Michael would have his car—and hopefully some happy memories to go with it. Wasn't that worth it?

Anna set the table with her everyday dishes, which were actually very nice. She had everything ready to go for Michael's welcome-home dinner when she noticed the snow coming down harder now. She also noticed that Huntley was antsy, just like her second graders would be under the same circumstances. Her old beagle knew there was some exciting weather going on outside, and he needed to check it out. "You want to go for a walk?" she asked, and he wagged his tail. "Okay, just a quick one . . . long enough

271

for you to taste some snow." She put on her heavy coat, wrapped a scarf around her head and neck, and shoved her feet into her boots, and they were ready to go.

It really was beautiful out. The sky had a dusky purple cast to it, and the snowflakes illuminated in the streetlights were tumbling down. Huntley sniffed at the snow and even bit at some of the falling flakes, and Anna simply looked up in wonder. They really were going to have a white Christmas after all. Maybe she had given up too soon. Maybe this really was going to be the best Christmas ever. She walked along happily, admiring how ordinary things like cars and houses and trees took on a completely new and wonderful appearance with a fine white coat of snow. Maybe that was like forgiveness . . . or how love covered a multitude of sins. Maybe that's how she needed to see Michael tonight. Not that he had even sinned. She didn't know that for sure. And the more she thought about it, the less likely it seemed. Still, she decided as she walked back to the house, if he had sinned, she would choose to forgive him. Oh, definitely, she'd need God's help. But she would do her best to forgive him. And, really, she'd wanted to give him the best Christmas present ever . . . what could be better than forgiveness?

As she turned the corner to their house, she hoped that Michael's car would be parked out front. His flight should've gotten in by now. But the street was empty and white. She shook the snow off her coat and scarf and brushed it from Huntley's back, then went inside to see that the message light on the phone was flashing. She pushed the message button and listened.

"Anna," a crackly voice that sounded like Michael said. "I'm stuck at Sea-Tac right now. All the flights are delayed thanks to this winter storm. I'm trying to get out, but it's not looking good. I may be stuck in Seattle until morning. I'd call you on my cell, but it was dead when I got to the airport. I'll try to find an outlet to charge it. But this place is a madhouse. Just be thankful you're not here, sweetie. Talk to you later."

Later, when Anna didn't hear back from him, she tried to call his cell but only got his voicemail. So she told him she missed him and she loved him and to take care, and then she cried herself to sleep. She knew that she was being silly and melodramatic and that things would probably look much better in the morning, but she just couldn't help herself. It all seemed so hopeless. She wondered why she even tried. And when she attempted to pray, she felt like every ounce of faith had already been spent. It wasn't that she'd given up on God, but she just didn't have the energy or the words to hold on anymore. Hopefully he was holding on to her.

16

As it turned out, things did look better in the morning. Not only was the sun shining down on about four inches of crisp, white snow, but David called to announce that Michael's engine had arrived last night. "It's at British Motors right now," he told her. "Ron said that it's a beauty."

"Really?" she cried. "That's awesome."

"I was thinking that I could pick up the car when you guys are heading over to Dad's tonight."

"You don't mind?"

"No, I'm having fun with this. Besides, I'm earning my chance to take it out for a spin, right?"

"Of course."

"So, I thought I could drop Celeste at Dad and Donna's and then make an excuse to run some errand. By then you guys will be on your way, and Ron will meet me to trailer it up."

"He doesn't mind?"

"He thinks what you're doing is so cool, Anna. In fact, he can't wait to meet you."

"Really?"

"Yeah. Just make sure you leave the garage door unlocked, okay?"

"No problem. We never lock it anyway."

"Michael is going to be so jazzed."

"That is, if he gets home."

"Huh?"

She explained about the weather and cancellations.

"Oh, yeah, I heard the storm really messed with some West Coast flights."

"I haven't heard from him this morning," she said.

"Maybe that means he's on his way."

"Maybe . . ."

"Well, whenever he does get here, he's gonna love his Christmas present, Anna. You can count on that."

"I hope so."

When Michael finally did call, it was past noon. "It looks like the flight is going to go," he told her. "I would've called you sooner, but I wanted to wait until I was sure. We've been sitting on this plane since 8:30."

"You're kidding."

"Nope. And it's getting old. But I should be home around three . . . well, maybe four by the time I get out of the airport."

"Dad's expecting everyone at six."

"I'm looking forward to it."

"I love you, Michael," she said, feeling a little uncertain . . . as if he might not feel the same way about her anymore.

"I love you too, Anna. I can't wait to wish you Merry Christmas."

"Me too. Fly safely."

Anna hung up and, as usual, whispered a prayer for his safe return home. That struck her as slightly ironic, because she'd always been the one to fret over airline safety, worrying that his flight would go down and she would lose him. She was always on pins and needles when he traveled, particularly if it was a cross-country flight. How many times had she endured the anxiety of Michael being taken from her? How many times had she prayed? And now everything felt different. He would be the one left to deal with losing her.

Anna distracted herself by getting things ready for the Christmas dinner tomorrow. She lined up the dry ingredients for turkey dressing—all ready to go. She even made the Jell-O salad that her dad so loved but everyone else made jokes about. Then, with the kitchen prepped for tomorrow, she busied herself by bagging and boxing the Christmas presents she'd gotten for her family, pausing to examine her meticulously wrapped gifts, knowing full well that the pretty packages would simply be torn open, the paper and ribbons tossed aside. But she had enjoyed putting them together, carefully choosing the type of wrapping paper that suited each member of her family. In her mind, the gifts were perfect—inside and out. She just hoped her relatives would appreciate them.

Then she put on her parka and loaded everything into her car. It took several trips, and each time she went out, Huntley gave her that look—that "why can't I go outside too?" look. "Later," she told him. "I'm sure your papa will take you out." This way she felt assured that, even if Michael got home in the nick of time, everything would be ready to go. The main thing was to get out of there before David and Ron came to pick up the car.

Finally, she put the finishing touches on the enormous fruit salad she was taking for tonight's buffet and put together an attractive plate of homemade cookies to share with Dad and Donna. She'd already taken cookie plates to her neighbors, including Bernice across the street, reminding her that they expected her to join them for Christmas Day tomorrow. Bernice had promised to "be there with bells on."

Michael made it home just in time to dump his bags, grab a shower, and make some quick phone calls, which she hoped were business related but couldn't be certain, since she couldn't hear him as he talked on his cell phone in the bathroom. *Stop being so suspicious*, she told herself as she fed Huntley and filled his water dish, promising him a walk tomorrow morning. Then she gave him a new rawhide bone. "Merry Christmas, old boy," she said as she scratched him behind the ear.

"Ready to go?" Michael said.

"Yes, I already loaded everything in my car."

"Such a smart woman." Then he hugged and kissed her in such a way that she felt certain that her suspicions about another woman must be wrong. Either that or her husband deserved an Oscar for his performance.

She handed him her car keys. "Want to drive?"

"Sure. That snow's getting pretty messy in town. I actually slid coming off Arbor Drive. After that I slowed down."

Anna glanced down their street as Michael pulled out. She wondered if David and Ron might be lurking around the corner just waiting for them to go. She also wondered how Michael would react when he found out that it was just a matter of days before his beloved MG was up and running. Suddenly the old excitement of pulling off a great Christmas grabbed her again. She felt like she was about six years old and waiting for Santa to arrive.

"This is so beautiful out here," she gushed as he drove through their neighborhood. "I love snow."

"I do too—at least I do right now. I wasn't too crazy about it when I was stuck in Sea-Tac."

"I guess it was a good thing I didn't go with you after all. Hey, how did your presentation go?"

He grinned. "Pretty well, I think. We won't know until after Christmas. But if we get this account, Anna . . . well, things are really going to change for us."

She nodded. "That's great." Unfortunately the things that she expected to change wouldn't be good things. But Anna didn't want to think about that tonight. She wasn't going to let anything ruin this Christmas.

"You're here!" Donna said as Anna and Michael came into the house loaded down with packages.

"Not that it matters," Celeste said. "Since everyone else isn't."

"Who's not here?" Anna asked as she handed a bag to Donna and peeled off her coat.

"Your brother," Celeste said. "He just dumped me and took off."

Anna patted Celeste's shoulder. "Sorry about that. But how are you doing? How's baby?"

Celeste brightened. "I'm okay, considering. And I finally got some real maternity clothes." She held out her hands to model a form-fitting pale pink maternity top, sticking out her tiny tummy. "See?"

"Pretty."

"And your dad's been missing in action for the past hour," Donna said. "He said he had some last-minute errands to do, but I thought he'd be back by now."

"Well, it is Christmas," Michael said, winking at Donna. "You know how those last-minute errands can be."

"Yeah, he probably forgot to get you a present," Celeste teased.

Donna's face fell. "Oh, good grief," she said. "Surely he's not out there trying to shop tonight."

"I don't think so . . ." Anna said. "And I happen to know a little something about it."

Donna smiled. "Well, sometimes I think we make too much about gifts at Christmastime. One of these years I'm going to call a Christmas truce—no gift exchanging—period."

"Well, not this year," Michael said as he set a bag of gifts beneath the tree.

"Hey, where's Meri?" Anna asked, looking around.

"They're running late," Donna said, "but the grandmas are in the living room watching *White Christmas*."

Celeste feigned a yawn, patting her mouth for drama.

"Need any help in the kitchen?" Anna said, although she happened to like that movie.

"Sure," Donna said. "I never refuse an offer of help."

"Guess I'll go keep the grandmas company," Celeste said.

"And I'll finish unloading the car," Michael said.

Anna chatted with Donna as they worked together in the kitchen. Then the phone rang. "That's probably your dad," Donna said as she picked it up. "Oh, hi, David. What's up? Oh, you want to speak to Anna? Sure. She's right here." She handed the receiver to Anna with a curious expression.

"Anna?" David said. *"Where is the car?"*

"Huh?"

"The MG? Where is it?"

"In the garage, like I said."

"We're *in* the garage right now. The car is not here, Anna."

"What do you mean?"

"I mean *it's not here*. I'm telling you the car is gone."

"It can't be gone." Anna felt sick to her stomach again. She sat down on a stool and tried to understand what was happening. "It has to be there, David."

"Well, it's not. The dustcover is folded neatly in the corner, almost like the car resurrected itself and flew off to car heaven."

"Very funny."

"Do you think someone stole it?"

"Well, we don't lock the door. But the car doesn't run. It's not like anyone could hot-wire it and zip off. We were never worried about thieves."

"Well, you can be worried now."

"This is a total catastrophe."

"I know. So what do I do now?"

"I guess there's nothing you can do, David." Anna sighed. "Just tell Ron I'm sorry to have wasted his time and get yourself back here. After all, it is still Christmas."

"I know, but the car and the engine and what about the—"

"Just let it go for now."

"Okay."

Then Anna hung up and turned to Donna, who now looked extremely curious. "Everything okay?"

Anna just shook her head. "Not exactly."

"Is David having some kind of car troubles?"

"Not exactly," she said again. "More like I'm having car troubles. But I'll explain it all to you later. Okay?" Then Anna went out to speak to Michael, but to her surprise he didn't seem to be around. And when she looked outside, her car was gone too. "Where'd my hubby go?" she asked Celeste.

Celeste just shrugged. "He said he needed to pick up some ice cream."

"Ice cream?"

"Yeah. If you ask me, all these guys are nuttier than Grandma Lily's fruitcake."

"You don't like my fruitcake?" Grandma Lily asked.

Celeste patted her hand. "Of course I do. After all, you spike it with rum, don't you?"

Giving up on Michael, Anna returned to the kitchen to help Donna. And as they worked, she relieved Donna's curiosity by explaining about Michael's MG and her grand plan to give him the best Christmas gift ever. "Please don't tell anyone though. Not yet anyway," she said. "Not until we figure this out."

"So you really don't know where the car went?" Donna asked.

"No, I don't have a clue. Hopefully it's not stolen. Who would steal a car that doesn't even run?"

"When did you last see the car?"

Anna shrugged. "Goodness, I don't know. I hardly ever go out to the garage."

"Poor Michael."

"Yes, not only does this ruin his present, but he's also out a very sweet car. He loved that car, Donna."

"Are you going to tell him tonight?"

"I don't know. Maybe not until we get home, or maybe even not until after Christmas. No need to spoil his evening. He was in such good spirits. Although I don't know why he went out to get ice cream like that."

"Maybe he's having a rendezvous with your dad." Donna shook her head. "I can't figure out what got into Kenneth, taking off like that."

"Yeah, and I thought Dad said we were eating at six o'clock sharp." She pointed to the clock.

"He did." Donna frowned. "And it's nearly seven. But I can't get mad just at your dad. Not with most of the menfolk AWOL right now."

"Well, it sounds like Meri and Todd just got here," Anna said. "I can hear Jackson running down the hallway."

Donna glanced out the kitchen window. "Oh, good. And that looks like your dad's pickup pulling up right now."

Before long, all the missing players were present and accounted for, and after Dad said a sweet Christmas blessing, they all lined up for the buffet dinner.

"This looks totally great, Donna," Meredith said as she took a generous serving of mashed potatoes. "Thanks for going to all this effort."

"Yeah," Michael said. "After scrounging on airport food for twenty-four hours, I can't wait to sink my teeth into a slice of that ham."

"Did you really spend the night in the airport?" David asked.

"I did."

"Seriously?" Meri said. "What did you do? Sleep on the floor?"

"Yuck," Celeste said. "Can you imagine the cooties?"

"The airlines actually brought us some of those flimsy blankets and pillows." Michael laughed. "Like that made everything so much better."

"You must be exhausted," Todd said.

"I'm looking forward to my own bed tonight." Michael winked at Anna, but at the same time, Anna felt Meredith jabbing her with her fork. Anna glared at her sister, but Meri just smirked like she still thought Michael was guilty.

Anna felt torn as the evening wore on. On one hand, she had no desire to break the news of the missing car to Michael. But on the other hand, she felt totally drained. Her last hope of making this Christmas special seemed to have totally evaporated with David's phone call. She knew that Christmas should be about more than just giving gifts. But she couldn't believe that she'd sacrificed Great-Gran's Meissen china for—for what? An expensive engine that was no longer needed and a gift certificate that could never be used? Or perhaps Michael's car wasn't gone for good. Maybe Michael had sent it out for something—like a new paint job? Oh, she knew that was ridiculous. But she wasn't quite ready to give up. Not yet.

Finally, the food was eaten or put away, the packages had been opened with wrappings still strewn all over the floor, polite thank-yous had been exchanged whether or not they were sincere, old familiar carols had been sung with gusto while Donna played the piano, and eventually everyone seemed ready to call it a night.

"Your house tomorrow," Donna said to Anna and Michael as she handed them their coats.

"Two o'clock sharp," Michael said in a cheerful voice, and then the two of them wished everyone Merry Christmas and stepped outside into the winter wonderland. Michael slipped an arm around Anna's waist as they went down the snow-cleared walk to the car. "Just to keep you safe," he said as he drew her closer. Then he opened the passenger door, but before he released her, he bent over and kissed her soundly. "Merry Christmas, sweetie."

"Merry Christmas to you too," she murmured back.

Then once they were both in the car he started humming "Jingle Bells."

"You're certainly in a good mood," she said, knowing full well that she would ruin his happy spirits once she informed him of the missing MG.

"I certainly am."

"Is it just Christmas in general?"

"Maybe . . ." He turned and grinned at her. "Or maybe it's because I have a special Christmas present waiting for you at home."

She tried to look pleased with this announcement, but all she could think of was that she had nothing for him. Nothing he would want anyway. Nothing but a mess she still had to unravel. Could engines be returned?

When they got home, Michael told her she had to close her eyes as they went into the house, so she complied. Then he walked her through the living room, until they finally stopped in what she knew must be the dining room. "Okay to look now," he said. "Merry Christmas, Anna!"

She opened her eyes and was stunned to see a gorgeous set of dining room furniture in front of her. A long, rectangular table with eight marvelous chairs. "Oh, Michael," she gushed as she ran a hand over the smooth surface of the table. "It's Craftsman style . . . and it's absolutely perfect."

"It's Stickley."

"No way!"

"The table and chairs anyway." He nodded over to a china cabinet that was against the wall. "That's not."

"Oh!" she cried. "I didn't even see that. Oh, it's so beautiful. But how can we afford these pieces? They must've cost a fortune, and we promised not to go into more debt."

"No new debt has been incurred, my love."

"Did you win some lottery then?"

"Nope." He grinned even bigger.

"Oh, Michael, it's all so beautiful. I don't know what to say." She threw her arms around him and broke into tears.

"Well, don't cry, sweetie. Or are those tears of happiness?"

"I'm just so shocked. How could you possibly afford this?"

"Well, I couldn't afford the whole set. I figured out a way to pay for the table and chairs after I found them at Emery's Fine Furniture—but it was the china cabinet that I really wanted, and it was a small fortune. But remember how I've always wanted to learn woodworking?"

She nodded, wiping tears from her cheeks with the backs of her hands.

"Well, there was a night class at the college last semester. I signed up, and the next thing you know, I was building this Craftsman-style china cabinet."

Anna felt dizzy now, like the dining room was starting to spin. She sat down in a chair and stared up at the magnificent cabinet. "You built this?"

He smiled proudly. "I did. With the help of a master. Joe Farns-worth."

"I've heard of him."

"He taught the class and really helped me a lot with my project. But I didn't want you to know what I was up to, so I kept pretending to be working late. I hated lying to you, Anna, but I wanted this to be a surprise."

She nodded, taking in a deep breath. "It's a huge surprise. And I love it. But I have to know . . . how *did* you pay for everything?"

He shrugged. "Well, you know, the old MG was just sitting there in the garage and—"

"No way!" Anna shot to her feet. "You sold your car?"

"I didn't think you'd mind. I mean, it was just gathering dust and—"

"No!" Anna waved her hand in front of him, trying to stop his words.

"What's wrong?"

"Just a minute," she told him, turning to dash to the bedroom. "Let me get your present for you now." Within seconds, she returned with her envelope, waiting with a pounding heart as he opened it . . . watching as he examined the card, the photo, the gift certificate . . . and seeing realization set in.

He looked at her with a creased forehead and misty eyes. "Anna, Anna . . . what did you do?"

"I bought you an engine," she said. And suddenly she was starting to chuckle. "And I was going to get it put in your car." She giggled a bit more as she pointed to the gift certificate. "And I wanted it all done by Christmas, but it didn't work out. Then David came over here this evening to get the car, and—" She burst out into loud laughter now. "And it wasn't here! He called me at Dad's and we were both so upset and I thought it had been stolen and it's—you—you sold it!" She realized she probably sounded hysterical as she continued to laugh. But Michael just gathered her up into his arms.

"I can't believe you," he said softly. "But I have a question for you now. We promised no more debt, Anna. How could you possibly pay for an engine as well as this gift certificate?"

"My china," she whispered, glancing at the empty cabinet. "I sold it."

"You sold it?" Michael held her back and stared down at her.

284

"But you loved that china. It was Great-Gran's. It's the reason I made you the china cabinet."

She nodded. "I know, I know. But I love you way more than the china, Michael. I did it for you."

"I cannot believe how blessed I am," he said as he wrapped an arm around her waist.

She looked up at the beautiful cabinet again and sighed. "I can't believe you made that for me, Michael." She thought of all her suspicions and felt terrible. How could she have been so wrong? How she had misjudged him. And the whole time he was doing this for her.

Michael shook his head. "I can't believe you have no beautiful china to put inside of it now."

"I'm sorry."

"You should've seen your dad and me running all over the house, searching for your china. I was fit to be tied."

"Dad was in on this?"

"Yep. He helped to get the stuff delivered here, and then I sneaked over to make sure it was all set up okay. I wanted to get some of your china out and put it in the cabinet and on the table, but when I couldn't find it, I figured you must've stored it somewhere. I never dreamed you'd sold it."

"Merry Christmas, Michael."

"Merry Christmas, darling." And then they kissed and they kissed some more. And by the time they said good night a couple of hours later, Anna thought that perhaps this really had been the best Christmas ever.

17

Anna woke to the sound of someone ringing the doorbell—again and again as if their finger was stuck. She glanced at the clock to see that it wasn't even seven yet. And wasn't this a holiday? What was going on?

"Who's that?" Michael said groggily.

"Santa?"

"I'll go see."

Michael took off, and Anna grabbed up her bathrobe, suddenly worried that something might be wrong. Who would possibly be ringing their doorbell at this hour, and on Christmas Day, unless something was terribly wrong?

"Anna," Michael called. "Your sister's here."

"Coming," Anna said. She prepared herself for the worst now. Had Meredith already told Todd the bad news about wanting a divorce? Had Todd gone into a rage and thrown her and Jackson out? What was happening? But when Anna got to the living room, it was only Meri standing there, still wearing her pajamas beneath her ski parka, along with a big grin.

"Meri?" Anna stared at her. "What's going on?"

Meredith held out a plain brown paper bag. "Merry Christmas, Anna banana."

"Huh?" Anna wanted to ask her sister if she'd lost her mind or taken up drinking recently.

"Just a little something for you." Meri winked at her now.

"What?" Michael said, peering to see what was inside of the bag. "Oh, Meri," he said. "That is in totally bad taste. What on earth are you think—"

"It's for Anna, not you." Meredith held the bag toward Anna. "Here, Anna."

So Anna stepped forward, took the bag from her, and looked inside. "Meredith!"

"Let me explain. I just got this—"

"If you think this is funny, it is not." Anna pulled out an all-too-familiar-looking EPT box—the same brand of pregnancy testing kit that she had used while they underwent all those fertility treatments. "This is just plain mean, Meri."

"Seriously, Meredith," Michael said. "You've pulled some stunts in your—"

"Let me explain!"

"Fine," Michael said. "Explain."

Meredith tossed Anna a glance, then stuck her chin out and began. "Anna thinks she has ovarian cancer, Michael."

Michael turned to look at Anna with a shocked expression. "Is that true?"

"I don't actually know . . . I mean, I haven't been to the doctor yet."

"Why not?" He went to her now, put his arm around her shoulders.

"We don't have insurance."

"That doesn't matter. I mean, this is serious. What about your mom?"

"Exactly," Meredith said. "That's what I told her."

"I have an appointment," Anna said weakly.

"Well, never mind for now," Meredith said. "Let me explain the kit. I got to thinking, Anna. All the symptoms of ovarian cancer are very similar to pregnancy symptoms—"

"No, Meri," Anna said. "That's not it. I've been pregnant before, and I never felt like this. These are real symptoms and—"

"Wait a minute, will you?" Meredith stood in front of Anna now. "I've been pregnant too, Anna. Remember? And when I got pregnant, I thought I had ovarian cancer at first. I never told you, but I had quite a scare."

"Really?" Anna peered curiously at her. "But my—my last pregnancy . . ." Anna tried to remember. "I never got sick or anything. I felt fine the whole time."

"Every pregnancy is different, Anna."

"I know, but—"

"Think about it, Anna. Feeling bloated, having stomach problems, needing to use the bathroom frequently . . . that's how lots of pregnant women feel."

"But I already took a home pregnancy test, and—"

"When?"

"It doesn't matter. It was negative, Meri."

"Maybe you did something wrong, or maybe it was defective."

Anna considered this. "It was an old kit . . ."

"And I'll bet you only tried it once."

"Yes, but—"

"Okay, Anna, here's what pushed me over the edge. Remember when we were trying on dresses at the boutique?" She pointed her finger at Michael now. "Wasn't Anna something in that red dress?"

He nodded. "Yeah. She looked fantastic."

"Exactly! Now, I don't mean to pick on you, Anna. But you've never been terribly well-endowed in the bosom area, and you were like popping out of—"

"Oh my gosh!" Anna screamed, looking down at her fuller-than-usual chest.

Meredith tapped her finger on the box. "Please, Anna. Just go try it. Really, what could it hurt?"

"Besides one more disappointment," Michael said as he pulled Anna closer to him. "You don't have to if you don't want to, sweetie."

"But what if Meri is right?" Anna said. "I mean, she makes a good point."

"Come on," Meredith yelled as she pulled Anna by the arm and off toward the bathroom. "What are you waiting for?"

"Okay, okay." Anna felt a rush of excitement combined with a heavy sense of foreboding. "But let me do it alone, okay?"

"Okay. Just do it."

So Anna went into the bathroom and performed the task as she had so many times before. And, as she waited for the results, she prayed. She didn't ask for a miracle, she simply asked for God's will. And when she checked the testing stick, it was positive. She stared at it in disbelief, then realized there were two more tests in the box, so she decided to try it again. Maybe she'd done something wrong the first time. But the second time showed the same result. Still, she wanted to be certain.

"Everything okay in there?" Meri called.

"Don't bug her," Michael said. "She knows what she's doing."

Without answering, Anna did the test a third time. As she waited she could hear Meri and Michael talking. He was telling her about their strange gift exchange. And finally the third test was done, and it too was positive. She burst out of the bathroom door, running toward them. "Merry Christmas!" she cried. Then she threw her arms around both of them at the same time.

"Are you?" Michael's eyes grew wide.

"I did the test three times," she said. "Just to be sure."

"And?" Meredith grabbed Anna's hand.

"*I am pregnant!*" she cried. "Merry Christmas!"

And the three of them sang and danced and shouted so loudly that Anna was worried that the neighbors might actually complain. But she didn't even care. Because this truly was, without a doubt, the best Christmas ever!

The Gift of the Magi

The magi, as you know, were wise men—wonderfully wise men—who brought gifts to the Babe in the manger. They invented the art of giving Christmas presents. Being wise, their gifts were no doubt wise ones, possibly bearing the privilege of exchange in case of duplication. And here I have lamely related to you the uneventful chronicle of two foolish children in a flat who most unwisely sacrificed for each other the greatest treasures of their house. But in a last word to the wise of these days let it be said that of all who give gifts these two were the wisest. Of all who give and receive gifts, such as they are wisest. Everywhere they are wisest. They are the magi.

O. Henry

The
CHRISTMAS
DOG

1

|||||||||||||||

As Betty Kowalski drove home from church on Sunday, she realized she was guilty of two sins. First of all, she felt envious—perhaps even lustful—of Marsha Deerwood's new leather jacket. But, in Betty's defense, the coat was exquisite. A three-quarter-length jacket, it was beautifully cut, constructed of a dove-gray lambskin, and softer than homemade butter. Betty knew this for a fact since she had touched the sleeve of Marsha's jacket and audibly sighed just as Pastor Gordon had invited the congregation to rise and bow their heads in prayer.

"It's an early anniversary present from Jim," Marsha had whispered after the pastor proclaimed a hearty "Amen." As usual, the two old friends sat together in the third pew from the front. On Marsha's other side, next to the aisle so he could help with the collection plates, sat Marsha's husband, James Deerwood, a recently retired physician and respected member of the congregation.

Naturally Betty didn't show even the slightest sign of jealousy. Years of practice made this small performance no great challenge. Instead, Betty simply smiled, complimented Marsha on the lovely garment, and pretended not to notice the worn cuffs of her own winter coat, a charcoal-colored Harris Tweed that had served her well for several decades now. Still, it was classic and timeless, and a new silk scarf or a pair of sleek leather gloves might dress it up a bit. Not that she could afford such little luxuries right now. Besides, she did not care to dwell on such superficialities (especially during the service). Nor would she want anyone to suspect how thoughts such as these distracted her while Pastor Gordon preached with such fiery intensity about the necessity of loving one's neighbors today. He even pounded his fist on the pulpit a couple of times, something the congregation rarely witnessed in their small, dignified church.

But now, as Betty drove her old car toward her neighborhood, she was mindful of Pastor Gordon's words. And thus she became cognizant of her second sin. Not only did Betty *not* love her neighbor, she was afraid that she hated him wholeheartedly. But then again, she reminded herself, it wasn't as if Jack Jones lived *right* next to her. He wasn't her *next-door* neighbor. Not that it made much difference, since only a decrepit cedar fence separated their backyards. It was, in fact, that rotten old fence that had started their dispute in the first place.

"This fence is encroaching on my property," Jack had said to her in October. She'd been peacefully minding her own business, enjoying the crisp sunny day as she raked leaves in her backyard.

"What do you mean?" She set her bamboo rake aside and went over to hear him better, which wasn't easy since his music, as usual, was blaring.

"I mean I've studied the property lines in our neighborhood, and that fence is at least eight feet into my yard," he said.

"That fence is on your property line, fair and square." She looked him straight in the eyes. "It's the public access strip that's—"

"No way!" He pointed toward the neighboring yards where the public access strip had been split right down the middle. "See what I mean? Your yard has encroached over the whole public access strip and—"

"Excuse me," she said, shaking her finger at him like he was in grade school. "But the original owners agreed to build that fence right where it is. No one has encroached on anyone."

He rubbed his hand through his straggly dark hair, jutted out his unshaved chin, narrowed his eyes. "It's over the line, lady."

Betty did not like being called "lady." But instead of losing her temper, she pressed her lips together tightly and mentally counted to ten.

"And it's falling down," he added.

"Well," she retorted, "since it's on your property, I suggest you fix it." As she turned and walked away, she felt certain that he increased the volume on his music just to spite her. It seemed clear the battle lines were drawn.

Fortunately, the weather turned cold after that. Consequently, Betty no longer cared to spend time in her backyard, and her windows remained tightly closed to shut out Jack's noise and music.

Now Betty tightened her grip on the steering wheel, keeping her gaze straight ahead as she drove down Persimmon Lane, the street on which Jack lived. She did not want that insufferable young man to observe her looking his way. Although it was hard *not* to stare at the run-down house with the filthy red pickup truck parked right on the front lawn. Obviously, the old vehicle couldn't be parked in the driveway. That space was buried in a mountain of junk covered with ugly blue tarps, which were anchored with old plastic milk bottles. She assumed the bottles were filled with dirty water, although another neighbor (who suspected their young neighbor was up to no good) had suggested the mysterious brown liquid in the containers might be a toxic chemical used in the manufacturing of some kind of illegal drugs.

Betty sighed and continued her attempt to avert her gaze as she slowed down for the intersection of her street, Nutmeg Lane. But despite her resolve, she glanced sideways and let out a loud groan. Oh, to think that the Spencer house had once been the prettiest home in the neighborhood!

As she turned the corner, she remembered how that house used to look. For years it had been painted a lovely sky blue with clean white trim, and the weed-free lawn had always been neatly cut and perfectly edged. The flower beds had bloomed profusely with annuals and perennials, and Gladys Spencer's roses had even won prizes at the county fair. Who ever would've guessed it would come to this?

The original owners, Al and Gladys Spencer, had taken great pride in their home. And they had been excellent neighbors and wonderful friends for decades. But over the past five years, the elderly couple had suffered a variety of serious health problems. Gladys had gone into a nursing home, then Al had followed her, and eventually they both passed away within months of each other. The house had sat vacant for a few years.

Then, out of the blue, this Jack character had shown up and taken over. Without saying a word to anyone, he began tearing into the house as if he was intent on destroying it. And even when well-meaning neighbors tried to meet him or find out who he was, he made it perfectly clear that he had absolutely no interest in speaking to any of them. He was a rude young man and didn't care who knew it.

As Betty pulled into her own driveway, she wondered not for the first time if Jack Jones actually owned that house. No one had ever seen a For Sale sign go up. And no one had witnessed a moving van arrive. Her secret suspicion was that Jack Jones was a squatter.

It had been late last summer when this obnoxious upstart took occupancy of the house, and according to Penny Horton, the retired schoolteacher who lived next door, the scruffy character had brought only a duffle bag and three large plastic crates with him. But the next day, without so much as a howdy-do, he began tearing the house apart. Penny, who was currently in Costa Rica, was the one who informed Betty of the young man's name, and only because she discovered a piece of his mail that had been delivered mistakenly to her mailbox. "It looked like something official," Penny had confided to Betty. "It seemed to be from the government. Do you suppose he's in the witness protection program?" *Or perhaps he's out on parole,* Betty had wanted to suggest, but had kept these thoughts to herself.

Out of concern, Betty had attempted to reach the Spencers' daughter, Donna, by calling the old number that was still in her little blue address book. But apparently that number had been changed, and the man who answered the phone had never heard of anyone by that name. Even when Betty called information, citing the last town she knew Donna had lived in, she came up empty-handed. So she gave up.

Betty frowned as she bent to open her old garage door. The wind was blowing bitter and cold now, and she had forgotten her wool gloves in the car but didn't want to go back for them. She didn't usually park in the garage, but the weatherman had predicted unusually low temperatures, and her car's battery was getting old. She gripped the cold metal handle on the single-car garage door and, not for the first time, longed for a garage-door opener—like the one Marsha and Jim had on their triple-car garage. One simply pushed the remote's button and the door magically went up, and once the car was inside, down the door went again. How she wished for one now.

Her grandmother's old saying went through her head as she struggled to hoist up the stubborn door. "If wishes were fishes, we'd all have a fry." Oh, yes, wouldn't she!

Betty shivered as she got back into her car. She still couldn't get that obnoxious neighbor out of her head—all thanks to this morning's sermon! But what was she supposed to do? How could she love someone so despicable? How was it even possible? Oh, she'd heard that with God all things were possible . . . but this?

She decided to commit the dilemma to prayer. She bowed her head until it thumped the top of the steering wheel, asking God to help her love her loathsome neighbor and to give her the strength she lacked. "Amen," she said. Then she tried to focus her full attention on carefully navigating her old Buick forward into the snug garage, although she was still thinking about that thoughtless Jack Jones—if that was his real name.

The next thing she knew, she heard a loud scratching sound and realized she'd gotten too close to the right side of the garage door. She took in a sharp breath and quickly backed up, readjusted the wheel, and went forward again, but when she turned off her engine, she knew it was too late. The damage was done. And, really, wasn't this also Jack Jones's fault? He was a bad egg—and had probably been one from the very beginning.

As Betty sat there, unwilling to get out and see what the scrape on her car looked like, she replayed the man's list of faults. And they were many. Right from the start, he'd stepped on people's toes. With absolutely no consideration for his neighbors' ears or sleeping habits, he had used his noisy power tools in the middle of the night and played his music loudly during the day. Of course, these habits weren't quite so obnoxious when winter came and everyone kept their windows shut. But how many times had Betty gotten up for her late-night glass of milk only to observe strange lights and flashes going on behind Jack's closed blinds? Sometimes she worried that Jack's house was about to go up in flames, and perhaps the whole neighborhood along with it. She would ponder over what that madman could possibly be doing. And why did he need to do it at night? What if it was something immoral or illegal? For all she knew, Jack Jones could be a wanted felon who was creating bombs to blow up things like the county courthouse or even the grade school.

Betty removed her keys from the ignition and reached for her purse and Bible. She slowly got out of the car, and out of habit ever since that notorious Jack Jones had moved into the neighborhood, she securely locked her car's doors. Then she sat her purse and Bible on the hood of the car and peeked around the right side to see the front fender. The horizontal gash was about a foot long with a hook on one end, causing it, strangely enough, to resemble the letter J. Betty just shook her head. It figured . . . J for Jack.

So she continued to obsess over him—and over today's sermon and her futile prayer. How *was* it possible to love someone so completely disagreeable and inconsiderate and downright evil? She grunted as she struggled to lower the garage door. *Really,* she thought as she stood up straight, *even Pastor Gordon would be singing a different tune if he was forced to live next to Jack Jones.*

Betty let herself into the house, turning the deadbolt behind her—another habit she had never felt the need to do before Jack Jones had entered the picture. She set her purse and Bible on the kitchen table, then went to the sink and just stood there. She gazed blankly out the window. It was a bleak time of year with bare trees, browning grass, dead leaves—all in sepia tones. A nice coat of snow would make it look much prettier.

But she wasn't looking at her own yard. Her eyes were fixed on her neighbor's backyard. As usual, it looked more like a dump site than a delightful place where flowers once flourished and children once played. The dilapidated deck was heaped with black plastic trash bags filled with only God knew what. And as if that were not bad enough, there were pieces of rubbish and rubble strewn about. But the item that caught Betty's eye today, the thing that made her blink, was the pink toilet!

Betty recognized this toilet as the one that had once graced Gladys Spencer's prized guest bathroom. It had been a small, tidy bathroom with pink and black tiles, a pink sink, and a matching toilet. Betty had used it many a time when she'd joined Gladys and their friends for bridge club or baby showers or just a neighborly cup of coffee. Gladys had always taken great pride in her dainty pink guest soaps and her pink fingertip towels with a monogrammed *S* in silver metallic thread.

As Betty stared at that toilet, so forlorn and out of place in the scruffy backyard, she realized that time had definitely moved on. Betty could relate to that toilet on many levels. She too was old and outdated. She too felt unnecessary . . . and perhaps even unwanted.

Betty shook her head in an attempt to get rid of those negative thoughts. Then she frowned to see that last night's high winds must've pushed the deteriorating fence even further over into what once had been the Spencers' yard. Jack Jones would not be the least bit pleased about that. Not that she cared particularly.

Betty had long since decided that the fence, whether it was her responsibility or his, could wait until next summer to resolve. But if she could have her way, she would erect a tall, impenetrable stone wall between the two properties.

She filled her old stainless teakettle and tried to remember happier days—a time when she'd been happy to live in her house. She thought back to when Chuck was still alive and when they'd just moved into their new house in Gary Meadows. It had seemed like a dream come true. Finally, after renting and saving for eight years, they were able to afford a home of their own. And it was brand-new!

Al and Gladys Spencer had immediately befriended Chuck and Betty as well as their two small children with a dinner of burgers and baked beans. And that's when the two men began making plans to build a fence. "Good fences make good neighbors," Al said. Since Chuck and Betty's children were still young, whereas Al and Gladys had only one child still at home who was about to graduate, it was decided that they'd put the fence directly on the Spencers' property line, allowing the Kowalskis the slightly larger yard. "And less mowing for me," Al joked. And since the city had no plans to use the public access strip, and there was no alley, it had all been settled quite simply and congenially. That is, until Jack Jones moved in.

Not for the first time, Betty thought she should consider selling her house. Depressed market or not, she didn't need this much space. Besides that, the neighborhood seemed to be spiraling downward steadily. Perhaps this was related to tenants like Jack Jones, or simply the fact that people were stretched too thin these days, and as a result, home maintenance chores got neglected. Whatever the case, there seemed to be a noticeable decline in neighborhood morale and general friendliness.

It didn't help matters that both her middle-aged children, Susan and Gary, lived hundreds of miles away. They were busy with their own lives, careers, and families and consequently rarely visited anymore. These days they preferred to send her airline tickets to come and spend time with them. But every time she went away, she felt a bit more concerned about leaving her home unattended—and with Jack Jones on the other side of the fence, she would worry even more now. Perhaps she should cancel her visit to Susan's next month. She usually spent most of January down there in the warm Florida sun, but who knew what kind of stunts that crazy neighbor might pull in her absence? And who would call her to let her know if anything was amiss? There could be a fire or a burglary or vandalism, and she probably wouldn't hear about it until she returned. A sad state of affairs indeed.

The shrill sound of the teakettle's whistle made her jump, and she knocked her favorite porcelain tea mug off the counter, where it promptly shattered into pieces on the faded yellow linoleum floor. "Oh, bother!" She turned off the stove, then went to fetch the broom and dustpan and clean up her mess. She had never been this edgy before—at least not before Jack Jones had moved into the neighborhood. And she was supposed to love her neighbor?

2

Betty opened an Earl Grey teabag and dropped it in a porcelain mug that was still in one piece. As she poured the steaming water over it, she just shook her head. "Love your neighbor, bah humbug," she muttered as she went to the dining room. This was the spot where she normally enjoyed her afternoon cup of tea and looked out into her yard as the afternoon light came through the branches of the old maple tree. But she had barely sat down by the sliding glass door when she glimpsed a streak of blackish fur darting across her backyard like a hairy little demon. She blinked, then stood to peer out the window. "What in tarnation?"

There, hoisting his leg next to her beloved dogwood tree, a tree she'd nurtured and babied for years in a shady corner of her yard, was a scruffy-looking blackish-brown dog. At least she thought it was a dog. But it was a very ugly dog and not one she'd seen in the neighborhood before, although she couldn't be certain that it was a stray. With each passing year, it became harder and harder to keep track of people and pets.

She opened the sliding door and stepped out. "Shoo, shoo!" she called out. The dog looked at her with startled eyes as he lowered his leg, but he didn't run. "Go away," she yelled, waving her arms to scare him out of her yard. "Go home, you bad dog!" She clapped her hands and stomped her feet, and she was just about to either give up or throw something (perhaps the stupid dog was deaf and *very* dumb) when he took off running. He made a beeline straight for the fallen-down fence, neatly squeezing beneath the gap where fence boards had broken off, and escaped into Jack Jones's yard—just like he lived there!

"Well, of course," she said as she shut the door, locked it, and pulled her drapes closed. She picked up her teacup and went into the living room. "A mongrel dog for a mongrel man. Why should that surprise me in the least?"

She sat down in her favorite rocker-recliner and pondered her situation. What could possibly be done? How could she manage to survive not merely her loutish neighbor but his nasty little dog as well? It almost seemed as if Jack had sent the dog her way just to torture her some more. If a person couldn't feel comfortable and at home in their own house, what was the point of staying? What was keeping her here?

It was as if the writing were on the wall—a day of reckoning. Betty knew what she would do. She would sell her house and move away. That was the only way out of this dilemma. She wondered why she hadn't considered this solution last summer, back when Jack had first taken occupancy in the Spencer home. Didn't houses sell better in the warmer months? But perhaps it didn't matter. Still, she wasn't sure it made much sense to put up a For Sale sign during the holidays. Who would be out house shopping with less than two weeks before Christmas?

"Christmas . . ." She sighed, then sipped her lukewarm tea. How could it possibly be that time of year again? And what did she need to do in preparation for it? Or perhaps she didn't need to do anything. Who would really care if she baked cookies or not? Who would even notice if she didn't get out her old decorations? Christmas seemed like much ado about nothing. Oh, she didn't think the birth of Christ was nothing. But all the hullabaloo and overspending and commercialism that seemed to come with the holiday these days . . . When had it gone from being a wholesome family celebration to a stressful, jam-packed holiday that left everyone totally exhausted and up to their eyeballs in debt when it was over and done?

Betty used to love Christmastime. She would begin planning for

"Remember when Mom died?" she said suddenly.

"Well, yeah, of course."

"There were times when I wanted to talk about things then, Dad. But most of the time you didn't want to. Why was that?"

"I just didn't see the point in dwelling on things."

"Or showing emotion?"

"It's probably just the way I was raised," he said. "Back when I was growing up, men and boys were expected to keep their emotions in check."

"Did you ever cry for Mom?"

He looked down at his coffee and frowned, but he didn't answer. And for some reason that just really irritated her.

"Well, if something happened to me, I'd want Michael to cry," she announced.

"And I'm sure that Michael would cry if something happened to you."

She scowled. "Well, I'm not so sure."

"Why not?" Now Dad looked really concerned.

"Just because . . ."

"But Michael loves you, Anna."

"Did you love Mom?"

"Of course."

"But you didn't cry."

"But Michael is different from me. If anything happened to you, I'm sure he'd feel it deeply. I'm sure he'd cry."

She shook her head and broke off a piece of her donut, holding it in her fingers, trying to decide whether to take a bite or not.

"Just because I didn't cry when your mother died does not mean I didn't love her, Anna. I loved her more than anyone will ever know. And I still miss her today."

Anna looked up in time to see his eyes getting misty. "I'm sorry, Dad," she said quickly. "I'm sure you do."

Now he smiled. "You look so much like her, Anna. You two are like two peas in a pod."

"In more ways than you know."

A shadow crossed his face and he cocked his head ever so slightly, it long in advance. Even the year that Chuck had died suddenly and unexpectedly just two days after Thanksgiving, Betty had somehow mustered the strength to give her children a fairly merry Christmas. They'd been grade schoolers at the time and felt just as confused and bereaved as she had. Still, she had known it was up to her to put forth her best effort. And so, shortly after the funeral, Betty had worn a brave smile and climbed up the rickety ladder to hang colorful strings of Christmas lights on the eaves of the house, "just like Daddy used to do." And then she got and decorated a six-foot fir tree, baked some cookies, wrapped a few gifts . . . all for the sake of her children. Somehow they made it through Christmas that year. And the Christmases thereafter.

When her son Gary was old enough (and taller than Betty), he eagerly took over the task of hanging lights on the house. And Susan happily took over the trimming of the tree. Each year the three of them would gather in the kitchen to bake all sorts of goodies, and then they would deliver festive cookie platters to everyone in the neighborhood. It became an expected tradition. And always their threesome family was lovingly welcomed into neighbors' homes, often with hot cocoa and glad tidings.

But times had changed since then. Betty had taken cookie platters to only a couple of neighbors last year. And perhaps this year she would take none. What difference would it make?

Betty set her empty tea mug aside and leaned back in her recliner. She reached down to pull out the footrest and soon felt herself drifting to sleep. She wished that she, like Rip Van Winkle, could simply close her eyes and sleep, sleep, sleep. She'd be perfectly happy if she were able to sleep right through Christmas. And then January would come, and she would figure out a way to sell this house and get out of this neighborhood. She would escape that horrid Jack Jones as well as the ugly mutt that most likely intended to turn her backyard into a doggy dump site.

3

A little before seven on Monday morning, Betty woke to the sound of someone trying to break into her house. At least that was what it sounded like to her. She got out of bed and pulled on her old chenille robe, then reached for the cordless phone as she shoved her feet into her slippers. Some people, like her friend Marsha, would've been scared to death by something like this, but Betty had lived alone for so many years that she'd long since given up panic attacks. Besides, they weren't good for one's blood pressure.

But the screen door banged again, and she knew that someone was definitely on her porch. And so she shuffled out of her bedroom and peered through the peephole on the front door. But try as she might, she saw no one. Then she heard a whimpering sound and knew that it was an animal. Perhaps a raccoon or a possum, which often wandered into the neighborhood. She knew it could be dangerous, so she cautiously opened the front door. She quickly reached out to hook the screen door firmly before she looked down to see that it wasn't a raccoon or possum. It was that scruffy dog again. Jack Jones's mongrel. The dog crouched down, whimpering, and despite Betty's bitter feelings toward her neighbor, she felt a tinge of pity for the poor, dirty animal. And Betty didn't even like dogs.

"Go home, you foolish thing," she said. "Go bother your owner."

The dog just whined.

Betty knelt down with the screen still between her and the dog. "Go home," she said again. "Shoo!"

But the dog didn't budge. And now Betty didn't know what to do. So she closed the door and just stood there. If she knew Jack's phone number, she would call him and complain. But she didn't. She suspected the dog was hungry and cold, but she had no intention of letting the mongrel into her house. He looked as if he'd been rolling in the mud, and she'd just cleaned her floors on Saturday. But perhaps it wouldn't hurt to feed him a bit. Who knew when Jack had last given him a meal?

She went to look in her refrigerator, trying to determine what a hungry dog might eat. Finally, she decided on lunch meat. She peeled off several slices of processed turkey, then cautiously unlocked and opened the screen door just wide enough for her hand to slip out and toss the slices onto the porch. The dog was on them in seconds.

Betty went to her bedroom and took her time getting dressed, hoping that Jack's mutt would be gone by the time she finished. Perhaps he would beg food from another neighbor. But when she went to check her porch, he was still there. So she went to the laundry room and found a piece of clothesline to use as a leash.

"I hope you're friendly," she said. She bent over, hoping to tie the cord to the mutt's collar. But the dog had no collar. Instead he had a piece of string tied tightly around his neck. What kind of cruel gesture was that? She broke the dirty string and fashioned a looser sort of collar from the clothesline cord, looping it around his neck. To her relief, the mutt didn't make it difficult, didn't growl, didn't pull away. He simply looked up at her with sad brown eyes.

She stepped down from the porch and said, "Come!" The dog obeyed, walking obediently beside her. "Well, at least Jack has taught you some obedience," she said as she headed down the footpath to the sidewalk. "I'm taking you home now." Then she turned and marched down the sidewalk toward Jack's house. But now she wasn't so sure. What if this *wasn't* Jack's dog?

"Hello, Betty," Katie Gilmore called out. She stepped away from where the school bus had just picked up her twin girls. "How are you today?"

Betty smiled. "I'm fine, thank you."

Katie frowned down at the dog, then lowered her voice. "Does that dog belong to, uh, Jack Jones?"

"That's what I assume," Betty said. "I saw him in Jack's back-yard yesterday."

"Yes, I noticed him over there too." Katie looked uneasy. "I hadn't known Jack had a dog. I hope he's friendly."

"I'm sure there's a lot we don't know about Jack." Betty forced a wry smile as she looked down at the dog. "But the dog seems to be friendly enough."

Katie frowned at the animal. "Poor thing."

Betty suspected Katie meant "poor thing" in relation to having Jack Jones as an owner. Everyone knew that Katie's husband, Martin, had experienced a bit of go-around with Jack last summer. Quiet Martin Gilmore had walked over and politely asked Jack to turn down his music one day. But according to Penny Horton, who'd been home at the time, Martin had been answered with a raised power tool and some rough language.

"Are you taking the dog to Jack's house?" Katie glanced over her shoulder toward the shabby-looking house.

"Yes. And I intend to give him a piece of my mind too."

Katie's brows arched. "Oh . . ." Then she reached in her coat pocket and pulled out a cell phone. "Want me to stick around, just in case?"

Betty wanted to dismiss Katie's offer as unnecessary, but then reconsidered. "I suppose that's not a bad idea."

"He can be a little unpredictable," Katie said quietly. "That's the main reason I've been making sure the girls get safely on and off the school bus these days."

Betty nodded. "I see."

"I'll just wait here," Katie said. "I'll keep an eye on you while you return the dog." She shook her head. "It looks neglected . . . and like it needs a bath."

Betty thought that wasn't the only thing the dog needed, and she intended to say as much to Jack Jones. Naturally, she would control her temper, but she would also let him know that organizations like the Humane Society or ASPCA would not be the least bit impressed with Jack's dog-owner skills.

When she got to Jack's house and knocked on the door, no one answered. However, his pickup was still parked in the front yard, so she suspected he was home and knocked again, louder this time. But still no answer. Finally, she didn't know what to do, so she simply tied the makeshift leash to a rickety-looking porch railing and left.

"He didn't answer the door?" Katie asked when Betty rejoined her.

"No." Betty turned and scowled at Jack's house. "I've a mind to call the Humane Society."

"It seems cruel to leave the dog tied to the porch," Katie said.

Betty shrugged. "I don't know what else to do."

"Well, I can see Jack's porch from my house. I'll keep an eye on the dog, and if Jack doesn't come out and let the dog inside or care for it, I'll give you a call."

Betty wanted to protest this idea. After all, why should that dog be her concern or responsibility? But she knew that would sound heartless and mean, so she just thanked Katie.

"Martin and I just don't know what to do about him," Katie said as she walked Betty back to her house. "I'll admit we didn't get off on the best foot with him, but we've tried to be friendly since then, and he just shuts us down."

"I know," Betty said. "He shuts everyone down."

"Now Martin is talking about moving. He's worried about the girls. He even did one of those police checks on Jack—you know, where you go online to see if the person has a record for being a sexual predator."

Betty's eyes opened wide. "Did he discover anything?"

"No." Katie looked dismal. "But now Martin is worried that Jack Jones might not be his real name."

Betty nodded. "The thought crossed my mind too."

"So what do you do about something like this?" Katie's tone

was desperate now. "Do you simply allow some nutcase to ruin your neighborhood and drive you out of your home? Do you just give in?"

Betty sighed as she paused in front of her house. "I don't know what to tell you, Katie. I wish I did. And even though I've lived in this neighborhood for nearly forty years, I really don't have any answers. The truth is, I'm considering moving myself."

Katie shook her head. "That's just not fair."

"Well, I'm getting old." Betty forced a weak smile. "My house and yard are a lot of work for me, and the winters are long. Really, it might be for the best."

"Maybe so. But I have to say that Jack Jones has put a real damper on the holidays for me. The girls' last day of school is Wednesday, and I told Martin that I'm thinking about taking them to my mother's for all of winter break. Martin wasn't happy about that. He still has to work and isn't looking forward to coming home to an empty house while we're gone. But I told him that I didn't look forward to two weeks of being home with the girls with someone like Jack next door."

"That's too bad."

"I'll say. It's too bad that we don't feel safe or comfortable in our home."

Betty just shook her head. What was this neighborhood coming to?

"Anyway, I'll let you know how it goes with that poor dog," Katie said. And then they said good-bye and went their separate ways.

Once inside her house, Betty decided to call her daughter. Susan had always been sensible, not to mention a strong Christian woman. Plus she was a family counselor with a practice in her home. Surely she would have some words of wisdom to share. Some sage advice for her poor old mother. Betty planned to explain the situation in a calm and controlled manner, but once they got past the perfunctory greetings, Betty simply blurted out her plan to sell her home as soon as possible.

"When did you think you'd list it?" Susan sounded a little concerned.

"I'd like to put up a sign right now. But it probably makes more sense to wait until after the New Year."

"So . . . in January?"

"Yes. I didn't think anyone would want to buy a house right before Christmas."

"But you're coming here in January."

"Yes, I know. I'll put my house up for sale and leave."

"But the market is so low right now, Mom."

"I don't care."

"And I'll bet you haven't fixed anything up, have you?"

"I'll sell it as is."

"Yes . . . you could do that."

But Betty could hear the doubtful tone in Susan's voice growing stronger. "You think it's a bad idea, don't you?"

"I don't think it's a bad idea to sell your house. But I suppose I'm just questioning your timing. January isn't a good time to sell a house. The market is low right now. And I know you have some deferred maintenance issues to deal with and—"

"You think I should wait?"

"I think waiting until summer would be smarter."

"Oh."

"Why are you in this sudden rush, Mom?"

Betty felt silly now. To admit that it was her rude neighbor sounded so childish. And yet it was the truth. So she spilled the whole story, clear down to the scratch on her car, the broken tea mug, and the dirty dog.

Susan actually laughed.

"It is *not* funny."

"I'm sorry, Mom. I'm sure it's not funny to you. But hearing you tell it, well . . ." She chortled again. "It is kind of humorous."

"Humph."

"What kind of a dog was it?"

"What *kind* of a dog?" Betty frowned. "Good grief, how would I know? It was a mutt, a mongrel, a filthy dog that I would never allow inside my house. I can only imagine what Jack Jones's house must look like inside. It's a dump site outside. Did you know that

310

there is a pink toilet in his backyard right this moment?" Betty went on to tell her daughter that Katie Gilmore was considering evacuating for Christmas and that Martin had actually done a criminal check on Jack.

"Oh dear," Susan said. "Do you think he's dangerous?"

"I don't know about that, but I do know he's very rude and inconsiderate and strange. I can only imagine what he's doing to the Spencer house. For all I know, he might even be a squatter or an escapee from the nut hatch, hiding out until the men in white coats show up to cart him away."

"Seriously?"

"Oh, I don't know."

"Have you even given him a chance, Mom? Maybe he's just lonely."

"Of course he's lonely. He pushes everyone away from him."

"But it sounds as if everyone is being confrontational."

"He invites confrontation!"

"Have you tried being kind to him?"

Betty didn't answer.

"I remember how we used to take cookies to our neighbors . . ."

Betty laughed now, but it was edged with bitterness. "I do not think Jack Jones would appreciate cookies, Susan. You don't understand the situation at all."

"Maybe not. But I do remember that my mother once told me that kindness builds bridges."

"All I want to build is a tall brick wall between Jack's house and mine." Betty mentioned the falling-down fence and disputed property line.

"See, that's just one more reason why it's not time to sell right now, Mom. You need to resolve those issues first."

"Maybe so."

Then Susan changed the subject by talking about the grandsons. Seth was still on a church missions trip, where they were putting in wells and septic systems in Africa.

"He just loves what he's doing there," Susan said, "and he loves the people. In fact, he's extended his stay until March now."

"And what about Marcus?" Betty asked. "How's school?"

"School is going fine. I think this is finals week. And, oh yeah, he has a girlfriend."

"A girlfriend? Have you met her?"

"No. But it sounds like he may be going to her house for Christmas."

"So you and Tim will be alone for Christmas?" Betty had booked her flight to Florida months ago, but now she considered changing the dates so that she could be with her daughter during the holidays too. Why hadn't she thought of that sooner? Oh yes, she remembered—her commitment to help with the Deerwood anniversary party just days before Christmas.

"Not exactly alone . . ." Susan explained how Tim had put together a plan to share the expenses of a small yacht with some other couples while they toured the Florida Keys together during the holidays.

"That sounds like fun." Betty frowned out the back window. Jack's dog was in her backyard again!

"I wasn't sure at first, but I'm getting excited now."

"Well, I'm excited too," Betty said in an angry voice. "That mongrel dog has sneaked into my backyard again!" The mutt was making a doggy deposit right next to her beloved dogwood tree! Did the mongrel think that because it was a *dog*wood tree, it was open season for dogs? "That horrible animal! I think I'll take a broom to him."

"Oh, Mom!" Susan sounded disappointed. "That's so mean. You've never been mean like that before."

"Are you suggesting it's not mean for Jack to force me to clean up after his dog? To remove nasty dog piles from my own backyard?"

"That's not the dog's fault, Mom. You said yourself that the fence is falling apart. What do you expect?"

"I expect the owner to take some responsibility for his animal. Maybe I should go throw something at the nasty dog."

"What happened to the sweet Christian woman I used to know?" Susan asked.

"Jack Jones is making her lose her mind."

"Oh, Mother, you can do better than that. Remember what you used to tell me when I was young and I'd get so angry that I'd feel like killing someone?"

"What?" Betty felt a headache coming on.

"You'd say, 'Why don't you kill them with kindness, Susan?'"

Betty rubbed her forehead as she remembered her own words.

"So, why don't you do that now, Mom? Why don't you kill Jack Jones with kindness?"

"And his little dog too?"

"Yes. And his little dog too."

Betty promised her daughter that she'd consider the challenge, and she was just about to say good-bye when Susan said quickly, "Hey, I almost forgot to tell you."

"What's that?"

"Have you heard from Gary lately?"

Suddenly Betty felt worried. She could tell by Susan's voice that something was wrong. Surely no harm had come to her son. "No . . . I haven't spoken to him since Thanksgiving. Is everything okay?"

"Well, I wasn't supposed to say anything to you . . ."

"Anything about what?" Betty was really concerned now.

"It's Avery."

"Oh." Avery was Gary's stepdaughter. She was in her mid-twenties and still acted like an adolescent. "What's happened with Avery?"

"She's gone missing."

"Missing?"

"Gary called awhile back and told me they haven't heard from her since October."

"October?" Betty considered this. "Gary didn't mention this when he called me at Thanksgiving."

"He probably didn't want to worry you."

"I see."

"But they're starting to get concerned. I mean, Avery's been known to take off and do some irresponsible things before, but not for this long. And she usually checks in from time to time."

"And she hasn't checked in?"

"No." Susan sighed. "Apparently Avery got into a big fight with Stephanie."

Stephanie was Avery's mom, Gary's second wife. She was an intelligent woman and very beautiful, but her temper was a little volatile, and this sometimes worried Betty. "When was the fight?" Betty asked.

"Mid-October."

"Naturally, Avery's been missing since then?"

"Pretty much so."

"Oh dear, that's quite a while. I hope she's okay."

"I'm sure she's fine. Avery probably just wants to teach her mom a lesson. Anyway, I've really been praying for her, and I thought you might want to also."

"Yes, of course I'll be praying for her."

"And I'll assume you're praying for your neighbor too?" Susan's voice sounded a tiny bit sarcastic now.

"I'm *trying* to pray for him," Betty said. "But it's not easy."

"Well, I'll start praying for him too, Mom. Keep me posted."

"And you keep me posted on Avery."

"Sure, just don't let Gary know that I mentioned it. And in the meantime, remember what I told you."

"What's that?" Now Betty felt confused. They'd talked of so much—to sell or not to sell the house, Avery's disappearance.

"You know, take your own advice—kill him with kindness."

Betty looked out at her backyard only to see that the stupid dog was now digging in her favorite tulip bed. "I'll kill him, all right," she snapped.

"Mom!"

"Yes, yes, like you said, with kindness. I have to go now, dear."

But after she hung up and went outside, Betty did not have kindness in her heart. And when she saw that someone—and it could only be Jack—had hammered a board over the opening in the fence, on his side of the fence, she felt outraged. Had he allowed his dog to pass through and then sealed off the doggy escape route? What was wrong with that man?

She marched out to the woodshed and got an old ax. The dog followed her, watching as she took the ax to the fence and chopped an even bigger hole. Fortunately, the fence was so rotten that it wasn't much of a challenge. The challenge came with getting the dumb dog to pass back through the hole onto his own side of the fence. She went back to the house and utilized another piece of lunch meat to entice the mutt into Jack's yard. Once he was there, she shoved several pieces of firewood in the hole to block the new opening of the fence.

She let out a tired sigh as she looked across the sagging and now somewhat ravaged-looking fence. The dog just sat there in the yard and looked at her with those sad brown eyes.

"I'm sorry," she said. "Dogs don't get to pick their masters, just like I don't get to pick my neighbors. We both need to make the best of it."

But as she walked away, she felt guilty on several levels. And the expression on the poor mutt's face seemed to be imprinted in her mind. When had she become so mean?

4

Betty finally had to pull the drapes on the windows that faced her backyard because she could still see the dog sitting out there in the bitter cold just staring toward her house in the most pitiful way. She picked up the phone and considered calling information for the number of the Humane Society. Why shouldn't she turn Jack Jones in for dog neglect? He deserved it. But then she remembered her daughter's words. And so she replaced the phone and decided to go to the grocery store instead.

With Susan's challenge running through her mind, Betty decided she would give this her best attempt. She would do all she could to "kill Jack and his dog with kindness." And, although she normally lived on a fairly frugal grocery budget, today she would throw caution to the wind. So, along with her normal groceries, Betty also gathered up the ingredients for cookies and fudge. After that she stopped in the pet aisle, where she added to her shopping cart a red nylon collar and matching leash, some dog shampoo, a couple of cans of dog food, and even a red and green plaid bed.

"Looks like somebody is getting a dog for Christmas." The cashier winked at her as he bagged up her purchases.

"Looks that way, doesn't it?"

"Or maybe the family pooch is getting something from Santa?" he asked.

She just gave him a stiff smile and paid in cash from her envelope. This was a habit she'd developed years ago when the children still

316

lived at home. But today's shopping had used up the remainder of her December grocery budget. The month was only half over, and she usually went shopping once a week. But perhaps it would be worth it. Perhaps this was how she would buy peace. And, if the kindness plan didn't work, she would simply sell her house, and she might even toss budgeting out the window. Maybe she'd do like Susan—board a boat and just sail away into the sunset. Why not?

But as Betty loaded her unusual purchases into her car, trying to ignore the J-shaped gash on the front right fender, she felt rather foolish. What on earth was she doing with this doggy paraphernalia anyway? As she closed her trunk, she feared she might be getting senile. Or maybe she had simply lost her mind. Had Jack Jones driven her mad?

To distract herself from Jack, she focused her attention on praying for Avery. Although they weren't related by blood, Avery had started calling Betty "Grandma" shortly after her mother married Betty's son Gary a dozen years ago. And Betty had adopted Avery into her heart as a granddaughter.

Betty remembered the first time she'd met the quiet, preadolescent girl. It had been shortly before the wedding, and Betty had suspected that Avery wasn't too pleased with her mother's marriage. But during the reception, Betty and Avery seemed to bond, which was a good thing since Betty was to keep Avery while Gary and Stephanie honeymooned in the Caribbean. Naturally, Avery had been reluctant to be away from her friends, and Betty had been a bit apprehensive about caring for a girl she barely knew, but by the end of the two weeks, they'd become fast friends. Avery had even cried when it was time to go home.

Over the following few years, Avery usually spent at least two weeks of her summer vacation at Betty's home. And sometimes spring break as well. But everything seemed to change when Avery turned sixteen. That was when, according to Betty's son, Avery became a "wild child." And Gary worried that his stepdaughter's strong will would be too much for his aging mother. Just the same, Betty missed those visits, and over the years she continued to send Avery cards and gifts, and occasionally money, for birthdays, holidays, and graduation. Betty seldom got a thank-you in return, but she figured young people weren't trained in the social graces very much these days.

As Betty pulled into her driveway, then carefully parked her car in the garage again, her thoughts returned to Jack Jones. Suddenly she wondered just how she planned to present her eccentric "gifts" to her neighbor. More than that, she wondered how he would receive them. Besides being rude and inconsiderate and painfully private, Jack Jones struck her as being an extremely proud young man, and stubborn too. For all she knew, he might throw her silly purchases right back in her face. Really, it was a crazy idea—what had she been thinking? Perhaps the best plan would be to simply forget the whole thing and take the items back tomorrow. Even if the store refused to refund her money, they could probably give her a credit. And so she carried her groceries into the house but left the doggy items in her car to be returned later.

Still feeling a bit silly, she stowed her groceries away—all except for the baking ingredients, which she lined up on the counter by the stove, just like she used to do before a full day of holiday baking. Then she stood there staring at the bags of chocolate chips, nuts, dried fruits, and powdered and brown sugar, and finally just shook her head. Had she lost her mind?

Did she really plan on making Christmas goodies to give to her neighbors—people she barely knew? And to share her homemade treats with the likes of Jack Jones? Was that even sensible? What if she were setting herself up for trouble? What if Jack Jones was a dangerous man? A criminal? It was one thing to love her neighbor, but what if her neighbor was a murderer, or a pedophile, or a sociopath? Should she take cookies to a man like that?

With a little more than a week still left until Christmas, she decided to think about these things later. Right now she was too tired to think clearly, let alone bake cookies.

Betty awoke to the sound of something knocking on the front door. She blinked and slowly pushed herself out of her recliner, thinking it must be that mongrel dog again. Why wouldn't he just leave her alone? Didn't he know where he lived? She groaned as she made her way through the living room. Her arthritis was acting up, probably as a result of this cold, damp weather.

But when she looked through the peephole, not expecting to see anyone, she saw what appeared to be an attractive, dark-haired young woman. A scarlet-red scarf was wound so high up her neck that it concealed the lower half of her face, so it was hard to tell who it was. Feeling slightly befuddled and not completely awake, Betty just stared at the person, thinking to herself that those dark brown eyes looked oddly familiar.

"Avery!" Betty fumbled with the deadbolt and opened the door so she could unlock and open the screen door. "Avery!" she cried again as she embraced the girl in a warm hug and pulled her into the house. "I almost didn't recognize you. It's been so long."

As Betty closed the front door and relocked the deadbolt, Avery began to unwind the scarf from around her neck. "Hi, Grandma," she said in a tired voice. "Sorry to bust in on you like this, but I was, uh, in the neighborhood . . ."

"I'm glad you came! I'm so happy to see you." Betty took the girl's slightly damp parka and hung it on the hall tree to dry out, along with the snagged-up scarf that appeared to be nearly six feet long. "How are you?"

"Oh, I'm okay . . . I guess." Avery pushed some loose strands of dark hair away from her face. The rest of her hair was pulled back into a long and messy ponytail. Her skin seemed pale, there were dark smudges under her eyes, and without her parka, she seemed very thin and waiflike.

"Come in and sit down and get warm." Betty motioned Avery toward the living room.

"Wow, everything looks just the same, Grandma." Avery looked around the room with hungry eyes. "Nothing has changed."

Betty laughed. "I guess that's how it is when we get old. We're comforted by keeping things the same."

"I'm comforted too." Avery sat on the couch and picked up a pillow with a crocheted covering that Betty's mother had made for her years ago. Avery just stared at the pattern of colors—roses, lilacs, and periwinkle. "I always loved this pillow, Grandma."

Betty smiled. "I'll make sure to leave it to you in my will."

Now Avery looked sad as she set the pillow aside. "Don't say that. I'd hate to think of you dying. I don't want the pillow that bad."

"Don't worry, I don't plan on going anytime soon."

Avery nodded. "Good."

"So, what brings you into my neck of the woods?"

Avery sighed. "I don't know . . ."

Betty considered the situation. She didn't want to press too hard, didn't want to make Avery so uncomfortable that she'd be tempted to run off again. Better just to keep things light. "Say, are you hungry?"

Avery looked up with eager eyes. "Yes! I'm starving."

"Well, I just went to the grocery store today. And I haven't had lunch yet either. Why don't we see what we can find?"

Before long, Betty had grilled cheese sandwiches cooking on one burner, and Avery was stirring cream of tomato soup on another.

"This feels good," Avery said.

"Cooking?"

"Yes. Being in a real kitchen, smelling food . . . it feels kinda homey."

Betty had noticed how grimy Avery's hands and nails looked. Like she hadn't bathed in days, maybe even weeks. "Well, everything's about ready," she told her. "Maybe you'd like to go wash up before we eat."

Avery nodded. "Yeah, that's a good idea."

Soon they were both sitting at the kitchen table, and, as usual, Betty bowed her head to say grace.

"Just like always," Avery said after Betty finished. "You still thank God every time you eat?"

"I try to."

"That's nice." Avery smiled and took a big bite of her sandwich, then another, and then, in no time, her sandwich was gone and she was shoveling down her soup.

"I'll bet you could eat another sandwich," Betty said.

"Do you mind?"

"Not at all." Betty got up to fix another.

"Grandma?"

"Yes?" Betty paused from slicing the cheese.

"Why is it so dark in here? Why are the curtains all shut?"

"Oh." Betty frowned. "It's a long story."

"I've got time."

So, as Betty grilled the second sandwich, she began to explain about her unpredictable and somewhat thoughtless neighbor. She tried not to paint too horrible a picture of him. After all, she didn't want to frighten Avery. But she did want her to understand that the man was a bit of a loose cannon. "And now that he's got this crazy dog, well, it's getting to be even more complicated."

"What kind of a dog?"

"Who knows? A mutt."

Avery laughed. "Oh."

Betty reached over to open the drapes that had been blocking the view of the backyard. But to her pleasant surprise, the dog was not anywhere in sight. "Hopefully, Jack has enough sense to put his dog inside," she said. "Because it looks like it's about to rain again. And as cold as it is out there, I expect it might turn into a freezing rain by tonight."

Avery stood and began to clear the table. "I'll clean these things up."

"Thank you," Betty said. "I appreciate that."

"You go put your feet up," Avery said. "Leave everything to me."

"Now that's an offer I cannot refuse."

For the second time that day, Betty got into her recliner and put her feet up and was about to doze off when she heard something at the door. Avery was still in the kitchen, so Betty slowly made her way out of her chair, went to the door, and realized that this time it really was that dog again. In Betty's excitement over seeing Avery, she'd forgotten to lock the screen door, and now the dog had wedged itself between the loose screen door and the front door, almost as if he thought it was a place to seek shelter. Betty had barely opened the door and was about to shoo it away, but the dog shot between her legs and right into the house.

"No! No!" Betty waved her hands. "Out of my house, you mongrel! Get out of here! Get out! Get out!" But the dog ran down the hallway and headed back toward the bedrooms.

"What?" Avery came out holding a sudsy saucepan. "Do you want me to leave?"

"No, not you. That darn dog sneaked into my house. I was yelling at it to go away."

"Oh, I thought you meant me."

"No, of course not." Betty pointed down the hallway. "He went that way. Help me catch him."

They finally cornered the runaway dog in the bathroom, where it cowered on Betty's pale pink bath mat. Or what used to be pale pink before being spotted with muddy smudges.

"Bad dog!" Betty shouted.

But Avery knelt down beside the dog, holding its head in her hands and looking into its face. "Poor thing. Look how dirty and cold it is."

"Yes, Jack Jones is a very bad man. He should be arrested for pet neglect, among other things."

"Can I give him a bath?" Avery asked with hopeful eyes.

"A *bath*?" Betty gasped. "You mean right here in my bathtub?" Avery nodded.

Betty wrung her hands. "But he's filthy. It will be such a mess, the whole bathroom will smell like a dog."

"I'll clean everything up when I'm done." Avery looked sad now. "Look, he's so cold . . . he's shivering." She touched his muddy brown coat. "And he's so dirty and matted and sad. Please, Grandma, we can't let him go back like this."

Betty got an idea. "Okay, you can bathe him, but not in here. You can put him in the laundry sink. That won't be such a mess."

"Okay!" Avery scooped up the dirt-encrusted dog and carried him through the house with Betty trailing behind her, carrying the half-washed saucepan in one hand and the soiled bath mat in the other. Betty deposited these items, then dug through her linen closet to find two old towels to give to Avery. By now the laundry sink was nearly full.

"Do you have any soap to use on him?" Avery asked.

Betty remembered her recent doggy purchases. "As a matter of fact, I have just the thing." She headed out to the garage to get the shampoo and returned with all the doggy items in tow.

Avery's eyes grew wide. "Where did you get all that stuff?"

"At the store."

"For *this* dog?"

"I wanted to be a good neighbor." Now Betty felt a little sheepish to admit this, since she'd just tried to chase the mutt out of her house. "I thought Jack Jones needed some help with his dog."

"I'll say." Avery reached for the bottle of shampoo and began to lather up the wet dog. "I have a feeling this is going to take awhile."

"I'll leave you to it," Betty said. She went to finish up the nearly cleaned kitchen, then on to the hallway and bathroom to mop up the dirt the dog had tracked in, and finally back to her recliner, where she collapsed in exhaustion and closed her eyes.

When Betty opened her eyes about an hour later, she saw a clean brown dog lying in the plaid bed, wearing a red collar and snoozing comfortably. But where was Avery? Surely she hadn't left. Not in this weather. And not after dark. Betty went down the hallway and noticed the bathroom door was shut with a light coming from beneath it, and she could hear water running. Avery had probably discovered that after bathing the filthy dog, she needed a bath as well. Hopefully, this meant she planned to stay awhile.

And if Betty had her way, Avery would at least spend the night here. Not that she could force her to stay longer than that. But Betty would certainly put her foot down if Avery made any attempt to leave this evening. And so Betty went to check on the guest room, the same room Avery had inhabited so many years before. She turned the baseboard heater up, fluffed the pillows, and added an extra quilt at the end of the bed. Avery hadn't brought any luggage with her, nothing besides an oversized bag. Was it possible she had only the clothes on her back? And if so, why?

Betty went to her own room and retrieved a pair of pretty pink pajamas that Susan had given her last Christmas. She'd never even worn them. Not because she didn't like them, but probably because she'd been saving them. But saving them for what? Well, she didn't know. It's just the way she was about some things. Perhaps she'd been saving them for Avery. Whatever the reason, she neatly refolded them and placed them by Avery's pillow. Then she turned on the small light on the bedside table and smiled in satisfaction. Very welcoming.

"I hope you don't mind that I took a shower," Avery said when she emerged from the bathroom with wet hair. "But I was kind of a mess."

"You did a good job of cleaning up that dog." Betty nodded to where the mutt was still sleeping. Then she frowned at Avery's soiled T-shirt and jeans. "But why did you put on your dirty clothes again?"

"Because they're all I have."

"You don't have any other clothes?"

Avery just shrugged. "I'll be okay."

Betty shook her head. "No, you will not be okay, Avery. I know you're smaller than I am, at least around, and I think you might be a bit taller. But I might have something for you to wear while we wash your clothes."

"Okay." Avery smiled.

"And the guest room is all ready for you. In fact, if you like you can simply put on the pajamas I laid out for you."

"Okay," Avery said again.

"And then we'll sit down and talk."

Avery bent down to pat the dog, and he looked up with what almost seemed a grateful expression.

"He looks like he's got some terrier in him," Betty said.

"Yeah, that's what I thought too."

"Well, I need to figure out how to get him back to Jack now."

Avery frowned. "I don't think that horrible Jack person deserves to own this dog. He's got a really sweet disposition, and Jack sounds like a total monster. The poor dog's hair was so matted and filthy that it took a bunch of shampooing and rinsing to get him clean. And the whole time he was totally patient. I could tell he liked the attention. But I could feel his ribs. I think he hasn't been fed properly."

Betty nodded. "I'm sure you're right about Jack not being a fit pet owner, but I don't know what we should do about it."

"We should report him to the ASPCA."

"That thought has crossed my mind." Betty pressed her lips together firmly. She wondered what kind of a Christian witness it would be for her to turn in her neighbor. On the other hand, what kind of a Christian allows an innocent animal to suffer that kind of neglect?

She looked at Avery's dripping hair and dirty clothes. "We'll figure out the doggy dilemma later. In the meantime, why don't you change out of those dirty things and get your hair dried before you catch pneumonia."

Avery patted the dog one more time, then left the room. Betty sighed loudly as she sat back down in her recliner. Rocking back and forth, she pondered over what should be done—not so much about the dog as about her wayward granddaughter. Why had Avery shown up like this? And where had she been these past months? Should Betty call Avery's parents? Or should she simply encourage Avery to let them know she was okay?

Betty looked over to where the dog was sleeping again. What was her responsibility for that poor dog? Avery was probably right, he did seem like a nice dog. Not that Betty wanted or needed a dog—she most definitely did not!

And then there was Jack to consider. Betty leaned her head back and closed her eyes. Only yesterday, her biggest challenge was to stop envying her friend's new coat and to make an attempt to love her unlovable neighbor. But her problems seemed to have multiplied. Now she had not only Jack to contend with but a neglected dog and a troubled granddaughter as well. Oh my!

5

||||||||||||||

"It will serve him right," Avery said. They had just agreed to keep Jack's dog overnight. Perhaps he'd be worried about his animal and want to take better care of him. Or so they hoped.

"And when I return the dog to him tomorrow morning, I'll warn Jack that this neglect cannot continue." Betty stirred the simmering rolled oats, relieved that Avery didn't mind having oatmeal for dinner. It was one of Betty's favorites.

"Tell Jack that you'll report him if he doesn't treat his dog right," Avery said.

Betty nodded. "I'll try to make that clear. But I don't want to be too confrontational with him."

"Why not? He's a total jerk, Grandma."

"Yes, he is a jerk. But he's also my neighbor. And the Bible teaches us to love our neighbors." Betty turned off the stove and removed the pan.

"Even when they're jerks?"

"Even when they're jerks, and even if they're our worst enemies."

"That doesn't sound possible."

Betty smiled. "Yes, I've felt like that myself. It's a challenge."

Avery was studying the calendar that was taped to Betty's fridge. "Wow, is this what day it is?"

Betty looked to where Avery's finger was pointing and nodded. "That's right."

"It's like eight days until Christmas."

Betty spooned out the oatmeal and set the bowls on the kitchen table. She'd already put out brown sugar, raisins, walnuts, and milk to go with it. "I can hardly believe it myself," she said as she sat down.

"Whose fiftieth anniversary is this?" Avery asked as she continued to study the calendar.

"My good friends Marsha and Jim Deerwood."

"Oh, I thought maybe it was yours." Avery kind of laughed and joined Betty at the Formica-topped table. "But I guess you don't celebrate anniversaries if you're not both around."

"To be honest, I do." Betty bowed her head and said a quick blessing over their oatmeal. When she looked up, Avery had a curious expression.

"You celebrate your anniversary?"

"I know it sounds silly. In fact, I've never told anyone before. But yes, I do. I fix a special little dinner, set the table for two, and think about Chuck, and I remember our wedding day."

"What day did you get married?"

"June 20. Last summer would've been our fiftieth anniversary."

"Wow. That's a long time."

Betty nodded as she chewed a bite.

"Why didn't you ever remarry?"

Betty considered this. It was a question she used to get asked a lot. But not so much as the years piled on. "I just never met the right man. It was hard to measure up to Chuck."

"But don't you get lonely?"

"I suppose . . . a little. Especially after I retired from the electric company. But I've had plenty of time to get used to being alone. Also I have my church, my friends, my neighbors."

"Some of your neighbors sound awful."

Betty forced a smile. "The neighborhood has changed over the years."

"So, are you going anywhere for Christmas?" Avery asked.

"No. I plan to stay home this year." Betty poured more milk on her oatmeal. "I offered to help with my friends' fiftieth anniversary, and it's just a few days before Christmas. Then I'm scheduled to go to Susan's shortly after the New Year."

"Oh."

"What about you, Avery? Do you have special plans for the holidays?"

Avery stirred her oatmeal without looking up.

"I know that you had a fight with your mother."

"Did they call you?"

"No . . ." Betty wasn't sure how much she should press Avery.

"Well, I guess I'm kind of like Jack's dog."

"How's that?"

"If you don't treat me right, I run away."

Betty chuckled.

"Do you know how many times my mom's been married?"

"I thought Gary was her second husband."

"That's what she *wanted* you to think."

"So, he's not?"

"Nope. She was married *three times* before Gary. He's her fourth."

Betty tried not to look too surprised.

"Gary knows about it now."

"But he didn't before?"

"Nope."

Betty wondered how Gary had reacted to this news but didn't want to ask.

"And I'm the one who told him."

Betty lifted her brows. "And how did your mother feel about that?"

"That's what started our big fight. Actually, the fight was already in motion, but that's what made it really take off. Mom told me to leave and never come back."

"Your mother said that?"

"Pretty much so."

"But she was probably speaking out of her emotions, Avery. I doubt that she really meant it."

Avery shrugged as she stuck her spoon back in her bowl. "I think she meant it."

Now Betty didn't know what to say. Really, what could she say? It wasn't as if this was her business. And she'd heard enough about Avery's adolescence to know there were probably two sides to this story. Still, Betty felt disappointed that Stephanie had deceived her as well as her son. She really was curious as to how Gary had reacted to this bit of news. She knew Gary loved Stephanie. But she also knew he had a strong sense of propriety. He would not like discovering he'd been lied to.

"Anyway," Avery continued, "I do not plan to be home for the holidays. I doubt that I'd even be welcome there."

"You're welcome to stay with me."

Avery brightened. "Thanks!"

"But on one condition."

Now she frowned slightly. "What?"

"Let your parents know where you are."

Avery seemed to be thinking about this.

"I realize you're not a child, Avery. How old are you now, anyway?"

"I turned twenty-three in September."

Betty shook her head. "And I completely forgot to send you a card."

"That's okay."

"But as I was saying, you're not a child. You're an adult, but that means you need to be responsible. And a responsible adult lets family members know that she's okay."

"Yeah, you're probably right."

"So if you take care of that, you're welcome to stay here during the holidays."

Avery nodded.

Betty wasn't sure what more she should say to the girl. She certainly had questions, but she didn't want to make Avery feel like she was participating in the Spanish Inquisition tonight. Nor did she want to lecture her or drive her away. Betty suspected that Avery was broke. And it appeared that she had nothing more than what was on her back and in the oversized bag she'd tossed into the guest room.

Betty knew enough about Avery's past to know that, much to her parents' dismay, she'd dropped out of college at the end of her junior year. Avery had claimed that a degree would not guarantee a job. But since leaving school, her employment history had been splotchy at best. According to Susan—Betty's best news source since Gary preferred to keep his mother in the dark—Avery had held a variety of low-paying and unimpressive jobs. And she seemed to bounce back and forth between living at home and staying with friends. Now she was here.

But the truth was, Betty was grateful for the company. And she didn't mind that Avery would be with her through the holidays. Just as long as she informed her parents of her whereabouts. Betty did not want to find herself in the center of a family feud.

Betty glanced at the kitchen clock to see that it was past seven. "I suppose you should wait to call your parents until tomorrow since it's pretty late where they live."

Avery looked relieved. "Yeah. I'll call in the morning."

Just then the dog wandered into the kitchen, going straight to Avery as if they were old friends. "I think we should set the dog's bed and things up in the laundry room," Betty said.

"Is it okay if I feed him again?" Avery asked. "He seemed pretty hungry."

"I'll leave that up to you. Just make sure he has a chance to go out and do his business before you tell him good night."

Betty awoke to a high-pitched whining the next morning. It took her a moment to figure out that the sound was coming from the laundry room, more specifically from the dog. And then she realized that the dog needed to go outside for a potty break. She let him out into the backyard and watched from the open doorway as the dog started to hike up his leg on the trunk of the dogwood tree again.

"No, no!" Betty yelled from where she was standing in the house.

330

The dog looked at her but didn't seem to understand. She just shook her head, tightened the belt of her robe, and waited for him to finish his business.

Betty let the dog back in through the sliding door. "Don't get too comfortable here," she warned as she attempted to usher him back to the laundry room. But since he didn't seem very eager to go, she resorted to using an opened can of dog food to entice him. Holding it in front of his nose, she led him into the room.

"Now, as bad as your master may be, he's still your owner." Betty spooned some food into the bowl. "And like it or not, you're going back to him today."

Betty went to check on Avery, only to discover that she was still sound asleep. Probably exhausted from her travels or whatever it was she'd been doing. Betty decided to just let the girl rest. Besides, it might make it easier to return the dog without Avery around to stir things up.

Betty knew that Avery was outraged by Jack's attitude toward his dog. Perhaps it had to do with Avery's feelings about how her mother was treating her. Or maybe it was just empathy. Whatever the case, Betty knew this was something she should handle on her own. So she gathered up the dog things and put them in an oversized trash bag, then leashed up the dog and proceeded down the street and around the corner toward Jack's house.

As usual, his pickup was parked diagonally across the front yard, and the place still looked like a wreck. And just like yesterday, no one answered when she rang the doorbell. Then it occurred to her that the doorbell, like the rest of the house, could be out of order. And so she knocked loudly. But as she knocked, she noticed that the door was ajar. She pushed it open slightly and was tempted to peek inside, but she worried that she might be caught and accused of trespassing, so she controlled herself. Instead, she simply unlatched the leash from the little dog's collar and shoved the unsuspecting pooch through the open door, then closed it firmly. She left the leash and the bag of doggy things on the front porch. Resisting the urge to brush off her hands or shake the dust off her feet, Betty turned and marched away. Mission accomplished.

Betty went home and cleaned up the laundry room, trying to eradicate the damp doggy odor that seemed to permeate the tight area. She put in a load of laundry, including Avery's soiled clothes and the smelly dog towels, and then she straightened the house and gave the kitchen a good scrub down.

Eventually she went to check on Avery again. It was nearly eleven, and the girl was still fast asleep. But Betty remembered the dark circles she'd noticed beneath Avery's eyes last night. She probably needed a good rest. And Betty needed to put her feet up. But first she called Susan. When she got Susan's answering service, she left a message, explaining that Avery was safe and with her, and that she'd make sure Avery called Gary and Stephanie as soon as possible.

It was almost one by the time Avery made an appearance. By then Betty had enjoyed a short nap and come up with a plan for their day. She explained her idea to Avery as she set a peanut butter and jelly sandwich and glass of milk in front of her. That used to be Avery's favorite lunch, but that had been quite some time ago. She hoped it didn't look too childish now.

"I've got errands to run for my friends' anniversary party," Betty said as she refilled Avery's milk glass. "And then I thought we'd take you shopping for some clothes."

"Cool." Avery's eyes lit up like she'd just won the lottery or an all-expense-paid shopping trip.

Betty cleared her throat. "But since I live on a pretty tight budget, I'm taking you to a thrift store to shop. In fact, Goodwill is located in the same strip mall as the party store where I need to shop. We'll save on gas money as well. I hope you don't mind secondhand clothing."

"That's okay," Avery said with her mouth full. "I like retro clothes."

"Retro?" Betty thought about this. "Well, that's a good thing."

"You're probably wondering where my other clothes are." Avery took a long swig of milk.

"Yes, I suppose I was."

As Avery devoured the second half of her sandwich, she told Betty a crazy story about traveling with a friend named Kendra. They ran out of money and panhandled until they could afford bus tickets to L.A., where they planned to stay with a friend for a while, but there was some kind of disturbance on the bus during the night.

"It was all this old dude's fault." Avery shook her head as she set her milk glass in the sink. "He was like forty, and he'd been coming on to both of us, so Kendra got fed up and smacked him in the nose." Avery made a face. "So this jerk made a big fuss, telling the driver that we were propositioning him, which was so not true, and the driver put Kendra and me off the bus, right out in the middle of nowhere. So we hitchhiked, and the guy who picked us up offered to buy us breakfast in this little town. We left our backpacks in his car, and while we were using the bathroom, he took off with our stuff."

"Oh my." Betty just shook her head. "You should be thankful he didn't hurt you girls. Hitchhiking sounds very dangerous."

"I guess. After that, Kendra and I got in a huge fight and went our separate ways. Since I wasn't too far from your place, I caught a ride into town . . . and now here I am." She smiled. "I was so glad to see they still hang those candy cane decorations on the streetlights here. So old-fashioned and sweet."

Betty nodded. "Yes, that's one way to look at it. Some people just think it's because the city is cheap." She pointed to Avery's dirty dishes in the clean sink. "I'd appreciate it if you picked up after yourself while you're here, Avery. The dishes in the dishwasher are dirty."

"Uh, sure, okay."

"Thank you." Betty watched as Avery rinsed the dishes and put them in the dishwasher. She didn't want to sound like an old curmudgeon. But she didn't want to encourage laziness in the girl either.

"No problem." Avery closed the dishwasher and turned to look at her. "Now what?"

"Your clothes should be clean and ready for you," Betty said. "I heard the dryer buzzer a few minutes ago."

"Thanks."

Betty glanced up at the clock. "And if you don't mind, I'd like to leave by two. I want to get back home before it starts to get dark. That's around four thirty these days."

"No problem."

As Avery got dressed, Betty went to fetch her coat and purse but was interrupted by a banging on the front door.

And there on the porch was that dog again!

"What on earth are you doing back here?" she said. Naturally, the dog didn't answer, but his tail waved back and forth with canine enthusiasm. And there on a corner of her porch was the same garbage bag Betty had left at Jack's house. That's when Betty noticed a piece of paper taped on the dog's red collar. Stooping to examine it more closely, Betty saw some words scribbled in pencil: "Thanks, but NO thanks!"

She blinked and stood up. Well, it just figured. She must've insulted Jack Jones with her generosity. Fine, if he didn't want the doggy things, she didn't care. Why had she expected a normal reaction from the foolish young man in the first place? Still, it seemed irresponsible to send his dog like this to inform her. And it did seem a waste of money since she certainly couldn't return these used items to the store. Besides, it appeared obvious that Jack needed some help in the doggy department.

"Your owner doesn't have a lick of sense!" Betty frowned at the dog. His tail stopped wagging, and he looked somewhat confused by the tone of Betty's voice. "Oh, I'm not scolding you. It's just that your master is very stubborn." Betty thought for a moment. "But then, so am I."

Betty went into the house and dug out a small white index card, then wrote "Merry Christmas" in bold letters with a red felt pen. She stuck a hole in one corner and threaded a piece of yarn, then tied it securely around the dog's collar. "We'll see who wins this little battle of the wills."

She gathered up the bag containing the dog paraphernalia and threw it over one shoulder like a grumpy Santa. Taking the leash in her other hand, Betty marched back to Jack's house. His pickup was still there, but this time the door was firmly closed, and she could hear his power tools running inside. Just the same, she tried knocking on the door, then banging loudly, but to no avail. So she retrieved the plaid dog bed from the bag, shook it out, and set it on a protected corner of the porch. She tied the leash to the nearby post, leaving enough slack so the dog could move around a bit.

Betty did feel a bit sorry for leaving the dog like that, but it was better than him running loose in the neighborhood or being hit by a car. And she and Avery could check on his welfare when they returned from their shopping and errands in a couple of hours. Hopefully the dog would bark and make some kind of fuss to get his owner's attention before long. Betty just hoped that Jack would take the hint that the doggy goodies were intended to be a gift and simply keep them.

6

||||||||||||||||

"What happened to the dog?" Avery asked as they got into the car.

"He went home."

"To Jack?" Avery's voice was laced with disgust.

"Yes." Betty slowly pulled out of the garage.

"Did you talk to him first?"

"The dog?"

Avery laughed. "No, Grandma. I mean Jack. Did you talk to the beast? Did you tell him that he needs to take better care of his dog?"

"Not exactly." Betty sighed. "Would you mind hopping out and closing the garage door, dear?"

"Where's your remote?"

"What?"

"For the door."

"This is a very old-fashioned door."

Betty frowned as she waited for Avery to close the door. She felt like she was in over her head. Not just with Avery, but with Jack and the dog and just everything.

"Thank you," Betty said as Avery hopped back in the car.

"So, was Jack happy to see his dog?" Avery persisted.

"I . . . I don't know."

"What do you mean you don't know?"

"I mean I didn't actually see him."

"But you took the dog back?"

"Yes. He didn't answer the door." Betty considered explaining how she'd taken the dog back twice but figured that would only muddy the already murky waters.

"How could you possibly give the dog back without seeing his lame owner, Grandma?"

Betty grimaced. Why was this so complicated? "Avery . . ." Betty suddenly remembered a good distraction technique. "Did you remember to call your parents?"

"No . . ."

"Well, you promised me you'd do that."

"Can I use your phone?"

"Of course you can use my phone. I already told you that."

"Okay." Avery held out her hand.

"What?"

"Your phone."

"But it's not here, Avery. We're in the car." Betty wondered if the girl had lost her senses.

"You mean you don't have a cell phone?"

"Oh." Betty shook her head as she stopped for a red light. "No, of course not. Why would I need one of those foolish things?"

Avery looked astonished. "Are you serious?"

"Of course I'm serious. I do not understand what all the fuss is about. We've all gotten along fine without those little phones for a long time. In fact, I think people who use their phones in public—in restaurants or movie theaters or even church—well, they are very inconsiderate."

"You really are old-fashioned, Grandma."

Betty peered at Avery. "Shall I assume you have a cell phone?"

"The light's green."

Betty pulled forward.

"I *had* one. But I lost it."

"Oh yes, the great hitchhiking heist."

Avery laughed.

"Well, you must promise me that you'll call your parents as soon as we get home, Avery." They shook on it.

Avery shadowed Betty as they perused the party store for golden anniversary items. Betty had offered in early November to do this for Marsha and Jim. And she'd meant to take care of it long before now, but she'd been hit with a nasty cold that had hung on much longer than usual. She just hoped that she hadn't waited too late. Fortunately, she'd had the foresight to order the napkins earlier. She just hoped there would be no shortage on paper plates and cups now.

"How about helium balloons?" Avery asked.

"Balloons?" Betty looked up at the gaudily decorated Mylar confections displayed along the wall and frowned. There were rainbows, kitty cats, dinosaurs, and cartoon characters, but nothing very appropriate for a golden anniversary. "I don't think so, dear."

"Why not?" Avery reached into a basket of regular balloons. The old-fashioned kind. "You could do the plain metallic-gold ones mixed with some pearly whites. Put a bunch of them together in balloon bouquets. It would be pretty."

Betty considered this, trying not to look shocked as Avery raised the balloon to her lips and proceeded to inflate it.

"And cheap," Avery said as she proudly held up the filled balloon. It was actually rather attractive, and it did look like gold.

Betty nodded. "Yes, I suppose balloons might be nice after all."

"Where are you having this little shindig anyway?" Avery let go of the balloon and it went flying through the store, making a long series of sputtering sounds.

Betty looked over her shoulder nervously. "The church."

"Down in the basement?"

"Yes, of course. That's where we have social functions."

"Then you'll need lots of balloons and all kinds of things to brighten it up."

"I've only budgeted fifty dollars for this," Betty said.

"Fifty bucks?" Avery frowned. "For how many people?"

"We've estimated around eighty to a hundred. Fortunately, I've already paid for the napkins."

They headed to the paper plate section.

"So what all do you need to get with your fifty bucks?"

Betty pulled out her list. "Paper plates, coffee cups, plastic punch glasses, and forks. Oh yes, and a few decorations."

Avery picked up a package of gold paper plates and shook her head. "I'm not a math whiz, Grandma, but these plates alone are going to eat up a big chunk of your budget."

Betty felt a headache coming on. Avery was probably right. Oh, why hadn't she considered this earlier? "I suppose I'll just have to increase my budget."

"Or . . ."

"Or what?"

"Let me help you, Grandma."

Betty blinked. "That's very sweet, Avery. But how do you intend to help me?"

Avery got a sly look. "Back in high school, I loved doing set design in drama. I was always able to take a tiny budget and make it go a long way. Everyone was impressed. One year we did a pirate musical, and you should've seen how realistic it was."

Betty didn't know what drama or pirates had to do with golden anniversaries, but her head was beginning to throb more now. "I think I need an aspirin," she muttered as she opened her purse to peer inside.

"Are you sick?"

"Just a headache."

"I know," Avery said suddenly. "I saw a coffee shop next door. Why don't you go and sit down, take your aspirin, have a cup of coffee, and just relax. I'll do your shopping for you."

Betty knew this was a bad idea, but she didn't want to offend Avery. "Oh, I don't think that's necessary. I just—"

"No, Grandma." Avery snatched the list from Betty. "Let me do this for you. Just trust me, okay?"

Betty reached up and rubbed her temples.

"I promise you won't be disappointed."

"I just don't think it's a good idea, dear."

"You liked the balloon idea, didn't you?"

"Well, yes, but—"

"No buts."

Betty felt too flustered to think clearly. On one hand, it would be an enormous relief to hand this off to Avery, go and sit down, have a cup of tea, and take it easy. On the other hand, what if the whole thing turned into a complete mess?

"Really, Grandma, I *know* I can do this." Avery's eyes were so bright and hopeful that Betty decided she wanted to give the girl this chance. Really, what could it hurt? So she opened her purse, extracted the money she had put into an envelope marked "Deerwoods' Fiftieth," and handed the bills to Avery.

"And I can go to Goodwill too," Avery said. "You know, to pick up some clothes."

"Oh, yes." Betty had nearly forgotten that part of the plan. She reached into her purse again and took out her old, worn billfold. She pulled out two twenty-dollar bills. She knew that wasn't much for clothes shopping, but it was the remainder of her December grocery money. Still, she thought that perhaps this month's budget would need to be increased a bit. After all, she hadn't planned on having a houseguest. She could make adjustments for it later. It was always such a challenge living on a fixed and very limited income. But she had made it this far in life, and always the good Lord provided.

"Here you go, dear. I hope you can stretch this."

"Now you just go next door and relax, Grandma. Let me take care of everything."

Betty closed her purse and nodded. But the movement only made her head throb more. All she wanted was to sit down, take an aspirin, and sip a nice, hot cup of tea.

Before long, that was exactly what she was doing. And after about thirty minutes, she began to feel more like herself again.

"More hot water for your tea?" the middle-aged waitress asked.

Betty glanced at her watch. "Yes, I suppose that would be nice."

"Doing some Christmas shopping today?" The waitress refilled the metal teapot, snapping the lid shut.

"Not exactly." Betty smiled at her. She explained about her friends' fiftieth wedding anniversary and how her granddaughter had offered to help with the shopping.

"Your granddaughter must be delightful," the woman said. "What a relief when so many young people are so messed up. Did you hear the news today?"

"What's that?"

"Big drug bust over on 17th Street. Cocaine, meth, marijuana . . . there were even a bunch of firearms."

"In our town?" Betty clutched her coffee mug.

"Oh yeah." The waitress lowered her voice. "I actually recognized one of the young men. He'd been in here a number of times. I never would've guessed he was involved in something like that." She shook her head. "You just never know."

"No, I suppose not." Of course, this only made Betty think about Jack Jones again. Suspicions such as these had gone through her head more than once in regard to him. For all she knew, he could've ripped the house apart in order to grow marijuana inside. She'd heard of things like that before. And what if he had guns? Oh, it was too horrible to think about.

But what about that poor dog? Perhaps she'd been cruel to leave him there with Jack. She hoped that Jack wasn't cruel to the poor animal. And then she thought about her granddaughter and how upset she would be if any harm came to that dog. What had Betty been thinking?

Betty looked at her watch again. She was surprised to see that an hour had passed with no sign of Avery. She finished the last sip of tea and wondered what she should do. The strip mall wasn't so large that Betty couldn't go look for Avery. But it was cold outside. And what if Betty went to the wrong place and Avery showed up at the coffee shop?

"Everything okay?" the waitress asked with a concerned expression.

"Yes. I just thought my granddaughter would be finished by now."

"Have you tried to call her?"

Betty frowned. "No . . . but I'm sure she'll be along any minute now."

"Yes, I'm sure she will."

But as soon as the waitress returned to the kitchen, Betty began to get worried. Really, what did she know about Avery? She hadn't spent time with her in years. Betty knew that she'd run away from home. And she hadn't even called her parents to say she was alive. Then she'd hitchhiked with a friend, gotten her things stolen, and eventually wound up on Betty's doorstep. Not exactly the profile of a responsible young woman. And not exactly like the picture Betty had concocted for the waitress.

For all Betty knew, Avery could be involved in something horrible. Something frightening like drugs. And hadn't Betty just given Avery a handful of cash? What if Avery was long gone by now? What if she'd simply pocketed Betty's money and run?

Betty sighed. It wouldn't be the money so much. But to think that Avery had tricked her, deceived her into believing that she wanted to help, when she was really taking advantage of her . . . Well, it wasn't only disheartening; it made Betty feel sick. She closed her eyes and took a deep breath, willing herself to relax, to let these worries go, and to put her trust in God. It was an old habit she'd adopted long ago—a way of dealing with life's stresses.

As she sat there with her eyes closed, she heard the familiar strain of Bing Crosby crooning, "I'll be home for Christmas, you can count on me . . ." Funny how the old tunes from her era were becoming popular among young people again.

She relaxed as she listened to the words, remembering how she and Chuck had been separated for one Christmas while he was serving in Korea. How many times had she listened to the song and cried? But then he'd come home, they'd gotten married, and she had never again expected to be separated from him during the holidays. Little had she known that they would have only a dozen Christmases to share. And then he'd be gone.

The song ended, and Betty opened her eyes to discover that her cheeks were damp with tears. Embarrassed by this display of emotion, she quickly reached for the paper napkin and dabbed at her face. So silly, after all these years, to still be missing him like that.

She sighed and looked outside. It was starting to get dusky, and she had told Avery she wanted to be home while it was still light since she didn't see well after dark. She put out the money to pay for her tea and slowly stood.

"No sign of your granddaughter yet?" The waitress frowned.

Betty just shook her head and slowly walked toward the door. It felt as if someone had tied large rocks around her ankles. And she knew she was a very foolish old woman to have trusted Avery like that. At least she hadn't given her the car keys. That was something to be thankful for.

7

||||||||||||||||

"Grandma!" Avery called. She rushed toward the coffee shop with what looked like dozens of shopping bags hanging from her shoulders, arms, and hands.

"Avery!" Betty couldn't believe her eyes. "Where have you been?"

"Shopping, of course."

"But you took so long." Betty peered at her. "How did you manage to buy so much . . . stuff?"

"Goodwill, the Dollar Store, and a craft shop around the corner."

"Oh?" Betty opened the trunk of her car, watching as Avery piled in her purchases.

"Yeah. I found all sorts of cool things, Grandma. It's going to be so awesome."

Betty blinked to see some magenta and lime-colored artificial flowers tumbling out of a large plastic bag. She couldn't imagine what those bright blooms might be for—perhaps a Mexican fiesta. But they certainly weren't appropriate for a dignified fiftieth anniversary party. Even so, she was so relieved to see Avery again, to know that she hadn't run off and that she actually had been shopping—well, Betty didn't even care what kind of frivolities Avery had wasted her money on. At least she was safe.

Avery was very secretive about her purchases when they got home. She asked if she could keep the decorations in her room while she worked on them. Betty had no idea what that meant, but she was too tired to protest, so she agreed.

"But don't forget your promise," Betty said. "To call your parents."

"Yeah." Avery nodded as she went into her room. "I'll do it."

"I'm going to begin fixing dinner. I have decided that I'll do the cooking and you'll be on cleanup. Does that sound fair?"

Avery grinned. "Sure. I love your cooking, Grandma."

Betty smiled. Maybe Avery hadn't changed that much after all. Still, it was a bit stressful having a young person suddenly thrust into your life. One didn't know what to expect, how to react.

Tonight Betty was making macaroni and cheese, but not the boxed kind that turned out orange and salty. Avery had talked her into getting some of the boxed kind at the store when she'd been visiting Betty one summer. One bite and Betty had decided that Avery needed to learn a better way. Avery had been cautious at first, complaining that Betty's macaroni "looked funny," but after she tasted it, she declared it to be the "bestest macaroni and cheese ever." Betty made it with real cheese and butter and cream, and she always baked it in the oven, removing the foil for the last few minutes so the bread crumbs turned crispy and golden brown. Betty hadn't made macaroni and cheese in ages, but her mouth was watering when she finally slid the heavy casserole dish into the oven.

She looked at her messy kitchen, then smiled to herself. This was one of the benefits of having Avery here. Betty could cook what she liked, and her granddaughter would clean up the mess. Not a bad little setup.

"Grandma," Avery said from the living room. "Someone's at the door. Want me to get it?"

"I'm coming." Betty untied her apron and went out to see who was there. It was nearly six now, and most respectable people would be having dinner.

"Oh!" Avery said. She opened the front door wide enough for Betty to see Jack standing there, a somber expression on his face and a familiar-looking garbage bag in his hand. The dog stood at his feet, wagging his tail and looking into the house like he expected to be invited in for dinner.

"What do you want?" Avery put her hands on her hips and scowled at Jack.

Jack studied her for a moment, then turned toward Betty. "I don't know what your game is, but I do not want a dog."

Avery stepped forward and stared up into Jack's face. "Seems like you should've thought of that sooner."

"Huh?" He frowned. "Who are you anyway?"

"This is my granddaughter, Avery," Betty said. "Avery, I'd like you to meet my neighbor Jack."

"I know all about you, Jack," Avery said. "I wanted to report you to the Humane Society, but Grandma wouldn't let me."

"What?"

Avery pointed down at the dog. "You're a grown man. You should know better than to treat an animal the way you've treated him. He's a sweet dog, and you have totally neglected and—"

"You're crazy," he said. "This isn't my dog."

"He was filthy and cold and half-starved and—"

"And he's not my dog," Jack said. He looked over at Betty again. "I thought he was your dog. I saw him in your yard."

"And I saw him in your yard," Betty said. "I assumed he belonged to you."

"Looks like we both assumed wrong." Jack dropped the plastic bag in her house. "Here you go."

"What do you mean, 'here you go'?" Betty said.

"You got him this stuff." Jack glared at her. "I guess that means he belongs to you."

"He does *not* belong to me." Betty stepped closer, glaring back at him now.

"Looks to me like he does. You got him the collar and leash and—"

"But he is *not* my dog. I only got those things because I thought you were—"

"So you admit that you purchased the dog paraphernalia?"

"I felt sorry for the dog."

346

"And they say possession is nine-tenths of the law, right?"

Betty didn't know how to respond.

He kicked the plastic bag with the toe of his boot. "So this is your dog bed, and that must mean this is your dog."

"But I don't want a—"

"I'd appreciate it if you'd quit dropping your dog off at my house." He narrowed his eyes at Betty. "And if you do it again, I will report *you* to the Humane Society. Do you understand?"

Betty was too angry to respond.

"We understand," Avery snapped, "that you are a selfish, mean man. And you don't deserve a dog like this." She reached down and picked up the mutt, holding him protectively in her arms. "He is lucky to escape you."

"You got that right!" Jack turned and slammed the door shut behind him.

"What a beast!" Avery said.

"Good riddance," Betty said.

"You poor thing," Avery cooed to the dog. "I'll bet you're hungry."

Betty just stared at her granddaughter and the dog. She wanted to tell Avery in no uncertain terms that the dog was not welcome in her home. But Avery looked so happy and hopeful that Betty just couldn't bring herself to say those words. Not yet anyway. Besides, there wasn't much they could do about the situation tonight. The animal shelter would probably be closed by now. And Betty didn't like to drive after dark anyway. She would deal with the dog tomorrow.

"Don't forget to call your parents," Betty said as she headed back to the kitchen to make a salad.

While Betty was in the kitchen, she overheard Avery talking on the phone. She could tell she was talking to her mother and that it wasn't an easy conversation.

"I want to stay *here* for Christmas," Avery said. There was a long pause, and Betty imagined what Stephanie was probably saying to her daughter. So often she had used accusatory words, negativity, blame, and guilt to pressure her daughter into complying with her wishes. Betty had witnessed these awkward conversations before. But because Stephanie wasn't her daughter and Betty had no actual blood relation to Avery, she had always kept her mouth shut. Still, it had troubled her. It seemed unhealthy. And sad.

"I'm a grown-up," Avery said. "And I can—" She was obviously cut off again. No surprises there. "I'm sorry you feel that way, Mother. Merry Christmas to you!" There was a loud bang as Avery slammed the receiver down. Good thing that old phone was tough.

"My mother is a moron," Avery said as she joined Betty in the kitchen. "Man, something smells really good in here." She peeked in the oven. "Mac and cheese?"

"Yes. I was hankering for some."

Avery smacked her lips. "All right."

"So . . . how are your parents?" Betty asked with hesitation.

"I don't know about Gary. But my mom is as messed up as ever."

"I'm sure they've been worried about you."

"My mom is more worried about how it looks to have a missing daughter." Avery began to imitate her mother. "'Oh dear, what *will* people think if Avery is still AWOL at Christmas? It will completely ruin our hallowed Christmas celebrations if Avery doesn't show up looking like the perfect little princess daughter. Oh my, we must keep up appearances.'"

Betty smiled. Avery actually did sound a lot like Stephanie. Not that Betty intended to say as much.

"I gave the dog some food, Grandma. But he hasn't even touched it. Do you think he's okay?"

"I have no idea. I've never had a dog before."

"Me neither. But he's so sweet. If he really doesn't belong to Jack, I think I'll keep him."

As they set the table together, Betty wanted to point out how unrealistic Avery's adopt-a-dog plan was, but she decided to hold her tongue for now. Of course, the dog would need to go to the animal shelter tomorrow. But Betty would see to that. In the meantime, it wouldn't hurt to postpone that conversation. And Avery seemed so happy tonight, chatting cheerfully as they ate dinner. Betty felt there was no sense in hurrying up what would surely come as a disappointment later.

While Avery was cleaning up the dinner things, the phone rang. Betty always had a tendency to jump when the phone rang. Maybe it was because she didn't get that many calls in the evening. Or maybe it was just an old reaction from a time when a ringing phone could bring bad news. But she hurried to pick up the extension in the hallway, out of the noise of the kitchen.

"Hi, Mom."

"Oh, Gary." Betty smiled as she sat in the straight-backed chair. "It's so nice to hear your voice."

"You too. I hear that Avery paid you a surprise visit."

"Yes, she's here. And I'm thoroughly enjoying her."

"I'm sure she's enjoying you too." There was a pause, and Betty thought she could hear another voice in the background. "But, uh, Stephanie is not too happy."

"Oh?"

"She really wants Avery home for Christmas."

"That's what Avery said."

"And she wants me to tell you that you should send her home."

"I should *send* her home?" Betty blinked as she imagined packing her granddaughter in a large cardboard box and shipping her out to Atlanta on a UPS truck.

"Naturally, we'll pay for her airline ticket," he said quickly. "But if you could just make Avery see that she needs to—"

"I doubt that I can *make* Avery do anything she doesn't want to do."

"Okay, Mom, *make* was not the right word. But I know that you could influence her. Avery would listen to you."

"Avery is an adult, Gary."

"An adult who can act very childish."

"Perhaps she acts childish because she is so often treated as a child."

There was a long pause. "You make a good point."

349

"Avery seems to want to stay here," Betty said. "She has offered to help me with the Deerwoods' fiftieth anniversary celebration."

"They've been married fifty years?"

"Yes." Betty wanted to point out that she and Gary's father would've been beyond that milestone by now if Chuck was still alive. But she realized there was no reason to.

"Tell them congratulations for me."

"I will. But, you see, Avery has helped me to get things. And she's going to work on them and—"

"Sorry, Mom," he said quickly. "But Stephanie wants the phone. Do you mind talking to her?"

"Not at all." But Betty wasn't the one to do the talking. When Stephanie got on the other end, she immediately began to rant and rave about how Avery needed to come home—right now. About how she'd been gone away too long. And about how it was wrong for Betty to keep her away from her family.

"Excuse me," Betty said. "I am *not* keeping Avery from anyone."

"You're making it easier for her to avoid facing up to her responsibilities."

"Her responsibilities?"

"To her family."

"What responsibilities does she have to her family?"

"To be here with us. To be with our friends. It's what we do every year. Avery knows that."

"But Avery is an adult," she said for the second time. "She should be able to make up her own mind about—"

"Avery has the mind of a child," Stephanie snapped. "She proved that by running off and doing God only knows what with God only knows who."

"That may be. But she's here with me now. She's in no danger."

"And I suppose you can promise me that, Betty? You're prepared to take personal responsibility for my daughter's welfare?"

"I'm only saying that she is just fine. And she's welcome to stay with me for as long as—"

"So you're choosing her side. You're taking a stand against me while you enable her."

Betty wasn't exactly sure what *enabling* meant these days, but the way Stephanie slung the term, like it was an accusation, worried Betty. Why didn't game shows like *Jeopardy* talk about words like this? Just the same, Betty decided to give it a try. "Wouldn't *enabling* mean that I'm *helping* a person to do something . . . as in making them *able*?"

Stephanie laughed so loudly that Betty's ear rang, and she had to hold the receiver away. "Of course that's what you'd think, Betty. But no, enabling is making it easy for a person to avoid what they really need to be doing. You enable them to fail."

"Oh." Betty had no response to that.

"But if you're determined to position yourself between us and Avery"—Stephanie made a sniffling sound, although Betty did not think she was really crying—"then I suppose I can't stop you."

"I'm not taking a position," Betty said.

"Oh yes you are."

"I've simply told Avery she can stay with me through the holidays if she wants to and—"

"Fine. Have it your way. I hope you both have a very merry Christmas!" Of course, with the tone of her voice and the way she said this, she could've been using foul language and the meaning would not have been much different. And before Betty could respond, she heard the dull buzz of the dial tone in her ear.

"Let me guess," Avery said as she appeared in the hallway with a dish towel hanging limply in her hand. "My mom?"

Betty just nodded as she replaced the phone.

"Now she's mad at you too?"

"I'm afraid so."

Avery grinned. "Well, join the club, Grandma."

"Apparently my dues are all paid up in full."

"My mother would've made a good dictator."

Betty stifled a smile.

"She wants to rule the world, you know."

"I just hope you're sure you're making the right decision to stay here for the holidays."

Avery frowned. "You don't want me?"

Betty hesitated. Of course she wanted her. But was she wrong to keep Avery from returning home? Was she an enabler—the bad kind?

"I'll leave if you want me to," Avery said quietly.

"No, of course I don't want you to leave." Betty put a hand on her shoulder. "I only want what's best for you, dear."

Avery nodded, but there was a flicker of hurt in her eyes. Betty wondered if she should say more to reassure her granddaughter. But what could she say? It was true that Betty only wanted what was best for Avery. The problem was that Betty didn't have a clue as to what that was. Should Avery stay here and risk angering her mother? Or go home and face whatever it was she needed to face? Really, what was best? And it seemed unlikely that an old woman like herself—living on a very frugal budget and on the verge of selling her home and fleeing from a questionable neighborhood— was truly the best resource for someone like Avery.

8

Then next morning, Betty got up at her usual time, just a bit past seven. But when she went to the laundry room to check on the dog, she was surprised to discover that he was not there. The door was firmly shut, just like it had been last night, and his bed and food dishes were still there, but the dog was missing. Betty checked around the house and even looked out into the backyard, but the mutt was nowhere to be seen.

Finally, worried that Jack had sneaked over and broken into her house in the middle of the night, she decided to check on the welfare of her granddaughter. And there, in the guest bed, were both Avery and the dog. The dog looked up from where he was comfortably curled up against Avery's back, but Avery continued to snooze. Betty just shook her head and quietly closed the door. She hoped the dog didn't have fleas.

Thanks to the dog's need to go outside, Avery got up before eight. Betty sipped her coffee, watching as Avery waited by the sliding door for the dog to finish up his business. To Betty's relief he had found another part of the yard—not the dogwood tree—to relieve himself this time.

"It's freezing out there," Avery said as she let the dog back inside. "Do you think it'll snow?"

"I'm sure it's a possibility." Betty set her coffee mug down.

"I've always wanted to see a white Christmas," she said dreamily. "Maybe this will be the year."

"Maybe." Betty smiled at Avery. "Now, if you don't mind, I'd like to hear more about what you got for the Deerwoods' anniversary party."

Avery's mouth twisted to one side. "But I wanted to surprise you, Grandma."

"Surprise me?"

"Yes. I have to work on everything. But I don't want you to see it until I'm done."

"That's very sweet of you, dear. But I'd really like to have some sort of an idea of what you're—"

"I used your list," Avery said. "And I can guarantee you that I got enough plates and cups and things for a hundred people. And I've got what I need for decorations too. So can't you just let me work on it and surprise you? I promise you it'll be awesome. You won't be disappointed."

Betty thought of those loud magenta and lime flowers she'd spied in the trunk and wasn't so sure. What if the Deerwood party turned into a luau or a fiesta or a pirate party? How would Betty explain it?

"Please?" Avery asked.

Betty remembered how many times Avery's mother had questioned Avery's abilities, belittled her skills, and treated her like a child. "All right." Betty nodded. "I will trust you with this, Avery."

Avery threw her arms around Betty. "Thank you, Grandma! I won't let you down."

After breakfast, Avery remained barricaded in her room. Occasionally, she'd emerge in search of things like glue, scissors, staplers, and tape. Sometimes she would carry plastic bags out to the garage, warning Betty not to come out and peek while she worked on something out there. Avery reminded Betty of some mad scientist, secretly creating . . . what? Frankenstein? A bomb? Hopefully the Deerwoods' fiftieth anniversary would survive whatever it was she was putting together.

To distract herself, Betty decided to proceed with her Christmas baking. Just as she was attempting to fit a pan of fudge into the fridge, she felt a nudge on the back of her leg. She jumped and nearly dropped the pan before she realized it was the dog.

"Oh!" she exclaimed. "You scared me."

The dog looked hopefully at her, wagging his tail, then he ran toward the sliding glass door.

"You need to go out?" she said as she slid the fudge pan onto the lower shelf. "I'm coming, I'm coming." She opened the door and let the dog out, but as she was waiting she heard the oven timer ring. She hurried back to the kitchen, worried that her walnut squares might be getting overdone, which would ruin them completely. But she removed the pan to see that they looked just about perfect. And smelled even better.

She got out the waxed paper, tore off a sheet, and laid it on the cutting board. Then she sifted a layer of powdered sugar onto this and went back to see that the pan had cooled just slightly, so she carefully turned it upside down and dumped the squares onto the waxed paper. She sifted more powdered sugar over the top while the squares were still warm.

Finally they were finished. She couldn't resist trying a square just to be sure. And then, of course, she needed a cup of coffee to go with it. She poured the last one from the morning pot, then sat down to enjoy this lovely little treat.

She had just finished it up when she looked out into the backyard to realize that the dog didn't appear to be there. She stood and looked more closely, peering to the left and the right. Then she went outside to call for him. But he didn't come. That's when she noticed the hole in the back fence. Had the foolish dog gone off and wandered into Jack's yard again? She peered into Jack's yard, which was just as messy as ever, but she didn't see any sign of the dog. Still, she felt certain that was where he had gone.

Betty returned to the house and wondered what to do. Really, the sooner she took the dog to the pound, the better they'd all be. Besides, it had occurred to her that it was entirely possible the dog already had an owner who was looking for him. In the meantime, she didn't want to give Jack enough time to follow through with last night's threat to call the Humane Society and turn her in as a negligent pet owner. Not that he could prove such an outrageous accusation, but even so, she didn't wish to invite trouble.

She got her walking jacket and the dog leash, and on her way through the kitchen she paused to look at the walnut squares. Suddenly she remembered what her daughter Susan had said: "Kill him with kindness." Fine, that was just what she would do. Or at least try.

Betty got into her holiday cupboard, dug out a festive plastic Christmas plate, and carefully arranged walnut squares and fudge on it. It would've been prettier with a few more kinds of cookies, but this would have to do. She covered it tightly with plastic wrap and hoped that this would do the trick. Then she slipped on her gloves, and armed with leash and cookies, she was ready for her mission.

Before she left, she knocked on Avery's door.

"Don't come in!" Avery yelled.

"I won't. I'm just going next door."

"Okay!"

Betty considered giving her granddaughter a fuller explanation about the missing dog but didn't want to involve her in what could easily turn into another nasty dispute. Who knew how Jack would react? Would he assume that Betty had purposely sent the dog to his house in order to harass him? Just what she didn't need right now. Hopefully her sugary peace offering would help to smooth things over.

As she walked to Jack's house, Betty wondered how she might use the dog's runabout habits to her advantage today. She was well aware that Avery wanted to keep the dog. But perhaps she could convince her that the reason the dog had run away was to search for its real owner. And that the responsible thing to do was to reunite the mutt with his family. Surely Avery would understand.

Today Jack's front yard was cluttered with what appeared to be the Spencers' old wall-to-wall carpeting. Betty frowned down at a strip of olive-green rug. Gladys had always kept her home immaculate, and Betty suspected that the carpet still had many years of serviceable use left in it. Not that Jack seemed to care about such things.

Not for the first time, Betty was curious as to the interior state of the house. She stepped over the carpet strip and rang the doorbell. She could hear a power tool running inside, whirring noisily. She rang the bell again and then knocked. But the sound of the machine continued steadily, and Betty knew that it was hopeless. She was tempted to try the door but knew that could easily backfire. The last thing she needed was for Jack to accuse her of breaking and entering.

She considered leaving the cookie plate behind, but Jack would probably assume it was one of his neighbors attempting to poison him and toss it into the trash. And she wasn't about to waste perfectly good cookies.

Why was this so frustrating?

She turned on her heel and marched back to her house. Really, why did she even bother? As for the dog, well, he was on his own as far as Betty was concerned.

"Where's Ralph?" Avery asked as Betty came into the house.

"Ralph?" Betty set the cookie plate aside and removed her gloves.

"The dog."

"You named him Ralph?" Betty blinked. "Why?"

"It was my grandpa's name."

"Oh. Well . . ." Betty hung up her coat.

"I looked in the laundry room and in the backyard, but I didn't see him anywhere. Do you know where he is?" Avery looked worried.

"I was looking for him myself. I thought maybe he'd gone to Jack's house."

"Did he?"

"I don't know for sure. Jack's not answering his door."

"But you think Ralph is there?"

Betty shrugged. "Or perhaps he ran away to search for his owner."

"His owner?" Avery scowled. "Do you really think Ralph has an owner, Grandma? He looked like he'd been abandoned or was a runaway."

"Or maybe he's just lost. It occurred to me that he could have a family who loves him. Someone might be looking for him."

"He didn't have a collar. And you said there'd been a string tied around his neck, almost like someone wanted to strangle him."

"We don't know that for sure, Avery."

"Well, I'm going out to look for him." Avery reached for the door.

"Wear a coat," Betty told her. "It's freezing out there."

So Avery grabbed her coat, took the leash, and then was gone. Betty stood by Avery's closed bedroom door and considered taking a peek, but she knew that would offend her granddaughter. Instead, she returned to her baking.

She was just rolling out sugar cookie dough when Avery appeared—with the dog. "I found Ralph!" she said.

Betty peered down at the dog. He was wagging his tail happily, sniffing the floor and eagerly licking up spilled crumbs from Betty's baking spree. "Where did you find him?"

"You were right, Grandma." Avery tossed her parka over a kitchen chair. "He was at Jack's house."

"Jack answered the door?"

"Nope."

Betty frowned.

"I rang the bell and knocked, and finally I just opened the door and went in."

"You went *into* Jack's house?" Betty's hand flew to her mouth.

"Yep. Walked right in. Man, what a mess."

"What was going on inside?"

"Major demolition."

"He's tearing the place apart?"

"It sure looked like it."

"Did you see anything, uh, unusual?" Betty wanted to ask specifically about dangerous things like drugs or firearms, but knew that sounded a bit paranoid.

"I didn't get far enough to see much."

"Jack stopped you?"

"Yeah. But not before I spotted Ralph."

Betty shook her head.

"So I snatched up Ralph and gave Jack a piece of my mind."

"Oh dear."

"I told Jack that he was rude and selfish and mean, and that you were a nice person and that he had no right to make your life miserable."

Betty held on to a kitchen chair to brace herself. "You said all that?"

"I sure did."

"Oh my."

Avery took a piece of cookie dough and popped it in her mouth. "Yum!"

"And what did Jack say to you?" Betty asked. "I mean in response to all you said to him?"

Avery laughed. "Nothing. I think he was speechless."

"Did you ask him why he let the dog in his house?"

"I accused him of dognapping."

"Dognapping?"

"Yeah. I told him since he'd made it clear that Ralph didn't belong to him, he had no right taking him into his house."

"I am curious as to why he'd do that. Especially after all he said last night. He seemed to genuinely dislike the dog."

Avery nodded. "Yeah. I think it's suspicious, Grandma. I don't trust Jack."

Now Betty remembered her previous strategy. "But I'm also curious as to why the dog took off like that, Avery. It makes me think that he could be looking for his family."

"We're his family now, Grandma."

Betty frowned. "But what if someone out there is missing him, Avery? Perhaps a family with children? What if they want their pup home for Christmas?"

Avery bit her lip.

"We wouldn't want to be responsible for someone's sorrow."

Avery nodded. "You're right. I'll make 'found dog' posters. I'll put them in the neighborhood and—"

"But I thought we should take him to the dog shelter."

Avery shook her head stubbornly. "No, that would be cruel."

Betty didn't know what to say.

"Let me handle this, Grandma. Please."

Betty looked down at the dog and sighed. "I'll tell you what, Avery. I'll give you until the weekend to find his owners."

Avery nodded. "Okay. I'll do my best."

"In the meantime, the dog—"

"Ralph."

"Fine. In the meantime, Ralph will be your responsibility."

"No problem."

"And I suggest you fix that hole in the fence unless you want to go looking for him at Jack's house again."

"I'll handle it." Avery reached for another clump of cookie dough and popped it in her mouth, then turned to the dog. "Come on, Ralph."

Betty watched as the dog, tail wagging, followed Avery out of the kitchen just like he'd been doing it his whole life. Still, this was not reassuring. Already it seemed that Avery had bonded with the dog. What would happen when she'd be forced to part with him?

9

||||||||||||||||

Avery, true to her word, made "found dog" posters and hung them around the neighborhood. But, just to be sure, Betty called the animal shelter and local vets to let them know about Ralph as well. Naturally, she did this while Avery was holed up in her room, where she was working on the anniversary things and unable to hear. But so far there hadn't been a single inquiry about the dog. Betty didn't know what to make of it.

Then late on Thursday afternoon, the dog went missing again. Avery was fit to be tied, and Betty felt a mixture of relief and regret. On one hand, it would be easier for everyone if the dog simply exited their lives as quickly as he'd entered. Yet at the same time, Betty realized she'd grown a tad bit fond of the mutt. She didn't mind when he nestled down at her feet while she sat at the kitchen table. And she liked how nicely he would sit to wait for a treat—just like someone had taught him manners. Sometimes she thought he was a right nice little dog. This, of course, worried her—she had no intention of becoming attached to a pet.

"I'll bet Jack took him again," Avery said as she pulled on her parka. "I'm going to find out."

"I don't think you should go alone." Betty pushed herself up from her recliner.

"You sit tight, Grandma," Avery said. "I can handle this."

Betty wasn't so sure. "But Jack is a bit unpredictable, dear."

"I can deal with him."

361

"Wait," Betty said. "Why don't you take him a cookie plate?"

"A cookie plate?" Avery frowned. "Why would I want to do that?"

Betty took Avery by the elbow and walked her to the kitchen as she explained the "kill him with kindness" theory. "Your Aunt Susan reminded me of it a few days ago. And I think it's worth a try."

"I don't know."

But Betty was already loading up a Christmas platter. "I don't think it could hurt," she said as she wrapped it in plastic wrap. "And if it doesn't sweeten him up, well, at least we can tell Susan that we gave it a try."

"Okay." But as Avery took the plate, she still looked skeptical.

"Are you sure you don't want me to come along?"

"No, I'll be fine."

"Just be careful." Betty shook her finger in warning.

"Yeah, yeah." Avery was already halfway out the door.

Betty sighed as she returned to her recliner and the task of untangling an old string of Christmas lights. Earlier that morning Avery had decided to venture into the attic, then happily came down with two boxes of Christmas decorations. After that, she'd been determined that the house should be decorated to the hilt.

At first, Betty had opposed the idea. She had imagined being alone when it was time to take everything down, struggling to get it all put away before her trip to Florida. However, it wasn't long before the youthful enthusiasm infected Betty, and it was fun to see Avery enjoying herself. Betty watched with fascination as her granddaughter tried out new ways of using old decorations. For instance, Betty never would've hung her mother's old handblown glass ornaments on the dining room chandelier, but they actually looked quite lovely there, reflecting and refracting the light. Very clever indeed.

Betty set aside the hopelessly tangled lights and frowned out the front window. Had she been foolish to allow her granddaughter to go to that man's house? She got up and hurried to the kitchen, nervously staring at Jack's mess of a house as if she thought she could help Avery should trouble erupt. Just then the phone rang, and she was forced to turn away from the window.

She'd barely said hello when the female voice on the other end demanded to know if Avery was there.

"Hello, Stephanie," Betty said cheerfully, hoping she could warm up her daughter-in-law. "How are you doing, dear?"

"How do you think I'm doing when my only daughter refuses to come home for Christmas?"

"I really don't see why that should be such an—"

"That's just it. You really don't see, do you, Betty?"

"Avery is a grown woman, Stephanie. Shouldn't she be allowed to make her own choices about where—"

"Talk to your son," Stephanie snapped.

And then Gary was on the line. "Hi, Mom," he said.

"Hello, Gary."

"Stephanie wants me to persuade you to send Avery home."

"Is that what you want too?"

"I suppose." His voice sounded flat.

"But why? I don't understand why it's so important."

He didn't answer right away, and when he did, his voice was quiet. "Stephanie's mom is coming for Christmas. And, as you know, Evelyn is, uh, well, rather jealous."

"Oh?" Betty was well aware that Evelyn had often resented Betty's relationship with Avery in the past. But that was when Avery had been a little girl, a long time ago.

"I know it probably sounds silly to you."

"I just don't really understand."

"Well, Evelyn wants us to help her with her will. And Stephanie is worried that if Avery isn't here, and if Evelyn figures out that she's with you . . . well, Stephanie feels this could present a problem."

Betty was speechless. Did they plan to use Avery as some sort of bargaining chip, a form of insurance to assure them they would be properly compensated for in Evelyn's will? This just seemed so ridiculous.

"I know what you're thinking, Mom."

"Really?"

"I can guess."

"Well, I must admit that I'm a bit surprised."

"Anyway, I'm not telling you what to do." His voice was gentle now. More like the old Gary. "I'm just telling you how it is here. Frankly, I'm glad that Avery is with you. I think you're a whole-some influence in her life."

"Well, thank you."

"I just wanted you to know that Steph is very determined."

"I see."

"So if Avery could give her a call, just talk things through, I'd appreciate it."

"I'll tell Avery."

"And I apologize for how Steph just spoke to you. All I can say is that she's very upset. And she's been hurt deeply by Avery's little disappearing act."

"I'm sure it's been difficult for her."

"But I realize Avery is an adult. At least according to her birth date."

"If it's any encouragement, Avery is acting very much like an adult." Betty described how Avery had taken full responsibility for the anniversary preparations and how she'd put up "found dog" posters. "And this morning she even got me to help in decorating the house for Christmas. I'd been feeling a bit like Scrooge. But she's so enthusiastic that I finally gave in. And she's actually quite clever." Betty rambled on until Gary said he needed to go.

"I'll tell Avery to call her mother," Betty said. Then she hung up and looked out across the backyard toward Jack's house. It was dusky now, and suddenly Betty felt concerned. How long had Avery been gone? Shouldn't she be back by now? Betty could see light coming from what had once been the dining room window. But there was something like a sheet draped over it, so she couldn't see inside.

Betty began pacing in the kitchen. Should she go and check on the girl? Or would that seem like interfering? Would it send the message that Avery wasn't mature? That she wasn't capable of taking care of herself?

Betty looked up at the clock. It was about four forty now. Perhaps she should wait until five. But what might happen in twenty minutes? And then, if something really was wrong, wouldn't it be foolish for Betty to go over there? Wouldn't it be better to call the police? But if she called the police, what would she say to them? That her grown granddaughter had been at the neighbor's house for more than thirty minutes? They'd probably just laugh or write her off as crazy.

She considered calling the Gilmores, but what would she say to them? Katie was already fearful about Jack. Why alarm them further? Or maybe Katie and the girls had fled to her mother's by now. In that case, what would Betty say to poor Martin? He'd already endured several confrontations with their contrary neighbor. Why would he want to have another?

Betty continued to pace, staring out the window and trying to replace her worry with prayer. But her prayers sounded feeble. "Protect Avery," she said again and again.

Finally, it was nearly five o'clock, and she could stand it no longer. She went for her coat and took off to discover what was wrong. If all else failed, she might be able to scream loudly enough to disturb a neighbor. But Betty had barely rounded the corner when she spied Avery and the dog strolling her way.

"What happened?" Betty said. "Are you okay?"

"Sure." Avery smiled.

"But you were gone so long." Betty realized that her hands were shaking. Perhaps it was from the cold, but she thought otherwise.

"You were right, Grandma."

"Right?"

"Jack seemed to appreciate the cookies."

"Really?" Betty wasn't sure how to respond. She should be happy about that, but instead she felt suspicious.

"And we had a nice talk."

"Is that so?" Betty imagined Jack's dark countenance as he

eyed her granddaughter. Sizing her up, making his plans for evil. Avery was a beautiful young woman. And vulnerable too. What if Jack were a rapist, a serial killer, or both? Oh, why had Betty been such a fool as to let her go over there by herself?

"He's lonely, Grandma."

"Is that what he told you?"

"Yes, and—"

"I don't want you going over there by yourself again," Betty said quickly. "I'm afraid he could be dangerous and—"

"He's not dangerous." Avery laughed.

"You don't know that."

"Oh, Grandma, you're just being paranoid. Jack told me about the misunderstandings you've had and how he's tried to talk sense into you, but how you just won't listen, and now the whole neighborhood has turned against him."

"And you believe him?" Betty stopped walking and turned to peer at Avery. Her face was illuminated by the streetlight, and she looked confused.

"Why shouldn't I believe him?"

"Because he's not trustworthy, Avery."

"But you're the one who said to be kind to him. And I think that's just what he needed."

Betty was too flustered to respond. So they both walked back to the house with only the clicking of the dog's toenails on the sidewalk to break the silence.

Why hadn't Betty seen the danger in this situation? Why had she allowed Avery to walk right into what could have easily been a trap? Wasn't that how criminals worked? They earned the victim's trust, and then they went to work. What would Avery's mother think if she knew?

"Your mother called," Betty said as they went into the house.

"So?"

"She wants you to call her back." Betty removed her jacket. "She said it's urgent."

"Big surprise there."

"But you'll call her, won't you?"

366

"I guess."

"I promised that you would."

Avery groaned. "I wish she'd just leave me alone."

"I'm going to start dinner," Betty said. She headed for the kitchen, but once she got there, she just stood and looked out the window toward Jack's house. As she looked, it appeared more frightening and sinister than ever. And so she prayed again. Only this time she prayed that somehow Stephanie would convince her daughter to come home for Christmas. And, as much as Betty would miss the girl, she felt certain that Avery would be safer there than here.

Because they'd had a good-sized lunch, with a snack of Christmas cookies and tea in midafternoon, Betty decided to fix oatmeal for dinner. This with whole wheat toast and home-canned peaches should be sufficient for both of them. She was just taking the oatmeal off the stove when Avery appeared.

"My mother is losing her mind." Avery sat down at the kitchen table, which Betty had already set for their simple meal.

"How so?" Betty avoided Avery's eyes as she spooned the hot cereal into the bowls.

"She says Grandma Evelyn is dying."

"Is she?"

"I seriously don't think so."

Betty sat down, bowed her head, and asked the blessing. Then she looked at Avery. "So why does your mother think Evelyn is dying?"

"Because she's old."

Betty nodded. "But what if your mother is right?"

Avery just shrugged and stuck her spoon into the brown sugar, dumping two heaping spoonfuls onto her oatmeal.

"Would you feel bad if you didn't get to see your grandmother . . . if she were to die?"

"I guess."

Betty felt a stab of guilt. She knew she was being somewhat insincere with her granddaughter. But she was doing it for Avery's own good. She wanted Avery out of harm's way. More specifically, out of Jack's way.

"I still regret not making one last trip out to see my own mother," Betty said slowly. "I knew she'd been having some health problems, but I just didn't believe it was terribly serious. I considered going out to visit in June. But then I changed my mind. I don't even recall why exactly. The next thing I knew, she was gone. I never got another chance."

Avery nodded. "I'm sorry."

"Thank you, dear."

"But that was your mother. Not your grandmother."

"That's true."

"And I assume you had a good relationship with her?"

"Yes, very good."

"Well, it's not like that with me and my grandmother."

"Perhaps that's an even better reason to spend time with her."

"So that she can torture me?"

Betty didn't know what to say.

"Grandma Evelyn and my mom will probably gang up on me, Grandma. They'll get on my case for taking off. They'll lecture me about going back to school. They'll remind me that I'm a failure, and then they'll rub my nose in it." Avery seemed on the verge of tears now. She set down her spoon with a clank. "And I just can't take that—that's not a happy way to spend Christmas." She scooted her chair back and ran out of the kitchen, slamming her bedroom door behind her.

Betty felt like a villain. And her few bites of oatmeal now sat like hard little stones in her stomach. She just sat there with her hands laid flat on the kitchen table and wondered how she had managed to make such a mess of things. How was it possible to hurt someone so deeply when you only wished to help them?

Betty realized she was crying for the second time in one week. The tears surprised her. She was a woman who usually kept her emotions in check. But what surprised her even more was the feeling of something warm pressing against her leg. She looked down to see the dog sitting right next to her, looking up at her with the most compassionate brown eyes she'd ever seen.

368

Reaching down, she stroked his smooth head. "You really are a good dog, aren't you?" She stood slowly. "But there is someone else who needs you more than I do right now. Come on, boy." He obediently followed as she walked to Avery's room and quietly opened the door. Betty let him into the darkened room, where the quiet sobs of a hurting girl cut through her like a knife. She knew the animal's presence would just be a Band-Aid—a temporary solution to a problem that was much bigger than a little brown dog. But at the moment, it was all Betty had to offer.

10

|||||||||||||||||||||||||

Avery's mother called again the next morning. Betty tried not to eavesdrop as she took over the chore of cleaning up the breakfast things, but she could tell that Avery was trying to be reasonable. She could hear the strained patience in Avery's voice. She had to give the girl credit—she was trying.

"I'll call you tonight," Avery promised. "Yes, Mom, I love you too."

Betty was just putting the last dish in the dishwasher when Avery came back to the kitchen. "Hey, Grandma, you weren't supposed to clean up."

"It's all right." Betty smiled as she gave the speckled Formica countertop one last swipe with the sponge. "I didn't mind."

"I told my mom that I'd make a decision by tonight."

Betty just nodded.

Avery looked at her hopefully. "What do you want me to do, Grandma?"

"I want you to do what's best for you."

"But you think I need to be with my family?"

Betty pressed her lips together tightly.

"You're not going to tell me, are you?"

"I think it's a decision you need to make, Avery."

"Well, I'm not going to think about it today." Avery brightened. "Today I'm going to go decorate the church basement for the Deerwood party."

Betty blinked in surprise. "Goodness, I'd nearly forgotten that today's Friday."

"And tomorrow's the big event," Avery said. "The church secretary told me that I could come anytime after eleven today to get everything all set up for tomorrow."

Betty tried not to look too concerned. But she was feeling more than a little worried that she'd still not seen what Avery had been secretly preparing in her room. "Do I get to have a sneak peek?" she asked.

"Nope."

Betty frowned.

"Don't you trust me?"

"Yes, you know I do, Avery."

"Do you trust me to drive your car today?"

Suddenly, Betty wasn't so sure.

"I'm a good driver."

"I'm sure you are."

"And I need to load and unload everything without you seeing it," Avery continued, "or else that'll spoil the surprise. So you'll have to let me use your car, Grandma."

Just then the dog barked from outside. "You'd better let him in," Betty said, "before he wanders off."

Avery went to open the door, then came back and asked again to use the car.

"Well, I suppose I don't have much of a choice," Betty finally said.

"No, I suppose you don't." Avery grinned. "You won't be sorry."

Betty wanted to say, "I hope not," but she knew that would sound rather pessimistic. And so she just smiled and tried not to think about lime- or magenta-colored flowers. She tried not to imagine piñatas or pirates or multicolored balloons. No, she trusted Avery with this. Her granddaughter would not let her down.

"I still have some things to get ready," Avery said.

"And I have a hair appointment at nine," Betty suddenly

remembered. She had booked the appointment a month ago. Going to the beauty parlor was a luxury that Betty budgeted for only twice a year. One time before Christmas and again before Easter. The rest of the time, Betty tended to her own hair. Whether it was cutting or curling it, she'd become rather adept at it over the years. Still, it always looked nicer when it was done professionally.

For nearly two blissful hours, Betty sat and listened to the hairdresser talk about everything and nothing while she worked on Betty's hair. Betty welcomed this break from thinking about runaway dogs, mixed-up granddaughters, frightening neighbors, angry daughters-in-law, and circus-like anniversary parties. And when she left the salon, she told herself that somehow everything was going to be okay. She could just feel it.

But when she got home, she found a flustered and unhappy Avery. "It's after eleven," Avery said. "And I need to get the stuff to the church."

"I know, but you can use as much time as you like to do your decor—"

"And Ralph is gone again. I checked at Jack's, but his pickup is gone too."

"Now, don't worry," Betty said. "You just go ahead and pack your things up in the car and head on over to the church. I'll find the dog, and everything will be just fine when you get back."

Avery seemed somewhat relieved, and then she smiled. "Hey, your hair looks pretty, Grandma."

Betty patted her hair. "Why, thank you."

"So, do you mind waiting in the living room while I get things loaded into the car? So that you don't see anything?"

"I'll just go and put my feet up."

"Thanks. It should only take about fifteen minutes."

"That's fine."

"And then you'll go and look for Ralph?"

Betty nodded. "I will do my best to find him."

By the time Betty heard Avery backing out of the driveway, it was close to noon. And despite being on the verge of a nap, Betty forced herself up, put on her jacket and gloves, got the dog leash, and headed out to search for the dog. She called up and down the street but didn't see the dog anywhere. And Avery was right, Jack's pickup was gone.

Betty stood on the street, looking at Jack's house and wondering if he might've possibly kidnapped the dog and then dumped him somewhere. Perhaps he'd been irked at the dog for wandering into his yard and relieving himself on the grass.

"Hey, Betty," Katie called out as she took her mail out of the box.

Betty waved and smiled. "I thought you'd have taken the girls to your mother's by now."

Katie came down the walk toward her. "That was the plan. But then my mother came down with that nasty flu, and I didn't want the girls to be exposed to it."

"I understand." Betty nodded, then frowned as she glanced over at Jack's house again. Just what was that man up to anyway? Had he taken the dog? And, if so, how would Avery react?

"Is something wrong?" Katie looked worried. "Tell me, Betty, has Jack done something again?"

Instead of voicing her concerns about Jack's interest in her granddaughter, Betty quickly explained about the missing dog. "He's shown up at Jack's more than once, so I thought maybe he'd be there today."

"You still have that dog? I saw all those dog posters around, and I figured the owners must've called you by now."

"No." Betty shook her head. "And I'm not sure what to do about it. My granddaughter, who's staying with me right now, is getting very attached to the mutt, but we will most definitely have to find a home for him soon."

"You mean if you find him at all."

"Yes, I suppose that's true." Betty sighed. "He's a nice little dog, but he's also a bit of a nuisance with all this running-off business."

"I know what you mean." Katie pulled her knit hat down over her ears. "We had a runaway cat for a while—every time Fiona took off, the girls' hearts were just broken. I could hardly stand it. I'd waste hours on end just hunting all over for her."

"I remember," Betty said. "She was a little black and white cat. Sometimes she'd be in my yard."

Katie nodded. "We got her spayed and everything, but it made no difference. She had absolutely no sense of boundaries. She'd be gone for a week and we'd be almost ready to give up on her, then she'd come home again. Naturally, the girls would be deliriously happy, and for a while everything would be fine. And then foolish Fiona would pull her little disappearing act again. I finally decided it was in the best interest of the girls' emotional welfare if that crazy cat was gone for good." Katie had a sly expression now. "The next time she ran away . . . she never came back."

Betty blinked.

"I simply took her to the pound, Betty. And I told them that the cat needed to be out on a farm where she could roam freely."

"How did the girls feel about not seeing Fiona again?"

"Naturally, they were sad. But they got over it. In the long run, it was really the kindest solution. Better to deal with these things early on—less pain that way."

Betty nodded. "That makes sense."

"Anyway, I'll let you know if I see your funny little dog around," Katie said.

Betty placed a hand on Katie's arm. "Say, I'll bet your girls would love to get a dog for Christmas."

Katie just laughed. "A runaway dog, Betty? Weren't you listening?"

"Well, I thought it was worth a try."

"Thanks anyway."

They parted ways, and Betty made a mental note to take the Gilmores a cookie plate—a small consolation for being stuck in this neighborhood during the holidays.

Betty walked up and down the street one more time, calling and looking, but with no luck. As she walked, she replayed Katie's story about the runaway Fiona. Maybe Katie was right about this. Maybe it was better to just get it over with, get rid of the dog before anyone—specifically, Avery—had time to become too attached. Yes, it made perfect sense. And if she were lucky, the dog would go away and stay away on his own. Maybe that's what he had already done. He certainly seemed the type.

She was about to turn the corner to go home and forget all about the mutt when she saw that familiar red pickup coming down the street. She waited for Jack to slow down and then watched him drive right up on the curb, over the sidewalk, and park right in the middle of his brown yard. Such a lovely sight.

"Hey," he called out to her. "I got your dog."

Betty hurried over, ready to demand to know why in the world this thoughtless young man felt it was okay to nab someone's dog and then drive him around in his truck. Furthermore, if he thought that was acceptable behavior, where did he draw the line? Would he be kidnapping Avery next and—

"I found him out in the street," Jack said as he climbed out of the pickup. The dog hopped out behind him, looking none the worse for wear. "I drove by your house earlier to drop him off, but your garage was open and your car was gone."

"I was getting my hair done." She realized that this had probably come out sounding rather snippy. But she was angry and getting angrier.

"Yeah, well, it didn't look like anyone was home. So I decided to take Ralph to the lumberyard with me."

"Ralph?" Betty was surprised that Jack actually knew the dog's name.

"Yeah, that's what Avery said she's calling him."

"Avery can call him whatever she likes, but he'll be going to the dog shelter before the day is over."

Jack scowled at her. "Shouldn't that be up to Avery?"

Betty wanted to tell him to mind his own business but decided to go another route. "Avery will be returning to Atlanta for Christmas, and with holiday travel costs what they are these days, and this being at the last minute, I seriously doubt her parents will be willing to pay airfare for this stray dog as well." She bent down and clipped the leash onto his collar.

Jack's dark eyes felt like drills boring into her now. "Does Avery know you're taking Ralph to the pound?"

Betty blinked. "I told my granddaughter that I'd give the dog a few days to be picked up by his owners. Since that does not appear to be the case, she will surely understand about this."

Jack just pressed his lips together and shook his head.

"I am in no position to be adopting a pet," she said. Not that it was any of his business or that she needed to defend herself to the likes of him.

"I'm not suggesting you are." He just shrugged.

"Come on," she said to the dog, jerking firmly on the leash.

Jack watched her with obvious disapproval.

"Come on," she said again. Fortunately, this time the dog listened and began to move.

"Anyway," Jack called as she began to walk away, "thanks for the cookies."

She turned and looked back at him in surprise. "You . . . you're welcome."

Then he smiled. But, for the life of her, she could not read what was behind that smile. In some ways it seemed genuine, but the more she thought about it, the more convinced she became that it was a mocking smile. As if he knew something she didn't. And it was unnerving.

Betty took the dog into the house, put him in the laundry room, securely closed the door, and proceeded to look up the number for the animal shelter. As the phone rang, she reminded herself of Katie's story, of runaway animals and broken hearts. Really, it would be for the best.

Finally, a man answered, and she quickly explained her situation.

"We're pretty full up right now," he said.

"I'm very sorry about that," Betty said. "But this is not my dog. I've allowed him to stay with me, but I can't continue this. He had no ID or collar or anything. And it's been almost a week. I've already called the local vets and posted 'found dog' signs, and I even offered him to my neighbor as a Christmas present for her little girls."

The man chuckled. "That didn't go over?"

"Not too well." She almost told him about the runaway part but thought that might not present the dog in the best light. "So, you see," she said, "I really need to bring him in. Before the weekend, if possible."

"We're open until six."

"Thank you." Betty hung up and just hoped that Avery would get home from the church in time to make it to the shelter before six. She also hoped that Avery wouldn't be too upset or try to put the brakes on this solution. Because, really, it was for the best. It made no sense for either Betty or Avery to hang on to this mutt any longer.

And yet, if it truly was for the best, why did she feel so uncertain? Why did she feel somewhat guilty?

Just then the phone rang, causing Betty to jump.

"How are you, dear?" Marsha asked.

"Oh my! Do you really want to know?"

"Of course I do. What's the matter?"

So Betty poured out the whole frustrating story about the stray dog and the unexpected granddaughter and everything. Almost. The only part she left out was in regard to Jack. But that was only because she knew Marsha lived a protected life. With a gated neighborhood and a modern security system in her home, Marsha couldn't possibly understand a neighbor like Jack.

"Is there anything I can do for you?"

"As a matter of fact, yes." Betty told her about the need to take the dog to the shelter. "I'd drive him myself, but I let Avery use my car so she could set things up for your anniversary party tomorrow."

"Avery is setting things up?"

Betty could hear the concern in Marsha's voice. "Oh, she's very talented," Betty said. "Much more creative than I am."

"Really?"

"She's been working on it for the past few days."

"The past few days?" Now Marsha sounded impressed, and Betty worried that she may have overstated things. "Isn't that nice."

"So, you see, I'm without a car. And I'm worried the shelter may close before Avery gets back. And then we'd be stuck with the dog all weekend, and I just don't know what to—"

"Well, I was just on my way out to pick up Jim's favorite suit at the cleaner's. How about if I come and pick you up?"

"Oh, I would be so grateful, Marsha. You're sure you don't mind?"

"What are friends for?"

Betty waited on pins and needles, watching eagerly for Marsha's silver Cadillac to pull up. She so wanted to take care of this business before Avery got back from the church. She'd already put on her coat, and the dog was on his leash. Her purse and gloves were ready to grab up in order to make her getaway.

It was nearly two when she saw Marsha's car coming down her street, and even before she pulled into the driveway, Betty and Ralph were out the door and heading toward her.

"My, but you are eager," Marsha said as Betty opened the door on the passenger side.

"I didn't want to waste any of your time."

Marsha frowned slightly. "I don't suppose you have a doggy carrier for him, do you?"

"I'm sorry." Betty bent down to pick up the dog, then eased herself backward onto the seat and planted the dog securely on her lap before turning her legs around. "But I'm sure he'll be no trouble."

"I just don't want him to scratch the leather upholstery. Jim wouldn't appreciate that."

"I'll be very careful."

"Very wise of you to take care of this doggy business before the holidays," Marsha said. "Pets can be such a nuisance, underfoot, breaking things."

Betty felt unexpectedly defensive of the little dog just then. And she almost told Marsha that this animal was different, that he didn't break things or get underfoot, and he certainly would not scratch up Marsha's upholstery. At least she hoped not. And he didn't disappoint her—he sat perfectly quiet as Marsha drove them across town.

"I'm so looking forward to the celebration tomorrow," Marsha said. "I can't wait to see who comes." She explained that her daughter Karen had let it slip that they'd received some unexpected RSVPs. "She wouldn't say specifically from whom, but I could tell by the way Karen said it that we'd be pleasantly surprised."

"How nice." Betty patted the dog on the head and tried not to feel guilty for what she was about to do. Surely the dog would find a good home. Besides, what choice did she have? Avery would be returning to Atlanta soon. Having the dog around would only make it harder on everyone. Betty was doing her granddaughter a favor. Not only would it please Avery's parents, but it would keep her out of harm's way where Jack was concerned.

"Here we are," Marsha said as she pulled up to a cinderblock structure that looked more like a prison than a shelter. "Would you like me to come in with you?"

Betty considered this. The truth was that moral support would be most welcome right now. But then she looked at Marsha's lovely leather jacket and considered the animal smells that would most likely permeate the building, combined with Marsha's general disapproval of pets. "No," she finally said. "I'll be fine. But thanks for offering."

Betty picked up the dog and set him outside the car, but she could tell by his quivering body that he was just as nervous as she. And he was probably even more frightened. Still, she suppressed these troublesome thoughts as she walked toward the entrance. This really was in the best interest of everyone, she told herself as she reached for the door. Katie had said as much, and so had Marsha. Betty was foolish to think otherwise.

As she entered the building, hearing barks and yelps of other dogs, she knew that she'd done Avery a big favor by handling this on her own. It took strength to do something like this.

"May I help you?" asked a young woman in blue jeans and a sweatshirt.

Betty quickly explained her phone call and how a man had told her she could bring the dog in. The woman asked her some questions and finally handed her a rather lengthy form. Betty carefully filled it in and gave it back to her.

The woman studied the form, then frowned at Betty. "You're sure you wouldn't want to keep this dog?"

Betty glanced down at the dog. He looked up with such trusting brown eyes that she forced herself to turn away. She shook her head. "No, no. I can't have a dog. You see, I go to Florida next month, and I don't have anyone to care for him . . ." She continued rambling about how she planned to sell her house and perhaps look into some kind of retirement home. Even to her own ears it all sounded rather lonely and sad . . . and perhaps a little bit phony.

The woman took the leash from Betty's hand. "It's not required, but we like to recommend that people who leave pets in the shelter make some kind of a donation toward the welfare of the animal."

Betty tried not to look too surprised as she opened her purse. "I live on a fixed income," she explained as she extracted a ten-dollar bill and several ones. "Will this be enough?"

"Thank you." The woman smiled. "That will help to buy pet food."

Betty nodded and backed away from the woman and the dog. "Yes . . . I suppose it will." She turned and made her way to the front door, realizing that everything looked blurry now. She reached for the doorknob but couldn't actually see it. She fumbled until it turned in her hand. Then, as she went out into the cold air, she realized she had tears running down her cheeks. She was crying again. The third time this week. And this time, she was crying harder.

She paused to reach for a handkerchief, drying her tears and blowing her nose before getting back into Marsha's warm car. *Goodness*, she thought as she tucked her hanky back in her coat pocket, *all this emotion—just for a dog?*

11

Betty was relieved to see that her car was not in the garage when Marsha pulled into her driveway.

"You seem very quiet today," Marsha said as she put her car into park. "Are you sure you're okay?"

Betty sniffed. "As I said, it's been a little stressful this week."

"I hope our anniversary party hasn't added to your stress."

"No, not at all. In fact, Avery seems to have thoroughly enjoyed helping."

"I'm so excited to see what she's done."

Betty nodded. "So am I."

"And now I better get over to the cleaner's." Marsha looked at her watch. "Can you believe that I'm still not finished packing yet?"

"Oh, I nearly forgot about the cruise Jim booked." Betty gathered her purse and reached for the door handle. "When do you leave again?"

"Sunday morning. We'll miss the Christmas service in church."

"I'll miss you too." Betty sighed as she opened the door.

"At least you'll have Avery to keep you company." Marsha reached over and patted Betty's shoulder. "That's a real comfort to me. I told Jim that I felt sad to think of you spending Christmas alone this year."

Betty forced a smile. She did not intend to tell Marsha that Avery might be going home after all. Why cause her concern?

"Avery has decorated the house and wants us to cook a turkey. Do you know I haven't cooked a turkey in years?" Betty was out of the car now. "I'll see you tomorrow, Marsha. Thank you again for helping me with the dog."

Marsha waved as she backed out of the driveway.

Betty went through the garage into the house. She paused by the laundry room, where the dog's things were still in their place, as if the dog would be coming home any moment. Betty quickly gathered up the dog bed and bowls and stashed them on a low shelf in the garage. Out of sight, out of mind. Or so she hoped.

Then she made a cup of tea and sat down in her recliner to relax. But as she sat there, all she could think about was that silly little dog. And even when she closed her eyes, hoping for a nap, she felt as if those liquid-brown canine eyes were indelibly printed inside her head. Finally, she reached for the remote and turned on the TV, flipping through the familiar channels until a figure skater appeared.

❦

"I'm home," Avery called as she came into the living room.

Betty opened her eyes, blinking into the light.

"Sorry, Grandma. Did I wake you?"

"It's okay." She smiled at her granddaughter, watching as Avery removed her parka and unwound the bright scarf from around her neck.

"It's so cold out." Avery rubbed her hands together. "I really think it's going to snow."

"You might be right." Betty put the footrest down and sat up straight. "So, tell me, how did the decorating go?"

Avery's eyes lit up. "It was awesome, Grandma. It looks really, really cool."

"Cool?" Betty nodded, taking this in.

"Way better than I expected. No one will even remember they're in the church basement. It's like another world down there now."

"Another world?" Betty wasn't sure what to make of that. Was

382

it another world like Mexico, or a pirate's cove, or Mars perhaps? Still, she was determined not to show the slightest sign of distrust.

"Where's Ralph?" Avery asked.

Betty stood slowly.

"Grandma?" Avery's voice sounded worried now. "Where is he? Did you find him? Is he okay?"

"Avery . . ." Betty looked into her granddaughter's eyes. "I have something to tell you."

"Has he been hurt?" Avery looked truly upset now.

"No, he's perfectly fine."

Avery looked relieved. "Oh, good. But where is he? Outside?"

"He's not here."

Avery frowned. "Where is he, Grandma?"

Betty walked into the kitchen. She knew she was stalling, but she just hadn't thought this through properly. How was she going to explain to Avery what she'd done? How was she going to make her understand?

"Grandma?" Avery followed her.

"The dog had run away again," Betty began. "I looked all over the neighborhood for him, Avery. I was quite worried. Finally, I found him. It turned out he was with Jack, in his truck."

"Did Jack take Ralph?"

"No."

"Then what?" Avery said. "Where is Ralph?"

"I knew that you were considering going home for Christmas, Avery. In fact, I think that's probably just what you need to do, and—"

"What does that have to do with Ralph?"

"Well, as you know, I can't keep a dog. I'll be going to Susan's in January. And I may even sell my—"

"Please, Grandma, just cut to the chase. Where is Ralph?"

"I took him to the animal shelter."

"To the pound? You took him to the pound?"

"It's an animal shelter," Betty corrected. "They'll take good care of him and find him a home or perhaps his original own—"

383

"Unless the pound is overcrowded," Avery snapped. "And then they might just kill him."

"Oh, no," Betty said quickly. "They are good people. And I gave them money for dog food. They won't hurt him." But even as she said this, she didn't know it for certain. And the idea of those people hurting that dog, or that Betty was responsible, cut through her like a knife.

Avery was crying now. She sank down into a kitchen chair, holding her head in her hands and sobbing. "I love that dog, Grandma. I needed him."

Betty didn't know what to say. And when the phone rang, she was relieved for the distraction. Until she realized it was Avery's mother on the other end. She'd completely forgotten about Avery's promise to make a decision by tonight.

"Hello, Stephanie." Betty's voice was flat.

"May I speak to Avery, please?"

Betty glanced to where Avery was still sobbing at the kitchen table. "Avery is, uh, well, she's unable to come to the phone right now."

"Unable? Or unwilling?"

"She's a bit upset," Betty said.

"Upset? Why? What's going on there, Betty?"

"She's sad that I took a stray dog to the animal shelter."

"Is that all? Well, put her on the line, please. I need to speak to her."

Betty stretched the cord of the phone over to where Avery was sitting. Covering the mouthpiece, Betty said quietly, "It's your mother, dear. She wants to speak to you."

Avery looked up with watery eyes. "I don't want to speak to her." Then she stood, but before she left the room, she added, "Or you either."

Betty felt a lump in her throat as she put the phone back to her ear. "I'm sorry, Stephanie, but Avery really doesn't want to talk right now."

"Well, when does Avery want to talk?"

"I really can't say, dear." Betty heard the front door open and close.

"Because we need to figure this out. Gary just found an airline ticket online. It's not cheap, but it's better than we expected."

"That's good."

"That's only good if Avery is coming home."

"Yes, that's true." Betty looked out the kitchen window, peering out into the darkness and worrying about her granddaughter being out on the streets alone on a cold winter night.

"And we don't know if Avery is coming home. There is no point in wasting good money on air fare if Avery has no intention of coming home. Do you understand what I'm saying to you, Betty?" Stephanie said as if she were speaking to a child.

"Of course."

"So, can you tell me what we should do? Should I tell Gary to get the ticket?"

"I really don't know."

"Can you promise me that you'll see to it that Avery gets to the airport and gets on the plane? It's a red-eye flight."

"A red-eye flight?"

"Yes. The plane leaves at 10:15 p.m. your time."

"At night?"

"P.m. means night, Betty."

"Yes, I know that." She imagined herself driving Avery to the airport at night. Betty did not see well after dark. And the airport was nearly an hour away.

"So, do we book the flight or not, Betty?" Stephanie's voice was sounding more and more impatient. She reminded Betty of a rubber band that was stretched too tightly.

"I just don't see how I can possibly make that decision," Betty said.

"Well, someone needs to."

"And I believe that someone is Avery."

"Then put Avery on the phone!"

"I can't."

"Why not?"

"Because she's not here."

"But you said—"

"She stepped out."

"But it's nighttime. Even in your time zone it must be dark out."

"Yes, it is. I'm sorry, Stephanie, but I really don't see how I can help you. You and Gary will have to make your own decision about the plane ticket."

Somehow Betty managed to extract herself from the phone conversation, then she hurriedly put on her coat and went outside to see if she could find Avery. She went up and down the street, looking this way and that, feeling foolish, old, and tired. Really, what chance did she have of catching up with a young girl?

Finally, she returned home in defeat. Out of curiosity, she checked Avery's room. It was something of a relief to see that Avery had taken nothing with her. Not even her purse. Perhaps she was just taking a walk to cool off. But with temperatures dropping below freezing tonight, she would cool off quickly.

It was nearly eight when Betty finally made some oatmeal for her dinner, but even then she didn't feel hungry. Where was Avery? Was she okay? Should Betty call the police and report her as missing? Would they even be concerned? Wasn't there some kind of rule about a person being missing more than one day before they would search? But perhaps Betty could explain that her granddaughter was distraught, possibly even depressed. Would they go and look for her then? If Marsha and Jim weren't busy packing and preparing for their big day tomorrow as well as their anniversary cruise, Betty would call them and ask for help.

After only a few bites, Betty dumped her oatmeal and began to clean the kitchen. By nine, she decided to call the local police. Really, what could it hurt? But as she expected, they did not want to file a missing persons report yet.

"Most cases like this resolve themselves," the woman told her. "Your granddaughter is probably on her way home right now."

"But—"

"If it makes you feel better, I'll let our patrolmen know that she's out there."

"Oh, yes, I would appreciate that." Betty gave her a description of Avery, thanked her again, and hung up. She looked out the living room window, staring out into the darkened street and hoping that, like the policewoman had assured her, Avery would suddenly show up at the door.

Finally, Betty attempted to watch some TV. And eventually she just went to bed, but she was too worried to sleep. And so she prayed. She prayed that somehow God would unravel this tangled mess that she felt responsible for creating. She prayed that God would somehow take what appeared to be evil and transform it into good.

At just a few minutes past eleven, Betty heard the front door open and close. She'd purposely left it unlocked in the hopes that Avery would return. But now she was worried. What if a perfect stranger had just walked into her home? Perhaps her strange neighbor Jack?

Betty remained motionless, almost afraid to breathe as she listened to quiet footsteps. Then she heard someone using the bathroom. And then going into Avery's room and closing the door. Of course, it had to be Avery. But just to be sure, Betty slipped out of bed and tiptoed to the living room. Hanging limply over the back of an armchair was Avery's parka and bright red scarf. She was safe.

12

Betty slept in later than usual on Saturday morning. Probably due to her late night and worries about her granddaughter. Still, she felt hopeful as she got out of bed. She was optimistic as she did her morning stretches, then pulled on her thick, quilted robe. Avery was home, and this morning they would talk. Betty would apologize for taking Ralph (yes, she was calling the dog by his name now) to the shelter. And perhaps she and Avery could figure this whole thing out together. Maybe there was a way that Avery could keep the dog. Even if it meant Betty had to use some of her savings to pay for the dog to fly to Atlanta with Avery. Oh, some might think it foolish on Betty's part, but maybe it was just what the girl needed.

Avery's bedroom door was open, but Avery was not in her room. Her bed was neatly made, and some of her clothes were folded and sitting at the foot of it.

"Avery?" Betty tapped lightly on the partially opened bathroom door. But Avery wasn't in there. Betty continued to look through the house, only to discover that Avery wasn't there at all. But where could she be? Suddenly Betty realized that she'd never gotten her car keys back from Avery last night. But when she hurried out to the garage, she found the car parked there as usual.

As Betty made coffee—a full pot since she told herself that Avery had simply taken a morning stroll—the phone rang again. This time it was Gary, and all Betty could tell him was that Avery had come home safely last night but had gone out again this morning.

"This isn't helpful, Mother."

"I'm sorry, but that's all I know."

"Steph is really bugging me to get that ticket."

"Like I told her yesterday, that is up to you. I don't know how to advise you."

"Well, when Avery comes in, please ask her to call."

She promised to do that and hung up. A part of her was tempted to jerk the cord out of the wall, but she knew that wasn't a very responsible thing to do. Instead, she sat down and drank her coffee and prayed that Avery would come home soon. Surely she'd want to go to Jim and Marsha's anniversary celebration this afternoon. She had worked so hard on those decorations and had been so excited about everything. Betty remembered how her face had lit up while she was talking about it yesterday. Yes, Avery would certainly want to go to the party.

But at one twenty, Avery was still not back. The party was supposed to start at two, but Betty had planned to get there early to check on things. So she left Avery a note along with bus fare, saying that she looked forward to seeing her at the celebration.

Betty grew increasingly nervous as she drove toward the church. Suddenly she was remembering those gaudy flowers again, those mysterious bags, and how Avery had holed up in her room. What if she'd actually created a monstrosity? What if Avery was too embarrassed to show her face at the church now? How would Betty explain it? How could she possibly apologize or make it up to her good friends?

Betty parked in the back, thankful that no other cars were there yet. It was barely one thirty now. If the decorations were truly a disaster, Betty might have enough time to make changes, to cover up for her granddaughter's lack of discretion.

She entered the church and headed straight down the stairs, bracing herself. She was about to turn on the lights when she realized there was already some light down there. Not bright, but enough to see.

Betty entered the room and was stunned to find that the basement had been transformed into a gold and white fairyland. So pretty it literally took her breath away. How was it possible that Avery had done this? And on such a frugal budget? It seemed nothing short of miraculous.

Betty walked through the room, admiring a concoction of gauzy white fabric that was hung like an arbor over the main table. The folds of fabric were sprinkled with gold sparkles and tiny stars and intertwined with small white Christmas lights. There were pearly white and gold balloons here and there, and an abundance of gold and white flowers artfully arranged. Upon closer investigation, Betty discovered that spray paint had been involved—Avery had used metallic gold and white spray paint to transform the previously bright-colored artificial blooms into something much more dignified and fitting for a golden anniversary.

Paper doilies were painted gold, arranged beautifully beneath small stacks of white paper plates and embossed napkins. If Avery had told Betty she was using plain paper plates, Betty would've been concerned. But the way Avery had placed and arranged everything—it was all perfectly elegant. It was truly a work of art. Betty wished she'd thought to bring a camera. But surely someone would have one.

Now Betty noticed a number of white candles that had touches of gold spray paint, like gilt, to make them lovelier. And nearby was a box of matches and what appeared to be a folded note with "Betty Kowalski" written on it.

Dear Grandma,

I came by and turned the light strings on. All you need to do is light the candles and it should be all set for Jim and Marsha. I'm sorry to miss it. And I'm sorry I've been so much trouble for you. I know I need to figure out my own life, and that's what I plan to do. Thank you for putting up with me.

Love,
Avery

Betty refolded the note and slipped it into her purse. Avery must've stopped by here sometime earlier. Perhaps just to make sure that everything was still okay. But why hadn't she stayed for the party? What difference would a few more hours make? Why had Avery been in such a hurry?

Of course, Betty knew why. It was because of her . . . and what she'd done to Ralph.

Betty put her coat and purse in the closet and slowly went about the room, lighting the various candles and pausing to admire the beauty of her granddaughter's handiwork. The flickering candlelight, which was reflected on surfaces of metallic gold, made the room even more magical than it had been before. It was a masterpiece. And Betty knew that Marsha and Jim would appreciate it.

As she stood off to one side, looking at the scene from a distance, she realized that once again she was crying. She went into the bathroom, blew her nose, and dried her tears, telling herself that she was too old for such melodrama.

And, really, shouldn't she be happy for her granddaughter? Avery's note had actually sounded very mature. As if she had finally decided to take responsibility for her own life. To stand on her own two feet. Yet Betty couldn't help but wonder how Avery would accomplish this with little or no money. How could Avery possibly take care of herself? What would she eat? Where would she sleep? How would she manage to get by?

Betty heard some young-sounding voices outside of the bathroom and suddenly felt hopeful. Perhaps Avery had changed her mind and come back. Maybe she'd give Betty a chance to start over again after all. Eagerly, Betty went out into the room to discover Jim and Marsha and their children and grandchildren. They were going around the room oohing and aahing, obviously pleased with Avery's creation. Betty forced a smile to cover her disappointment as she said, "Happy anniversary!"

"Oh, Betty," Marsha gushed, "it's so beautiful!"

"Did you do this?" asked Marsha's younger daughter, Lynn.

"No, not me," Betty said quickly.

"It was Betty's granddaughter, Avery," Marsha said.

"Well, it's incredible," Lynn said.

"Is your granddaughter an artist?" one of the grandchildren asked. Betty didn't recall the little girl's name.

Betty nodded proudly. "Yes, I think she is."

"Is she here?" she asked eagerly.

Betty sighed. "No, unfortunately, she had to leave."

"I want to get photos of this before anything gets messed up," Lynn said. "Mom and Dad, you go stand over there beneath that arbor thing, and let's get some shots."

Soon the cake arrived, and although Betty wasn't on the refreshment committee or the cleanup committee, she spent most of her time helping in the kitchen. Oh, she made an appearance now and then, smiling and visiting congenially, but mostly she wanted to remain behind the scenes, alone with her thoughts. She didn't wish to spoil her friends' fun, so she hid her broken heart behind busyness.

Finally, the party was winding down. Jim and Marsha came into the kitchen and thanked Betty again. "It was so beautiful," Marsha said. "I wish Avery had been able to come. I would've loved to tell her in person how brilliant I think she is."

"I'm sure Betty will pass that along," Jim said.

"Of course." Betty nodded.

"Will you join us for dinner?" Marsha asked. "Lynn surprised us by having it all catered at our house, and I know there's plenty for—"

"No thank you," Betty said quickly.

"Avery could come too," Jim said.

"Thanks, but we have other plans."

"Are you sure?" Marsha looked disappointed.

"Yes." Betty forced a smile.

Then Marsha and Jim hugged Betty and wished both her and Avery a merry Christmas. Betty told them to have a delightful cruise and to send a postcard.

"Count on it," Marsha said as she rejoined her family.

Betty remained in the kitchen just puttering around, wiping things that she'd already wiped, and waiting for everyone to depart on their merry ways. Finally, it was only the cleanup committee that remained, and they were getting right to work.

"Hey, Betty," Irene called out, "do you want to save any of these decorations?"

Betty went out and looked around the room. It no longer seemed magical with the harsh glare from the florescent overhead lights. Irene blew the last candle out, and others gathered up trash, plates with remnants of uneaten cake, plastic cups, and wadded-up napkins.

She was about to say no but then thought of Avery and all her hard work. She went to the main table and picked up a candle that was wreathed in gold and white flowers. "Yes," she told Irene. "I'll keep this as a memento."

"We'll put some of these other things in the wedding closet," Irene said. "You never know what might come in handy."

Betty nodded. "You never know." Then she got her coat and purse and went out to her car. It was just getting dusky out, and as Betty drove, she couldn't help but keep a lookout for Avery. How she longed to spot the girl, to pick her up, hug her tightly, and take her home. But there was no sign of her.

As Betty turned down her street, she saw that it was beginning to snow. Perhaps Avery's much-longed-for white Christmas was about to become a reality. But where was Avery?

Suddenly, Betty grew hopeful again. Perhaps Avery was at home. Maybe she'd realized that being broke and homeless on a cold day like this was not all she'd hoped it would be. Maybe she'd come to her senses.

Betty was tempted to drive fast, but she knew the streets were getting slick, and her night vision was lacking, so she went slowly and carefully. But when she got into the house, it looked just as it had when she'd left. Avery's clothes were still folded neatly at the foot of her bed. This had given Betty some hope earlier, thinking that Avery had probably planned to return. But as Betty looked more closely, it seemed that most of Avery's things, including her oversized bag and personal items from the bathroom, were missing. As if she had packed up and left for good. Those few items of clothing still on the bed had probably been too bulky to stuff into her bag.

Betty picked up a wooly sweater that Avery had purchased for two dollars at Goodwill, and held it to her chest. Why hadn't Avery taken this with her? If it was too big to pack, she could've at least worn it under her parka. It would've been much warmer than some of those other lightweight blouses Avery often wore. Why hadn't she taken it with her? And why had she left at all?

13

At five thirty, Betty put together a cookie platter for the Gilmores. She'd been meaning to do this for a couple of days, but what with Avery, the dog, and the anniversary party, she had forgotten. But now, despite the weather and the hour, she was determined to get it delivered. And her determination was twofold. Naturally, she wanted to be neighborly. But she also wanted to know if, by any chance, they had observed Avery coming or going today. Perhaps Katie had spoken to her. Although it seemed unlikely.

There was a dusting of snow on the sidewalk as Betty made her way down the street, then knocked on the Gilmores' door.

"Oh!" Katie opened the door, holding a roll of Santa wrapping paper in her hand. "What are you doing out in this weather?"

Betty forced a smile. "Wishing my neighbors a merry Christmas!" She held out the cookie tray.

"Oh, thank you!" Katie stuck the roll of wrapping paper beneath her elbow to receive the platter of sweets. "Won't you come in?"

"Perhaps for a minute."

"Martin took the girls out to get a Christmas tree," Katie said as Betty came inside. "He grew up in a family that firmly believed respectable people never put up their trees *until* Christmas Eve. But the girls begged and begged, and he finally gave in. So this year our tree will be up two days before Christmas." She winked. "That's progress."

"Yes." Betty nodded and smiled.

Katie cleared away wrapping paper and ribbons to make a spot for the cookies on the dining room table. "Would you like some coffee or tea or—"

"No thank you. I really can't stay. I can see you're busy."

"And I know you have your granddaughter visiting . . ." Katie frowned slightly, as if something unpleasant just occurred to her.

"Yes? What about my granddaughter?" Betty leaned forward. "Have you seen her today?"

"I realize it's not really any of my business."

"What isn't your business?"

"Well, I did notice your granddaughter today. I was picking up the newspaper this morning, and I saw her."

Betty nodded. "And?"

"And . . . I couldn't help but notice she was with Jack."

"Oh?"

"Yes. I thought it was rather odd, Betty. I hadn't imagined that they'd be friends."

"Well, Avery has met Jack. And they actually had a nice little chat the other day. It seems he's lonely, and it's the holidays, and . . ." Betty didn't know what else to say. And despite her reassuring words, her heart was beginning to pound.

"Oh. Well, it just caught my attention to see her with him. They were getting into his truck."

"Jack's pickup?" For some reason, this struck Betty as strange. It was one thing to visit with a neighbor, something else altogether to let them take you somewhere in their vehicle.

Katie nodded. "Yes. And . . . I don't know how to say this, except to just spit it out in the open."

"Say what?"

"Your granddaughter seemed, uh, a little upset."

"Was Jack forcing her into his pickup?"

"I don't think so. But something about the whole thing just struck me wrong—I felt worried."

"Oh dear!" Betty's hand flew to her mouth.

"I'm sorry, Betty. I had meant to mention it to you earlier, just to make sure everything was okay. But then things got hectic, and Martin offered to watch the girls so I could do some last-minute Christmas shopping, and by the time I got back, you were gone. I got busy wrapping presents, and I guess I just forgot."

A rush of panic jolted through Betty. What if Avery, after a short conversation, had trusted Jack? And what if he'd turned out to be just the sort of person that Betty and everyone else in the neighborhood had feared? What if he had somehow tricked Avery? What if she was in trouble now?

"So, is everything okay? I mean with your granddaughter?"

"Actually . . . she's missing."

Katie's eyes grew wide. "Oh no! I'm so sorry, Betty. I knew I should've said something sooner."

"I'm sure everything is fine." But Betty could hear the tremor in her voice.

"Where do you think she is?"

Betty considered this. "I don't really know. But I know who I'm going to ask."

"Jack?" Katie looked slightly horrified.

"Yes."

"Oh, Betty, don't go over there alone. Not at night."

"I need to speak to him."

"Why don't you wait for Martin to get home? I'm sure he'd go over there with you."

"No, this can't wait." Betty's hand was on the door now.

"You can't go alone." Katie reached for her jacket. "I'm coming too."

"No, Katie." Betty shook her head. "You stay here."

"I can't. But wait and let me get my cell phone. I'll be ready to call 911 if it's necessary."

Betty decided not to argue, and they walked over to Jack's house. His pickup was there, and the lights were on inside the house.

"I'll knock on the door," Betty said.

"What if he doesn't answer?"

"I'll make him answer."

"I'm scared."

"You stay back," Betty said. "If anything goes awry, you make a run for it and call the police."

Katie just nodded. Her face looked pale in the streetlight.

Betty turned, took a deep breath, and marched up to Jack's door. First she rang the doorbell several times, then she pounded loudly with her fist. Suddenly the door opened, and she nearly struck Jack in the chest with her final blow.

"What's going on?" he said.

Betty stepped back, then remembered her mission. "I'm looking for my granddaughter," she said.

"She's not here."

"But you were seen with her. You took her somewhere in your truck this morning."

He shrugged. "Yeah, I gave her a ride."

"But she's missing." Betty stared at him, trying to see if there was evil in his countenance.

"Missing?" He looked slightly confused now.

"Yes. She never came home."

He nodded as if he knew something. "Of course not."

"What do you mean by that?"

"She didn't come home because I took her to the bus station."

"The bus station?"

"Look." He rubbed his hands on his bare arms. "It's cold out here. Why don't you come inside and we can discuss this calmly?"

Betty glanced over her shoulder to Katie, who was now standing directly behind her on the porch.

"You can both come in," he said.

"Fine," Katie said. "But first I'm calling Martin to let him know where I'm at."

They waited for Katie to make her call, and then the two women followed Jack into his house. He took them past the foyer and into what had once been a formal living room, but because some walls had been removed, it now seemed to be part of the kitchen, and it was also connected to the small family room and dining room. Instead of four rooms, it was now simply one. Did he plan to knock out all the walls and turn the house into a big barn?

"You've made some changes," Betty said.

"Wow," Katie said as she looked around. "This is exactly what I've been telling Martin that I want to do with our house. Have a great room."

"A great room?" Betty was confused. "It looks like a great big mess to me."

"No," Katie said. "It's opened up so that a family can be together in one space."

"That's right." Jack nodded toward a couple of folding lawn chairs. "I don't have much furniture, but you're welcome to sit down if you like."

"No thank you." Betty turned her attention back to Jack. "Let's cut right to the chase, Jack. What have you done with my granddaughter?"

"Like I said, I dropped her at the bus station. Well, that was after I took her by a church."

"A church?"

"She needed to leave a note with somebody."

Betty nodded. "And after that you took her to the bus station?"

"That's what I just told you."

"What time was it then?"

His brow creased. "I'm not sure. But it wasn't noon yet. Maybe not even eleven. Avery had come over to my place fairly early."

"She came to your house?" Katie asked.

"Yeah. We'd arranged to meet here in the morning."

"You *arranged* to meet her?" Betty frowned. "Why?"

"She wanted my help."

"Why?" Katie asked.

"Because she'd been over the night before. She was upset about losing the dog. We spent a long time talking things out. She decided that it was time for her to move on with her life, so she asked me to help her."

"To help her?" Betty said.

Jack shoved his hands in his jeans pockets but didn't answer.

"How exactly did you plan to help her?" Betty persisted. ·

"She was broke. She wanted to get away from here." He scowled at Betty. "And she wanted to get away from you too. She wasn't too pleased with what you did to her dog."

Betty felt her cheeks flush. "Yes, I know."

He shook his finger at her. "She really loved that dog."

Katie looked at Betty with an alarmed expression. "What did you do to the dog?"

"I took him to the animal shelter."

"Oh, well . . ." Katie shrugged. "That was probably for the best."

"Unless you're attached to the animal and want to keep it," Jack shot back at her. "Avery didn't even have a say in the matter. That wasn't fair."

"I know." Betty nodded again. "Jack's right about that. I regret what I did."

"You do?" Jack looked surprised.

"Yes, I do. But back to Avery. You say you took her to the bus station. Do you know where she was going?"

He shook his head. "I assumed she was going home, to her family."

Betty felt a small wave of relief. And yet she wasn't sure. How could she trust Jack? What if he'd concocted this whole story, and in the meantime, Avery was tied and gagged back there in one of the bedrooms?

Betty frowned. "Do you mind if I use your restroom?"

He gave her a funny look. "Seriously?"

"If it's okay with you."

"Well, the powder room is torn out right now."

"I know." Betty nodded toward the backyard. "I've been privileged to enjoy the pink commode with my morning coffee."

He kind of chuckled. "Sorry about that. I guess it's time to make a run to the dump again."

"I know where the other bathroom is," she told him as she headed down the hallway. Fortunately, the doors to the first two bedrooms were open. Except for some random boxes and building things, the rooms appeared to be empty. Betty paused by the master bedroom and was relieved to see that, except for a mattress topped with a sleeping bag in the center of the floor, it too appeared vacant. And since all the closet doors had been removed, there was no place else to hide a captive.

She went into the bathroom, which was surprisingly neat considering the state of the rest of the house, and after a few seconds, she flushed the toilet. Then, satisfied that Avery was not in the house, she returned to find Jack and Katie discussing, of all things, remodeling.

"The trick is not to change the plumbing and electrical," he was explaining to Katie. "That helps to keep costs down." He eyed Betty. "Did you have a good look around?"

Betty just cleared her throat. "Did you stay at the bus station to make sure Avery got onto the bus safely?"

He frowned. "She's not a baby. I'm pretty sure she knows how to take care of herself."

"But did she have enough money for the fare?" Betty frowned. "Atlanta is a long way."

"She had enough fare money as well as money for food."

Betty felt her shoulders relax. "I really should thank you, Jack."

"No problem."

"And I'd like to pay you back."

"Avery promised to pay me back."

"Well, okay. Then I suppose we should go. I need to let her parents know that she's on her way."

"Don't you think Avery would have done that by now?" he asked.

"Perhaps, but they've been quite worried."

He nodded. "I guess you'd know best, Mrs. Kowalski."

Betty was suddenly seeing this young man in a new light. Why had she been so hard on him before? So suspicious?

She stuck out her hand. "Just call me Betty, please." As they shook, it occurred to her that, like her, Jack had some challenges.

She also knew, better than some, how challenges sometimes led to grumpiness. Maybe everyone just needed to be a little more patient, a little more understanding. After all, wasn't it almost Christmas?

He released her hand and smiled. "Just call me Jack." His face was transformed by that smile. And for the first time, she realized that he was fairly attractive in a rugged sort of way. "Oh, yeah." He chuckled. "You already do call me Jack."

"Sorry to have bothered you," she said.

"It's okay."

"Thanks for the remodeling tips," Katie said as they went to the door.

"And thanks for the cookies, Betty," Jack called out. "They were great."

She turned and smiled at him. "I have more, if you'd like some."

He looked away and sort of shrugged, and suddenly she wondered if she'd stepped over some kind of invisible line again. "Thanks again," she said anyway. "I mean for helping Avery like you did."

Betty and Katie walked down the sidewalk until Katie finally spoke. "He seems kind of nice."

"Yes . . . perhaps we were wrong about him all along."

"Unless he's very good at covering something up." Katie lowered her voice. "I've read about serial killers, Betty, and some of them seem very nice on the surface. But they're actually coldhearted, psychopath murderers underneath."

Betty stopped walking and turned to face Katie. "Do you really think that Jack is a psychopath?"

"I honestly don't know . . . and I'll admit that sometimes I have an overactive imagination."

Betty shivered in the cold.

"But that's the problem with psychopaths, Betty. Most of the time people don't figure it out until it's too late."

Betty just shook her head and continued walking. Maybe it was a mistake to listen to Katie. After all, she was nearly a third Betty's age. What made her such an expert on anything?

"I'm sorry." Katie put a hand on Betty's shoulder as they paused by the Gilmores' house. "I'm sure Jack's not a psychopath serial killer. Like Martin says, I should quit reading those horrible books."

"Perhaps so . . ." Betty told Katie thank you and good night and hurried back to her own house, carefully locking the doors and the deadbolts once she was inside. She shuddered to think that she'd gone to bed with her front door unlocked last night. But that had been for Avery's sake. Surely there was no chance she'd try to slip in late tonight.

Betty still felt unsettled as she picked up the phone to call her son and daughter-in-law. But she was determined to remain calm and collected. Thankfully, it was Gary who answered, and she quickly told him what she'd just learned about Avery. Hopefully, it was the truth and not a cover-up.

"I can't tell you exactly when she'll get there," she said. "But the neighbor who told me made it sound as if she was heading your way."

"Well, that's a relief. That airline ticket didn't last long online, and I doubt that we'll find another one in time for Christmas now."

"So perhaps it's for the best."

"Maybe so. Thanks, Mom."

Betty controlled the urge to apologize. She longed to confess all and to tell her son that this foolish mess was all her fault. She wanted to admit how she'd failed Avery, how she'd betrayed her trust. But she suspected that would only make him feel more concerned for Avery's welfare. Better to wait until Avery was safely home, and then Betty would gladly take the blame. And hopefully, Avery would forgive her.

"I'll go online tonight and check the bus schedules from your town so we can have an idea of when to look for her," Gary said. "And we'll be sure to let you know when she arrives."

"Thanks, I appreciate that." But after they said good-bye, more doubts began to creep into Betty's frazzled mind. As much as she wanted to trust Jack, to believe what he had told her, how could she be certain? What if, like Katie had suggested, he really was a psychopath skilled at telling people what he thought they wanted to hear? What if Avery was actually in danger?

Once again, Betty knew her only answer, her only recourse, her only real lifeline, was to pray. And so she would pray and hope for the best.

14

Betty got up early on Sunday. But as she walked through her house, going through the paces of pulling on her old robe, slipping into her worn slippers, and putting on coffee, she felt more alone than ever. She looked at the Christmas decorations Avery had placed around the house. So jolly and festive just days ago, they seemed to be mocking her now. Who was she to expect a merry Christmas?

Betty looked out her kitchen window as she sipped her coffee. A white blanket of snow had turned her otherwise drab backyard into a winter wonderland. Avery's white Christmas was just two days away. Not that Avery would know or care now.

Betty looked beyond the fence toward Jack's house and was surprised to see that the pink toilet, as well as a few other things, had been removed from his backyard. Perhaps he had taken her comments to heart and made that trip to the dump after all. But when would he have done that? Last night? It seemed a little odd to make a trip to the dump on a dark, snowy night. Was the dump even open? And why the big rush?

Unless Jack had something else he needed to dispose of . . . something like criminal evidence.

Betty shook her head as if to shake away these horrible thoughts. She was being foolish. Katie's talk of psychopaths and murderers had poisoned her mind. Jack was a good man. He had befriended

Avery when she had no one to turn to. He had helped her out of a crisis. Betty should be very grateful. Not suspicious.

Betty jumped when the phone rang. Her heart raced as she picked it up. *Please, let nothing be wrong.* To her relief, it was Gary. And he sounded cheerful. "I checked the bus schedules, Mom," he said. "And it looks like Avery will be here in time for the Christmas Eve party tomorrow night."

"Oh, that's good." Betty sighed. "Did she call you?"

"No, but Steph thinks she's probably planning to surprise us. You know how unpredictable she can be."

"Oh, yes . . . of course."

"So it looks like our Christmas won't be spoiled after all."

"Oh, I'm so glad." Betty tried to insert a smile into her voice.

"Thanks for your help with this, Mom. We're just going into church now, so I'll have to hang up."

"Thank you for calling, dear."

When they hung up, Betty just sighed. Why was she feeling so emotional these days? Was it old age? The time of year? Senility?

She went into her bedroom to get ready for church. She always looked forward to the Christmas Sunday service. Their church didn't have an actual Christmas Eve or Christmas Day service like some did. But the Sunday prior to Christmas, they always did up right. At least that was something to look forward to.

Betty put on her favorite winter skirt, a red and black tartan plaid that Marsha had gotten for her in Scotland many years ago. Perhaps that had been the Deerwoods' twenty-fifth anniversary trip. She topped the skirt with a black cashmere sweater that had seen better days, then went to the bureau and opened her old jewelry box. But instead of retrieving her pearls, she paused to pick up an old photo of Chuck. He'd just enlisted in the army when it was taken. As hard as it was to see him leaving for Korea, she'd thought he looked so devastatingly handsome in that uniform. And when he'd offered her an engagement ring and the promise of marriage upon his return, she couldn't resist.

She studied his gentle brown eyes now and sighed. All these

years later, she still got a sweet, warm feeling just looking into those eyes. So much love, compassion, tenderness . . . Oh, how she missed him. But, she reminded herself, each passing year brought her closer to their reunion.

She replaced the photo on the lace runner and sighed. She picked up her pearls (the ones Chuck had brought her from the Orient) and put them around her neck, checking the clasp to make sure it was connected.

As she went to the hall closet for her wool coat, she was still remembering Chuck's eyes. For some strange reason—and it almost seemed disrespectful—something about her dearly departed husband's eyes made her think of that stray mutt, Ralph. Oh, she knew there was no real relationship between the two. But something about the mutt's eyes—maybe just the color or maybe even the warmth—reminded her of Chuck.

As she got into her car, she wondered what Chuck would think of an old woman who abandoned homeless dogs at the pound just days before Christmas. More than that, she wondered what she thought about such things herself—not that she cared to think about it anymore.

She drove slowly to church, relieved to find that the main streets had been plowed, and told herself it was ridiculous to think along these lines. Imagining that her dearly departed husband would want her to take in a stray dog was not simply ridiculous, it bordered on the verge of crazy. Perhaps even a symptom of early Alzheimer's or dementia, although she certainly hoped not. But silly enough anyway.

Betty arrived early for church. She knew that the sanctuary could be crowded during the holidays, and she wanted to be able to sit in her regular spot. But when she got to the third row, she was dismayed to see that not only was her place taken, but so were the places where Jim and Marsha usually sat. She knew her disappointment was childish, not to mention selfish, and that the fourth row would be just fine. But feeling displaced as well as old, she simply turned around, went to the rear of the church, and sat in the very back row. Alone.

She told herself she would not feel sorry for herself as the organ played Christmas hymns. She forced a smile, or what she hoped might pass as a smile. She leaned back and closed her eyes and just listened to the music. After a couple of pieces, the choir began to sing. And soon the seats around her filled up, and although she didn't know the people sitting next to her, there was a comfort in being invisible in the midst of strangers.

During the first part of the Christmas service, which was much the same as every year, she continued to feel distracted as she pondered over what it was in Chuck's eyes that had brought that silly dog to mind. Well, besides plain foolishness. She sat up straighter and forced herself to focus on the children, who were dressed for the nativity story and singing "Silent Night." She remembered when her own children did this very same thing during their grade school years. Gary had always wanted to be a shepherd, and one year, not long after Chuck had passed, their own Susan was chosen to play Mary. So long ago. So far away.

Betty used her clean hanky to dab her eyes. She had quit keeping count of how many times she'd cried this past week, and simply decided that it was just a new stage in aging. And that her best defense was to keep a handkerchief handy.

Pastor Gordon was at the pulpit now, and Betty willed herself to listen. He'd been the pastor of this church for more than two decades, and Betty had grown to respect him for both his biblical knowledge and his spiritual insights. She had missed the beginning of his Christmas sermon but was determined to listen carefully for the remainder.

"It was not so different then, more than two thousand years ago." He nodded toward the children dressed in their robes and angel wings, who now sat restlessly in the front row. "At the first nativity, the world was not expecting this holy guest either. They were not prepared to receive this heavenly visitor, this stranger who came in the form of an innocent child. A babe, a gift from God Almighty. And yet the world needed him. They needed this gift—desperately.

"We are no different today, friends. We get caught up in the season, busily making preparations for Christmas. We decorate, bake cookies, shop, and wrap presents, and yet we aren't truly ready. We aren't waiting with great expectations. Our hearts aren't prepared to receive this holy guest, this heavenly visitor. We have already settled into our preconceived notions. We have decided how this thing called Christmas is about to go down. We have our agendas, we've made our plans." He chuckled. "But you know what they say about the plans of mice and men."

Pastor Gordon leaned over the pulpit and paused, looking across the congregation as if he were about to disclose a great secret. "God's ways are higher than our ways, my friends." He held up a fist and raised his voice. "And God's love can come unexpectedly. It can rock your life and rattle your heart! Just like the world wasn't ready to receive God's love in the form of a child that was hurled from heaven to earth, we're not always ready to receive God's love. And we're not prepared to accept that it comes in a variety of ways. Often when we least expect it, God's love can show up in the form of something or someone we aren't happy to see—something or someone we want to push away or even run from. And, let me tell you, God's love can make us downright uncomfortable at times. Just like that newborn baby wailing in the night made some people in Bethlehem uncomfortable. And yet they needed him—desperately. And we need him. Desperately. Embrace God's love, my friends. Receive it. And then share it. Let us pray."

As Pastor Gordon prayed, Betty could think of only one thing. She had to get out of there. It wasn't that she wanted to escape her pastor or her friends or even the strangers sitting next to her. But what she wanted—what she truly, truly wanted—was to go straight to the animal shelter and get Ralph. Because it seemed entirely possible that God's love had come to her in the form of an unwanted little dog. And she had missed it. Oh, she'd probably missed lots of other things too. But she could do something about this. Ralph needed her, and she needed him.

When the service ended, she exchanged some hasty Christmas greetings and made her way to the exit, then left as quickly as she could. As she drove across town, she had no idea whether or not the shelter would even be open, but she was determined to find out. To her delight, the shelter was not only open, but Christmas music was playing and there were cookies out on the counter, and several people appeared to be shopping for pets. It was actually a very merry place.

Betty munched a sugar cookie as she waited for someone to help her.

"You're certainly busy," she said to the young man wearing a Santa hat who had just stepped behind the counter.

"That's because we had a spot on the local news this morning," he said. "We encouraged families to adopt unwanted animals rather than buying them from pet shops, which might support puppy farms where animals are not treated humanely."

"That's wonderful," Betty said.

"Except that we suggested they wait until *after* Christmas. But I guess we can't complain when our animals are finding good homes."

"No, of course not."

"So, what can we do for you? A cat perhaps? I have a nice tabby—"

"No thank you," she said. "I have something very specific in mind." She explained about dropping off Ralph recently. "It was a mistake, I'm afraid. And I'd like to have him back, if it's all right."

"Could you spot him?" the young man asked.

She smiled. "Of course."

He took her back to where dogs were barking and jumping in kennels. They walked up and down the aisle, and she studied all the dogs and finally shook her head. "I don't see him."

Just then the young woman who had helped her before walked by. Betty touched her arm and explained who she was and what she was looking for.

"Oh, that little brown terrier mix." The girl nodded. "Yes, he's been adopted."

Betty blinked. "Adopted?" Ralph had been adopted? How could this possibly happen?

The girl smiled. "Yes. He's such a sweet little dog, I'm not surprised someone wanted him. Now if you'll excuse me, I need to help this family with their paperwork."

"We have lots of other cool dogs," the young man said.

"Oh, yes . . . I see that you do." Betty just nodded.

"How about that schnauzer mix over—"

"No thank you."

"Are you sure?"

"Perhaps you're right about waiting until after the holidays . . ." She attempted to smile.

"Oh, yeah." He nodded. "It's better for the animal. So much is going on at Christmas. Pets get sick eating rich food or ornaments, or they get neglected or handled too much by guests—all kinds of holiday things that can be a threat to a new pet. You're wise to wait."

She thanked the young man for his help and then walked slowly out to her car. As she drove home, she tried to understand this whole strange chain of events. To start with, a dog she had never wanted and did not need had sneaked into her life. She had made many attempts to get rid of him and finally was successful. Or so she had thought. But as a result of dumping the dog—and wasn't that what she'd done?—she had hurt and then lost her granddaughter. Of course, she had wanted Avery to go home to her parents. But she hadn't wanted her to leave like that—not without at least saying good-bye. And what was the reason Betty had wanted Avery to leave? Jack. She had been fearful of Jack. She'd felt Avery would be safer at home.

Betty just shook her head to think of what a foolish woman she'd been.

And then she thought she'd figured things out while listening to Pastor Gordon's sermon—she knew that what she really wanted, what she needed, was that little dog. But now Ralph was gone. Adopted by someone else.

Love had come scratching at Betty's door in the form of a little brown dog, and she had completely missed it. She'd had her chance to welcome it, to receive it, and she had slammed the door in its face.

15

⁞⁞⁞⁞⁞⁞⁞⁞⁞⁞⁞⁞⁞⁞⁞⁞⁞

Betty woke up on Christmas Eve morning to the jarring sound of the phone ringing. It wasn't even seven yet, but she reached for the phone and tried to sound somewhat awake. "Hello?"

"Mom, this is Gary."

"Oh, Gary." She blinked and sat up. "How are you?"

"Not very well."

"Oh dear, what's wrong?"

"Steph was worried about Avery coming on that bus, afraid she wasn't going to get here in time or miss a connection. So I gave the route and schedule information to a cop friend of mine, and he checked the passenger list just to make sure everything was okay. And guess what?"

"I can't imagine."

"Avery was not a passenger."

"Oh?"

"She never even bought a ticket."

Betty was out of bed now. On her feet and pacing. "How can that be?"

"That's what we want to know. Where is Avery?"

"Goodness, I have no idea where she is, Gary."

"When did you last see her?"

Betty replayed the last several days for him, finally telling him about Ralph and how Avery had been hurt when she'd taken him to the shelter. "I was going to tell you this earlier," she said, "but I didn't want you to worry."

"We're worried now."

"I'm sorry."

"So who is this neighbor who supposedly put her on the bus?"

"Well, he didn't actually put her on the bus—"

"Who is he, Mom?"

"He lives in the old Spencer house. His name is Jack, and—"

"Crazy Jack?"

"What?"

"Susan told me you had a nutty neighbor who was tearing up his house and that you planned to move as soon as possible."

"Susan told you that?"

"Well, I might be exaggerating. We talked before she and Tim left for the Keys. She seemed to think the whole thing was rather humorous. I thought it sounded pretty bizarre. And I think you should sell your house."

"But I was wrong about Jack."

"How do you know?"

"Because I talked to him on Saturday. He helped Avery."

"Helped Avery do *what*?" Gary's voice was loud now. And sharp.

"He loaned her money and—"

"How do you know that, Mom? Did you *talk* to Avery?"

"Well, no."

"I'm sorry, Mom. I'm not mad at you. I know this isn't your fault. I'm just very frustrated. And Steph is coming unglued."

"I'm sorry." Betty didn't know what more to say. "But as you know, Avery has a mind and a will of her own. And she's not a child, Gary."

"Yes, so you've told me before."

"And I'm sure she's perfectly fine."

"I wish I felt as sure as you do." He sighed loudly. "My cop friend is going to help me figure out a way to look for her. We'll let you know if we find anything out. You do the same."

413

They said good-bye, and as she hung up, Betty felt her legs shaking as if they were going to give way. She sat down on her bed and just shook her head. What was going on? Where was Avery? And why didn't she get on that bus? Nothing made any sense. And now Betty was feeling frightened—and guilty. If anything had happened to Avery, if Jack was somehow to blame, Betty wouldn't be able to forgive herself.

She quickly got dressed, then pulled on her jacket and snow boots and walked toward Jack's house. But as she turned the corner, she saw that his pickup was gone. She stood there for a couple of minutes wondering what to do, and then she realized there was really nothing more she could do right now. Except pray.

As she trudged back to her house, she prayed for Avery—that she would be safe and that she would reveal her whereabouts to her family. Next she prayed for Ralph—that he'd found a good home and people who would love him. And finally she prayed for Jack. Or maybe she prayed more for herself. She asked God to show her how to be a good neighbor to Jack. Then, as if adding a postscript, she said, "And, dear Lord, if Jack is a dangerous criminal, please show me the best way to inform the authorities so that he might be arrested. Amen."

Now she realized that sounded like a doubtful sort of prayer. How could one pray to love her neighbor with one breath and then pray about turning him in with the next? She just hoped that God would understand.

Betty went into her house and sat down at the kitchen table to make a grocery list. It wasn't that she wanted to go to the store, but she was out of necessities like bread, milk, eggs, and even coffee. And although she didn't feel the least bit hungry, she knew the responsible thing was to take care of this chore.

But after the sparse list was made, she just sat there staring at it. She felt as if all energy had been drained from her, as if it were an enormous chore simply to stand. Yet somehow she forced herself up. Then she stood there for a moment, feeling disoriented. Finally, she went into her bedroom and climbed into her bed, fully clothed, then pulled the covers up and slipped into a deep sleep.

"Grandma!"

Betty looked up and blinked. There before her stood Avery. At least Betty thought it sounded like Avery. But this girl was dressed in white and hovered over her like . . . like an angel. Was it an angel? Or was it Avery? Betty squinted her eyes, but the bright light behind the girl framed her head like a halo and made it hard to see. "Avery?"

"Are you okay, Grandma?"

Betty nodded and sat up. "Avery?" she said again.

"I'm sorry if I scared you." Avery sat down on the side of Betty's bed and reached for her hand. "Actually, you scared me. I knocked on the door and no one answered. And then I saw it was unlocked, which made me really worried, so I came in. And then I found you in bed like this and I thought . . ." Avery shook her head. "I thought you were dead."

Betty smiled and squeezed Avery's hand. "Not quite dead—just a little rattled and tired I suppose. But I'm better now."

Avery hugged her. "I'm so sorry I was such a spoiled brat."

"You?" Betty held on to the girl. "I'm the one who should be sorry."

Avery released Betty and studied her face. "Why should *you* be sorry?"

Betty reached out to touch Avery's cheek, wanting to make sure she was real and not just a dream. "I have so many reasons to be sorry, Avery. Where do I begin?"

"With a cup of tea?" Avery suggested.

Betty nodded. "Yes, that sounds perfect."

"I'll go get it started."

"I'm right behind you." Betty stood and slipped on her shoes, then hurried into the kitchen, where Avery was already filling the kettle.

"I still can't believe it's you," Betty said. She watched Avery turn on the stove and reach for the tea mugs and tea canister. "I saw a girl dressed in white . . ." She chuckled. "And I thought that God had sent an angel to get me."

Avery laughed. "I'm hardly an angel. And this ugly white blouse is my uniform."

"Uniform?"

"Yeah. I got a job at the bus station café."

"The bus station café?" Betty sat down in a kitchen chair.

"Yes. It's a long story. I was so furious at you for giving Ralph away that I ran off to Jack's house and unloaded on him. I told him I was leaving that night, but he talked me into waiting until morning."

"And then he loaned you money and took you to the bus station?"

"Did you talk to him?"

"Yes. I was worried."

"He's really a sweet guy, Grandma. He even tried to talk me into staying with you. But I told him I was done with you." Avery made a sad smile. "I'm sorry."

"Don't worry, I understand. I've been a bit fed up with myself too."

"So anyway, I was at the bus station and about to get a ticket to take me home, but I just couldn't stand the idea of going back there. So I got a cup of coffee."

"At the bus station café?"

"Exactly. This girl was the only waitress there. And she was in the weeds."

"In the weeds?"

"You know, too many customers, too many orders, over her head."

"Oh. I see."

"And everyone was complaining, and this one dude was being really rude to her because his cheeseburger was probably getting cold, and she was about to start crying."

"Poor thing."

"That's what I thought, so I walked right past her and got his cheeseburger and handed it to him. And then I started taking orders and getting stuff and filling coffee cups, and the girl never even questioned it."

"Really?" Betty tried not to look too stunned. What nerve!

"Finally, it kind of slowed down, and the girl asked me who I was and if I'd come about the job." Avery put the teabags in the mugs.

"And so she hired you?"

"Her dad did. He's the cook and the manager. They'd just lost two waitresses earlier that week. And with holiday travelers, they were getting desperate."

"But how did you know how to do all that?" Betty studied Avery. "Taking orders and getting food. Don't you need to be trained or licensed or something?"

"Waitressing is waitressing. I've done it a lot of times." She filled the mugs with hot water and brought them over to the table.

"But it's been two nights since you left. Where did you stay?"

"Abby and Carl let me sleep on their couch."

"The waitress and the cook?"

"Yeah. But that couch was getting uncomfortable. And Abby's sister Laurel was coming home from school today, so the apartment was going to be crowded. They gave me tonight and tomorrow off since Laurel will help them out. So I thought I'd come check on you. Then you scared me half to death by playing possum in your bed. Were you feeling sick?"

"Just very tired." Betty took a slow sip of tea.

"Hey, how did you like my decorations for the anniversary party?"

Betty gushed about how much she loved them and how everyone else was extremely impressed as well. "Marsha and Jim were completely overwhelmed with how beautiful it was, and their grandchildren thought you must be a professional artist."

"I wish."

"So, do you want to continue with the waitress job?" Betty asked.

"Yeah. For a while. Until I figure something else out."

"Would you like to stay here?" Betty asked. "The city bus stop is only—"

"Two blocks from here." Avery grinned.

"You know that you're welcome."

"Thanks. I'd appreciate it."

"Would you mind calling your parents?"

Avery frowned.

"Or, if you don't mind, I can call them—just so they'll know you're safe."

"That's okay. I'll call them. I'm trying to act more like a grown-up. That's what Jack told me I should do."

"He told you that?"

"And a lot of other things. He's been through a lot, Grandma. You should get to know him better. I think you'll like him."

Betty nodded. "I'm sure you're right."

They finished their tea, and Avery, true to her word, called her mother. Betty could hear the tension in Avery's voice, and not wanting to eavesdrop, she hurried back into her bedroom and closed the door.

"It's safe to come out now," Avery called after a few minutes.

"I take it your mother wasn't too happy."

"That's a pretty safe guess."

"But she was relieved to hear you're okay?"

"I suppose."

"It's not easy being a parent, Avery."

Avery just shrugged with a hurt expression, and Betty decided to change the subject. "You'll never guess what I did yesterday."

"Let's see. It was Sunday . . . did you go to church?"

Betty smiled. "Yes, as a matter of fact, I did. But after that I went to the animal shelter. I wanted to get Ralph."

Avery's eyes lit up. "You got him back?"

Betty sighed. "No. I was too late. Someone else adopted him."

Now Avery looked sadder than ever.

"I'm sorry," Betty said quickly. "Maybe I shouldn't have told you that. But I just wanted you to know that I had a complete change of heart. I realized that Ralph was a wonderful, sweet little dog. And that I needed him. It almost seemed like God had sent him

418

to me, and then I'd stupidly turned him away. I can't even describe how sad that made me feel." She put a hand on Avery's shoulder. "Almost as sad as losing you."

"But I'm back."

"Yes, you are." Betty smiled. "And I need to go to the grocery store. I made a short list, but now that you're here, I think it's time to kill the fattened calf."

Avery looked confused.

"Or roast a turkey."

So they went to the grocery store, and since Betty had already spent her December budget, she decided to dip into January's. Of course, this would blow her grocery budget to pieces. But she didn't even care.

16

"This is a lot of food, Grandma." Avery surveyed the bags now lined up like soldiers on the kitchen counter.

Betty chuckled. "Well, yes, I suppose it is. We better get those cold items in the fridge."

"Can we invite Jack for Christmas dinner?" Avery handed Betty the turkey. "I mean, if he doesn't have other plans, which I'll bet he doesn't since he has no family around here anymore."

"Anymore?" Betty adjusted the lower shelf to make room for the turkey.

"Yeah. Jack's grandparents used to own his house."

"Jack's grandparents?" Betty scowled. "The only people who've ever lived in that house were the Spencers."

"Yeah. They must've been Jack's mom's parents. He said she grew up here. He even showed me her room. It's still painted pink."

"Donna Spencer is Jack's mom?" Betty dropped the package of celery in the vegetable bin and turned to stare at Avery. "Are you sure?"

"You know Jack's mom?"

"I knew her. Donna was a sweet girl. As a teenager, she used to babysit my children during the summers when I worked at the post office. Then she got married and moved away. Last time I saw her, she was on her second marriage." Betty strained her memory. "It seems to me that she had a little boy in her second marriage,

420

but they only came out to visit a few times. And I think his name was Johnny."

"Jack."

"Jack is Johnny?"

"Yeah. I guess he switched over to Jack while he was in Afghanistan."

"He was in Afghanistan?"

Avery nodded and handed Betty a bag of potatoes. "He said it was pretty rough over there. But it sounds like it's been almost as rough being home. He told me he has horrible nightmares, and that's why he likes to work on his house at night sometimes."

"Oh." Betty still remembered how Chuck had had bad dreams after he'd come back from Korea, but he'd never wanted to talk about his experience there. And to think Jack had been suffering too. Making noise in the night, with his neighbors all thinking the worst of him. She shook her head. "Poor boy."

"Anyway, his mom gave him that house," Avery said.

"Donna gave him the house?"

"Yeah. She and her brother inherited it. Only her brother didn't want it."

Betty just shook her head. "I still can't believe I didn't know that Jack was Gladys and Al's grandson. I wish he would've told me sooner."

Avery shrugged. "It sounds like he never got the chance."

"I suppose I never gave him the chance."

They were done putting things away now. "I think it's a lovely idea to invite Jack for Christmas dinner," Betty said. "How about if we invite the Gilmores too, unless they're busy. It's about time neighbors started getting acquainted."

"And we can serve dinner in the dining room," Avery said. "We'll use your pretty dishes. I'll get it all set up and—" Avery paused. "Can you hear that, Grandma?"

Betty stopped folding the paper bag and listened. "My old ears aren't too sharp."

"It sounds like someone at the door."

Betty tucked the bag into a drawer, then looked up in time to see Avery dashing out of the kitchen. "Grandma!" she screamed. "Com'ere quick!"

Frightened that there was an armed gunman at the door, Betty hurried to see Avery squatting on the floor with a familiar little brown dog licking her face.

"It's Ralph!" Avery said. "He's back!"

Betty couldn't believe her eyes. But it certainly did look like Ralph. "How on earth?"

"He found us, Grandma!" Avery scooped the dog into her arms. "He's home!"

Betty considered this. On many levels she wanted to agree with her granddaughter and say, "Yes, he's home, and all will be well." But at the same time, she was concerned. "But the people at the shelter said he'd been adopted, Avery."

"Maybe he didn't like his new owners."

Betty nodded. "Maybe."

"Can we keep him?"

"You know I want to keep him, Avery. But what if his new owners are looking for him right now? I'm sure they paid good money for him. He was probably meant to be someone's Christmas present. And certainly there's some kind of record at the shelter—"

"So what are you saying?"

"I'm saying that I'd better call the shelter. I'll explain everything to them, and I'll ask if we might possibly purchase Ralph back from his new owners. The shelter people care about animals, and I'm sure they'll understand that Ralph came looking for us, not the other way around. Ralph is more than welcome to stay with us, Avery, but I do think we need to go about this the right way."

Avery looked disappointed, but at least she agreed. Betty went to make the call. She carefully explained everything right from the beginning until how the dog had shown up of his own free will this afternoon. "I'm sure his new owners must be worried," Betty finished. "If I knew their phone number, I could give them a call." Betty decided not to mention her ulterior motive about wanting to purchase Ralph back from his new family.

"I can understand your problem," the woman said. "We're a

little shorthanded here today. But if it will help to reunite the dog to his family, I think it's okay for me to give you the name and phone number of the dog's owner."

"Thank you so much!"

The woman shared the information, and Betty thanked her and hung up.

"So?" Avery was waiting expectantly.

Betty just stood there, staring first at the dog and then at Avery.

"What's wrong, Grandma?"

"The owner . . ." Betty shook her head. "It's Jack."

"Our Jack?"

Betty nodded.

Avery sighed. "Oh."

"I had no idea Jack wanted the dog."

"He didn't."

"Well, to be fair, neither did I." Betty sighed. "Not at first."

Avery was clearly disappointed, but she just nodded. "Fine. I'll take Ralph back to Jack. Just let me run and use the bathroom first."

Betty reached down and patted Ralph's head. "It was nice of you to pop in to say hello," she said. "At least we're neighbors. And you're welcome to visit—"

Just then there was a loud knock on the door. Betty opened it to see Jack standing there. "Come on in, Jack."

He came in hesitantly. "Sorry to disturb you, Betty, but I'm, uh, looking for—" His brows lifted slightly when he noticed the dog. "Looks like Ralph decided to drop by."

Betty nodded. "And I just found out that he belongs to you now."

Jack looked slightly sheepish. "I just couldn't bear to think of him at the pound."

"He's a good dog."

Jack actually smiled now. "He is a good dog. But he seems a little confused about where he lives today."

Avery came into the room with her parka and bag over one arm. "Jack!"

"Avery!" Jack looked even happier to see her than she was to see him. "What are you doing here?"

With half sentences tumbling over each other, Avery explained about not going home, her new job, and her decision to stay in town. "Which reminds me, I want to pay you back the loan now."

He waved his hand. "That's okay, you—"

"No way," she said quickly, reaching for her bag. "I'm trying to do the grown-up, responsible thing. Remember?" She counted out the money into his hand. "Sorry about all the change, it's from tips. And you'll have to trust me for that last twenty. I had to use it for a city bus pass."

"Well, I better get out of your hair." Jack reached down to pick up Ralph. "Sorry to have bothered you."

"It's no bother," Betty said quickly. "In fact, we wanted to invite you for Christmas dinner tomorrow."

"Grandma got a turkey and all the trimmings." Avery smiled. "And I'm going to make a pumpkin pie."

"Do you have plans?" Betty asked.

"No . . ."

"Then we'll expect you at two."

Jack nodded. "All right then."

"And bring Ralph too," Avery said.

Jack chuckled. "My guess is that he'll beat me over here."

17

Jack guessed right. Shortly before noon on Christmas Day, Ralph came over to visit them again. "He must've smelled the turkey cooking," Avery told Betty. She led the little dog into the kitchen, then returned to where she'd been rolling out pie dough.

"Merry Christmas, Ralph." Betty plucked a turkey giblet out of the dressing she was mixing and tossed it to him.

"You're too early for dinner," Avery told him.

"Should we take him back?" Betty asked.

Avery paused with the rolling pin in her hand. "I suppose that's the right thing to do, Grandma. Although I'll bet Jack can guess where he is."

"How about if I take him," Betty offered as she wiped her hands on her apron. "That way you can finish the pie crust before it dries out. And I wanted to give Jack another cookie plate anyway."

Betty put together a generous goodie platter, but instead of putting the red bow on the plastic wrap like she usually did, she stuck it on Ralph's head. "Come on, boy," she called as she went for her coat. Acting as if he'd received top honors at doggy obedience school, Ralph stuck to her heels as she led him out the front door and down the walk.

Betty smiled as the little dog took the lead, trotting about a foot in front of her like he knew exactly where he was going and why. He turned the corner and headed straight to Jack's house just like he lived there. And, well, didn't he? Still, as Betty followed him, she couldn't help but wonder how a little stray dog like that had wandered into their lives, or how he had attached himself to not just one person in need, but two. Make that three. And she considered how this little dog had brought them all together. Really, in some ways, it seemed nothing short of a miracle.

"Merry Christmas," she told Jack when he opened the door.

"Hey, I was just looking for you, Ralphie." Jack grinned to see the red bow on his dog's head. "You're like a real party animal."

"He's a very special dog," Betty said. She handed Jack the cookies. "I think he just likes bringing people together."

"I guess so." Jack's expression grew thoughtful. "You know, Betty, I was wondering if it would be okay for me to give Ralph to Avery for Christmas. I know how much she loves him and everything. But then I got worried that you might not appreciate that—you might not want a dog in your house. And I sure don't want to rock your boat again."

Betty just laughed. "You know what I think, Jack?"

He looked slightly bewildered now. "What?"

"I think Ralph is a Christmas dog, and I think he's going to give himself to whoever he feels needs him the most."

Jack nodded. "I think you're right. Kinda like share the love?"

"And maybe we'll just have to share him too."

"Tell you what, Betty." Jack nodded toward the backyard. "I'm going to rebuild that fence—right where it's standing now, where my grandparents built it—but how about if we put a gate between the two yards?"

"And a doggy door too?"

"Absolutely." He stuck out his hand. "Deal?"

"It's a deal." Betty firmly shook his hand, then opened her arms to hug him, nearly toppling his cookie platter. "Welcome to the neighborhood, Jack!"

"Thanks, Betty. I think I'm starting to feel at home."

Betty patted Ralph's head again. "I thank you, little Christmas dog, for bringing us all together. And now I have a turkey to baste."

"We'll see you at two," Jack called. "Merry Christmas!"

"Merry Christmas," she called back. As she walked toward home, it occurred to her that her old neighborhood—which looked more spectacular than ever in its clean white blanket of fresh, fallen snow—was getting better all the time.

Melody Carlson is the author of more than two hundred books, including fiction, nonfiction, and gift books for adults, young adults, and children. She is also the author of *Christmas at Harrington's* and *The Treasure of Christmas: A 3-in-1 Collection.* Her writing has won many awards, including a Romance Writers of America Rita Award and the Romantic Times Career Achievement Award in the inspirational market for her many books. Her novel *Finding Alice* is currently in production as a Lifetime Television movie. Visit her website at www.melodycarlson.com.

A New Heartwarming Christmas Story from Bestselling Author
MELODY CARLSON

Lena, a woman down on her luck, finds a fresh start at Christmastime when a secondhand red coat unexpectedly lands her a job as Mrs. Santa at a department store. Lena thinks her luck is finally changing. But can she keep her past a secret?

Revell
a division of Baker Publishing Group
www.RevellBooks.com

Available wherever books are sold.

Another beautiful collection of Melody Carlson's best-loved Christmas stories.

Featuring the bestselling book
The Christmas Bus